VEIL RISING

VEIL RISING

THE STAR GUILD SAGA™ SERIES

BRANDON ELLIS

This book is a work of fiction. All of the characters, organizations, and events portrayed in this novel are either products of the author's imagination or are used fictitiously. Sometimes both.

LMBPN Publishing
PMB 196, 2540 South Maryland Pkwy
Las Vegas, NV 89109

First US edition, March 2020
ebook ISBN: 978-1-64202-803-4
Paperback ISBN: 978-1-64202-804-1

THE VEIL RISING TEAM

Thanks to our Beta Team:

Nicole Emens, Kelly O'Donnell, Mary Morris, John Ashmore, Larry Omans, Rachel Beckford

Thanks to our JIT Team:

Dave Hicks
Deb Mader
Dorothy Lloyd
Debi Sateren
Diane L. Smith
Veronica Stephan-Miller
Jeff Eaton
Peter Manis
Jeff Goode
Paul Westman

If I've missed anyone, please let me know!

THE VEIL RISING TEAM

Editor
SkyHunter Editing Team

1

ALI

Southern Iraq, 1939—Two Years BEFORE the United States Entry Into the War

Alison was only thirty-four years old, too young to die.

She had a theory that had, against her better judgment, dragged her far from the comforts of home and halfway around a war-torn world.

She believed in aliens, and today that belief was most likely going to get her killed.

Sweat rolled down her skin and under her clothes, the always unwelcome desert heat of Iraq sweltering inside the tomb.

Ali pushed her auburn hair from her sticky forehead. She leaned a torch against the sarcophagus, smoke wafting to her nostrils, and whisking toward the smooth granite ceiling.

As she ran her fingers over the lid's inscriptions, her lips twitched, trying to smile, and failed. The sarcophagus was the find of the century. William and the team left the day before on a rumor to find a key to open the sealed tomb in front of her.

The team wasn't supposed to be gone for long, but like this classified excavation, nothing ever went as planned.

She was alone, here in this recently dug-out tomb, waiting and studying the ruins of Madkhal in Southern Iraq.

A lean woman, her legs and arms toned from the work she had done as an archaeologist over the years, Ali was an only child to a military father who wanted more than anything to have a son, and he had instilled in her that exercise was just below defending country and family.

Morning sit-ups and push-ups were part of her daily ritual, no matter where in the world she was, be it Michigan or here in Iraq.

Closing her eyes, she took a deep breath. "Concentrate, Ali. Concentrate."

If it weren't for the damned Nazis combing the whole of the archaeological world for clues to uncover ancient alien technology and use what they found for their evil operations, Ali would be back at home in Michigan. She wouldn't be here worrying about German soldiers popping up at her dig to kill her and take what she found.

It had happened to colleagues before. There was no doubt it would happen again.

She pulled out a fountain pen and paper from a leather bag on the limestone floor and sat cross-legged, eyeing what she surmised was a keyway in the side of the sarcophagus, a place to insert the rumored key her team had gone to find, or rather, steal.

Her heart beat faster, and she wondered if her team was still alive. Had she sent them to their slaughter?

She shook her head. "Don't think that way, Ali. Picture them alive."

She pushed her hair behind her ear as nerves pricked along her spine.

Touching a hieroglyph, she traced it with her finger, noting a triangle inside a circle with a swirl in the center and replicated it with pen and paper in her lap.

It was a gateway. A portal.

Most archaeologists would look at a portal as a metaphor. Ali, on the other hand, figured it was real. Through the years of entrenching herself with Sumerian tablet translations, this was the spot—the ruins of Madkhal—the place where an extraterrestrial race in the Sumerian tablets, known as the Anunnaki, had extracted countless humans and taken them to God-knew-where.

She sighed.

No one believed her. Her theory was still only a theory, even to William and her own archaeology team.

A gunshot echoed across the wind in the distance, and Ali stood, the paper and pen falling to the floor. She rushed out of the tomb, up the stone steps, and onto the desert sand.

Another gunshot and Ali instinctively ducked, pressing her side against a half-buried granite wall, eyeing the horizon and squinting at the glaring sun. She reached into her pocket and pulled out a handkerchief. Dabbing her brow with it, her hand shook at each delicate touch.

She eyed the sand in front of her. It was everywhere and went on for kilometers. The sand she had come halfway around the world to see, just like her father had before he disappeared twenty-two years before.

Lost at sea, he had been the only U.S. admiral to have vanished aboard his flagship, and the highest-ranking casualty of the U.S. occupation in Haiti.

Only he hadn't really been a casualty, had he?

Suicide.

That's what the Navy investigation had said. She still had the letter, crumpled and tear-stained, in her dresser back home.

Suicide. Lost at sea. And here I am, practically lost in the desert, lost at the tomb, Alison thought bitterly. *Drowning in sand, dying in the heat. Like father, like daughter.*

She twisted around and gasped loudly as a camel's feet pounded across the desert. Ali swallowed a stab of nausea when William was the only one who showed. The camel came to a halt, its feet splashing sand against Ali's boots and loose cargo pants.

William hopped to the ground and handed her a long, thin cloth wrapped around what must have been the key to the portal. It was heavy, and she let out a gush of air. She hadn't realized she was holding her breath. "Where is the rest of the team?"

He gave her a look, his thick brown eyebrows furrowing, and his young crow's feet deepening. He was tall, handsome, athletic, and ten years younger than her. His expression told her everything, and the words rolled off his tongue like a dagger to her soul. "They're dead, Professor."

Her mouth gaped open. "All of them?" Her chest ached, and a rush of emotions filled her body, a mixture of guilt and sadness. She had placed her team in jeopardy, and now they were gone. She bit her quivering lower lip.

He nodded, his posture stooped. He quickly looked over his shoulder as if remembering something. "Hurry, Professor. The Nazi's are coming."

The Nazis.

She kicked the handkerchief to the side. Given to her by the dean of the university where she worked, it was he who'd gotten her into this mess. It was he who would take the brunt of her hot cursing if she lived through this nightmare.

He couldn't wait to conduct this dig until the war was over, a top-secret agreement between him and the Joint Chiefs of Staff. Even over her pleadings that waiting for the war to end would give her more time at the dig, to test out her theories.

And now all but she and William were dead.

It had been her bullheaded mind hell-bent on uncovering ancient codes and glyphs and the need for a woman in the field to be right that made her say, "Thanks, Dean. You won't regret it."

A job created for men, she knew. The dean and the Joint Chiefs of Staff gave her the dangerous project because nobody expected a woman would lead an excavation, and she'd be under the radar.

They were wrong.

William slipped a gun from his satchel, his eyes on the horizon at a forming sand cloud. It wasn't a storm. "Professor, we do this now or never."

"Right." She rushed toward the excavated opening in the sand and the group of steps down to an arched granite doorway.

"They'll be here soon," barked William.

Ali hurried down the limestone steps and through the arched entrance with William on her heels.

"Is this worth us dying over?" said William.

Ali shook her head. "We have time. We'll get out of here and on your camel in five minutes. That's all the time I'm giving us."

The cloth-covered item William gave her pulled forward as if someone had given it a tug.

She paused. "Did you see that?"

William hurried to the torch set against the sarcophagus. "See what?" His breaths were fast and heavy.

"Someone pulled the key in my hand." The item lurched forward again, pulling Ali toward the sarcophagus.

William looked around. "We're the only ones in here, Professor."

Ali held the key in her palm and unwrapped the cloth. The key was black and metallic with a hexagonal-shaped tip and a wide head where one would hold it. It was twice the size of a regular key. Notches and ridges made up both edges. "Okay, get the camera ready."

William placed the torch against a wall near the sarcophagus and set his gun down next to the leather bag on the floor. He reached into the bag and pulled out a small Leica thirty-five millimeter rangefinder camera, and readied the snapshot.

Ali bent, and the key flew out of her hand and into the keyhole. Ali lurched back, her eyes widening. Were the key and the keyway magnetic?

"How in the world did the key do that?" asked William.

"Anunnaki technology," Ali muttered under her breath, not knowing if that was entirely true. She'd studied the Sumerian tablets for years. The Lost Book of Enki, and the tablets, claimed the Anunnaki were the ones who created humans through advanced technology, just like a key which could be pulled perfectly into a keyhole.

Those tablets led her to this sarcophagus, where she might learn the truth.

If she had translated correctly, the Anunnaki had taken humans by the tens of thousands, eons ago, to unknown stars in the galaxy.

This portal was the link to it all. Perhaps a direct link to the kidnapped humans.

Ali reached forward and folded her fingers around the key. "Are you ready, William?"

"Ready as can be, Professor."

She twisted the key.

A loud pop sounded, and the lid moved upward as if levitating. Steam seeped around the edges, curling and dissipating as it neared the ceiling.

The lid moved behind the sarcophagus and slowly descended to land on the floor. A light shot from the opening and lit the room with a pale-white glow.

Ali stepped back, her jaw slackening, her eyes fixed on what was happening in front of her.

Lightning dazzled in the glow, spitting tendrils outward as if it wanted to grab something or someone.

"Haraje," came a whisper.

Ali jumped back. "Was that you, William?"

William shook his head. "No."

"Are you taking pictures of this?"

William nodded.

The light transformed, changing from a glow to an image of a planetary system with a golden planet and moons orbiting it.

The image began to fade, and a man transposed over it. His thick, muscular arms were crossed, his eyes were narrowed as though he was observing them. He had red hair and a beard, and his lips formed a smirk.

A bang vibrated across the main entrance door, and William yelped loudly, his hand touching the side of his neck as the camera fell to the floor.

He twisted around as blood coated his hand, and went to his knees. A thick flash and another bang reverberated in the room. William jerked and fell on his back, his eyes open as blood pooled around his neck.

William was dead.

Ali lunged for William, her heart sinking when a hot, searing pain grabbed hold of her chest. She backpedaled and hit the wall, sliding down to her rear.

As she held her chest, thin streaks of blood oozed down her shirt. She looked up. Three men wearing lightweight olive-colored fatigues and the trademark tropical pith Nazi helmet stood highlighted in the dim light from the sarcophagus.

How long had she been staring at the portal? It couldn't have been more than five minutes, could it?

The soldiers held their guns out, their eyes darting between Ali and the sarcophagus.

One man stepped toward her, his lips pursed. "*Was hast du gemacht?*" He pointed his hand toward the sarcophagus, his entire body shaking with rage, nostrils flaring. "*Was hast du gemacht?*"

Ali didn't know German, and if she had, she wouldn't have replied anyway. She pushed up into a more seated position, her lips tight as her wound pulsed in agony.

She eyed the Nazis, her fingers curling into a fist. They had killed her entire team, her friend, and trusted student, William, and she was next.

She eyed the gun on the floor. If she could reach it, maybe she could take a shot and pick off a Nazi swine.

If not, at least she'd die trying instead of watching these men study her hard work while her body slowly slipped into the next transition in life—death.

She went to move, but a stabbing pain gripped her, spasming her neck and chest and forcing her back down.

A Nazi strolled to her as he holstered his gun. He bent over and pushed her chin up. Smiling, he looked over his shoulder at his friends. "*Amerikanische Frauen sind schön, nein?*"

They nodded and laughed.

A clack accompanied by a streak of light echoed in the room. Blood splattered over Ali's face, and she lurched away.

The Nazi's eyes rolled to the back of his head, and he toppled over, a bullet hole in the side of his skull.

A giant of a man, the same one who had been staring at her through the portal, now stood next to the sarcophagus. He held a large black gun, the likes of which Ali had never seen before, and pointed it at the two men near the tomb's entrance.

He pulled the trigger again and again. Smoke swirled from the gun's muzzle and sent multiple slugs into the two soldiers. The men reeled back and forth, their arms and legs flailing until the giant stopped, and the men fell to the floor, limp and lifeless.

The giant, twice her width and height, pivoted and walked to Ali. He crouched in front of her and intertwined his fingers around her hair and whispered, "Haraje."

He sniffed and stood back, glaring at her as if she were important. He pulled out a short silver stick with yellow lights on either end and waved it over her. It beeped, and the yellow lights turned amber. A holographic image extended with data and words Ali's fading vision couldn't comprehend.

She was dying. Her breathing slowed, and sleep was taking over, life's last attempt to ease her out of existence.

The giant scratched his chin and nodded. He pulled out another device, this one oval, and moved it in a circle a few inches from her chest.

A deep cold enveloped her, and she unconsciously took a deep breath. She convulsed, her legs and arms twitching. Her eyelids fluttered, and her jaw clenched tightly.

Ali's vision sharpened, and her energy soared, sending her heartbeat into overdrive as it pumped vital blood through her body. She screamed and rolled, then twisted and turned.

Then everything calmed, and her body eased as she lay on her back, staring up at the red-headed beast looming over her.

Ali blinked and shook her head, her eyelids doing their best to shut and take her into a long, deep slumber. "Please fix...William."

The giant picked her up and set her over his shoulder. He stepped toward the portal as a sharp pinching sensation pricked her leg. She closed her eyes, and blackness overcame her.

2

ALI

Planet Eos, West of the Radiation Zone — Adarta System, Orion Spur

FOUR YEARS LATER

Chief Petty Officer Alison Johnson bit on a strand of her auburn hair and stood inside of her six-ton, four-meter tall mech.

A recurring dream inundated her thoughts, a dream that had terrorized her for four years now. She was in a sandy environment with a torrid, blue sky. Nazis had found and shot her in the chest.

But what in the galaxy were Nazis?

It felt real. Too real.

Get back to work, she told herself.

She turned her body and lifted her arm, the mech mimicking her movement. The hip and shoulder gyros hummed, counterbalancing the mech's displacement.

She swung her arm down, and the mech's arm followed, smashing a giant mound of red ebb rock—a heavy ore that, when melted and cooled, created the most durable metal known to humankind.

All spacecraft and mechs were made of this substance.

She bent, gathering the pieces with her mech's thick metallic hands and flinging the rock into a cart hovering next to her. If she could hear anything outside of her soundproofed cockpit, it would be the deafening sounds of rock pounding against the cart's metal.

Lifting the mech's arms again, she broke off another piece and tossed it into the cart. She did this over and over, frequently looking at the time on the HDC, the Holographic Display Console, just below the large cockpit window in front of her.

She counted the minutes until quitting time.

She blinked several times as she tried to get the stinging sweat out of her eyes. She glanced at the clock again. Only an hour left.

The feeling wouldn't leave her and never had. Why was she the only one she knew who had constant recurring dreams, and the same Guild'n dream just about every night? Everyone she'd asked rarely had a dream, and if they did, it was never recurring.

She shook the uncomfortable feeling away. She needed to concentrate.

"Focus, Ali," she mumbled as she finished filling her cart. "Complete," she called.

The hovercart moved forward, zipping ahead at a high rate of speed toward a large warehouse a few kilometers away.

Ali watched through the mech's window as the cart maneuvered around red boulders, successfully missing any obstacles in its way. She chewed her lower lip and surveyed the monotonous landscape while she waited for another hovercart to appear by her side. "Next." When, after several minutes, no hovercart appeared, she scowled. "Hendricks, I said, 'Next.'"

No response.

Hanging her head, she shrugged. What's the matter with him? "Hendricks, are you—"

She threw a dismissive hand in the air. Instead of berating him, she stared at the fading light over the horizon. It was beautiful. The sky was a canvas of purples and pinks, perhaps the only attractive thing about this planet, Eos.

The rest of this world was way too still for her taste. There were some trees, little vegetation, and rarely ever any wind. All water was underground in the form of streams and lakes, which provided her crew and the rest of the Star Guild fleet orbiting the planet with an unlimited supply of fresh water.

Water.

She pressed her lips against the soft tube that hung from the ceiling and sucked down a few chugs. Clearing her throat, she pressed the mech's parrot switch to the off position. Brushing her auburn hair out of her eyes, she leaned into the comm. "Next."

When the cart didn't arrive, she pressed the parrot switch back on and turned her torso. About ten meters behind her stood Hendricks' mech, tilting its head toward the sky, an empty cart hovering next to him.

"Are you daydreaming, Hendricks?"

No response.

Ali bent her mech down and grabbed a small wad of rocks. She brought her arm back and tossed the rocks in the air. A few slammed into his mech, and a dirt cloud burst outward upon impact.

"What the—" said Hendricks, his mech stepping back, his arms jolting outward.

"Did I surprise you, slacker? What are you doing? You're the last person I want to report to the upper brass for not doing his job."

"Uh," replied Hendricks over the commlink, his voice quiet. "You better take a look at what I'm seeing, Chief."

She sighed and tilted her head, causing the mech's head to do the same. Expecting to ask Hendricks what she was supposed to be seeing, perhaps another mythical elephant-cloud formation he always talked about, or maybe a cloud that looked like the snowmen everyone used to make back in Starbase Matrona's biosphere when they'd create a snow day, which happened only a couple of times a year.

Ali's eyes widened, and her mouth gaped open. What she was looking at had nothing to do with clouds.

Up above, higher than the atmosphere, was Starbase Matrona. A normal sight since the starbase had been like a daytime moon for this planet for a long time. What was occurring on Matrona and around it wasn't normal at all.

Explosions?

"Are you seeing what I'm seeing?" asked Hendricks, his voice trembling through the commlink. "What do you think is happening, Chief?"

Ali didn't want to say the first thing that popped into her mind because it couldn't be, but the words slipped out anyway. The last time a battle had taken place was years ago, and since then, Star Guild had been at peace. "Someone's attacking us."

World War Two echoed in her head, and she pushed the thought away as soon as it came. These types of words and thoughts came to her every so often, and they didn't make any sense. What the hell was World War Two, or world war in the first place?

She almost laughed at what she said, but deep inside, she knew what she was seeing, a massive attack of an intensity the Star Guild and Starbase Matrona had never seen.

"What?" Hendricks' disbelief boomed through the comm. "Who would attack Matrona?" He let out a quick but nervous laugh.

"The Nontoc Belt Pirates," she blurted out. But it couldn't be. They didn't have this much firepower unless they'd spent the years during peace expanding their fleet on the periphery of the star system.

Other than the Nontoc Belt Pirates, Ali knew of no other group of humans advanced enough to take on Star Guild and blast away at Starbase Matrona.

"Chief," said a woman's voice over the comm. "Look up."

This person's voice always scratched Ali the wrong way, but the event above was scratching her a bit more. "I am Daf. Do you know what's happening?"

"Not a clue. Maybe the Star Guild Academy Games got a little out of hand?"

It was true the Games were occurring, but starfighters and starships never used live rounds.

An explosion filled the sky, and streaks of fire blasted through the atmosphere, arcing over the horizon.

Ali stiffened. That didn't happen in the Games either. "Daf, where are you positioned?"

"Two kilometers east of you, gathering ebb at the Androse Quarry." There was a pause. "Chief, seriously, what are we looking at? Pirates?"

A drop of sweat dripped down Ali's cheek and fell from her chin to her chest. She didn't know how to answer Daf's question, and she didn't want to answer the way she had with Hendricks. This was beyond pirates. "Daf, listen to me. I need you to gather up the rest of team eleven and get them back to the warehouse. Hendricks and I will meet you there soon."

"But what's up with—"

"That's an order," snapped Ali.

"Roger that, Chief," responded Daf.

Ali pulled her eyes from the starbase and focused on the mountains of red ebb and rock lying in front of her. She had to get to the warehouse to contact Central Command, her mother, a captain in the fleet, anyone, and find out what was happening.

There had to be a reasonable explanation.

Haraje appeared on her holoscreen.

She did a double-take and froze. "Haraje?" What the Guild?

"Haraje?" asked Hendricks.

"Nothing. Let's get going."

More words flashed on her screen.

You're learning too much, Chief Petty Officer Alison Johnson. I've been watching you. I'm not pleased with what I've observed.

"What?" Ali reached forward and swiped the holodisplay. The message disappeared.

"Are you okay, Ali?"

"Never mind." She pressed her mech forward, her mind spinning.

She glanced up and saw more eruptions around the starbase.

Were people dying, or was this a simulation or a Star Guild Academy Games live event, something they planned and forgot to tell everyone?

She searched her mind, remembering when she was a starfighter pilot and flying in the Star Guild Academy Games. She couldn't remember any event like this happening before.

She pounded her mech's legs forward into a run and moved quickly across the terrain, not caring if she trampled important mounds of the vertically twisted ebb.

Hendricks' heavy breathing came over the comm. She pursed her lips and wrinkled her brows. "Hendricks, calm down. It's probably nothing." She bit down on her lie. It sure as hell *was* something.

The breathing grew heavier, and loud clanks filled Ali's commlink. She winced. "What the Guild, Hendricks? Are you pounding your HDC? Calm yourself, man. And do me a favor, turn off your commlink until you've settled down."

"Chief, something is after me. I can't–"

More clanks sounded through the comm, then silence. "Hendricks? You there? Hendricks?"

No reply.

Ali halted and spun around. Her jaw nearly hit her chest, and she flung her hand to her mouth. Her mech parroted her and pushed its head back, jerking Ali's body on impact, her restraints barely keeping her from hitting the back of the cockpit.

A billow of smoke rose from a pile of metal twenty meters away. It was Hendricks' mech, or what was left of it.

A roar zipped overhead, and metallic blasts slammed into the ground near Hendricks. Rock burst upward, exploding in a hot, molten mess.

Ali let out a gush of air, her thoughts scrambling chaotically as she did her best to make sense of what she was seeing.

"Hendricks?"

She froze, her feet rooted in her cockpit's ebb floor. Hendricks was dead, and a fire was consuming his downed mech.

No one could have survived whatever onslaught had just taken him and his mech out. Ali held back a scream and backed away.

Ali twisted her mech around and pressed forward as fast as she could get it going, her cockpit jostling up and down and her sweat flinging off her face at every hammering step.

She looked at her heat sensors. "Oh, Guild." She was pushing her mech too hard, the temperature gauge nearing the red.

She slowed to a jog, her breaths now heavy like Hendricks'.

Opening all comm channels, her voice thundered over the comm-link. "If anyone can hear me, get out of the quarries and stay away from the warehouses because they will come and kill you there. I repeat, they will come and kill you. This is no joke. Find cover where you can. Hendricks is dead, and we're under attack. I repeat we're under attack."

A burst of flame erupted in front of her, and rocks cracked apart as they were thrown into the air. She spun, moving away from what was assuredly cannon fire from something, somewhere.

Her mech jostled, an alarm sensor beeped, and a red light blared in her cockpit. Another blast, this time a direct hit, connected with her mech's inner leg and locked up her hip gyros.

Her mech lost balance, its arms flinging wildly along with Ali's.

Pressing several buttons on her HDC, she moved quickly, her fingers more used to the holographic buttons on the control panel than the back of her hand. She rerouted power, sending an overload to hydraulics and hip actuators.

She positioned her leg wide on the cockpit floor, her mech doing the same, planting its foot on the rocky ground and keeping her upright.

The mech shuddered, its back arching, as it absorbed a second cannon slug. All systems shut off, and the alarms silenced, the red light ceasing.

Her mech went limp and fell, landing on its side. Ali jerked in her restraints, her neck whiplashing from the concussion.

The mech bounced and turned when it struck the ground, tumbling onto its face and smashing onto a large piece of ebb and cracking the cockpit's windshield.

She instinctively reached for the window, wanting to cover the crack to prevent oxygen leak. Her arms smacked across her face as her mech rolled again, flipping like a crab on its back.

The mech shook one last time and hissed. Steam filled the cockpit, covering the window and blinding her from seeing anything outside.

Adrenaline pulsed through her body, and nausea rose to her throat. She swallowed it down and blinked several times as she gathered herself.

"Focus, Ali, focus. Get this mech up and go," she demanded.

Turning the parrot switch on, she moved her arms, expecting the mech to do the same.

Nothing.

Checking the switch to see if it was indeed on, she attempted to move the mech again.

No response.

Her mech was offline, and her HDC holoscreen blinked **INOPERABLE**.

She screamed and kicked at the column supporting the HDC. "Turn on, dammit."

Nothing.

She spoke into the comm. "Open all lines."

There was a crackle of static.

"Hello? Anyone?"

The line faded and went dead.

She flipped on the generator. The cabin dome light turned on and then off a second later.

She pursed her lips. The generator was damaged as well.

The mech was non-functional, and a non-functional mech wasn't a good thing to have on this planet, especially while being attacked.

She glanced at the steam-covered window and pressed her hand against it, feeling the dampness on her palm. She wiped away the newly formed droplets, creating a streak across the glass pane that allowed her to see beyond.

There it was as if waiting to see the terror streaking through her.

She narrowed her eyes and raised her middle finger. Even though it wasn't a hateful gesture during her life here in Star Guild and on Starbase Matrona, she knew it was hateful on another planet.

She held her finger out, shaking it at an enemy she'd never seen before because the ship before her was not a Nontoc Belt Pirate starfighter. "Do it. End it already. Let it blaze."

A lone, triangular-shaped craft hovered just above her. A burst of blue air shot from its underbelly as it better positioned itself.

A man's face came on her HDC screen. Ali's eyebrows rose high.

He had a red beard and red hair. He grinned. "Haraje," he said. "I tried to warn you, Ali. I tried. But you are smart, as our bloodline is, and you started to see through the illusion."

It was the man from her dreams.

"Goodbye, Ali. And good riddance. It was a mistake bringing you here, but I thought I was doing you and my bloodline a favor."

The inner portion of the ship's wings opened as black tubes protruded outward. Bursts of red-and-yellow flames erupted, and the clang of the mech's metal rattled through Ali's ears. She knew she was about to experience what Hendricks had, so she closed her eyes and braced for the inevitable.

3

SHAE

Biosphere, Starbase Matrona—Planet Eos Orbit

Fleet Admiral Shae Lutz sat on a blanket in the middle of a lush green meadow. It was something he'd not experienced in several years. He took a deep breath, relaxing and doing his best to enjoy the first few minutes of a much needed week-long vacation.

It had been years since he'd had to deal with pirates on the periphery, so constant fleet training, ship upgrades, and the usual holocomp keypad punching, holosignature dotted line pressing crap was on his mind.

It never ended, hence his reason for never having a relationship that lasted more than six months.

From a long line of Admirals, his father, and his grandfather before him, to say he had been prepped for military life from the day he was born was an understatement.

Going from military school to military school, fighting pirates on the periphery, and keeping Star Guild and Starbase Matrona safe from the pirate filth on the outer system belt were his accomplishments.

His memory blurred on everything farther than the last twenty years, though. He remembered graduating Star Guild Academy, fighting the pirates, and then making his way to admiral. His parents and his early schooling were a fog that hadn't lifted.

For some reason, he didn't remember his parents much, if at all. Again, a blur. They had died a year before he entered Star Guild Academy. Told he'd made a grand speech during both of their funerals, he couldn't remember and couldn't blame it on alcohol, because he didn't drink and never had.

Only his grandfather was still alive to see him graduate from the academy and had died shortly after. Shae's only brother had died in a mission against the pirate sector while Shae was in the academy.

All Shae had left was a nephew. He smiled at the image of the handsome young man in his mind, glad to have at least one relative alive and active in his life.

A cool breeze drifted across Shae's body, pulling him out of his thoughts. "Just relax, Shae," he said under his breath.

He lifted his necklace over his shirt and gazed at the pendant he'd worn most of his life. It had belonged to his grandfather. He looked at the mystical figures carved on it. Two men were riding one horse, both carrying a spear and shield. He pulled it to his heart and held it there for several moments, revisiting a fond memory. Then, carefully, he dropped it under his collar and shivered at the cold metal against his chest.

I better take advantage of this damn vacation.

He twisted in his sitting position. Behind him was a gift from the Prime Director, the highest political figure in the governance. The gift was a small table with gourmet food, dessert, and lemonade.

He raised a glass to his lips.

A loud cracking sound echoed around the biosphere, and the ground shook violently. Shae lost his grip on the glass, splashing lemonade down his chest. The glass bounced off his thigh and rolled off the blanket to the grassy field.

A boom roared across the field, and the ground shook again, this time with more intensity. The admiral fell to his side and moved to his stomach, gripping the grass at the edge of his blanket. His vision blurred and doubled from the trembling ground.

The shuddering stopped.

He eyed his surroundings, watching the trees and branches begin to slow their sway. Shae started to push himself off the ground but paused as he made eye contact with a deer frozen in fear at the edge of the forest.

He stood. "What the hell is happening—"

He was tossed onto his back from another tremor. A ferocious bang accompanied the shaking.

Then stillness.

The admiral stood, wiping the lemonade from his clothing.

Loud footsteps came through the meadow behind him. Before he could turn around to see who was approaching, he was thrown off his feet by another quake.

Landing hard on his back, he heard the cracks and pops of his bones absorbing the impact. He lay still for a moment, staring at the domed biosphere holographic Chanas while he waited for the ground to stop moving. When it did, he wiggled his toes and hands.

He sighed and touched his pendant. "Son of a Guild." He rolled onto his side, thinking Matrona had just undergone a major malfunction, probably in the core reactor compartment of the starbase.

As he turned, he eyed black boots less than a meter from his nose.

"Admiral, we have a problem."

His eyes followed the boots up the seam of a pant leg to the dark-blue Star Guild uniform he recognized. A young woman with hazel eyes stared down at him, her brown hair stuck to the sweat on her forehead, her chest heaving in and out.

Shae stiffened. From her wrinkled brow and her flitting gaze, something was wrong. "Major Gaines? Why are you here? What is going on?"

Eden Gaines extended a hand, her scowl deepening. She pulled him quickly to his feet. "The fleet is under attack, Admiral."

Dusting himself off, Shae frowned. "Is this a joke?"

Eden returned his glare. "I'm afraid not, sir." She grabbed his arm and started to run, guiding and pulling him toward the forest.

Shae yanked his arm away and leaned over to catch his breath.

"The Nontoc Belt Pirates?" He almost bit his tongue. Who else would it be? Those bastards couldn't take the fact they got their asses whooped last time, so they were coming back for more.

Another jolt rocked the biosphere, and he grabbed onto a low-hanging pine branch to keep himself upright.

Since when did the pirates have weapons this powerful?

Shae turned as soon as the shaking stopped. Eden was hanging onto a branch from a nearby tree as well. "Do they have new weaponry?"

Eden quickly shook her head. "No. It's not the pirates. We have to go now."

Another blast and the ground rocked back and forth. Eden grabbed Shae's shirt, forcing him onward. "We need to get you to your vehicle and then to the flight deck immediately."

Shae's mind raced, and he rushed forward, following Eden. This wasn't making sense. "Then who is attacking us?"

Eden looked over her shoulder at him as she ran. There was fear in her eyes. "They came at us quickly, sir."

He jumped over a small shrub. "Who, dammit. Who?"

She shook her head and pushed a fern aside. "We saw it as a blip on the holoscreen, then more blips, then more. There were hundreds of them, maybe thousands—crafts we've never seen before. When our sensors detected they were armed and targeting us, we didn't know what to do. They fired, so we fired back. We're still engaged." She skidded to a halt, gasping for breath. "Starship *Contrebis* is down, and Starship *Sirona* has taken heavy damage, many casualties, and—"

He interrupted her. "Slow down, Eden, and back up. What do you mean Starship *Contrebis* is down?"

"Gone, sir."

His eyes widened. "What? Destroyed?"

Eden nodded, and this time Shae grabbed her arm and practically dragged her through the biosphere's forest.

Jumping over logs, dodging branches, and tromping through bushes, they made their way to a central door. He punched in his code and slapped his hand on the control panel next to the door for further identification.

The door slid open, and their feet pounded on an ebb surface roadway to his hover vehicle parked down the street. Eden's was parked just behind his.

He put his hand on the hood, sliding his fingers across the smooth surface of the door to identify his fingerprints. "Engine, on."

The car purred to life as he leaped over to the driver's side and curled his fingers around the steering wheel.

The car rose, and Shae looked behind him to see Eden jumping into her vehicle. He admired Eden's athleticism. She was just like his daughter: strong, determined, and athletic.

He shook his head and paused for a moment, knocking his knuckles on his forehead. This attack must be shaking the sense out of him, enough so that he imagined he had a daughter.

He narrowed his eyes and pushed out a gush of air. Slamming his foot down on the pedal, he sped toward Flight Deck twenty-one.

4

ALI

Planet Eos, West of the Radiation Zone—Adarta System, Orion Spur

Ali stretched her limbs, then rubbed the back of her head. It was pounding and aching like she had a migraine.

"What the Guild just happened?"

Her mech jostled.

Then she remembered, and her heart skipped a beat. How was she still alive?

Her mech lifted, and Ali dropped her hands, gasping loudly.

The mech rose higher, resting at an angle. Someone or something was holding her mech by its shoulders. She looked up but was unable to see anything through the cockpit's domed ceiling.

Her mech began moving, its feet dragging on the rocky ground as it was pulled along the mining field. She looked out the windshield at the all too familiar red rocks.

Unstrapping, she grasped the HDC console's support column and pulled herself closer to the window. She glanced down at her mech's feet. They were shredded and battered, scraping across the ground and shooting sparks in every direction.

She swiped her hand across her HDC. "Open commlink." The HDC didn't respond. "Dammit."

She folded her arms and focused on whatever was pulling her along. Pushing her head against the cockpit window, she still wasn't able to see the bastard. "You think I'm going to let you take me without a fight?"

When the enemy opened her mech's hatch, she'd scratch, punch, and kick the Guild out of it until it screamed for mercy. She wasn't going to be a prisoner or slave or whatever these Beings wanted from her people.

She exhaled loudly and cracked her knuckles while she continued to glare out of the window. She squeezed her pants tightly and twisted the material. She wanted to break something, but most importantly, she wanted to end the red-bearded man's life. The guy was haunting her in her dreams, and now in real life?

His image had popped up on her screen before he took down her mech. Thoughts she might be going crazy ran through her mind. Perhaps stress had taken over, and her brain was creating hallucinations and displaying them on the screen.

But if she hadn't hallucinated, then it was most likely him pulling her mech along, taking it to who-knows-where.

Mount Gabriel came into view, and she took a step back as whispered words entered her mind: *Earth. Michigan. Professor. Madkhal Tomb.*

She pulled the back of her hair. Those words sounded familiar but felt so far away. Where did she know those words from?

Haraje.

"You asshole," she yelled, releasing her hair. "Get out of my thoughts."

The mech hit a large, jutting rock, vibrating and jolting her cockpit, and bouncing her against a wall.

She pushed off and crouched next to the HDC column, rubbing her arm and wishing she'd never unstrapped from her restraints. Glancing at the dome of her cockpit, Ali knew she couldn't jump out of the mech unless she wanted to die from lack of oxygen.

Maybe when the red-headed prick eventually pried open the cockpit hatch, she could send a fist and a knee to his groin.

Her shoulders fell. If it were the guy from her dreams, he was massive and could easily out-muscle her.

She crossed her arms and leaned against the column, waiting while the mech shook at every boulder and jutting rock it was dragged over.

The cockpit dimmed, and Ali glanced at the window. A shadow loomed over the ground she'd seen countless times, the mech storage warehouse.

Her mech's feet met the level ebb surface and began to slide smoothly.

She was now inside the warehouse.

Of all places, why would he take her here? And how would he possibly know the code to open the warehouse door?

Maybe it was open when he got here.

The light transitioned from soft shadows to near black as the large warehouse door shut behind them. Steam rose when fresh, breathable air activated, and the warehouse fans turned on.

If she escaped, she would be able to breathe, but she would be trapped in a warehouse with a lone killer who wanted to make her as bloody as he made the Nazis. Or as bloody as the Nazis made William.

Nazis? William?

She pushed the thought away.

"I had a crush on you the day I met you," William said. His young face stared down at hers as he moved in for a kiss. She pressed her lips against his and leaned against a tree, the wind blowing gently against her as she stood on soft green grass. Her heart felt like it would burst open, and she grabbed him, pulling him closer.

She shook her head.

Where did that thought come from? And why did it feel so real?

She touched her lips where his lips had pressed against hers.

"No, get out of my mind." There were more pressing issues than fixing her mind right now. Survival, for one.

She reached toward the ceiling where a button unlocked the hatch, her only way of escape.

She stopped, a finger hovering just below it. Maybe she needed to wait it out, to think of a better plan?

A jolt vibrated the mech, and it lowered. She slid across the cockpit, her butt slamming against the back wall.

A clank echoed throughout, and she glanced out the cockpit window, now above her.

Another clank, this time against the mech's exit hatch. It reverberated against the mech's inner walls and sounded like metal on metal.

Ali crouched, her breaths shallow and quiet.

It would take special and strong tools to open the hatch unless they blasted it like they had done with Hendricks' mech only an hour ago.

She narrowed her eyes and looked out the window. "You piece of crap. I can't wait to get my hands on you."

She looked around for a knife or any kind of blade to cut up the enemy.

She squeezed her hands into fists. "Damn regulations." She was just a mech pilot in Star Guild's mining operations, not authorized to carry weapons while operating a mech.

A second pounding struck the mech's dome, the sound almost deafening. Ali brought her hands over her ears. She closed her eyes and smelled her sweat filling the cockpit.

She pleaded to the mech gods to have this guy show himself so she could rip his testicles off.

How many of her friends had he killed?

She was willing to wait this out, and stay in her mech until the giant gave up and left the warehouse to find something else to do. Hopefully, that something else was to go off and die a painful death.

She eyed the window again and realized a simple truth, and she cringed and wanted to melt into the wall and hide.

The window was right in front of her. She could see out, which meant someone could see in.

She didn't want to look. The window was large, and that was a problem. If the giant looked through, she wouldn't be able to avoid eye contact, and she wouldn't be able to ignore him either. She was trained to look, trained to notice everything, and had a screwed up urge to explore and discover.

Looking would be a natural response.

The pounding stopped. The engineers had designed mechs to be impenetrable to almost anything, with its double-thick ebbed armor, the strongest metal known to humanity.

Even the window was made of more than a thousand long thin strips of clear ebb. How the engineers had accomplished that, she didn't know. Yet, it wasn't as durable or as strong as the thick armor making up the mech, as evidenced by the crack in the window.

She tucked her elbows into her sides and tried to make herself small. She wasn't sure why the giant, or whoever it was, hadn't chosen the cockpit window to break into first.

She took a deep breath, wondering when she'd draw her last.

A shadow appeared. It loomed and came closer.

She glanced up at the dome ceiling. If the evil prick peered in at her, that would leave the hatch unguarded.

She slowly slid her body closer to the hatch. This might be her chance. She'd pop it open and run as fast as her feet would take her into an office she knew was only about twenty steps away.

Out of the corner of her eye, the shadow grew.

Placing her finger lightly on the hatch button, she held her breath and waited for the right moment.

Something with large eyes and its palm outstretched came into view, pressing against the window.

5

SHAE

Starbase Matrona, Planet Eos Orbit—Flight Deck, Bay Twenty-One

Shae raced his hovercar through Sphere One, zipping around a corner to see Flight Deck Bay twenty-one's doors open and ready. He slammed his foot on the brake, and the hovercar fishtailed and slowed to a stop. He looked in his rearview mirror. Eden was halting right behind him.

He jumped out of his car, Eden close on his heels. Another shudder rocked the starbase, and he instinctively ducked and grunted loudly, more from anger at not understanding what was happening than anything else.

Shae looked over his shoulder at Eden as he took his first steps on the tarmac.

She had tears in her eyes and wiped them with her sleeve. She gave a curt nod, pressing her lips together. "I'm okay."

This was all too surreal. Things like this only happened in holo-movies, not real life. "Do we have any intel on the attackers?" asked Shae.

"Negative, sir."

Eden led him toward two empty Thunderbird Z-class starfighters perched like falcons on the flight deck.

"VTeb Squadron 2 is terminated," someone yelled from the flight deck as they rushed to Bay twenty-one's command room.

A mechanic raced by, wrenches in hand and grease covering his face, barking orders to several other mechanics hastily fixing Thunderbirds and Starhawk Transport ships.

"Get your gear on, Admiral," screamed Eden, her voice barely audible over the commotion in the bay.

"My gear?" He had been on Starbase Matrona for a vacation, not flight training.

"Any gear."

Shae's eyes widened. "What for?" It was protocol to transport Admirals via transports, not starfighters.

"I'm sorry, Admiral." She pointed toward a starfighter. "Right now, that's all we've got."

"Shit." Shae bolted toward the locker room and pulled open a locker, finding a flight suit and helmet. "Hope these fit."

He stripped off his clothes, threw on the flight suit, and snagged the helmet from the rack inside the locker.

He ran back into the bay, moving his feet across the ebb floor as quickly as his legs could take him. Eden was ascending her ladder and jumping into her Thunderbird. She gave Shae a thumbs-up just before lowering her cockpit window.

"We'll need more than a thumbs-up," muttered Shae.

He reached his Thunderbird's ladder, his boots clanging up each rung as he made it to the top. He swung one leg over the lip of the cockpit and pushed off with his other, landing in the pilot's seat. He threw his helmet on, then gave Eden his own thumbs-up.

He pulled up the HDC and pressed the engine drives. The Thunderbird revved like a lion, shaking the bird's wings that were tucked back like a diving eagle. He ran his finger across the holographic screen, initiating flight mode and opening the wings. He quickly checked his weapons, noting a forty-millimeter G-9 Wedger gun, equipped with impulse shield-penetrating slugs and mounted on the tip of the craft's nose along with two G-4 Smashup cannons fully loaded and ready in each wing. Loaded under the wings, half a dozen space-to-space missiles were ready to rip some enemy tail to shreds.

He turned on his commlink. "Flight Deck, this is Admiral Lutz. Ready for takeoff." He squeezed his fingers around the control stick.

The bay door leading out into the deep, dark cosmos remained shut.

Shae grimaced. "Flight Deck, do you copy?"

Silence.

His skin tingled, and a chill struck his core.

He looked around. The bay crew was in chaos, performing their jobs because they didn't know what else to do, yet ignoring him and Eden.

He clenched his jaw and slammed his fist against the rounded cockpit window. "Hurry up, people. Get us off the deck."

The bay quaked, and the starbase shifted, dipping a few degrees on its side. Shae's Thunderbird slid on its skids, heading toward the wall. The bay whined, and the starbase righted itself. His bird slowed to a halt.

"Flight Deck, this is Admiral Lutz. Do you read?"

No response.

He switched to private comm, patching into Eden's craft. "We need to get off the Guild'n deck, Major."

"Affirmative, Admiral. I'm bypassing Flight Deck and going straight to Command. I'll get them on the line."

Turning off his commlink, he covered his mouth with a hand and looked down. He wanted to gun it out of there, but slamming into the bay door wouldn't be a good idea.

"Admiral," said Eden. "After we launch, I'll be on your nine. You'll arrive safe and sound on *Brigantia*."

Starship *Brigantia*—his starship—his home. He couldn't wait to get back to his boat and command.

He glanced to the side; Eden was frantically talking with someone over the comm.

People began pouring out of the bay and to their stations. A crackle came over the commlink, and a tense voice spoke, "I'm sorry for the delay, Admiral. The Flight Deck is now clear. You're free to ride." The bay doors opened. The scene outside was chaotic, and a heaviness filled Shae's stomach.

Thousands of triangular-shaped crafts zipped by, shooting yellowish-red flames from their wings, followed by cannon slugs blasting into his fleet's starships, destroyers, cruisers, frigates, and the list of ships went on and on. In the distance, he spotted his ship, his baby, Starship *Brigantia*.

His starship was kilometers away, but because of its size, it looked much closer. Starships in the fleet were as big as small cities: cigar-shaped and equipped with immense ion boosters and thermal rockets built into their sides, connected to immense core reactors and operators.

His fleet was exchanging fire with the attackers, sending several bogeys into fiery flames. The fire snuffed out by the vacuum of space moments later.

"Thrusters," ordered Shae.

The Thunderbird rumbled, its thermal rockets initiating. "Lift." The Thunderbird rose a meter off the ebb flooring, hovering in position, ready for takeoff.

He looked again at Eden, then nodded and pushed the throttle forward. Gravity pressed his back firmly against his seat, the open bay door, and space approaching quickly.

Within seconds, he rocketed past the gravity field at the bay's launch exit and out of Matrona. He pushed the control stick to the left, heading for a heavily damaged Starship *Brigantia*.

"Hard right," yelled Eden.

Shae pulled the control stick to the right, barely missing another Thunderbird being chased by an attacker. Before Shae could assist, the fleeing Thunderbird exploded into a mess of engine parts and chunks of armor, fanning out into space.

Shae lit up the ion boosters accompanying his rockets, propelling him faster. "Zigzag," ordered Shae.

"I'm on your nine, Admiral. What you do, I do."

Shae guided his control stick back and forth, flying in a zigzag pattern toward *Brigantia*.

Shae's sensors beeped. He was being targeted. "Are you still back there, Eden?"

"Falling to your six, targeting him now, Admiral. Missiles locked. And launched."

From the HDC's radar, he locked eyes on a blip directly behind his craft. Then two blips, one with the Star Guild signature and a dot for a missile chasing the bandit on Shae's tail.

His bandit disappeared.

He brought up rear cams, eyeing the remnants of an explosion in his wake.

"Target deleted, sir."

"We're not out of this yet, Major," yelled Shae. One hand on the control stick, the other on the cockpit window, he pressed hard as he pulled a sharp turn.

Two bandits flew by and quickly looped around, steadying themselves in front of Shae.

"How did they..." he swallowed the rest of his sentence, then blurted out, "Split."

He veered left, and Eden veered right. The enemy flew by a second time, almost as if playing with them.

"Fifteen seconds and we're in *Brigantia*'s docking bay," informed Eden, her words quick and short.

A crackle came over the commlink. "Admiral, this is First Lieutenant Brigger. You are clear for landing. Bay Seventeen, sir."

An explosion rocked the bay he was headed for, enemy missiles and cannon fire making contact.

A warning beep sounded in his cockpit, and a blueprint of Starship *Brigantia* came on his display screen. Red highlighted Bay Seventeen on the ship. He was headed toward an unopened, malfunctioned bay.

"Negative, Brigger, the bay is compromised. Get that thing fixed, and now."

The cigar-shaped starship had bays on both sides of the behemoth and just aft of the main reactor. The bays were more like large tubes, all geared for different sized crafts arriving and departing. The closed tubes were getting larger as Shae pushed his Thunderbird toward *Brigantia*.

"Affirmative, Admiral. Pull up immediately, bay doors jammed, unresponsive. I repeat, pull up."

Shae yanked his control stick hard as an enemy starfighter crossed his path. Shae pulled the trigger, and shield-penetrating, armor-piercing cannon slugs charged through space to collide with the starfighter and crack it in two.

He flew through the fiery blast and veered left, coming around and above *Brigantia*. He eyed an enemy ship pulling behind Eden, its wing-mounted cannons sucking in and pushing out, shooting tracer-like fire.

He pushed the control stick forward, inching in behind the bogey. "You have a bandit on your six, Eden."

"I see him."

He eyed the holodisplay, and the crosshairs zeroed in on the target and flashed red. "Weapons lock. On my mark, break left. Now."

He pulled the trigger, and Eden broke left.

Nothing expelled.

"What happened?" Eden hollered.

Shae blinked, doing his best to clear his mind and let the blur of the moment slip away. Maybe he didn't press the trigger hard enough? He pressed it a second time.

Again, nothing.

He gritted his teeth, his nostrils flaring. "Damn Star Guild piece of crap. It's jammed and won't fire."

The bogey followed Eden and continued firing, missing as she pushed hard left, then a hard right.

"I've got to get this bogey off my back, Admiral. He's closing in."

Shae switched to space-to-space missiles. These better fire or Eden would be dead sooner rather than later. That wasn't something he was willing to let happen. "Again, on my mark."

The enemy ship shot several blasts, and Eden pulled up and twisted. The shots went wide.

Shae tightened his grip on the control stick, readying his finger on the trigger, waiting for target lock.

A loud beep sounded, and the red crosshairs lit up.

"Break right."

Eden's Thunderbird broke right, and Shae squeezed the trigger. A red-and-orange blast of fire rocketed from his wing.

An explosion erupted in front of him, sending debris in all directions, some absorbing into his graviton shields.

He spun away and let out a thick breath, his jumpsuit sticking to his body's sweat.

He glanced at the battle, and a weight descended on him, wanting to crush his shoulders and eat at his heart.

Destruction was everywhere. Shae's Star Guild family, young and old, were dying right before him, and here he was, barely making a dent in the enemy.

A Star Guild starfighter ripped apart several kilometers away, and his throat tightened. It was his duty to get everyone to safety, and he wasn't yet on deck to command his ships.

Eden's voice blasted through his comm. "A bogey is on your six, Admiral. Pull up, now."

Shae pushed his feet into the floorboard as he pulled back on the stick, looping upward. He saw his attacker come into view and then turn into a cloud of fire and debris. Eden's Thunderbird flew through the flames, and he let out another exasperated breath. "Thank you, Eden."

"My pleasure, sir. Although we do have another problem."

"Yes?"

"We have more inbound." She paused then coughed, clearing her throat. "I don't know what those things are, but they don't look friendly, and unless the Nontoc Belt Pirates have new technology, this is not the pirates. Coordinates one-one-seven moving by planet Eos."

Yes, two blips, no—four blips—filled his flight radar. He eyed the direction of the coordinates, straining to see through the explosions and battling starfighters, destroyers, and cruisers. He squinted. "What in Eos' name are those?"

Several gold pyramid-like ships rounded the planet like triangular suns.

"Those are massive, sir," Eden said.

"Admiral," said Brigger. "They are coming our way. Orders, sir?"

Get the hell out of there is what he wanted to order. He had no idea what those giant ships were packing.

"Are the bay doors operational?" Shae asked.

"Not yet, sir," replied Brigger.

A fireball lit up the area in front of Shae. He changed course, looping and twisting his Thunderbird as he rounded the Starship *Brigantia*. "How many fighters do we have out here, Brigger?"

"All of them."

Shae's eyebrows drew together. From what he'd seen, he assumed less than half of the pilots were in flight. "You're sure?"

"Yes, Admiral."

He swallowed hard. "Where are they, Brigger? I see very few of them."

Brigger's voice came quiet and heavy, "Most of them gave their lives for the fleet."

Shae bit his lower lip, nearly pressing his upper teeth all the way through. "What? That's more than two thousand pilots dead." The question hung in the air unanswered. If the fleet had been decimated this badly in such a short time, there was little chance of survival for any of them.

"Bay Seventeen operational and open, Admiral," shouted Brigger. "Free to land."

"Thank Guild," hollered Eden. "I'm right behind you, Admiral. Take the lead and land your bird."

6

SHAE

Starship Brigantia—Adarta System, Orion Spur

Shae entered Starship *Brigantia's* bridge with Eden by his side. Fear imbued the eyes of the men and women scattered around the deck. Some looked ready to burst out of their skin, while others seemed ready to break down.

Saluting them, Shae dropped his arm to his side. The command chair he had occupied for the last eighteen years was in the middle of the bridge. Next to his chair was the navigation station where the executive officer, XO Louise Stripe, stood. Straight blonde hair in a bun, her steely blue eyes were staring into his, her body rigid and jaw clenched.

"Everyone, get to your stations and get all our craft on board. It's a massacre out there," Shae ordered.

There were a few nods before crew members scuttled off to their stations.

He wanted to be in the operations room, better known as the CIC, Combat Information Center, the true heart of the ship. But it would be suicide to continue this defense, and killing more of his people wasn't in his best interests. They had to jump out of here with Starbase Matrona and the rest of the fleet, and soon, then regroup and come back to fight another day.

Shae hurried to his chair as a loud boom rushed to his ears. The ship rocked, and Shae was flung on his back, his head whipping hard against the floor. He stood at once, then stumbled as another shudder nearly took him off his feet a second time. He braced against Brigger's station just as his arms flew up, doing his best to catch Shae and coincidentally Eden but without success. They both fell onto the floor, Eden tripping over Shae and tumbling on her side.

Eden stumbled to her feet and went to her flight commander station to monitor what was left of her pilots.

Shae made it to his seat and sat on the soft chair. His heart beat quickly as he studied the main screen on the bridge. The vidscreen encompassed the entire wall and resembled a large cockpit window. "What's the damage report?"

"Shields more than half depleted. The hull is—"

Shae turned, spit coming out of his mouth. "Exact percentages, Brigger."

Brigger sat straighter. "Shields at thirty-eight percent, rail guns and bore cannons one-hundred percent offline, space-to-space torpedoes fully functional, NMJ drives, rocket boosters, rocket thrusters, and ion engines fully functional, hangar deck fully functional, je—"

The ship tossed, and Brigger bit his words.

"How many starships remain, Brigger?"

"Four, including this one, sir."

The admiral gave Brigger a double-take, then glanced at XO Louise Stripe, silently seeking an explanation.

Louise turned her attention to the battle raging over the vidscreen. "Five starships have been destroyed, Admiral. Countless destroyers and cruisers are gone, as well. We're less than half a fleet."

How were the starships and the rest of the ships taken out so quickly? If the pirates had new tech and new ships, how did they get it?

Shae stiffened. "Are we positive these aren't the Nontoc Belt Pirates?"

Louise nodded. "Yes, sir. Our incursion scouts monitoring patrol of the pirates sent back holovids of the pirates also being attacked and all but annihilated. Our scouts soon had the same demise."

Shae wanted to ask who these attackers were, but understood the question wouldn't get an answer.

His eyes darted back and forth over the bright lights flashing on the vidscreen and the debris floating and spinning away in the cosmos in front of him.

This attack was a nightmare beyond anything he'd ever imagined. "Open all commlinks to the captains of each remaining starship."

Holographic images appeared on a holostage several meters in front of Shae. Only three captains appeared, the only high captains left in the standing Star Guild fleet.

All three nodded to their fleet admiral. "Admiral Lutz," they said in almost perfect unison as if practiced too often.

Shae took another quick look at the battle raging outside and then back at the captains. "Get all starfighters inside your ships and let the rest of your assigned ships know we'll jump on my mark."

"Aye, Admiral," replied the two male admirals in the hologram, both old and tired, stress consuming them like a hammer smashing a thumb. The third one, a female with dark-brown hair and a hint of silver at the roots, remained silent. Even though her face didn't match the wrinkles of her fellow captains, it reflected the wear of long nights, stressful meetings, and tiresome training, plus a war that suddenly popped into existence.

She was Captain Diana Johnson. They rarely saw eye to eye, though she usually held her tongue because of ranking.

She widened her stance, her arms behind her back. "I have a request."

Shae gazed around the room, annoyed. He had far more pressing issues at hand, and a discussion wasn't one of them, no matter how short it might be. His face reddened, and he raised his chin high. "Captain Johnson, do you challenge my orders?" He noted her expression, and there was more than worry in her eyes, more than the fate of humanity resting on her shoulders. Yes, it was something more, something personal.

The two other captains blinked out, their holograms vanishing. Starship *Brigantia* rocked, and the lights on the bridge blinked off and on.

Shae grasped his chair's armrests, squeezing his fingers tightly while eyeing Diana.

She took a step forward, her blue eyes focused, not bending away from Shae's unwavering stare. "Yes."

Her hologram faded in and out, and she fell to the floor as her starship jostled violently. She collected herself and stood, clutching the side of her pants.

"Hurry, Diana. Spit it out."

"I'm keeping Starship *Sirona* here. As you know, all the men and women working on Eos, except for a few, are from my starship and my battle group. We plan on extracting them planet-side before we jump. We will meet your selected coordinates as soon as possible."

Shae gave a quick shake of his head. "Negative, Captain. You will take Starship *Sirona* and your battlegroup with us, and we'll come back for those on Eos when we're ready."

"Yes, my battlegroup will go with you, but Starship *Sirona* will not." Her lips straightened.

Shae tensed as heat flushed through his cheeks. She was disobeying an order. It was grounds for immediate removal. "You are sworn by oath to obey a fleet admiral's orders. It's cut-and-dried, Captain."

"I'm sorry, Admiral." She pointed to the floor as if it were planet Eos below. "Our family members are down there. We intend to retrieve them. Once we do, we will rendezvous with you. I'll then hand you my resignation."

He felt like squeezing Diana's neck. "Captain Johnson, you are relieved of your duties. Commander Paulic will take over."

Diana bared her teeth. "My daughter is down there."

The thought shot at him like an arrow to his gut. If his daughter were down there, he might do the same. His daughter was everything to him.

My daughter.

A yearning sensation took over. He wanted nothing more than to reach out and embrace his child.

He looked off for a moment. Was he going crazy? He didn't have a daughter.

He cleared his throat loudly and lowered his chin, his voice stern. "Captain, you are relieved."

He eyed the vidscreen. Though thousands of kilometers away, the golden pyramid ships were approaching port-forward quarters. Starfighters were pounding other fighters, destroyers were crumbling apart, and Shae couldn't tell who was who.

He looked over his shoulder at Eden. "Have you notified the starfighters and the rest of the fleet to get the Guild out of there and on *Brigantia*?"

Eden went to speak, but Diana interrupted her. "The rest of the crew on Starship *Sirona* are in agreement. We will retrieve our sons and daughters on Eos."

A tally of votes from the nearly ten thousand inhabitants on *Sirona* could not have taken place in such a short amount of time, especially during combat. Shae saw through her act and her reason for wanting to stay.

Another blast impacted the ship, and it shook back and forth. Shae gripped the chair's armrests more forcefully, his knuckles going white. "You are relieved of your duties. Get Commander Paulic on the holostage now."

Diana nodded, dropping her eyes to the floor. When she looked up, a trail of tears slid down her cheeks. She touched her thick dark-blue command suit above her left breast and unclipped her silver star. She held the star in her hand, staring at it for a moment, then dropped it on the ground. "I'm taking over Starship *Sirona* and hereby removing it from Star Guild."

"You can't do that." Shae rocked to the side, another explosion jostling the ship. "This is mutiny, Captain." Spit sprayed out of his mouth.

She bowed her head. "I'm sorry, Admiral." Her image blinked out, and the bluish-white screen in front of the holostage disappeared.

"Brigger, give the coordinates to the entire fleet and Starbase Matrona. Once all Thunderbirds land, we jump." Shae shifted his eyes to Eden's station. "And, Eden, I don't care what you have to tell them, get them here now."

Shae stood and paced toward the vidscreen, cringing over the fact that Diana had just disobeyed and then stole a starship. If she survived, he'd personally throw her into the brig.

He glared at the screen. The pyramids were nearing, and starfighters were chasing starfighters, flashes of red and orange painting the universe before him.

This was nuts. Who were these attackers? And why? What had his people done to deserve this?

"All remaining Thunderbirds are accounted for and in the nest, Admiral," said Brigger.

Shae twisted around and wiped away the beads of sweat from his forehead as he walked toward his seat. "Get ready to jump." He sat and looked at Louise. "Are the NMJ drives still operational?"

"Yes, Admiral."

"Patch me into all comms. We jump on my mark." And without Starship *Sirona*.

They had jumped many times before either chasing pirates or on exploratory missions, never finding much but uninhabitable planets. Yet, they had never jumped the entire fleet at once, let alone Starbase Matrona.

The thought of the starbase jumping sounded impossible, but it was equipped with NMJ drives too. Maybe it would work, maybe it wouldn't.

There had never been a need to jump Matrona.

Now there was.

Sitting at the helm next to the admiral, Louise leaned over. "I have to remind you, Admiral, Starbase Matrona has never before made a jump of this magnitude. We don't know if it will stay intact."

He took in a deep breath, closed his eyes tightly, and opened them slowly. "I have to trust the technology, Louise. That's all I can do."

"Understood, Admiral."

Another blast jostled the ship, and sparks sprinkled down from the ceiling.

Shae placed his hand on Louise's forearm, squeezing it gently. "Trust me."

Louise's blonde eyebrows rose, and she clutched her uniform's collar. "I trust you, sir. You know that more than anyone else."

"On my mark, XO." He stared at Louise. "Three...Two..."

"Starship *Intrabus* down, sir!" yelled Brigger, eyes meeting Shae's. "It's gone."

Shae's stomach clenched. Hope and luck had deserted them. "All remaining fleet," ordered Shae. "Jump at will."

7

ALI

Planet Eos, West of the Radiation Zone—Adarta System, Orion Spur

Ali crawled backward and hit her head against the metal cockpit hatch. She swiped hair out of her eyes, kicking at the window and putting her fists up.

"Daf?"

She dropped her guard, her jaw slackening.

Her fellow miner and mech pilot blinked frantically, peering through the cockpit window at Ali.

It was Daf who had pulled Ali's mech to the warehouse? She could have only done it with her own mech, but holy crap, for the first time in her life, Daf helped her, and in the process, saved her life.

"Did anyone else make it?"

Realizing Daf couldn't hear a word she was saying, she reached up and pressed the hatch button. A hiss echoed in the cockpit, and a clank reverberated against the walls as the hatch unsealed and opened. Cool air rushed in, and the familiar smell of the warehouse ebb flooring filled her nostrils.

Ali crawled out, and hands grabbed her by the collar. "Daf, what are you doing?"

Daf pulled, dragging Ali across the ebb floor to a door that led to the warehouse offices and cafeteria. Daf's breathing was labored and fast.

Ali spun around, swatting at Daf's hands, jarring them loose from her collar. "Get your hands—"

Ali cut herself off when she saw Daf's ghostly pale face, almost as white as snow in Starbase Matrona's winter biosphere. "Daf?"

Daf mumbled, speaking incomprehensible words. She twisted on her heels and bolted toward the office door, her feet moving in short, quick steps.

Ali pushed to her feet and ran after her. "Daf, calm down. We need to assess the situation and notify the authorities, especially my mom. They have to know what happened down here."

Daf halted, her voice coming out in a breathy whisper. "They. Killed. Everyone. All the mechs are scrapped, and nothing is left, and the mech pilots inside...dead. Who are they, Ali? Why did they kill them? Why? What do we do now? Will Star Guild send a rescue team after us?"

Ali pursed her lips and snapped her fingers in front of Daf's face. "I know this is upsetting and doesn't make sense, but we need to concentrate."

Daf pushed Ali away, her eyes frantic. She dashed to the door, pressing buttons on the wall panel, her fingers trembling. "What's the code? I can't remember the code. Why can't I remember the code?"

"Three-two-two-one. The code is three-two-two-one."

Daf's lips quivered, her arms shaking. She blinked in rapid succession.

Ali sucked in a gush of air, knowing what was about to happen. She moved quickly as Daf fell forward and into Ali's arms.

Ali pushed Daf against a wall, sliding her down to sit on the floor.

Ali gently slapped Daf's face. "Daf, wake up. Daf?" Ali grunted.

She paused, remembering Starbase Matrona. The last she saw, it was being bombarded by cannon and missile fire. From Eos, it looked like a fireworks display.

Were they the pirates? She shook her head. It was a definite no.

She reached down and pulled Daf up, holding her in one arm and pinning Daf against the wall with her leg. Ali typed in the code.

The office door opened.

She turned Daf around, grabbed her by the underarms, and pulled her through the doorway. An automatic switch activated when she entered, and the lights blared on. "No, for Guild's sake." The last thing she wanted to do was draw more attention to the warehouse.

She dragged Daf across the office, pushing a desk out of the way with her hip. She dipped below the next desk and pulled Daf behind it, hiding.

The light. The damn light. She'd have to turn it off.

A loud thud pounded against the mech bay door and reverberated through the warehouse. Ali froze, every hair on her body standing on end. She peered around the desk and looked through the office window. The bay door was dented inward. Someone wanted in from the outside, and they wanted in badly.

Another thud sounded, and Ali snapped into action, racing across the office and switching off the light. She saw a door labeled Security on a side wall.

"Yes. The security vids."

She punched in the code and burst into the office, plopped on a seat next to a desk with an HDC built into it, and switched on the outside cameras.

The holomonitor was black.

She scanned the room. "Where is everyone?"

Not a single soul was manning the warehouse or performing their normal routines for military ebb operations. Where did they all go? The mech pilots wouldn't be there because they were usually outside in their mechs collecting ebb. They were probably dead or running their mechs across Eos' ebb rock terrain, trying to survive.

But the warehousemen and women, the Star Guild officers, the boss man, engineers, and the techs—where were they?

There was no evidence of a struggle. It was as if they had just disappeared. They couldn't have gone outside without a mech. Or had they?

She went rigid. There was a back door with a terminal ramp that led to a docked transport ship. If they ran out that way, leaving regardless of no breathable oxygen, they'd be dead and lying lifeless on the ground.

There was a back window. Ali moved to get up, to look, to make sure no one had tried to escape and perhaps had found a place to hide somewhere in the structure. Yet, she might see dozens dead, her superiors, and some of her work buddies, not that they liked her anyway.

A third pound slammed against the bay door, deforming it even more. Looking out back could wait. Living for another day couldn't.

She bit her lip and pressed several buttons. The vidscreen blipped and crackled to life. "Good. I'm getting somewhere."

She slid her finger over a few icons. She turned on the audio command sequence. "Reroute all security vids to the nearest Eos satellite. Sync into mech warehouse Eleven and display."

The bay door jostled.

"Holovid," she said, bringing up a holographic display of the planet and seeing its rich golden color glow across space.

The satellite cam zoomed in, passing through the atmosphere and rushing toward red ebb rock, large mountains, and thick rock formations spiking upward, with quarries as far as the eye could see.

"Zoom in on warehouse Eleven."

The bay door whined as another large dent poked inward. She pounded the holographic display. "Hurry, hurry."

It zoomed in.

"Stop."

The camera halted its zoom and showed the exterior of the warehouse.

"Mech bay door," she ordered.

The satellite panned in and stopped. She tilted her head and glared as she let her arms fall to her side. "What is that?" There was no way she could defend herself against that monster.

She rushed to Daf. "Get up, Daf. We have to go. Now. We have to get into our mechs."

The bay door screeched, its wheels coming off its torsion springs, the anchor brackets snapping in half, loudly clanging as they fell and bounced on the ebb flooring. The bay door pushed forward, then kicked back, smacking against the ground.

A giant humanoid, wearing a green and gray mask and a thick suit the same colors, stood where the bay door had been.

An Anunnaki, thought Ali, then wondered where she'd heard that word, somehow knowing it was the name of the alien race.

A race she had studied...somewhere.

Earth?

She frantically shook her head. She didn't know what "Earth" meant, other than the ground the warehouse stood upon.

She brought her attention where it needed to be, at the figure standing in the large warehouse doorway.

He turned and faced in her direction, his muscles flexed. He went into a defensive position, and aimed a spear, the tip lighting up molten red. A singeing projectile expelled, headed toward Ali.

8

SHAE

Unknown Sector, Orion Spur

The jump sequence initiated, and everything slowed down as if time had become a gooey, thick substance instead of a fluid stream, and everyone on the bridge seemed to stretch—faces, fingers, noses—and all sound ceased. The vidscreen lit up in white streaking stars that zoomed by, to become lines, bright and thick.

Space compressed in front of them and expanded behind them using the NMJ drive, a Negative Matter Jump drive, installed on Starship *Brigantia*'s engine deck.

It was like riding on a tidal wave of warped space, allowing the ship to traverse distances by contracting and expanding, resulting in faster-than-light travel.

An instant later, everything calmed and was right again.

Shae stood from his admiral's chair and studied the green planet, its emerald haze shining against the stars. "Where *exactly* are we, Brigger?"

Brigger eyed a holoscreen at his station. "We picked coordinates zero-seven-nine. We're still in the Adarta System, Orion Spur, three light-years from Eos, Admiral."

An image of the remaining Star Guild fleet entered Shae's mind, nearly puncturing a hole in his gut. Did Starbase Matrona make it? If not, millions were dead, and he might as well have joined them for screwing up his responsibility—keeping his people alive.

He swallowed hard, not wanting to ask the most important question. "Have any of them made it?"

"Yes, sir."

Shae jerked his head back, and his eyes widening. "Thank Gui—"

"Wait." Brigger dropped his forehead to his hand. "No."

Shae pushed out of his seat and hurried to Brigger's station. He placed his fingers around the edge of Brigger's backrest and gripped hard, his knuckles turning pale. He wanted to rip through the upholstery and tear the enemy's spines from their necks for what they had done. He peered at the station's HDC. "What do you mean, 'No?' Where are they?"

Brigger's head moved up and down. "Yes and no. Starship *Taranis* made it along with her battle group." His voice cracked. "I'm sorry to say Starbase Matrona is nowhere to be seen."

Worry lines creased across Louise's forehead. "Orders, sir?"

Shae twisted around and glared at his XO. "We stand fast."

He walked to his chair and sat, narrowing his eyes at the vidscreen in search of any possible spark in space that might be the Starbase jumping to the coordinates. "She will come. I trust the technology. She'll arrive."

He slowly shook his head. A jump of this magnitude, or any magnitude, had never been tested on Matrona.

He tapped his finger on his chair display before him. "Over one thousand Thunderbird pilots dead with Starbase Matrona missing."

His mind spun. How had this happened? Who would attack his people, his family? There was no warning. Nothing. And so quickly? How could that be possible? Star Guild had satellites and radar, but the enemy had struck as if all his people's technology had been compromised, useless.

It had been confirmed these weren't periphery pirates. This was an entirely new monster, one more powerful than everything Star Guild had.

"Systems check, Brigger," Shae ordered.

Brigger placed his finger on the HDC and swiped across it. "We're not looking good, Admiral. Two percent shields, fifty percent power in the NMJ drive core reactor, ion engines at ninety-eight percent, ninety-nine percent hangar deck functioning, almost all long-and short-range sensors offline, aquaponics—" He gasped.

"Brigger?" questioned Shae.

"We need Matrona here, now, sir. This isn't good."

Shae twitched his nose, annoyed. He knew what they needed. They all knew what they needed.

Brigger shoved a finger at the HDC. "I need you to see this."

Shae marched over to the station to look at what Brigger was pointing at and dropped his head. "No. That's the last thing we need right now." He grimaced.

If he were alone, he would have punched a hole in the wall. On the bridge, an admiral that couldn't remain steady, calm, and in charge was no admiral at all.

Any chance of survival had just decreased tenfold.

Shae dipped his head, his lips in a tight line. "We need Matrona." He walked over to his command chair and slumped down onto the seat. "Open commlink to Starship *Taranis*."

Brigger pressed a holographic button. The holostage fizzed on, pixelating thousands of dots. The dots emerged, a low voice sounded through the comm, and an image appeared on the holostage. "Captain Jenkyns here."

Shae steepled his fingers together. "How's your ship?"

"Our ship has sustained heavy damage. Do you want me to go through the systems check with you?"

"No."

Jenkyns stiffened. "I hope Starship *Brigantia* has fared significantly better than us."

"Negative, Captain. Our ship is barely alive. We have at least a week of repairs to complete, if not more."

Shae eyed the vidscreen at the bridge's bow, seeking any change in the sector they were in, perhaps a blip, any indicator that Matrona had made the jump. "Captain, some of our sensors are down. Do you have Matrona on your radar?"

"That's a negative, Admiral," replied Jenkyns.

He brought his fingers to his forehead, rubbing his thick, tan skin. "We have a problem, Jenkyns. We lost all of our freshwater reserves. We're empty."

"You have water in Aquaponics, correct?" asked Jenkyns.

"Aquaponics is gone as well. A rupture in our agriculture deck wiped them out." He paused, correcting himself. "No, a rupture sucked out all our food and water. As you know, we have no starbase to bail us out."

"You were our lifeline, Admiral," stated Jenkyns. "We have a minimal amount of food and water. Our run to get more from Matrona was scheduled for later this evening."

"How much do you have on hand?"

A short pause. "About two days."

A loud blaring alarm sounded in the bridge.

"Incoming vessels," yelled Eden.

Shae's eyes shot to the vidscreen, and Captain Jenkyns' image blinked out.

"They're coming in fast, Admiral," warned Eden.

There was no way his people could survive another attack. He glanced at his shoes, seeing how clean they still were. An image of them blowing up and bursting into flames popped into his mind. "Captain Jenkyns, evasive actions. We can't leave this sector until our NMJ drives charge further."

"Aye, aye, Admiral," responded Jenkyns, blaring over the comm channel.

"Zoom in." Shae stood and walked toward the vidscreen to watch two large golden pyramid-like shapes flying toward them. "When will the NMJ drives be fully functional?"

Brigger moved his eyes over his station's HDC. "Yes, about four hours. Engineering is working on it."

"We don't have four hours. Tell them to speed it up."

"Yes, sir."

A loud beep sounded through the bridge, and the vidscreen narrowed in on three large objects speeding toward them.

Eden tensed. "Torpedoes launched and coming our way, sir."

"Launch countermeasures," said Shae.

A weapons tech typed in a few commands on his holoscreen. "Countermeasures launched."

The bridge hummed, and the temperature rose on the deck. The floor of the ship vibrated under Shae as hundreds of star-like projectiles expelled from *Brigantia*'s port and starboard-side tubes, rushing toward the torpedoes.

The admiral waited for the countermeasures to do their job.

They zipped toward the incoming torpedoes, narrowing in on their targets and making a thin debris field. The torpedoes impacted with the launched countermeasures, and burst into a flash of light, shooting off a wave of energy that spread outward and toward Starship *Brigantia*.

Louise stood, her face like stone. "That isn't supposed to happen. What type of weapons technology is that?"

Shae lowered his chin. "I don't know but brace for impact."

Shae clicked the restraining belt on his seat and held onto the armrests. Then, like a wave hitting a large ocean vessel, *Brigantia* rocked back as the rise of energy hit, moving the ship up and backward, fiercely shaking her.

Shae closed his eyes, gritting his teeth. Another wave was on its way. "Brace."

Brigantia rocked back, and the vidscreen blipped out, going black. The starship dipped to the side, and the starboard thrusters roared, teetering the ship back in place.

The tremors stopped, and Admiral Shae opened his eyes. "Get the vidscreen online."

Brigger dipped his head, working frantically at his HDC. "Already on it."

A beep echoed in the bridge, and Shae whipped his head around to Eden.

Eden scanned her HDC. "More torpedoes launched and heading our way."

The vidscreen blinked on, zooming in on the next wave of incoming torpedoes.

Shae let out a heavy breath. "Launch more countermeasures. Do we have enough power to turn around and escape?"

Brigger wiped his hair off a sweat-drenched forehead. "Negative, sir." He pressed a holographic button, eyeing the weapon's tech.

"Countermeasures launched."

Shae leaned forward, and looked off into deep space, past the torpedoes, past the pyramid-like ships and the stars beyond.

Two words repeated in his mind: *Space Templars.*

Over and over.

Space Templars.

Why would that pop into his mind? They were a myth, tall tales taught to children in school. His grandfather had told him they were real, and that during a classified exploration he'd met some when his transport had trouble after landing on an asteroid.

He didn't know if his grandfather was pulling his chain or not.

The Templars were known as saviors of lost explorers. They gave their lives to be in service to others. According to the legends, their oath was to help those less fortunate and to be a force of light in any darkness. Shae understood, along with the rest of the crew, that the Space Templars were a myth. But there were no other options, no other strategies. He couldn't hold off these attackers forever.

Star Guild military, now only consisting of Starship *Taranis* and Starship *Brigantia* and their battlegroups, were outgunned by the behemoths coming their way.

No matter how silly it seemed, he had to do it.

Shae spun in his chair and gazed into Brigger's eyes. "Press the distress beacon. Include a message in the beacon." He paused, not believing what he was about to say. "We, Star Guild, call upon you, the Space Templars."

A hush went over the bridge, as if everyone and everything, including the monitors, stopped at his last words, *Space Templars.*

"Y-yes, sir," said Brigger.

Louise cocked her head to the side, probably thinking he had lost his senses. Her eyes shifted to the vidscreen, her brows raised. "Countermeasures hit successfully. No energy wave formed. We're in the clear."

He pulled out his golden pendent and rubbed his thumb over the knight sitting on a horse, wondering why there was a second knight seated behind the first one. *If you're real, show yourselves. Please.*

An alert horn sounded.

Eden pounded her fist on the HDC control panel. "They are relentless. We have inbound fighters headed our way. It looks like hundreds. Between *Brigantia* and *Taranis,* we have half that many pilots remaining, if that."

Shae walked toward the vidscreen, fury rising in his belly. He wanted to rip the attackers apart, piece by piece, atom by atom. But it didn't matter what he wanted. He had to do what admirals do. Give orders and make the final decision. "Open intercom to all decks."

"They're open, sir," said Brigger.

Shae glared at the scene. Hundreds of incoming craft barreled toward them. "All pilots on deck, report to your Thunderbirds. And all remaining ships, prepare for battle."

"Brigger," barked Shae. "Did you send the distress call?"

"Yes, sir."

"Good." He rubbed the pendant and flipped it over to read the words inscribed on the back:

Equites non intercedere nisi invocatum. Knights Do Not Interfere Unless Called Upon.

9

SHAE

Unknown Sector, Orion Spur

"I repeat, pilots to your Thunderbirds," growled Shae over the comm channels.

Louise chimed in, "Three hours until we can jump again, Admiral."

Shae shot her a look, one brow raised. "It's better than the original report. The techs and engineers are working fast. Get Captain Jenkyns on the comm."

A buzz and Jenkyns' hologram appeared near Admiral Shae's command chair. Jenkyns gave a nod, sweat dotting his forehead. "Yes, Fleet Admiral?"

"Are your Thunderbirds and your battlegroup ready?"

"Ready on your mark."

"Launch your Thunderbirds and command."

"Aye, Admiral." Jenkyns' hologram faded out.

"First Thunderbird wave away, sir," shouted Eden. She stared intently at the HDC attached to her station. She lifted a hand as if she were conducting an orchestra. "Second wave away, sir."

Shae watched the vidscreen. Two groups, each with a dozen Thunderbirds, flew toward the oncoming enemy starfighters. Destroyers and cruisers reared around, their boosters engaging and blasting them forward. "Keep 'em coming, Eden."

Her arm still raised, Eden finally dropped it. "Third wave...fourth wave...fifth wave...sixth and final wave away."

Shae cocked his head as a sensation rushed through his body. He blinked it away a few times, but for a moment, he was watching a young girl playing the flute in a band. He was holding his wife's hand, a pleased smile on his face.

A flute? What the Guild was a flute? And a wife? He never wanted one nor had one for that matter.

Stress.

Shae rubbed his hands over his face, bringing himself to the present. "A view of Starship *Taranis*."

The image on the screen shifted from his Thunderbirds and battle groups flying toward the incoming onslaught, zipping by the green planet near them, to Starship *Taranis'* Thunderbirds exiting their launch bay, heading to join *Brigantia*'s Thunderbirds.

He looked over his shoulder. "Louise, how long before our Thunderbirds are within weapon's range?"

She glanced at her chair's small holovid. "Two minutes, although I'm already hearing reports of enemy weapons locking on our birds." She grimaced. "They have a more advanced targeting system than us."

This enemy was more advanced, and they wanted to commit genocide on the human race. But why? What reason to attack and kill every living person on Starbase Matrona and in the Star Guild military? Was it for the ebb?

"Bring up a closer view of the incoming bogeys."

The vid cams connected to *Brigantia* shifted and panned past the Thunderbirds. Sweeping across the starlit cosmos and floating rocks, they rested upon the enemy fighters. The enemy fighters were triangular, propelled by red rockets, which meant they were burning a different type of chemical than Star Guild starfighters, or it was a strange type of ionic propulsion.

Shae scanned the fighters, noting that the cockpit windows were wide and black. The wings carried cannons and projectiles, similar to the missiles the Thunderbirds carried, except the ones on the enemy craft were larger.

Yet, they were fast, hitting speeds the Thunderbirds had yet to reach.

Louise pressed a few holographic buttons. "Two minutes until they meet. May Star Guild guide their way."

Shae pulled out his pendant and rubbed it between his thumb and index finger. The Space Templars. He almost laughed, shaking his head in dismay. What a silly thought to send a distress call to a mythical group, written about for a thousand years in children's fantasy books. They didn't exist.

All it had done was make him look like an idiot, a putz, in front of the crew. The last thing an admiral should do is look incompetent.

He took in a deep breath and tapped his pendant. He needed to plan a quick strategy. He wanted to meet with the military council, and figure out what the best execution was for a situation like this.

They had prepared and battled the Nontoc Belt Pirates many times, and built a massive fleet to hold them off for years.

This battle, this war, was something he'd never thought he'd experience. No one had. An advanced race with tech that outmatched Star Guilds'?

What they needed was a miracle.

Eden's voice boomed through the bridge. "We've lost two birds, Admiral, and our Thunderbirds are still not in weapon's range."

"Brigger?" said Shae.

"Yes, Admiral?"

"Be Eden's second hand. We need help commanding the pilots. Move Thunderbird Squadron VTeB-14 into formation alongside VTeB-12."

"Aye, sir."

Eden pushed away from her station and hurried toward Shae, her chin high.

He'd seen this expression on her before, the last time during the Star Guild Academy Games when she wanted to join even though she was a few years past the age limit. She had been determined to change it and successfully did.

Shae crossed his arms. “Eden, what is it?”

“Permission to fly, sir.”

He cupped his hands behind his back and widened his stance. “Request denied.”

Eden took a step forward, her gaze flitting around the room, not settling on anyone. “Admiral, I must. Please.”

“Weapon’s lock,” interrupted Brigger. “We have engaged the enemy.” He smiled at the admiral, then dropped his gaze back to the HDC, his smile fading. Shae wasn’t looking for a smile. There was nothing happy about today.

“Thunderbirds down. Thunderbirds down,” said a pilot command officer.

Shae clenched his jaw. More young men and women, more innocent lives, lost. “I can’t let you go out there, Eden.” He pointed to the vidscreen, eyes trained on her. “I need your expertise. I need you here. I don’t want you to die out there, Eden.”

She was like his daughter. All brains and all courage, and that couldn’t be lost out in the battle and couldn’t be lost in his heart, the way he felt for his own child, who was somewhere…

He slapped his hands together. “I don’t have a daughter.”

Eden’s head jerked back. “Excuse me, sir?”

“Nothing.” He watched her for several moments, searching. Did she have what it took? Could she survive?

“I can do it, Admiral. I’m the best you have. I can command from my Thunderbird much better than from here. And I’ve noticed some interesting patterns from the way these…*others*…fly. I think I can expose their shortcomings, their weaknesses. I am much more suited to lead from my bird.”

“Three more Thunderbirds down,” came Brigger.

Admiral Shae’s nostrils flared. She was right. Of all people on the bridge beside Louise, Eden was like family. But an admiral must go with what was right, not what his emotions dictated.

He touched the pendant hanging from his neck and put it under his collar, where he felt the cold hardness touch his chest, his heart. "Suit up and command from your bird."

Eden's mouth gaped open a few centimeters, and she stood straighter. "You won't regret this."

"Leave before I change my mind." He turned and stared at the vidscreen, his heartstrings pulling every emotional cord known to humankind.

Eden rushed out of the bridge just as Shae turned to see her leave. He wanted to yell for her to stop, to be careful, to fly the other way and out of harm's disgusting reach.

Instead, he watched the door close behind her while rubbing the back of his sweaty neck. His stomach churned. Eden was too important, too intelligent, and too brave to be thrown to the wolves.

"Admiral, we're taking heavy losses," said Brigger.

Shae exhaled. "How's the enemy fairing?"

"They're taking losses too, though not many."

"Give me exacts, Brigger."

Brigger glared at the HDC in front of him. "Twenty-eight of ours...no, now twenty-nine of ours down. Only twelve of theirs, sir."

Shae clenched his fists, wanting to punch at the injustice of it all, at the piece-of-shit attackers killing everything he loved, everything he swore to protect.

"Eden away," sounded Brigger.

Louise left the helm and walked to Shae. She rested her hand on his shoulder and whispered, "We need a miracle."

He glanced at her hand, then at her thick lips, looking anywhere but into her eyes. "That's what I'm praying for."

He touched his pendant through his shirt. *Space Templars, if you're out there, fight for us.*

A tingling sensation enveloped his heart, and words came out of his mouth that didn't seem his own. "Executive Officer Louise Stripe, in times like these, act like hope is always on our side and that a miracle is on its way no matter what. It's called faith. We will survive. We will succeed."

"Thirty-six Thunderbirds down, sir, and seventeen bogeys," reported Brigger.

Louise shot Brigger a look, then turned back to Shae. "What's our next plan of action, sir?"

"Let's take *Brigantia* and *Taranis* for a ride. We meet head-on with those pyramid-flying pieces of starcrap and blow some holes in them. We will leave our impression on those bastards."

"That's a last stand, sir."

"We will succeed. Somehow. By Guild, we will."

She dipped her head.

Shae pointed to Brigger. "Contact *Taranis*."

Captain Jenkyns' hologram appeared on the holostage.

"Yes, Fleet Admiral?"

"We move on the pyramids, full speed ahead."

Jenkyns paused, clearly calculating strategies in his head. "Admiral, if you don't mind, we have another option."

"Yes?"

But Shae didn't see any other alternative. *Brigantia's* NMJ drives were down, and with the auxiliary power offline, they couldn't outrun the enemy. They had no other choice, but to blast the incoming pyramid starships while they still had squadrons of starfighters and groups of battleships alive and fighting.

The more confusion for the enemy, the harder for them to concentrate.

If they could pull this off, it would be a miracle. If they couldn't, at least they would die trying.

"We retreat. We run."

Shae swallowed hard. They couldn't. "Jenkyns, we have three hours until Negative Matter Jump drives are online and functional. Until then, we can't jump. We have nowhere to run. We have to fight."

Jenkyns touched his temple. "Our drives are functional."

Shae tilted his head. "I see where you're going."

"Yes, Admiral. If we move on the pyramids, we likely all die, although with honor. However, the human race can survive if *Taranis* jumps. We can give our species a chance."

Shae turned to Louise. She gave him a nod.

"Two more birds down," said Brigger.

"Orders, Admiral?" asked Jenkyns.

Shae glanced down at his feet for a moment and then at Jenkyns. The human race was more important than this fight. If Shae could save some, all the better. "You are to jump on my mark."

"What about the rest of my battle group, sir?"

Shae shook his head. "They stay. If we can last three more hours, we'll have all remaining Thunderbirds dock here, and will rendezvous with you at your coordinates. If, after approximately four hours, we don't show, jump again." Shae looked at Brigger. "Patch in *Taranis'* new jump coordinates."

Brigger pressed several buttons. "Done, sir."

"Captain Jenkyns, mark time at four hours."

Jenkyns took a deep breath, standing straight and tall, and touched two fingers to his brow in a quick salute. "It has been an honor, Admiral."

Shae bowed his head and pressed both hands flat on his chest. "And it will still be an honor when we jump to your coordinates." He stiffened and stood erect. "Jump on my mark, Captain." The hologram bleeped out. "Five. Four. Three. Two. One—jump."

Starship *Taranis* brightened like a small star, then collapsed into itself, dissolving right before Shae's eyes. Remnants of the energy disbursement remained, weaving in and out of space as if in and out of time. In minutes, the disbursements would fade away, but Shae didn't have minutes to watch the spectacle.

He walked to his seat and sat down, resting his arms on the armrests. His eyes remained on the vidscreen. "Full speed ahead."

10

ALI

Planet Eos, West of the Radiation Zone—Adarta System, Orion Spur

Ali dove to the floor, her hands cushioning her fall. The large giant holding the spear blasted a shot against the wall outside the office. She heard the crunch of rocks crash to the floor, her eyes nearly popping out of her skull.

Ali slid both hands under Daf's armpits and dropped to the floor as a second burst rocked the office.

Ali crouched and peeked over the desk, holding her breath. "We have to get out of here. Wake up, Daf." She jostled Daf. "Wake up."

Daf remained unconscious.

Ali peeked around the corner again. Through the office window into the main warehouse mech bay, she could see the humanoid crouched next to her downed mech, inspecting it.

He walked around to the open hatch. She couldn't tell if the being was green, blue, or her skin color but assumed it was the redhead from her dreams, perhaps wearing a suit and mask to breathe in the Eos environment.

If this guy was from her dreams, then her dreams had to be real.

Maybe it was a memory? If so, then how?

She couldn't worry about it now.

The giant touched the mech's hatch and poked his spear through the hatch's opening.

He slowly turned his head, then stood to peer through the window where Ali was watching. The individual's enormity was terrifying and almost surreal, tall as a four-meter mech and nearly as wide as one.

The guy was the same size as the man in her dreams, the one who took her, but to where?

Shock struck like lightning through her. To here? To Eos? To Starbase Matrona? Was she from a different world altogether?

No. I'm going crazy.

Ali ducked back behind the desk and patted Daf's cheek. "All you did was faint, so why are you still unconscious? Wake up, or I'm leaving you here."

Daf didn't move. Was she even alive? Ali pressed on Daf's neck, checking for a pulse and felt it against her fingertips. She was very much alive. "Get up, you worthless piece of ebb."

Nothing.

Ali rolled her eyes. Daf was more than just a pain in her ass. She dragged the unconscious woman across the floor, down an aisle of desks where she picked one—the biggest and widest desk—and hid Daf and herself behind it.

Directly behind her were long windows framing the walls, the Eos mountain range in the distance. She wished she could break the window and escape, but she knew what fate had in store for her if she did such a thing.

No oxygen equaled death.

The light coming through the back windows slightly dimmed. This was good. She'd be more hidden as darkness settled over Eos, though the sun never dipped entirely below the horizon this time of year.

The office shook, and a concussion buffeted the room. The door, including the frame that held it, exploded into a thousand pieces, throwing wood and thin ebb rock across the office, splattering pieces onto the desks and floor.

Ali covered Daf with her body as loud footsteps entered the room. Ali held in a gasp, not because of the killer coming in to end her but for the lack of oxygen. With the mech bay door blown open and the outside fully in view, and now the office door and a large portion of the wall destroyed, oxygen was leaking outside, leaving them to the mercy of the Eos atmosphere, where carbon dioxide and methane reigned supreme.

She only had minutes at most to get inside a mech where oxygen was plenty, making it breathable for both her and Daf.

Another step sounded in the office, and Ali peeked over the desk. The giant was hunched forward, doing its best not to hit its head on the ceiling. It was clearly searching for her, snooping under desks. He pushed one out of the way, then grabbed the next desk, flipping it over, the edge cracking off.

She closed her eyes for a second, doing her best to think of any way out.

There was only one way, and that was to the mech bay.

No more thinking.

She had to go.

The humanoid took another step, inching forward and pushing aside the desk she had been hiding behind moments before.

She had one attempt and one attempt only.

Taking several more steps, the being poked his spear into the security room and peeked inside, bending to move through the doorway.

That was her chance.

Ali grabbed Daf by the wrists and pulled her down the aisle. She reached the hole in the office wall and rushed through it into the mech bay, the cold rush of outside air chilling her skin.

She let out a gush of air, not able to hold it in any longer. She inhaled, surprised she found some more and filled her lungs.

Fresh oxygen?

Perhaps the air hadn't drained entirely out of the mech bay yet.

Ali looked over her shoulder at the standing mechs lining the warehouse wall. There were about twenty of them, and she saw one with an open hatch.

The staircase ladder to reach the mech's cockpit was across from the mech, butted up against a mech with its cockpit hatch closed.

She pulled Daf, her heart pumping. Daf's shoes screeched across the ebb floor.

Ali glanced behind her again.

In about ten meters, she'd be at the mech.

She shifted her attention and turned back around to look at the office. She gasped loudly, her eyes going wide.

There it was, the humanoid, running toward her with long, athletic strides, its spear moving back and forth with every pounding step.

Adrenaline pumped through her, and her biceps burned as she rushed to the mech. She released her grip on Daf's wrists and raced to the staircase ladder, quickly rolling it over to the open hatch. She kicked the staircase brake in place and grasped Daf under her armpits, pulling her up the stairs, straining and squinting, her muscles weakening under the effort.

She exhaled, then inhaled.

How was she getting any oxygen at all? It should have blasted out of the mech bay by now.

A loud bang echoed in the bay, and a tracer whizzed by her head and hit the mech, ricocheting off, leaving a gray mark. Smoke rose from the small indentation and wafted toward the ceiling lights.

The humanoid was getting closer with every passing second. He held out his spear and pointed it directly at Ali.

Energy surged through her body, and she moved as fast as she could, taking quick step after quick step up the ladder. At the top, she shoved Daf over the hatch and heard Daf's body thud against the bottom of the cockpit. She jumped up and over the opening as another flash of red tracer fire blew past the open hatch, barely missing her.

Landing on the cockpit floor, she grabbed the hatch's handle and slammed it shut, pressing the lock button. A hiss filled the cockpit as oxygen poured in.

She took several large breaths, taking in the air she desperately needed.

She scrambled into the straps and secured her body in position, clicking the restraining belt tightly. She waved her hand over the HDC, turning it on, and thanked her lucky stars she and Daf were still alive.

The mech growled on, vibrating as all systems came to life.

Shaking her head breathlessly, she stood on the footpads that instantly calibrated her body type to fit the mech's operational output, and allowed her to control the mech with her movements at the precise time she moved.

A loud pound sounded, and the mech jolted, leaning to the side. Ali moved her leg to balance the mech, the hip actuators mimicking her and keeping the mech upright.

Ali looked down at Daf sprawled on the floor next to her. Blood dripped from her mouth and the side of her head. The fall into the cockpit hadn't been nice to her, but it was better than being dead. "Stay with me, Daf."

Another loud clank and the mech shuddered.

Ali narrowed her eyes and bared her teeth. "You wanna fight?"

She turned her torso and swung her arms around and hit the humanoid hard across its chest. It fell backward, flinging its arms wildly until it hit the ground hard, its spear twirling across the floor.

Ali walked forward and lifted her mech's foot high over the giant. She dropped it onto the humanoid's chest, leaning in on the pressure and pressing hard on her footpad.

The humanoid grabbed the foot, wrapping its enormous hands around the sides, doing its best to push the foot away.

No luck.

The giant let go, letting his arms go wide and limp like a bird spreading its wings, ready to fly to its death. Ali was happy to comply and adjusted the mech's weight, cracking through the man's chest. If that didn't end his life, nothing would.

Her heart raced, and she lifted the foot off the man to see a lifeless body before her.

She looked at the being's face. The mask had ripped open, and the man before her was clearly dead but didn't have a beard, though his hair was red.

From the facial structure, this was not the man in her dreams.

She took a step back. She'd never killed a person and didn't like the emptiness it gave her.

She shook off the darkness encroaching on her heart and bounded her mech forward, moving as quickly as the mech was able, heading for the blown-out mech bay door where evening's dimming light poured through.

"What's...happening?" Daf rubbed her temple and winced. She let out a loud breath and looked at her fingers. "Why…" she coughed, "am I bleeding?"

Ali concentrated on the HDC and shifted her eyes to the cockpit window as they passed through the bay door and onto the red ebb ground.

"Ali is that…"

A beep sounded on the mech's HDC, and dots appeared on the holoscreen. Ali's shoulders drooped. "Can't talk right now. We've got unidentified craft heading our way."

"Huh?" Daf tried to stand but fell back down when Ali leaped her mech over a boulder and slid down a small embankment, landing skillfully in stride.

Ali turned and raced toward a large mountain in the distance, Mount Gabriel. She checked the heat gauge as she ran.

"Stay down, Daf, and hold on to something."

Daf pressed on the ridge of her nose. "I think it's broken."

"I *said,* hold on to something."

"Huh? Where are we?" Daf pinched her nostrils shut with her thumb and index finger.

"I'll explain later, hold on to the HDC column." How many times did she have to repeat herself?

Daf slid over and wrapped one arm around the column, using her other hand to maintain pressure on her nose.

Ali leaped the mech high into the air and jumped over a mound of ebb, reaching the mech's peak jumping capacity. The ground rose quickly toward her, and she pressed an air compression function on her HDC, causing air to blow out of two metal hoses attached to each side of the mech's ankles to slow its descent.

The mech's hydraulic shocks cushioned the landing, the impact soft and easy. Not something any rookie mech pilot could do, let alone many advanced pilots for that matter.

Sweat dripped from Ali's skin as she took the mech at a fast pace across the ebb terrain. Her HDC beeped; unidentified craft were looming closer.

"Where are we going, Chief?"

"To the mountain." Ali pointed, forgetting to turn the parrot switch off and saw her mech pointing as well. If she could get to the mountain before the shadow of night came, she could probably reach a tunnel she'd found on a previous visit and walk her mech inside.

Was that the best strategy? If she were found, she'd be trapped.

Daf stood up and peered through the cockpit window.

"Why are we going there? Take us back to the warehouse."

"I know some hiding places at the base of the mountain."

Ali pushed the mech to its next speed, a flash of heat expelling inside the cockpit.

"Hiding places?" asked Daf.

Ali shot her a look. "In case you forgot, we're under attack. For all I know, we're the only survivors."

Daf's mouth dropped open. "Wha—" She dropped her arm from the column. "It can't be."

"It is."

Daf covered her mouth. "It wasn't a nightmare. It was real. And your mech. I thought you were dead, but I hoped you weren't. That's why I dragged you to the warehouse."

"Thank you for that." Ali watched her HDC. The enemy craft was coming from the other side of the mountain and fast. She didn't know if the enemy used heat sensors to find their targets or if they were even tracking Ali's movements at all. If they were, Daf and Ali would be at the bad end of a strafing run and soon.

She sprang her mech over another boulder, again landing skillfully into a run. She glimpsed again at the HDC. "How much time until I'm to Mount Gabriel?"

The HDC computed and blinked twenty-four seconds.

"How much time until the unidentified craft reaches Mount Gabriel?"

Thirty-three seconds blinked on the HDC.

The starfighters were faster than her, so if they by chance picked up speed, they'd close the distance to the mountain quicker than her mech.

She didn't have a lot of time to find the entrance to the tunnel. She'd need another place to hide.

One popped up in her head. A place she had taken long mining breaks under she knew was nearby.

"Hurry up, mech. Go, go." Ali leaned forward, jumping her mech again.

She eyed the HDC.

Eleven seconds for her, eighteen seconds for the starfighters.

She moaned. "Son of a Guild."

She bounded left, placing her mech's foot on a boulder, and shoved off, pushing herself toward the hiding spot. She landed, running her mech up the base of Mount Gabriel. She located the area, a thick ebb formation with two large rocks jutting upward with a huge rock slab sitting horizontally on top of the two, which acted as a roof. It had been a place to rest when a rare storm came, a safe place where she parked her mech to watch the rain and lightning crash down from the sky.

A place she hoped would hide her well, though it wasn't the best hiding place anyone would choose. But it was the only one in the vicinity.

Luck had to be on her side.

She reached the rock formation and hid under it, immediately shutting down her engines and dampening her heat load, taking her HDC offline.

The problem? Her mech would be leaking heat, regardless.

Daf pointed to the sky. "Whoa..."

Enemy craft zipped overhead as Ali sucked in oxygen, not daring to let it out. She wiped the sweat from her brow with her jumpsuit sleeve, her heart pounding like a starfighter engine and her mouth as dry as an Eos above-ground lakebed.

She kept her eyes on the ships, hoping they didn't turn around and have her on their sensors.

11

EDEN

Unknown Sector, Orion Spur

Eden pushed her Thunderbird's throttle forward, bursting through Starship *Brigantia's* launch tube, heading for the battle.

She banked hard and glanced over her shoulder at a glowing beacon of light, *Brigantia*, shining in the ever-present darkness. Her home away from home shrank the farther she traveled, flying like a comet toward enemy attackers.

She swallowed hard thinking about her mentor, Fleet Admiral Shae Lutz. He let her out here, and she'd make sure he'd be proud he had, along with everyone else on that starship.

Those people on that ship, especially Admiral Lutz, were everything to her. They had been her *real* family. Being raised by a single drugged-up mother who had disregarded her like an old rag doll in the back of a closet, never seen, never played with, had made her and her mother nothing more than roommates, and nasty ones at that.

Her muscles tightened at the thought. She hadn't seen her mother in who knew how long. Was she even alive? Would she be proud that her daughter, Eden, was risking her life to save as many people as she could?

Probably not.

She eyed the coming swarm of frenzied activity: explosions, tracer fire, friend, and enemy dying.

Her stomach burned. She didn't like the idea her friends were blinking out of existence.

A lone straggler, an enemy breaking off from combat, beeped on her target lock.

She switched to missiles. The long beep told her it was time to fire. She pressed the trigger, and a missile blasted forward, slamming into the craft.

Eden's Thunderbird rocked as she propelled through a fiery cloud, the debris spinning away from her, and the fire burning to nothing a moment later.

She veered right and found herself behind another enemy starfighter.

She shifted her finger over the trigger. Her target lock beeped wildly, and her HDC's crosshairs hovered over its mark.

She switched to guns and pulled the trigger again, holding it down and sending cannon slugs the bandit's way.

She hit her mark and flew through the glittery entrails.

In front of her was the main battle, and no more enemy stragglers showed themselves on her HDC. Or they had realized she was too much to handle and entered the main fray.

Sweat seeped through her hair, wetting the soft inside lining of her striated ebb helmet. Outside, tracer fire and missiles dotted space, going on forever, hurtling toward nothing or something, preferably not her own team.

She tensed when an explosion lit up the cosmos. She hoped it wasn't a friendly Thunderbird hit and broken into fiery pieces, burned and then frozen in the deep, dark vacuum of space.

Unfortunately, a destroyer had cracked in half, one half spinning away from the other.

Her stomach jumped to her throat, and she pushed her starfighter forward. Her cockpit window heads-up display showed her distance from the beehive of activity, where the breadth of the battle loomed.

She was closer than she thought.

She cringed as chaotic shouts, screams, and incoherent orders carried through her commlink in a nonstop stream like demons scraping her inner ear. She couldn't stay back and roam the outskirts of the skirmish. She had to be with her friends, her allies, and her compatriots.

She turned down her comm audio dial, turning the combined voices into one monotonous cry.

She was the major, and she'd make sure to stay alive long enough to win the battle and get everyone back, even if she had to take the last bullet.

Checking her HDC, she spotted the signatures of *Brigantia*'s Thunderbird Squadron VTeB-12, VTeB-14, and VTeB-16, comprising fifty-two remaining Thunderbirds, all fighting for their lives. The *Taranis'* forces fared better, but not by much.

She wiped a clammy palm on her flight suit just as a beep sounded through her cockpit. She gasped, eyes widening, and spun her craft out of the way. An incoming attacker flew by quickly, its heavy cannons streaming red slugs and missing by meters.

Torquing her Thunderbird to the right, she pressed her throttle forward and punched her starfighter faster through the blackness.

She was wide of the major conflict and heading toward a small ring cloud of floating rocks. She noticed the enemy who had engaged were entering the firestorm of battle, ignoring Eden or coming back for her later.

She turned off the commlink. "Power down," she ordered, and her Thunderbird complied. Any heat or electrical signatures coming off her bird would be invisible to all sensors as soon as her ship cooled, which out here, would be fast. Most importantly, the rocks would disguise her from radar, she hoped.

She squeezed her eyes shut and knocked her helmet with her fist. "Think, Eden, think."

On her short trip here, she couldn't think of anything other than saving her people. That wasn't a plan. To save her pilots, she needed to think of something now, especially since she told Admiral Lutz that she was more competent out here than on *Brigantia*.

She opened her eyes and shifted them to the two red, glowing pyramids moving closer to the fight.

She lifted her visor and tapped the center of her forehead this time, something she used to do for tests to stay focused. It was also something she did when her mother was out cold on the couch and she needed to think of an excuse to tell the neighbors for them to help her.

"She fell and hit her head. Can you take her to the infirmary?"

"She didn't have enough water and fainted from heat exhaustion. Can you take her to the infirmary?"

"She had a seizure. Yeah, she has them all the time. Can you take her to the infirmary?"

Tapping helped her to think outside the box, and it usually worked. "What's the plan?" she said, continuing to tap.

The enemy fighters were precise, rarely making mistakes. They worked as a team. What was baffling was that for such elite attackers, these enemies didn't seem to evade very well when engaged from behind. It was as if they weren't as well trained in evasive maneuvering tactics.

"That's it."

But, no, could it be that simple?

It couldn't be that easy. They don't know what to do while being chased, or they don't understand the element of surprise?

They lock up? Why?

"Why" didn't matter. If simple worked, then she had to do it. If surprise worked, so much the better.

"Open commlink." She swiped the salty sweat from her lips, then slammed her visor shut. "This is Major Eden Gaines. VTeB-12, 14, and 16, we change our plan of action." She found an empty sector on a map on her HDC, one filled with more floating rocks, enough to hide hundreds of starfighters. "Disengage and fly to zero-one-six, I repeat, zero-one-six. Now."

She powered on her Thunderbird and pressed it to the coordinates. Eden watched as her starfighters immediately disengaged, taking evasive maneuvers as they headed for the rendezvous point.

"VTeB-12 and 14, form a flock. VTeB-16, create an arrow. When we meet at the specified coordinates, you better bet you'll have a hundred fighters on your asses." She'd be at zero-one-six in less than a minute, just before the squadrons. "VTeB-12, when I give the order to break left, I will say 'Twelve.' Confirm order."

VTeB-12 confirmed, and she continued, "VTeB-14, when I give the order to break right, I will say 'Fourteen.' Confirm."

Again, several voices confirmed. "VTeB-16, you are the closest group to the coordinates. Continue arrow formation and swing around behind me. I'll be at the coordinates before you. When you are there, turn off your Thunderbirds and float within the belt of rocks. We'll be invisible to their sensors. When the enemy flies by, we'll re-engage thrusters and blast them. Do you confirm?"

The problem was, she didn't know for sure if they'd be invisible. Most likely, the enemy would catch *something* on radar, but if the enemy were using a different type of sensors, then maybe the floating rocks would disguise Eden and the fleet, making them like ghosts ready to materialize.

She reached zero-one-six quicker than she thought and positioned her craft near a giant asteroid, flipping her craft so her guns would face the belly of the enemy fighters when they flew by, chasing her pilots.

"VTeB-16 spread out among the rocks and position your ships like mine. The rest of you, don't mind us and fly above the sector. Lead these bastards to the slaughter." She eyed her HDC. Hundreds of enemy fighters were hot on her pilots' tails.

Eden floated with the rocks, watching VTeB-16 flying directly at her.

The man in the lead zipped by her and turned on a dime, flipping one-hundred-eighty degrees. He boosted forward several meters, floating by Eden's side. He flashed an unsure grin, his eyes wide with fear. The guy had most likely witnessed death and destruction on a level unheard of in his life.

The rest arrived and found positions near dozens of rocks.

"Once 12 and 14 break, we open fire. Do you understand?"

"Yes, Major," came the replies.

This had to work. It would surprise and potentially throw the attacking assholes off for a minute, hopefully two. "Twenty seconds until we down some evil pricks," she blared over the comm.

She clenched her teeth. Setting up an ambush, the timing had to be perfect. If this worked, it would increase the odds of their survival. If she were wrong, she'd be another dust cloud in the memories of space. "They don't like to be surprised, ladies and gentlemen pilots. Get ready."

Well, who the hell liked to be surprised by missiles and flames?

Nine seconds displayed on her HDC. "Hold tight, everyone. Trust me on this. We lay waste to these guys on my mark."

The blips of her allies and the incoming enemy fighters soared closer to the coordinates on her holodisplay.

Four seconds.

Three seconds.

Two.

"Twelve," she shouted. "Fourteen."

VTeB-12 broke left and VTeB-14 broke right, separating like people parting for Prime Director Zim Noki making his way through a crowd.

The enemy craft hadn't detected her or squadron VTeB-16 and followed 12 and 14 banking above and away from the space rocks.

"Fire at will."

She switched on her Thunderbird and squeezed her trigger at an unknown enemy who deserved death tenfold.

The rest of 16 did the same. The bandits' fuselages cracked open, and internal fire shot out of the cockpits and rear boosters. Fireworks lit up the blackness in front of her, and debris shot wildly, spinning into the recesses of space.

"Some got through," came a voice over the comm.

The last of the enemy ships zipped overhead, and she checked the radar, nodding. "About two dozen blips made it alive, but we decimated them, boys and girls." She couldn't help but smile. "Let's get the rest." She pushed her starfighter to full throttle and switched to missiles.

She banked hard, veering behind an enemy. It dipped, and she followed her crosshairs lighting up in red and her target lock beeping. She pulled the trigger.

A missile launched from her wing, and an orange fire rocketed it forward, striking and bursting her target into chunks of armor and hundreds of parts.

Tracer fire and missiles from VTeB-16 tore more craft to shreds. The explosions and flames filled Eden's window, lighting her cockpit with yellow and reds, mirroring the external destruction only to extinguish in the vacuum of space seconds later.

To her amazement, the enemies weren't fazed. They continued their pursuit, ignoring the fact they'd just lost a dozen or so of their own craft in a single moment. It was as if they didn't know or care. They were not leaving their targets. They were either mad or brave, or who knew, maybe robots.

"Pursue and destroy. Stay on their backs."

VTeB-16 split. Some followed her and tailed the enemy chasing VTeB-14, others went after those chasing VTeB-12.

Eden veered around and slipped behind a bogey. Weapons lock beeped through the cockpit. She pinched her lips together, setting her finger on the trigger, and sent forth a missile that sliced through a bandit.

The tail broke apart, and the craft crashed into another enemy, sending both into a blaze of glory.

A crackle came over her comm. "Eden, move your team out of the way."

It was Admiral Lutz.

Taking her eyes off another target, she sighted *Brigantia* and a battle group of dozens of battleships, a handful of destroyers, and smaller crafts heading toward her formation. She glanced at her HDC. "All teams, coordinates zero-one-nine."

She pulled back on her control stick, the rest of her team doing the same. She turned her craft, swung around ninety degrees, and headed toward the new coordinates.

She gulped hard when she spotted the pyramids. *Brigantia* had covered a huge distance in a short time.

Hundreds of small blips on her radar told her that more enemy starfighters had launched and were coming her way, most likely to intercept *Brigantia*'s offensive play.

She gasped, and her arms flew up, her head jerking back. "What the hell?" A bright white light flashed between her and the pyramids, accompanied by a large object.

Eden froze. "Oh, no," she said under her breath.

Starbase Matrona, which for all she'd known was dead and out of commission, had jumped into the sector directly between *Brigantia* and the oncoming pyramids.

The technology worked, it actually worked. And at the worst time.

Two buzzes vibrated her seat, and her HDC lit up with warnings. Her mouth gaped open as she held back a scream.

She punched her fighter forward.

Two large torpedoes had launched from the pyramids headed directly for Matrona.

12

SHAE

Unknown Sector, Orion Spur

"*Matrona* jumped. I repeat, *Matrona* jumped."

Shae leaped out of his chair and rushed to Brigger's station, eyeing his holodisplay and ignoring the vidscreen's image of what Brigger was seeing. "Where are they?"

Brigger pointed to an area between *Brigantia* and the pyramid ships.

Two red dots blinked on the HDC. "What are those, Brigger? They are huge. Zoom in."

The screen zoomed in, displaying two comet-like orbs with fiery blue tails, measuring nearly half the size of the starship he was in, approaching Matrona quickly.

"Torpedoes, sir. And massive. But they're moving slower than usual."

Shae twisted around and glared at Louise. "Launch countermeasures."

Even though these torpedoes were slow, countermeasures most likely wouldn't get there in time.

Shae backed up and walked around to sit in his chair, slamming his fist against the armrest. "Let's get those torpedoes."

Louise nodded, her face white and pallid. Her chin trembled as if she wanted to personally show the attackers her fist. "Countermeasures launched, sir."

Shae rested his eyes on Matrona and saw a lone starfighter heading its way. "What starfighter signature is that?"

Brigger pulled it up on the holodisplay. "That's Major Eden Gaines, sir."

"Open commlink to Eden," said Shae.

13

EDEN

Unknown Sector, Orion Spur

"Eden, we have outbound countermeasures," said Shae over Eden's commlink.

She glanced at her HDC. She'd seen the torpedoes on her holodisplay the exact moment they were launched. She pushed her Thunderbird onward at a faster clip. "The countermeasures won't make it in time, Admiral."

"We have no choice," he replied. "Get the Thunderbirds out of there. If Starbase Matrona is destroyed, all nearby craft will be hit. Take your teams to our landing bays, but send some birds to launch as many missiles at the torpedoes as possible."

From the looks of her display, she was the only starfighter near enough to reach a distance to launch missiles at the oncoming projectiles.

"Yes, sir. I'm the closest to the torpedoes, and from what my sensors are telling me, no one would reach the launch point in time, so I'm the woman for the job." Eden clicked open all lines. "Attention birds, shake your attackers, finish your targets, and immediately head to *Brigantia*'s landing bay."

Eden pressed her throttle forward, speeding her Thunderbird toward the torpedoes.

She had to stop the torpedoes no matter the stakes, even if her life would end to save countless men, women, and children on that starbase, and ultimately on *Brigantia* as well.

Checking her HDC, she clicked her weapons on and locked them on the inbound torpedoes.

WEAPONS OFFLINE blinked across her screen.

"No...don't do this. Not now." She clicked on her weapons again.

WEAPONS OFFLINE

It was like a bad vid movie. This couldn't be happening. Did she melt her cannons somehow? Did she burn her weapons system?

"Eden," said Shae, his voice low and fierce like a father to a disobeying child. "We see that your weapons system is down. Turn around and head to *Brigantia,* now. There's nothing you can do to help from this point forward."

Eden pushed on the throttle, hurtling even faster through space, watching Matrona coming closer to her and the torpedoes moving ever closer to their target. She had to position herself between the starbase and the torpedoes.

She trembled and squeezed her muscles tightly, forcing herself to remain on course. This wasn't just a risk. This was a death sentence.

"Sir, I'm the only one who can stop this."

"Hold on and maintain course." There was a pause, then Shae continued, "You're correct. We have no other option." Another pause and Shae's breath echoed through her helmet. "What you're about to do is the bravest thing I've ever seen. If I had more of you, we wouldn't be losing this fight. Guild speed, Eden. Guild speed."

She heard his voice and listened to her heart beating rapidly, the blood pounding in her ears.

She knew Admiral Lutz would do the same if he were out here in her position and in the same situation—the only one close enough to potentially save a million people.

He'd do it. Her mom wouldn't, but she wasn't like her mom. Why did it matter? Admiral Lutz had taken care of her like she was his own daughter, the only one who had, so it wouldn't matter if Eden blinked out of existence. She wouldn't be missed by anybody except Shae.

She didn't have children, and no one would remember her when she ceased to exist.

Here she was, attempting to save her real mother, Starbase Matrona, and all the people inside who would never know Eden's name. That's what she was good at. Taking care of things and quietly leaving soon after.

Her lips quivered as tears welled in her eyes. She didn't want to say goodbye to the admiral, but she pressed forward anyway, pushing her throttle at full burn, her ion boosters propelling her at speeds she'd never reached before.

Matrona grew bigger, and the torpedoes were dead on target for the starbase's last breath. Eden had to get far enough in front of the starbase to limit the shock wave from hitting Matrona as much as possible.

She tapped on a few holographic buttons, pulling up distance and time.

Sixteen seconds and she'd blow by Starbase Matrona, probably looking like a string of fiery light as she passed, she thought.

"Eden," said Shae, his voice low, calm, and soft, like the father she had never known. "You're braver than anyone I've ever met and ever will. Thank you for your service and your life. You will be remembered for all time. I'll make sure of it."

His voice was like a song, a sad, depressing one. She didn't need that right now, didn't need any reason to turn back and head home, to console him and tell him everything would be all right. She didn't need a reason to help him and then move on to the next person, as she always had in relationships, with wounded plants, with abused animals - never keeping them, but fixing them up, loving them, and giving them away to more deserving people.

She flipped her commlink to the off position.

She passed Matrona, the moon-sized starbase a blur. If they could see her waving goodbye, she would do it. If she could get a glimpse of her childhood home, she would blow a kiss, thanking it for keeping a roof over her head, for being her family while her mother could not.

Blue light streamed into her cockpit. She was nearing the torpedoes.

She eyed the display on the flight console.

Eight seconds until impact. Eight seconds until her last heartbeat, her last moment to see the beauty of the deep, dark cosmos all around her.

She veered off, adjusting her flight trajectory for the torpedoes, her cockpit glowing bluer.

Impact in five seconds. She needed to go faster, to put as much distance as possible between her and Matrona.

For a brief instant, she wondered what she was doing. It was a bad idea. She deserved to live like everyone else. She could master herself, master life, and give to the remaining humans any wisdom stuck in her brain.

She shook her head.

It was too late.

It didn't matter.

The wisdom she'd pass down if she had any at all, would be that she was about to save an entire race, and that was more important than her own life.

Star Guild and Starbase Matrona, a family. My family.

She smiled at the thought. In her younger life, she had thought about having a partner and children, retiring as an admiral, living the rest of her life in nice quarters snuggled up to the biosphere inside the starbase where she could watch her children grow, then her grandchildren, and her grandchildren's children.

They would play in the biosphere forests, the beautiful meadows, the rivers, and hills, just as she had done alone while growing up.

Three seconds.

Her cockpit highlighted a deeper blue, and her head drew back stiffly. She thought about ejecting, pushing herself far away from the explosion, but who was she kidding? She'd be evaporated in seconds after the initial impact. If not, the waves that followed would turn her into space ash.

She gunned it, putting as much force against the throttle as she could.

One second.

Two silver egg-shaped orbs, as big as her Thunderbird, appeared on each side of her. Shining as if they were the most polished objects in the universe, she knew she was hallucinating, a fight or flight response from her brain to deal with her imminent death.

She let go of the control stick and placed her hands over her heart as she squeezed her eyes shut. Blue shone through her eyelids. In half a second, her life would be over, and she welcomed it.

14

SHAE

Unknown Sector, Orion Spur

On the vidscreen, Shae watched quietly with a thick lump in his throat and a heaviness in his heart as he waited for Eden to end her own life to stop torpedoes from ending Matrona's.

A second before impact, two unknown silver orbs jumped in on each side of Eden's Thunderbird.

A blue flash filled the bridge's vidscreen. Shae put his hands up to shield his face.

His first thought was Eden was gone, and he slumped against his seat. His next thought threw out a net of hope, *Survive, Matrona. Survive.*

The blue light disappeared just as the torpedoes detonated, sending a white translucent energy wave across the stars, an aura moving outward and heading toward Starbase Matrona.

Eden had been hit, vaporized upon contact. No pain. She did her job and her last one at that.

The energy wave dissipated as it reached Matrona, and the starbase stood its ground, not wavering or jostling.

"Thank Guild," Shae said to himself. "And thank you, Eden."

She was gone, and her Thunderbird with her, both incinerated.

The two egg-shaped ships were gone as well. It was either a strange suicide mission by those orbs or being in the wrong place at the wrong time.

Signatures indicated they had instrumentation and were piloted, but who the hell were they? Were they enemy ships? Or ships from another race, another species?

Shae and Star Guild may never know.

Shae's gaze dropped to the floor and he cleared his throat before bellowing out an order. "Turn the Thunderbirds and battle groups back around. Head for the remaining enemy craft. This isn't over yet."

"Admiral," said Brigger. "The enemy crafts are retreating."

"What?" Louise jumped from her station, leaning toward the vidscreen. "Why—"

She saw it, just as Shae did.

Shae stood at the vidscreen. The screen zoomed in on where the pyramids had been, showing debris spread in all directions. The pyramids had been demolished by something or by someone.

Louise hurried over, her eyes searching space. "What in the blazes? They didn't just blow themselves up." She shifted on her feet. "Reverse the vid feeds, Brigger. We need to see what hit them."

"Yes, ma'am." Brigger reversed the feeds. He pressed several more buttons, his eyebrows scrunching together. "I'm not allowed to reverse the feeds. Something is blocking me. But—" he jerked slightly back. "Uh, ma'am. The rest of the enemy ships are now jumping out of the sector."

Shae straightened. "Show me."

The vidscreen shifted from the destroyed pyramids to the enemy craft individually lighting up like stars, collapsing into themselves as they jumped out of the system.

Shae walked over and stood next to Louise, a sudden lightness coming over him. "Eden saved us."

Whatever else happened was strange luck, and the ridiculous miracle he requested, but the how of it didn't make any sense.

"Aye, Admiral. She lives forever among the stars now."

In truth, Starship *Brigantia* and Starbase Matrona shouldn't be alive and functioning. It wasn't just Eden who saved them. She had given them more time, but sacrificing her life hadn't killed those pyramid starships.

"Eden's the brightest star among them." Shae placed his hand on Louise's shoulder and squeezed, his voice soft. "Take over command and dock with Matrona. I'll be in my quarters preparing for the Prime Director to see what the hell is going on."

The admiral looked at the clock, counting down when *Taranis* would jump coordinates. They had three hours left. "Give Starship *Taranis'* coordinates to Matrona. We'll dock inside of Matrona when she jumps, taking all of us with her. Understood?"

The XO nodded. "Understood." She turned, taking over command.

Shae walked toward the bridge's exit with a mix of emotions he couldn't understand. None of what just happened was understandable by anybody, especially him.

"Ladies and gentlemen, prepare to dock on Matrona," the XO ordered.

15

ALI

<u>Planet Eos, West of the Radiation Zone—Adarta System, Orion Spur</u>

Ali placed the cockpit's water tube between her lips and took a sip.

Nothing but air.

"Dammit."

Daf had been peering out of the mech's window for as many hours as Ali had, watching the world turn pale blue as the last of the daylight dimmed. On Eos, the sun didn't fall much lower than the horizon this time of year.

Ali glanced at Daf. There was dried blood on the rims of her nostrils, and her eyes were sunken in.

"We don't have any water." Ali wanted to cut the silence of the last several hours.

Daf turned her head and looked at Ali, her face as pale as the many moons that circled the planet, her eyes bloodshot, and her long black hair a tangled mess. "What?"

"You look terrible, Daf."

Daf blinked a couple of times. "I just want...I just need to sleep."

"What's stopping you?" Ali checked the time on her HDC. It was 9:36 p.m. About this time, she should be on Starbase Matrona, in her living quarters sitting comfortably on her bed, watching an entertainment vid, and eating an apple or some other late-night fruit snack.

Daf's mouth slackened. "Um, well, we have enemies trying to crawl up our butts. Why else wouldn't I sleep?"

Ali's stomach tightened. She was talking to an inferior who suddenly had a bad attitude. "Don't speak to a superior in that tone."

Daf shot her a look. "I'm sorry, Chief, but I'm just stating the obvious."

This was why they never got along. Daf never respected Ali's higher rank and never cared enough to *act* like it. In truth, Ali's higher rank wasn't a military rank, but it was supposed to hold a tad more than a bucket of water.

Instead, Ali was more like a crew boss, just like all the Chief Petty Officers who ran mech mining teams on this planet.

Ali's eyes pierced Daf's, and she threw as many invisible daggers at the girl as possible. "What's obvious is that you're tired and cranky. I can handle staring out the window by myself. If anything happens, I'll wake you. Do you understand? I need you fully aware and awake, and right now, you're the opposite. Get some sleep."

Daf pursed her lips, let out a loud breath, and turned her head toward the cockpit window, again staring at the terrain in front of them.

They were on a hill that merged with the base of Mount Gabriel, making it easy to observe the land laid out before them, and allowing them to see farther than they could have from a lower location. Concealed under a strange rock formation that resembled a small lean-to, it was a nice hiding place among the ebb rocks jutting out everywhere, and with their mech shut down, they seemed to be invisible to the enemy.

Daf's stomach growled. "We need food." Her voice held no emotion, and she continued to stare out the window.

"And water," replied Ali.

Daf's shoulders slumped. "What else could go wrong?"

"Your attitude. Now, straighten up and act strong. I don't have the time or space for whiny underlings." She almost choked on her insult.

She didn't know what it was, but she couldn't stand being around Daf. Perhaps it was her beauty and the way she charmed men, the way their eyes twinkled when they looked at her.

In truth, though, Daf was right. They needed food almost as much as water.

Daf's brows V'd and her lips pursed, then she turned away from Ali.

Ali took a deep breath and told herself she couldn't let Daf or the stress get to her. It wouldn't be good for either one of them. "Look, I'm sorry. Like you, I'm a bit confused and scared. I don't know how many have died out there and how many we need to save."

"Save?" Daf jabbed a finger at the window. "Are you thinking about going around and searching for people?"

"We have warehouses Twelve and Thirteen a few klicks west of here. In a few hours, when the shadows are at their darkest, we sneak our mech over there."

Daf's mouth dropped open. "That's insane. We'll be caught and most likely tortured or killed."

Daf had a point, but they could also sit there and die from lack of food and water, and eventually, lack of oxygen as the tanks would run dry in under a day. Their best option was to travel to a warehouse at the darkest point of the night, find survivors, stock up, and refuel.

"We need to fill our oxygen tanks, too, Daf."

Daf thought for a moment and nodded. "All right. But did you see one?"

Ali tilted her head at the question. "If you mean the enemy, then yes, I did."

Daf picked at her shoe. "Those guys are big."

"Where the hell did you see one?"

"Ambrose Quarry." Daf picked harder at her shoe, trying to get the blood off the laces. "I looked up at the top of the quarry, and there were hundreds of those giants holding glowing spears staring down at us. I about crapped my pants. I thought it was a joke at first, you know, Warren's mech team shooting a hologram at the edge of our quarry, screwing with us like he usually does."

Ali's eyes widened, filling with hope. "Were there any survivors besides you?"

Daf shook her head, picking faster at her laces. "I don't know. The big guys shot their weapons, but it didn't seem to hurt our mechs. When their starfighters came, they ripped us to shreds. That's when I ran my mech's ass off."

"You didn't look to see if there were any survivors?"

Daf stopped picking and looked at her lap. "I was running for my life. I was scared to death. I don't even know how I survived. I ran—"

Ali raised her hand. "I understand. I was scared, too. I was certain that I *was* dead. You did more than I did." She looked Daf square in the eyes. "You saved my life. For that, I thank you."

"We got Guild'n lucky, Chief." Peering out the window again, she took a deep breath and cleared her throat. "Mount Gabriel is also called Forever Mountain. I've always wondered about that."

Forever Mountain. Ali had heard her dad call it that too. She shook her head. Her mom, her dad, there had always been something missing with her parents.

It was the lack of a real connection and an underlying sense her parents, Captain Diana Johnson and Major Gordon Johnson, were more strangers than anything else.

Always another presence hung around her, a shadow in the back of her mind, like a past life memory or something she couldn't quite put her finger on.

A father figure, as if she'd had another dad. She almost laughed at the thought that had consumed the last four or five years of her life.

Daf snapped her fingers. "Ali? You there?"

"Uh, yes. Mount Gabriel. It's the largest mountain on Eos. I think they named it that because it seems to go on forever."

"Oh." Daf shrugged. "That was uneventful."

"It could be called that because of another reason, though." Ali hesitated and wondered if she should continue.

"What is it?"

"I was wandering around a couple of weeks ago and stumbled across a large cave opening."

"During work hours?"

"Yes, I was investigating."

Daf perked up, a slow smile appearing on her face. "You were playing hooky?"

"No, investigating."

Daf rolled her eyes. "If you say so. Investigating what?"

"A blue light."

"A light?"

"Yes. I saw it blinking from the base of the mountain. Anyway, I went to search it out, and I found a tunnel."

"I've never seen a tunnel on this planet." Daf raised her brows and edged closer.

Ali gazed at the shadows across the land. They were getting darker, the color of the Star Guild's dark-blue uniforms she used to wear. "Yes, I—" Ali gasped and ducked, her knees hitting the cockpit floor.

The mech vibrated, and the earth trembled beneath its feet as a roar filled the sky.

Daf lurched back.

Ali quickly eyed the holomonitor to make sure her mech was off.

It was.

She took a few steps forward and leaned up against the cockpit glass to watch the new shadows zipping across the land from overhead.

Another roar, and then another.

Ali's lips moved, quietly counting the starfighters. "Eleven."

One banked right. A knot formed in Ali's throat. "Oh, no." It circled around.

Ali strapped in and got ready to activate her mech. "Hold on tight." She glared out of the window. "We have one coming in fast."

16

ALI

Planet Eos, West of the Radiation Zone—Adarta System, Orion Spur

Drops of sweat formed over Ali's lips as Daf held onto the HDC column and ducked low.

Ali caught her breath as the oncoming starfighter dipped its nose and angled its trajectory in Ali's direction.

She opened her mouth, ready to command her mech to power up.

The ground rumbled, and the starfighter changed its flight path. It spun high and away, displaying its underbelly. It looped and flew after its squadron, its afterburners lighting up a small portion of the sky.

She let out a deep breath. "It flew off." She relaxed. "Thank the galaxy."

"It flew low. I could practically feel its engines," replied Daf.

"I was wondering when they'd send a search party. I'm thanking everything under the stars they haven't located us yet." Ali rubbed her face to wash the fear off. "As you said, we're lucky." She leaned back against the bulkhead and let out a loud exhale.

Daf slumped back as well, her eyes darting over the ebb landscape.

They were going to be there for a little longer, so it would be best to get Daf's mind on something else, Ali thought. Something that used her brain, not that she had much of one in that beautiful head of hers.

It would help Ali get her own mind off the attackers and off her mentally abusive father, which always led to thoughts of her terrible mother.

She'd give anything to start her life over and be raised by loving parents.

Her father, now dead, lost in a Star Guild exploration or so she was told, was a piss-ant. She could hardly remember him, except the sharp, knife-pointed words he always had for her. It was as if he was caught in her memory fog, his face a mystery but his words screaming in her ears.

Her eyes shot wide, and she shook her head furiously. These thoughts and odd feelings shook at her brain like excavated earth through a soil sifter's mesh screen on an archeological dig.

Excavated earth? Soil sifter? Mesh screen? Archeological dig?

She was definitely going mad.

"Yo, Ali."

Ali lifted her chin. "Yes?"

"Are you all right? You look a little shell-shocked."

"Yes, sorry. Just lost in thought."

Daf leaned in. "What thought? Because whatever thought you were thinking must have been daunting, and I don't want to be thinking anymore fearful—"

Ali lifted her hand, shutting Daf up. She had to change the subject. "Where do you think they store all the ebb we collect?"

Daf shrugged. "I don't know. Perhaps back on Matrona or a starship? Why?"

"We've been collecting ebb ever since we've been orbiting Eos, a little over a thousand years, or longer, which is a little stupid if you ask me. Couldn't we find a new planet to live on by now? We should have enough ebb by now—more than enough—but I rarely see any new ships or bases being built, except after a pirate attack. Other than some repairs here and there, it doesn't account for how much ebb we collect." Ali huffed. "I find that a little strange, don't you? I always have, but," she put her fingers in air quotes, "'Don't question the governance. They know best.'"

"Well, they also use ebb on buildings, warehouses, floors, walls, just about everything. They're holding the ebb somewhere. What does that have to do with anything?"

"There are two-dozen warehouses holding forty-eight mechs each. We gather this stuff every day, and we don't have nearly the amount of repairs to use up all the ebb we collect and *have* collected for hundreds of years."

"So? They put it somewhere. Where? I don't know, and I couldn't care less."

Ali's eyes narrowed and her face flushed red. "Have you ever seen a pile of ebb after it's been transported off this planet? Have you ever even seen the pilots who fly the ebb transports, the Starhawks? Why are their windows tinted so dark we can never see inside? Have you ever met anyone who says they're on the Ebb Transport Team?" She didn't wait for Daf's reply. "Yeah, me either."

"Okay, so what are you saying, Ali?"

Ali wondered how Daf could be so dense. Perhaps this conversation used *too* much of Daf's brain. "I'm saying it's being taken someplace else. But where?" In exasperation, she threw her arms up in the air. "I don't know, and you don't know, nobody knows. I do know we are not using most of it. There's no doubt about that."

Ali glanced out the window and focused on a small mountain range silhouetted in the distance. Her life was always a shitstorm because there was always something missing she couldn't put her finger on.

Maybe it was why she questioned everything and why she trusted no one and did everything on her own terms, in her own way, and by herself. It could be why her memories faded into foggy picture-like flashbacks for anything past four years.

She felt like society, the governance, those who ran the starbase were lying about everything, including her. She didn't belong here with these people.

Perhaps her dream about the Nazis, the giant, and being shot, wasn't a dream after all.

She curled her fingers into a fist and pursed her lips. Her brain was likely shrinking and would be the size of Daf's someday as this was too much to process.

Ali continued her questioning. "Why is it mandatory to be over seven foot five inches in height if you want to run for the Prime Director position? They have all been over seven feet five inches. What the Eos is that about? And no one questions it?"

Ali rolled her eyes, again making air quotes. "'It's the way it's always been.'" She snorted. "Questions, questions, and never any answers."

Ali drooped at the enormity of it all. Through the years, she had come to see the people around her as robots. They did their best to live life happily, devoid of any real thoughts, even of dreaming. Why was dreaming rare for everyone except her?

She knew she wouldn't get much more out of Daf, let alone convince her the governance had a secret from everyone about their ebb storage, and about her.

"So, you mentioned a tunnel?" inquired Daf.

Ali looked down. "Uh, yep."

"Can I get a little more information there, Chief?"

Ali figured Daf was just another pawn, another thoughtless worker who wouldn't believe what she was about to say. It didn't matter. Ali never held her thoughts in for too long. "I found a tunnel system that went deep under Mount Gabriel. The tunnels seemed to go on forever, spiraling down. I walked my mech through them for a while and never came to a dead end. I did come on something strange, odd. An enormous, and I mean enormous, door with weird writing etched on it." She stopped, not wanting to waste her words on someone who would most likely think she was crazy.

"Huh. Who would build a door down there?"

"Who knows what Star Guild or the governance does when we're not looking."

Daf nodded, her lips curling up. "Yeah, that's where they must hide the ebb from us." She let out a soft laugh.

Ali shot her a dirty look. "Not funny, Daf."

Daf's lips formed an 'o,' and she gave a pointed expression. "You're serious?"

"As serious as George Washington. And he couldn't tell a lie."

"Huh?"

Ali blinked a couple of times. Who was George Washington? "I don't know what I'm saying."

"Ali, if you saw a tunnel in Mount Gabriel, why are we out here and not hiding in there?"

"We needed someplace fast to hide, and we weren't near the tunnel. We didn't have time, and besides, I only know of one way in which is also the same way out. Catch my drift? They find us, and we have no way to escape."

Daf nodded and turned her head to the window, again staring at the shadows and rocks.

"I saw something else down there," said Ali.

Daf looked a little suspicious. "Okay, I'll bite. What did you see?"

Ali shifted her weight from one leg to the other. She'd been standing for too long, so she unstrapped her restraining harness and sat down, crossing her legs. "The door. It said or showed we weren't created here. None of us. Not me. Not you. Not anyone."

"You got that from a door?"

Ali went rigid. "Yes. I saw images, and it was like it projected thoughts into my brain." Ali had wondered if it could have been a governance experiment. Her feelings told her otherwise, but who would create a massive door in the middle of a mountain?

Nothing was adding up. Not this war. Not her memories. Not that door.

"How could you have possibly determined all of that from a door?" Daf moved away from her, probably unconsciously, the way someone avoids discomfort or lies.

Ali tipped her head to the side and shrugged. She didn't blame Daf for not believing her. She wouldn't have believed someone if they told her the same story. It wasn't just a door. It was something else, something that changed the more you looked at it. She slapped her thighs and pointed at Daf, faking a grin. "Got you. I can't believe you fell for it."

"Okay. You're being an idiot, Chief."

"I know. I'm just trying to take our minds off what we're about to do."

"What are we going to do?"

Ali stood and strapped herself in. "Power up."

The mech activated, and the engines vibrated. She switched parrot mode on and glanced at Daf. "Hold on to something. We're heading west. It's time to get some food and water and find survivors."

17

SHAE

Starbase Matrona—Unknown Sector, Orion Spur

Shae stood at attention as several governance officials entered the conference room. One gave him a nod, his nephew Koda Lutz, the youngest political official of the group.

Three armed soldiers from the Matrona Guard entered next and walked around the massive table set in the middle of the room with a gigantic bowl of fruit at the center.

The guards held guns pointed at the admiral. They marched toward the back wall and stood as still as a statue.

A sudden chill hit Shae. This wasn't good. He pressed his hands together. They were cold and damp. He hadn't felt this way since his final exams at Star Guild Academy.

They had just been through a near genocide, and here was the Matrona Guard aiming their weapons at him in the same room Prime Director Zim Noki broadcast his speeches to everyone on Matrona.

Something was wrong. Hundreds of thousands were dead. They should be targeting the killers, not him.

Why didn't I bring my own sidearm?

Shae glared at the next person to join the group, the Prime Director, all seven foot five inches of him.

The Prime Director took a deep breath, his eyes fleeting to the green plants hanging from the walls. Vines climbed to the ceiling, flowers budding everywhere.

Shae cleared his throat loudly and gestured toward the military personnel. "What's going on, Prime Director?"

The Prime Director made Shae's six-foot six-inch frame seem insignificant. Zim was a beast, almost as thick in muscle as he was tall. Charismatic with a voice to match, his face was beautiful, chiseled where it needed to be. He was perfect for his high position in governance, always able to say the right things at the right time.

Zim approached Shae. His hand turned into a fist that slammed into Shae's stomach. Shae's breath escaped him as he doubled over, and his eyes popped wide as a growing ache filled his gut and went up to his chest.

Zim held Shae's curled body for a moment, then tossed him into a chair like a whipped dog.

Shae wheezed and leaned forward, pressing his forehead against the edge of the table. He gulped a couple of times and coughed several more. He tried to speak, to ask what was the deal, but nothing came out of his mouth.

Zim, an elected official who maintained his position by winning every political race held during the last three decades, was sometimes known to pack a punch to get his way.

Apparently, that punch was more literal than a metaphor.

Zim nonchalantly grabbed an apple and walked around the table to sit down across from Shae. Casually leaning back in his chair, he placed his feet on the table.

Zim took a bite, crunching it loudly for everyone to hear. His face reddened. "You left us high and dry, Admiral. You left us to die, you son-of-a-Guild. If I had it my way, I'd have you shot." He shook his head. "You abandoned us."

Shae, regaining his breath, lifted his eyes above the edge of the table. "I had no choice, Zim. We had to leave. They decimated my fleet." He sat up. "First Lieutenant Brigger patched through the coordinates to the entire fleet, including Starbase Matrona."

Zim dropped his feet and slapped the table with his hand. "We received no such communication, Admiral. And if we did, you should have waited until you saw Matrona jump. You risked millions of lives. Your fleet protects this starbase, not the fleet. The people come first. You are to serve and protect. You ran, you coward. You ran with your tail between your legs." He waved his hand, motioning for the other officials to join them at the table.

Shae had almost forgotten about them. As they took their seats, one of them nodded to him. She was an old friend, Prime Overseer Savanna Levens, and he was glad for her presence. She was the overseer of Sphere Six on Matrona, and one of her main functions was keeping the biosphere alive. The plants in the room were maintained by her office.

She sat straight, her gray hair falling over her aged eyes. She swiped her hair away. "Prime Director, the admiral would never knowingly do harm to you or the starbase. What you're doing here is absolutely insane."

"I agree," added Koda, frowning. His movie-star looks, short, styled black hair, and sparkling brown eyes shone at Zim.

Zim stared at Koda, then at Savanna. "He left us. He knowingly left us." He shook his head, his jaw set.

Shae put his hand up and attempted to calm the big man. "I left the coordinates with the entire fleet, Zim. I did everything in my power to help everyone in Star Guild and on Starbase Matrona get out of our sector alive. I thought Matrona would jump with us. You know me just as well as Savanna does. I would never knowingly harm you or anyone else in Star Guild."

Zim stiffened. "We're not Star Guild, Shae. All of us in here, including the Matrona Guards, are employees of Starbase Matrona. You, on the other hand, are Star Guild, and I'm above both Star Guild and Starbase Matrona. You had no authority over my position, including the military. You went over my head by taking over the fleet and jeopardizing millions of lives. Millions. You never once contacted me."

"We had no time to discuss options, Zim. We had to defend ourselves, and—"

"Defend?" Zim's eyes hardened. "You call that defending? You left. Plain and simple. You left us to fend for ourselves, though we had no defenses. If we'd had coordinates, we would have met you. The only explanation we have is a coup d'état."

Shae shot out of his chair. "What? By who?" He pointed to his chest. "By me?" He put his hands out, demanding an explanation. "A coup—a takeover?"

Shae felt like laughing. They had survived an invasion, and now he was witnessing something even more unbelievable than the attack. He changed to a more logical approach. "If you didn't have coordinates, how did you find us? You jumped Matrona to our exact coordinates, did you not?"

"We found you because of a distress signal coming from your ship. Who were you calling, Shae? The enemy?"

Savanna stood, the chair flinging out from behind her and tumbling to the side. "I've had enough, Zim. This meeting is over. What you're saying is absolutely crazy."

Koda pushed to his feet. "I second that. You're walking on ground you may not want to tread, Zim."

Zim ignored them, staring intently at the admiral. "Who were you calling?"

Shae sat down, wanting to bite his tongue but knowing he couldn't. "The Space Templars."

Zim stiffened. A twitch crossed his lower cheek as his eyes widened. Then he relaxed and smiled, the muscles around his eyes not contracting.

A fake smile.

Shae leaned in closer. Zim had twitched, not out of surprise, but out of fear. Was Zim hiding something?

The commonly held belief about the Space Templars was they were a myth. A normal response should have been a surprise-filled, quick laugh or confusion as if Shae had been joking.

Zim did none of that.

The Prime Director looked around the room, and his smile disappeared. He leaned back against his chair, his eyes cold. "A myth, Shae. It's a tale only children believe. Magical knights swooping in on majestic spacecraft are for action vids, not real life. Why did you *really* send it? Or do you want me to take your call to the Templars seriously?" Zim's question roused a chuckle around the room. "They are as fictitious as your lie. Who were you really calling, Shae?"

"A coup? That's what you're calling this?" Shae shook his head. He was being set up, and he knew this was just the beginning, the grand opening to the main attraction of finger-pointing. Shae had no interest in seizing control over the governance. Politicians were nuts. *This* was nuts.

"I didn't and *don't* have any intention of taking over the governance. You take me on my word, Zim, or shoot me now." He pointed at the military guard. "I have no patience for being dragged into a lengthy political scandal or whatever it is you're trying to create." He threw his hands up. "We were just attacked by an unknown force, something other than the Nontoc Belt pirates, and you want to play me into some type of political agenda?"

Zim raised one brow. "*Unknown* forces?" He released a phony laugh. "Oh, I think you know them well. I think you planned this attack, and until I can prove it, we have nothing more to discuss."

Zim stood. He nodded to his military guard and exited the room with all but a few of the officials following him like whipped pups after their master.

The pressures and panic of sudden war and the resulting mayhem had either rendered them so afraid that they would do anything for Zim, or they were spineless. Nonetheless, the timing was a perfect opportunity for Zim to perpetrate any political agenda of his choosing, pulling the wool over the eyes of the masses during the current chaos.

Across the room, Koda gave a thumbs-up. "I'm going to do everything I can to right this." He left the room, his eyes narrowed and determined.

Savanna strode to the door and turned, eyeing Shae. "I'm sorry. I don't know what's gotten into Zim. I've never seen him like this."

Shae stood and moved behind his chair, placing his hand on the top of the chair's backrest. He wiggled the chair back and forth, his knuckles turning white. "It's okay, Savanna." He looked at her and the green vines hanging down the wall behind her. They seemed to almost outline her face, making her glow.

"Everyone's alarmed by what happened," said Shae. "They need to point fingers at someone, and who better than me, the fleet admiral? Anything to clear Zim's name from this near genocide is going to be in Zim's best interest."

Savanna walked over to him and put her hand on his chest. "What happened?" She shook her head. Her mouth started to quiver as tears welled up. "Many of our friends and family are dead, Shae. Who were these criminals? Where did they come from?"

He placed his hand on hers. "I'll do everything I can to find out." He rubbed her hand, seeing there was more in her green eyes than she was telling him. "What happened to you, Savanna?"

She looked at her feet and started to sob. He pulled her into a hug.

"My son," she said.

He let go and grabbed her shoulders, lowering his head to meet her sobbing face. "Samuel?"

She nodded her head and slid into his arms again. "He was picking up his children at school when the first blast came." Her wrinkled hands started to shake as the sobs became stronger. "No, no," she wailed, punching his chest. "He was killed, saving his kids, my grandbabies."

Shae wanted to ask how it had happened, where exactly Samuel had been, at what school, but those questions were of no concern to Savanna. They wouldn't stop the grief from swallowing her. He couldn't imagine losing his daughter in a battle like this.

Shae stepped back, a pain enveloping his chest as if he had indeed lost a daughter, somewhere, and at some time. The problem? He never had a daughter, but he could see her, like a figure shrouded in mist.

He pushed the thought away as Savanna stepped back as well.

She patted his chest and gave a droopy smile. She wiped her tears. "I'm sorry. I don't want this to be too much for you." She waved a hand above her head and in a circle. "All of this."

"Don't apologize, Savanna."

"Do me a favor?" she asked, her chin quivering.

He nodded. "Anything for you."

"Find out who murdered my son."

He gave another nod. "I will. I'll bring them to justice."

She shook her head and backed toward the door. "Justice isn't what I'm looking for. I want to find a way to forgive them, to ask why they did what they did."

He gave a slight head shake.

How could she forgive them? Why would she? What did she want him to do, capture the enemy and present them to her so they could apologize?

He let the questions slip away. In her state, she wasn't thinking straight. How could he blame her?

Savanna turned and walked away, down the hall, and disappeared around a corner.

"Somehow, Savanna, I'll bring those bastards to your doorstep, dead or alive. I promise you."

He hurried out the door. There was no time to waste. He had to figure out what Zim was up to.

18

SHAE

Starship Brigantia, Starbase Matrona Docking Bay—Unknown Sector, Orion Spur

Shae put Eden's picture on his desk, then glanced out his two thickly lined clear-ebb windows. Usually, they displayed the universe —stars, a random comet, nebula clouds, and, of course, Eos with its golden aura.

But not today.

Today, he had a utilitarian view of Starbase Matrona's support columns in the inner docking station where his baby, Starship *Brigantia,* had been dry-docked for repairs.

He shifted his eyes back to Eden's picture and put his hands together in a prayer position. "Thank you."

He had sent Eden out, and she had saved countless lives. If he hadn't let her fly, more would be dead, and Matrona would've been a spectacle of eruptions.

"Eden. I'm so sorry." His stomach wrenched. He wanted to see her face again, to thank her in person, and throw her the military parade she deserved.

He made his way to his couch and sat. A holographic image of the most recent battle was displayed on his holovid, on pause.

"Play."

The holovid turned on.

"Stop." The vid paused. His mouth tightened as he studied the vid, his breathing slow and sharp.

In front of him, the sequence was stopped at the exact moment the two enormous pyramid ships erupted into a storm of fiery streams of debris, burning entrails blasting in every direction. Stars covered the background behind them, but there was a strange oval anomaly, translucent, and barely visible.

What is that?

"Reverse."

Shae scratched his head. He'd been at this for a while, doing his best to determine how the pyramids had been destroyed so quickly and so easily. Who, or what had destroyed them? Had it been the aftershock from the torpedo's impact on Eden's craft?

It couldn't be.

Could any of this lead back to Zim?

"Play."

Streaks of the fire pushed a handful of torpedoes onto the screen, followed by another handful, all coming from behind a group of asteroids near the pyramid ships.

The pyramid's armor sucked inward upon impact, the opposite side spitting out chunks of armor from the torpedo's exit. A secondary explosion went off, and a yellow flare erupted through the top of the pyramid like a volcano.

Both pyramids buckled in on themselves and splintered into pieces and formed a cloud of debris and shrapnel that covered everything in view.

"Stop. Zoom out."

There was that translucent oval-like craft again.

"Pull up grid."

A grid formed on the screen, showing horizontal and vertical lines, creating a pattern of squares with numbers in them.

"Zoom in on square twenty-one."

He squinted to make sure what he was seeing was correct. That was most assuredly a craft, an unsung hero.

"A surprise visitor we didn't know about." He sat up, looking intently at the craft. "Zoom in two more nodes."

"What the hell kind of craft is that?"

He'd never seen anything like it, an egg-shaped orb, not translucent like the first, but more silver in color, almost glowing.

No windows. No boosters. No wings.

That wasn't Star Guild technology, and if it were the attackers' technology, they had a traitor in their midst.

He stood and hurried to his desk. Turning on the commlink, he patched into *Brigantia*'s intercom on the bridge. "Executive Officer Louise Stripe, please report to the admiral's quarters."

He sat back down on the couch and stared intently at the paused vid.

"Reverse vid to the second hour, nineteen minutes twenty-eight seconds."

Eden's craft pulled up on the screen. Just before the torpedo impact, two silver egg-shaped orbs jumped in before a bright flash vanished them from existence.

Or so it seemed.

"Fast forward to the second hour, twenty-five minutes thirty-three seconds. Square section twenty-four. View in slow, zero-point-four speed."

He pinched his upper lip as he studied the vid.

Two silver egg-shaped orbs, accompanied by a Thunderbird, flew behind a floating space rock and disappeared from camera view.

What the hell was going on. Who was piloting those egg-ships? More importantly, how did they get a Thunderbird?

Was Eden in that Thunderbird?

He shook his head. "Impossible."

Any hope for Eden was gone. There was no way she survived.

He rewound and played it forward, watched, and reversed it again. He did this over and over as he attempted to piece everything together.

Part of him wondered if a malfunction was involved. This holovid had come from a camera at *Brigantia's* bow, near the bridge. Maybe the cam had been grazed by enemy fire, causing it to go haywire?

Secretly he hoped the Space Templars had answered his distress call, and they were the ones in the silver orbs.

He leaned his back against the couch cushion. "Don't be silly."

Zim was right. The Space Templars were magical heroes in children's fables, for kids to help them understand mythology and storytelling, and to uplift their spirits.

He shouldn't let his imagination get carried away.

Why did Zim hesitate when Shae mentioned the Space Templars? Zim's jaw had twitched, and his eyes clearly lied, but about what?

It was as if the Prime Director was hiding something.

He remembered his grandfather, the one who had given him the Space Templar pendant. He swore the Templars were real and had claimed they had once saved his starship after being struck by a rogue asteroid. All systems had been down, the fuel cells ruptured, and they couldn't communicate with anyone except inside the ship.

The mythical knights had arrived, appearing out of nowhere and repaired his grandfather's ship, saving everyone on board from a grizzly death.

Once the ship was repaired, the Templars vanished, and his grandfather and crew returned safely to Starbase Matrona. The only evidence left behind had been the repairs, and the pendant a knight had gifted his grandfather.

A buzz at the door startled Shae. "Come in, Louise."

The door slid open, and Louise walked in, her long blond hair bouncing with each step. She was a sight to see. Even though she was in her sixties, the Suficell Pods kept her young. She looked no older than a strong, elegant thirty-year-old woman, though being seen as a great beauty was not how she wanted to be perceived. She was a seasoned military leader, with the brains to match.

Louise stood next to the door as it closed and folded her hands in front of her. "The defenses are prepared. If there's another attack, we'll be ready." Her face tightened, and her eyes went cold. "Why won't Prime Director Zim let us jump out of here? We're in jeopardy by staying. Does he think the danger is over, simply because he thinks he's outing you?" She sighed. "Shae, you know he's not leaving this sector because of you."

"The Prime Director has every right to be suspicious of something, though I wish it weren't me. I'll have my day to make things right, but that's not why I called you here." He waved her over, inviting her to sit next to him. "I want you to see something."

She plopped down on the couch, her face hard and unwavering. "I heard what Zim did to you at the meeting."

Shae pointed to the holovid, ignoring her statement. "What do you see?"

She closed her eyes and rolled them around, no doubt to clear her tired and overstressed vision. She opened them. "Doesn't Zim realize we need to find a source of water since we're so far away from Eos? Matrona's reserves will only last us—"

She gasped. "What in Orion's Belt is that, Shae?" She stared at the still frame of the two orbs and the Thunderbird moving closer to the asteroids, pulling away from two exploding pyramids.

"You see it? Good. I'm not crazy."

"The Thunderbird and those orbs? Is that what you wanted me to see?"

"Yes. So you *do* see it."

"How could I miss it?" She looked confused. "Those orbs are the ships we caught on the radar just before Eden was hit. Who the hell are they? They jumped in for a second and then went off our radar a second later."

"And we thought they were incinerated along with Eden." He jabbed a finger at the screen. "Look at this." He cleared his throat. "Reverse. Play."

A pyramid released a squadron of starfighters, and all headed toward the small asteroid field near the pyramid, then they changed direction, moving evasively. A lone orb-ship shot out from behind an enormous rock and chased a handful of starfighters, launching dozens of missiles.

The starfighters exploded in a fireworks show, extinguishing a moment later to become charred debris. The orb and the remainder of the enemy starfighters accelerated off the cam view, but it wasn't hard for Shae to imagine the starfighters didn't fare so well.

Louise jumped back, wild-eyed. "Those...who..."

"Those orbs are the ones who blew up the pyramids."

Louise shot him a look. "Do you know who they are?"

"Not a clue." He rubbed the bridge of his nose.

Louise tilted her head, seeing his tell. "Don't play with me, Shae. I've been your XO for ten years now. You *do* have an idea."

He couldn't believe what he was about to say, especially in front of his executive officer. "They may be the Space Templars."

Louise sank into the couch. "You know how unpopular that explanation would be? The Prime Director is adamantly opposed to the idea, Shae. It's a career-ender. The Templar myth suggests we came from other worlds, other systems—"

"And they were the awakened ones who left us thousands of years ago," interrupted Shae. "Yes, I know how crazy it sounds."

"Oh, yeah, they could perform magic tricks, too." She frowned. "Don't get me started."

"The Prime Director is setting me up. How he explains history is the least of my concerns. I don't care if he believes me about the Templars or not."

Louise tightened her lips, holding back a reply, and shifted away from Shae.

"He's hiding something," Shae mumbled. "But what, exactly?"

"You're all over the vids, Shae."

Shae stood and walked to his desk, tapping his chin in thought.

"Did you hear me? You and this lie Prime Director Zim is pinning on you is all over the vids, being broadcast throughout Star Guild channels and Starbase Matrona. He said he suspects you're the head of a military coup attempt and that you set up this attack, and he means to prove it."

Starship Taranis, Shae thought.

He lunged at a holopad, quickly shuffling through applications and icons until he found what he was looking for. He pressed on a document and squinted. "Right here." He stomped over to Louise and dropped the holopad onto her lap. "Read this."

Louise skimmed through it, scrolling down the document, then glared at Shae. "This is the daily report of a travel log. It's for the fleet admiral's eyes only."

"Yes. I was looking over it earlier, and it shows two things that I find disturbing."

She shrugged as if there was no point in reading the log. It showed the comings and goings on Matrona. There were starfighter reports, Starhawk ebb transports, starjumpers, and other space vehicles logged earlier in the day.

She stopped and moved the holopad away from her, then puckered her lips as she paused. "Wait a second." She pulled the report back and blinked several times, her face turning pallid.

Shae raised his eyebrows. "You see it, don't you?"

"Plain as the bright sun I do." She stood, nostrils flaring. "Zim left Matrona on a starjumper before the attack, and *then* came back to Matrona just before Matrona jumped to our coordinates. Where did the son-of-a-Guild go?" She composed herself, embarrassed by her lack of self-control. "He could be plain lucky, leaving just before the attack began." She threw up air quotes with her fingers. "A mere coincidence."

"Keep looking, Louise."

She let out a huff. It was easy to tell she didn't want to get involved, but unable to resist, she cocked her head to one side and scrunched her nose as she read. "Wait, it says he wasn't on the starjumper when it returned to Matrona." She bit the side of her lip. "Uh...then where was he?"

"That's a question I want *him* to answer. He wasn't on his return ride home." Shae shrugged. "So, how did he get back on Matrona, especially after it had jumped into our new sector? The logs never show him coming back to the starbase. We know he had to have, but there is no record of it. Why is that, and when exactly did he return?"

She held the holopad close to her face. "Maybe he went to Starship *Taranis*?"

"*Taranis* jumped back into our coordinates an hour before we were to rendezvous with her. You heard me on the bridge give Captain Jenkyns a direct order to wait five hours." He splayed his open hand, showing five fingers. "After five hours, if we didn't make it, Jenkyns was to jump to a new set of coordinates somewhere in the outer periphery. I never told him to jump back here. Yet he did."

Louise stopped pacing. "Jenkyns said he came back to fight. To help us."

Shae quieted, and his shoulders relaxed. "He is a noble man. I give him that. I don't know him all too well, Louise, which makes this confusing. I doubt Zim went to *Taranis* since he wouldn't have known where *Taranis* had jumped to. Plus, I don't see any log entries of Zim entering Starship *Taranis* anywhere, so that's out of the question."

"Just like you don't see him entering Starbase Matrona," added Louise. "Why is Zim covering his trail? Better yet, *what* trail is he covering?"

Shae sat in his desk chair. "I need someone close to Zim to give me some answers because Zim sure as hell won't hand me the truth on a silver Star Guild platter."

Louise placed her hands on her hips. "You want a spy?" She shook her head. "Not me. No way."

"I wasn't asking you, Louise. You've never spoken but two words to Zim. I need someone inside the governance."

"Who?" She turned her eyes to the vidscreen.

"I'll figure it out, but until then, I need you—"

"Admiral." Louise shot both hands into the air. "It's erasing."

The admiral dashed over to the holovid to see the still frame of the explosions, the Thunderbird, and one orb. His brow furrowed. "Only one orb? Where's the other one?" The remaining orb started to fade until it disappeared a moment later. The Thunderbird vanished next.

"Reverse," Shae blurted.

The vid reversed. When it played back, it displayed exploding pyramids and nothing else. No torpedoes emerged from behind the asteroids, no orbs, and no Thunderbird; everything had been completely wiped from the holovid.

19

ALI

Planet Eos, West of the Radiation Zone—Adarta System, Orion Spur

Ali walked her mech westward, toward warehouse Twelve. Dusk's shadows loomed larger and longer as the sun descended below the horizon. If Ali took a stroll on this nearly windless planet without a mech, though not survivable, she imagined there would be nothing more than total silence.

There weren't very many animals here, other than the carbon dioxide breathing drudges, creatures that looked like biosphere squirrels the size of large dogs. They lived underground and popped out of burrowed holes here and there to eat the low shrubbery that grew in cracks in the ebb landscape.

She stepped her mech on a small spindly tree and cursed herself for doing so. Trees were few and far between, and here she was killing it like it was a measly human in the enemy attackers' way.

"Are we almost there yet?" Daf yawned, rubbing her eyes like a child and breaking the quiet Ali had been reveling in.

Ali yawned in return, and asked the HDC, "How much longer until we reach warehouse Twelve?"

Eleven minutes flashed on the holographic display.

They had been pressing their luck, hoping beyond Guild that no more enemy search parties would fly overhead. So far, none had.

She peered down at Daf, blinking the tired blur from her eyes and ignoring her overly active beating heart. "Eleven minutes. We'll be there soon enough, Daf."

Ali spotted a huge boulder and stomped toward it, the cockpit gently moving up and down with every step. She reached the boulder and positioned the mech alongside it, leaning its back against its breadth and hearing the metal armor scraping against the ebb rock.

The evening was fading into more darkness, and she slid her finger across the holodisplay to switch on her night vision.

She tilted forward and peered around the boulder.

"There it is," she muttered, her eyes sweeping over the terrain, making sure enemy soldiers weren't lurking. "I think we're clear."

She moved her mech toward the lights shining in the distance, maneuvering around a ridge.

Ali jerked back, slamming on the brakes in front of a descending slope. She dropped her arms by her side and bowed her head, a hot fury rising in her belly. "Those evil assholes."

Daf whipped her head around to the window to see what Ali referred to. She put her hand to her throat. "No."

Dusk couldn't hide the horrendous sight before them.

Ali swallowed vomit.

In front of them were blown off human limbs, corpses of men and women, littering the ground, along with destroyed mechs, burnt components, obliterated small craft with wings strewn about, and charred cockpits with burned bodies inside.

No survivors.

There couldn't be.

Ali pounded the HDC, enraged. "Those bastards. Those giant stick-shooting pieces of ebb-buckets." She clenched her teeth. Pressing her mech forward around the dead, she wanted to scream and take every one of the killers and hang them on spikes, their blood dripping to the ground as a warning never to attack her kind again.

"What are you doing?" cried Daf.

"There might be survivors in the warehouse."

"Don't be stupid. Turn around."

"No." Ali kept her eyes forward, her jaw set, and her muscles rigid. There wasn't a single person in the star sector who could change her mind. She half wished there was a giant inside so she could crush the evilness with her mech's foot.

She let out a gush of air and calmed herself, doing her best to stop her hands and body from shaking.

She halted her mech near someone lying on their back and brought the mech to one knee. She spoke through the gaps in her teeth, "Slit-lights on."

Two thin lights beamed from the mech's shoulders and highlighted a woman's face. Her skin was pale, and her eyes were open, lifeless. Dried blood crusted her lips, and there was a bruise over one eye. Blood had oozed all around her, now dried, and puddled from an exit wound near the woman's spine. She'd been hit in the torso by some type of projectile. Hopefully, it had killed her instantly, but it was doubtful.

Ali studied the woman's eyes. Her corneas were clouded, which meant the woman had been dead for at least two hours. In a day or so, the woman's eyes would be opaque.

"Slit-lights off."

Ali adjusted her mech's legs and brought it to a standing position. She continued toward the warehouse.

Daf threw her hand up, palm out. "Wait, stop going forward. We can't go in there."

She wanted to kick Daf in the throat. Anything to push some humanity in her.

Instead, Ali took another deep breath. A chief was calm in any scenario, bloodshed or not. In most cases, Ali wouldn't care how she came off in front of inferiors. Today, lives were at stake, even hers. "The woman has been dead a couple of hours. I don't think there's any danger here." She pointed her hand at the warehouse, the mech mimicking her movement.

Daf wiped her eyes. "You better be right, or we'll look like them in a few minutes."

Ali walked up a long slope and onto the ebb flooring in front of a closed mech bay door. A panel was fastened to the wall next to the door. Ali punched a holographic button on her console. "Connect to warehouse Twelve's south mech bay door panel."

The HDC complied. "Code one-eight-eight-one."

The bay door opened to a dimly lit room. Ali stepped inside. "Code one-eight-eight-one to close south mech bay door." The door closed behind them, and the room dimmed more.

A second door was in front of them, and stepping on the ramp opened it automatically, to reveal row upon row of mechs, some with their dome hatches open.

Ali surveyed the bay and cleared the entryway. A loud bang indicated the door had closed, and steam engulfed the area, fogging the cockpit window. It subsided seconds later, and the HDC beeped; oxygen levels in the bay now at an optimum level.

Ali went to move, then stopped, her heart skipping a beat. An overweight man wearing overalls was on the ground in a puddle of blood. He was a tech and appeared to have been shot in the stomach.

The blood had coagulated, so he'd died more than fifteen minutes before, and because the outer perimeter of the pool was already dried, Ali knew it had been more than an hour.

Daf pulled her brows together into a frown, and her eyes narrowed. "I don't like the looks of this, Chief. Let's get out now."

Ali didn't like the looks of it either. Who would? She wasn't turning around, though. They needed food and water, and their oxygen tanks refilled. "He's been dead for a while, Daf. I know what this looks like, but I don't detect anything out of the ordinary on radar. No unidentified ships around this structure's perimeter."

"How do you know?"

Ali tapped the HDC. "Radar."

"No, the guy. How do you know how long he's been dead?"

"The blood and the eyes—we had to learn about it at Star Guild Academy. I was really good. You know, with my sick and twisted mind."

Ali pressed her mech's unlock hatch button. A swoosh of air sounded, decompressing the hold from the hatch lock and making Daf jump.

Ali looked down at Daf with her hand pressed firmly against the hatch. "You stay here. I'm going to get us some water and food. I'll be back."

Daf shook her head. "Uh, no. You'll need help." She looked over her shoulder through the cockpit window, no doubt making sure the coast was clear. "I'm going with you."

Oh, brother. "Trust me, Daf. You should stay." The last thing Ali wanted was to be slowed down.

Daf ignored the order. "More hands to carry means more food and water."

Ali gave Daf a nod and pushed the hatch open, feeling fresh air comb through her hair and touch her face. It felt good to be out of the stuffy mech. She had forgotten how fresh the air was here, even fresher than on Starbase Matrona.

Ali moved up and out of the mech, crawling down its side and finding the floor with her toes. She stretched, getting some kinks out.

Ali waved for Daf to follow. She walked past the dead man and to the warehouse office door and punched in the code. The door beeped open.

Ali moved down an aisle of desks and stopped. "I think...yeah." She pointed to another door. "There's the cafeteria."

Daf nodded and walked hastily to the cafeteria door and opened it. Dozens of empty tables and chairs greeted them, everything clean and proper. It hadn't been used. How could it? The people here had probably been dead before noon.

Ali walked past Daf. She figured they'd just get food, hook their mech up to water, fill the tank to the brim, get fresh oxygen tanks, and then be out of here, maybe to find some survivors elsewhere.

They walked to the kitchen door and pushed it open. Food bags hung on the walls, cooling boxes were in the center of the room, and storage boxes sat under the hanging food bags.

Ali shoved a bag in Daf's face. "Here. Grab food as quickly as you can."

Ali moved to a cooling box and found apples, pears, oranges, and persimmons. She shoved armfuls into a bag and snatched carrots and celery from a counter. Not her favorites, but when you're hungry, the taste didn't matter.

A loud clang echoed through the kitchen. Ali froze.

"Sorry." Daf held up a metal spoon. "I dropped this. I thought we'd need some spoons with all the avocados I got."

Ali looked at Daf's bag. "That's all you have? Avocados?"

Daf gave a weak smile. "The cabinet was full of them."

They were in a hurry, and she didn't have time to argue.

"Let's go." Ali moved through the door, not looking back to see if Daf was following.

Ali entered the office and quickened her pace. She turned to move around a desk, then stopped dead in her tracks. A blue haze streamed through the office windows, coming from outside.

Daf stared out a window. "What the Guild is that?"

Ali narrowed her eyes. She knew exactly what that was.

Walking toward the window, Daf tried to get a better look.

Ali went for her arm to pull her back. "It doesn't matter. Let's go."

Daf shook her head. "I've never seen that coming from the mountain before."

Through the windows, Mount Gabriel stood tall and majestic in front of the dark clouds and fading sunlight. Rays of blue light beamed from its base.

Daf slowly shook her head. "Has anyone ever reported blue lights coming from Mount Gabriel?"

"No, but let's get out of here."

For all Ali knew, the light was alerting the enemy, wherever they were, and that was the last thing they needed.

The light brightened, and Ali stiffened. "It's probably the enemy. Let's get out of here and get to the next warehouse."

In truth, she wanted to visit the light. It called to her, creeping into her muscles and veins, trying to control her. It came from the tunnel door, she was sure. Regardless, that area would be crawling with giant soldiers and flying craft in a short time.

Ali turned and hurried out of the office to the mech bay, her breath coming fast. "Idea. Let's each grab a mech with a full water and oxygen tank. We'll split up the food. Two mechs are always better than one."

Plus, it wouldn't be so stifling inside, and the oxygen wouldn't be used as quickly.

Daf nodded, her face white. "The bad guys are coming, aren't they?"

"Probably." Ali climbed up a mech with a hatch already open, hopped down into the cockpit, and turned it on. The engine vibrated the cockpit, and the hip gyros and hydraulic shocks slightly bounced as if testing themselves.

She dropped the bag of food and pushed it to the side with her foot as she ran her finger over the holoscreen. "Water systems check." She dipped her head. "Good. They're full."

She looked up. Only one mech was on, hers.

"Dammit, Daf."

She climbed out and looked to see Daf running toward her, waving her hands wildly. "Help. I need your help."

20

ALI

Planet Eos, West of the Radiation Zone—Adarta System, Orion Spur

"There's a man in a mech over there. He's hurt, he's hurt," screamed Daf.

Ali's mouth flew open, and she climbed down her mech as fast as she could. "Where? Is he conscious?"

Daf grabbed Ali by the elbow, dragging her to a mech across the warehouse. "Yes, yes." Reaching the mech, Daf pointed at its open hatch. "In there."

Ali climbed the steps and peered over the edge to see a man sitting on the cockpit floor with one shoe on and the other off, holding his ankle. He looked up at her and blinked, his face contorted in pain. "Help."

She hopped into the cockpit and bent to place her hand on his shoulder.

He was young but not too young. Crow's feet had begun to form, and gray dotted his low-cut beard and mustache. His eyes were also gray, and even though he was in pain, they were relatively calm.

"Mister, can you walk?"

He shook his head, his face ashen. He was trembling. "I've broken my ankle. It's painful, but it's nothing compared to the carnage outside."

Ali jerked back at the enormity of his ankle. It was swollen and about the size of a grapefruit. "How long have you been here?"

He massaged his ankle just above the swollen area. "About two hours, I think."

"We need to set your ankle."

"The soft tissue damage is more what I'm worried about. It's a closed break, and I don't need it set, but a splint would be nice."

She pulled his sock down.

He recoiled. "Easy does it."

"No discoloration." That was a good sign, and no major blood vessel was severed, so there was no internal bleeding to worry about. Ali placed her hand a few inches above his break. "Heat. We should—"

"Do you need any help?" Daf asked from the top of the ladder.

Ali nodded. "Yeah, get me some things to make a splint. You know, thick tape from the tech shop and see if they have any pieces of wood about the length of your forearm."

"On it." Daf climbed down the mech.

"How did this happen?" Ali asked, still crouched next to the guy.

He stopped rubbing his lower leg and leaned back, sighing loudly. "They shot at us, and I stumbled over something. I don't know what it was that I trampled over, but I heard a snap the moment I tripped. I crawled up here, thinking I'd be followed, but I was the lucky one, I guess." He frowned, pointing at the mech's dome. "I tried to close that thing, but it wouldn't budge."

Ali frowned. "You have to press the hatch button over there."

He dropped his arm with a stressed chuckle. "Of course. It's that easy."

Ali stood, placing her hands on her hips. "What's your name?"

"Doctor William Simmons."

She tilted her head. *William?*

She looked at his thick bottom lip and touched hers. Had they kissed before? There was a William in her dream. No, in her memories.

She shook her head. She was thinking nonsense. "You said you're a doctor?"

He cringed and reached for his ankle, placing his hand gently upon it. "You look shocked. Sorry to disappoint."

"I'm a little shocked a doctor would be on Eos. We usually have therapists down here who know basic injury repair and first aid, but never a doctor."

"Right," said William, rubbing the top of his ankle.

"We need to get you to a Suficell Pod to heal your wound. But to do that, we'll need a ride to Star Guild or Matrona somehow, if the shuttles haven't been blasted out of the stars already."

The doctor eyed Ali intensely. "You don't know?"

"Know what?"

"There are plenty of Suficell Pods here on Eos."

Along with extending life by a hundred and forty years or so, Suficell Pods could heal all wounds and disease by emitting high-frequency waves that matched the frequency and vibration of the disease, thus shattering the diseased cells.

It tended to work wonders on broken bones as well, typically healing them within a day.

"A Suficell Pod on Eos? Where?"

"On Starship *Sirona*."

My mom's ship?

Ali cut off a chuckle. "That's crazy. That starship isn't here."

"It's here, right now on Eos. She came down here to save as many people as she could. I should know. I'm a doctor on that ship."

The shock was getting to the doctor. It had to be. There was no way Captain Diana Johnson, her mom, would be down here. That didn't make sense.

The doctor continued, "*Sirona* sent help to this warehouse. Shortly after we got here, the warehouse was attacked, and our ships lost." He swallowed hard. "As you can see, I was the only survivor."

That can't be. "Do you know *Sirona*'s coordinates?"

William nodded.

She doubted it, but if there was a small chance William was right,

Sirona could keep them safe more than any place on the planet. It was equipped with weapons and built with thick armor. Once they extracted as many survivors as possible, they could get off this planet.

"Then let's get you some help." She pulled herself up and over the hatch and glanced down at Daf, who was on her way up the steps carrying a bucket.

"I got your stuff, Chief. I think."

"Give me the bucket. I need you to drive the mech I was going to use. My food bags are in it, and the mech's water tank is full. We're heading to Starship *Sirona*."

Daf gave Ali a double-take. "We're headed where?"

21

EDEN

Unknown Location

The sweet smell of flowers wafted to Eden's nose, and the sound of rushing water trickled into her ears.

Where am I?

She was lying on something soft and delicate.

Sheets?

Whatever it was had to be the softest, smoothest material she'd ever touched.

Her mouth curled in a smile, and she took a deep breath, stretching her arms and yawning.

She shouldn't be alive.

She opened her eyes and bolted into a sitting position.

She was in a room lit by a small flame shaped like a tear. It danced on a glossy holder, its contents dripping down its own sides as if it were crying.

She looked around the room. It was enormous, fit for a Prime Director.

Ship quarters were a fraction of this size, which meant she wasn't on Starship *Brigantia*.

It was elegant with ornate tapestries draped around, some white, but most mixed with purples and violets. They hung from the ceiling, the walls, and on the posts at each corner of her bed.

A bed?

This was not her bunk.

She touched the sheets again, pinching and rubbing her fingers over them. They were delicate, comfortable, and the opposite of Star Guild linens.

She lifted herself and sat cross-legged and yawned, rubbing her eyes.

"Hello?"

Her voice echoed through the room, but no one answered.

She threw the sheets off, then halted, her eyes on two doors across from the foot of her bed. Flowers grew out of large terra-cotta pots next to the doorway.

Was she in a fantasy-land? "What is going on?" she whispered to herself, a hand over her pounding heart.

She placed her feet on the floor and stood, rubbing her lower back. Feeling soft fabric, smooth and light, against her hands and skin, she looked at her covered body. She wore a white robe.

She furrowed her brow. "How did I get into this?"

She shook her head and took a few steps, her feet touching a cushy, furry-like substance.

She looked at the floor and studied it. "Grass." She leaned over and caressed a single blade between her fingers, noticing tiny meadow flowers mixed throughout.

She stood and shrugged, feeling drawn to go outside, more or less pulled by the serenity of the environment. She gave another yawn as she reached the closed glass door.

The outside landscape was spectacular.

Large stone decking stretched to a cliff, where water rushed beneath the stone and spilled over into a canyon, a view she'd only seen in paintings.

Beyond the canyon were trees of various sizes. There were clouds at the top of a ridge, and the sky above was mixed with pinks, purples, and golds. Two moons, one large and yellow with silver rings and the other small and red, loomed above the horizon.

The glass doors slid open, and a gust of wind and cool mist hit her, dying down as quickly as it came.

She stepped back and looked at the door, her eyes darting left and right. "Hello?"

Her heart pounded faster, and she twisted around, feeling someone behind her.

No one was there.

She yawned again and shook her head, trying to wake herself. She wasn't dreaming, that she understood, but she was somewhere she'd never been before, on a different world, amidst a beauty she didn't deserve.

She walked forward and placed a foot on the stone decking. A coolness vibrated up her leg and through her spine. She shook at the intensity of it and relaxed her body.

That felt good.

She paused, crinkling her brow. The stone had done something to her. Her body now felt alive and awake, and her grogginess was gone entirely.

A loud squawk sounded, and Eden instinctively ducked, her hands above her head.

Rainbow-colored birds lifted into the air from the cliff's edge, calling loudly. They dove into the canyon and disappeared under the stone deck out of Eden's view.

They reminded her of her pilots and their formations.

Her heart dropped.

Are they alive? Did Star Guild and Starbase Matrona survive?

Her family, Star Guild, might be gone. She wanted to cry, something she had only done as a child.

She put her hands to her face and swallowed hard, holding back tears. She coughed it away. "Stupid. Crying does nothing. It's for sissies."

She wanted to scream. Fleet Admiral Shae Lutz, the XO Louise

Stripe, that odd guy, First Lieutenant Brigger Murphy, her pilots, her crew, her friends, may all be gone.

A zap went up her feet. A euphoric sensation grabbed hold of her and ran through her body.

She stood straight and breathed deeply, her mood changing.

Did it come from the stone? She bent and touched it. Cool energy radiated from the pavement, but nothing more.

She shrugged, happy for the fresh energy, and eyed the surroundings.

Domes, transparent like crystal, were set back from the cliffs and glistened in the dawning light.

Eden rubbed her eyes and blinked several times. "Are those homes?" She put her hands beside her mouth, creating a makeshift megaphone. "Hello?"

Her voice echoed, reverberating off the canyon walls.

No one replied.

She turned swiftly, spinning on her heel, and hurried toward the open doors. Stepping inside, she stopped in her tracks and yelped. Her foot slipped and came off the ground, and she landed on her back with a loud thump.

A shadow appeared.

She pushed up in a defensive stance, her fingers curled into fists and held them in front of her face.

A strange figure wearing a robe with a billowy hood covering its face stood in the corner of the room by her bed.

She shifted her back leg. If that *thing* approached her, the back of her heel would slam into the side of its face.

"Welcome," said the figure, the tenor of his voice strong and healthy. He respectfully nodded, the hood still concealing his features.

He motioned at each corner of the room and out stepped three more robed and hooded figures from the shadows.

"Don't even think about it," warned Eden, tightening her fists, her eyes darting from figure to figure. "I'm trained to defend myself, and I will beat the living Guild out of anyone who thinks I can't."

The man lowered his hood to reveal a handsome face with a beautiful smile, his white teeth shining.

He was young, with eyes as blue as the biosphere's sky, and chestnut-brown hair, the picture of health in its prime.

He bowed. "I'm Skye Vortek." He extended his hands to his hooded friends. "We're the Space Templars."

22

SHAE

Starship Brigantia, Starbase Matrona Docking Bay—Unknown Sector, Orion Spur

A rap on Shae's door woke him. He lifted his head off the pillow, his eyes blurry.

He was on his couch and didn't remember falling asleep. He sat up, pulling both hands through his hair and ruffling it up a bit.

He checked the time on the wall. It read 10:09 p.m.

The orbs. The Thunderbird...erased.

He stood in a hurry. Yes, the holovid. It had been tampered with, but by whom, and why?

Another rap on the door.

"Who is it?"

No answer.

He took a deep breath and rolled his eyes. Why wake him and not answer?

He yawned and wearily walked to the door, rubbing the sleep out of his eyes.

Another knock.

"For Guild sakes, I'm coming." He wiped a dab of slobber off the side of his mouth with his sleeve and spoke to the console next to the door. "Unlock and open."

The door slid open, and bright light beamed through the doorway. Shae crossed a forearm in front of his eyes to block it. "What's going on here?"

Chatter, full of questions, battered him, turning into noise he couldn't make sense of.

Shadows stood behind the light.

Reporters? No, it couldn't be.

He squinted his eyes at the invading brilliance.

Yes, indeed reporters, and too many to count.

How did they get permission to board?

He took a wobbly step back. "What's the meaning of this? Turn off those damn lights." He swung his arms in front of him, swiping at the people he likened to biosphere flies. "Get back."

A gorgeous woman with a sparkling necklace, a white dress, and a pretty smile pushed through the doorway.

She shoved an audio mic in front of his face. "Do you know why you're implicated in the coup? What do you have to say about the charges brought against you?"

Shae wanted to shove her out of the room. "I did no such thing. Get out." He placed his hands on the woman and tried to ease her back through the doorway.

A man slid by her and shoved another mic next to Shae's chin. "The Prime Director says he has proof you were the mastermind in the attack. Do you have a response for that, Admiral?"

Shae frowned. "It's absurd. No comment, and time for you to leave." He leaned against the man, pushing him against the wall of reporters outside.

Out of the corner of his eye, he saw Louise, her mouth open, clearly surprised at what was taking place.

She waved her arm at someone down the hall and then pointed at the reporters, her lips curled in anger. "Get them out of here."

Several *Brigantia* guards came down the hallway, their boots echoing loudly, and rounded up the reporters, pushing them away like a herd of unwilling cows in Matrona's agricultural center.

Shae hurried back into his office. "Close."

The door shut and muffled the harshness of the reporter's complaints to the *Brigantia* guard.

He wiped his hand over his mouth, dazed. The leading questions, the accusations, and assertions.

"I'm being set up." He shook his head. "What has Zim done?"

Was it now Shae against the governance? If so, then no telling what they would pull next.

He tapped a button on his desk. "Admiral Lutz to Brigger."

"Yes, sir?"

"How did the reporters get onto the ship?"

"They were allowed passage by the Prime Director and the Matrona Police. The police have jurisdiction over all Star Guild matters and ships. I'm sorry, sir. We tried to warn you."

Shae clicked the commlink off and paced as he thought. He knew the Matrona Police had the right to exercise authority, but to give free passage to the damn reporters?

He had to find a way out of this.

His starship was docked inside Starbase Matrona, which gave him easy access to all spheres within the starbase, but easy access also meant the reporters had easy access to his quarters, to his ship.

By now, Prime Director Zim probably had his starship locked down, forbidden to leave Starbase Matrona.

A thud on the door. "This is the Matrona Police. You are under arrest. Surrender any weapons you may have and step out peacefully."

Shae's heart skipped a beat.

No, this wasn't happening.

He marched to his desk and swiped his hand over the corner. A wooden panel opened, and a sizable two-muzzle pistol slid out. He picked it up.

Another bang on the door.

His eyes moved from the gun to the door.

"This is your last warning, Admiral. We will blast this door open if you do not come out immediately."

He gave a heavy sigh, and his shoulders slumped. The police were just doing their job. They had no clue they were following orders based on a lie. They didn't know Zim was pulling a blanket over their eyes.

He eyed his pistol and shook his head.

He placed the gun back into the panel, closed it, and slowly walked to the door and stood erect. He needed to look respectable in front of the cameras and demonstrate strength, honor, and most importantly, truth. He needed the people to see his face, the sincerity in his eyes, and to see through the deception Zim perpetrated right in front of them all.

He reached for the control panel, and his stomach lurched. "Wait," he said under his breath. "Koda, my nephew." He, along with Savanna, might be his only allies in the governance.

Dashing back to his desk, he clicked the auto-write function on the desk's HDC and spoke into it. "Koda, this is of the utmost importance and for the safety of Star Guild, the governance, and the people of Starbase Matrona. Zim is masterminding a lie, and I don't know why or what he is gaining from this. I need eyes on the inside. Please be them for me because we need all the help we can get. Find out what you can and report it to Executive Officer Louise Stripe. Your Uncle, Shae."

He pressed a button on the HDC, and a silver sheet with the admiral's seal embossed on it materialized on his desk, his words printed in black. He folded the note several times and curled his fingers around it, making a fist to hide it from view.

A physical copy was the safest way to get this information to Koda, and less likely to be tracked.

"Open," he yelled. The door whooshed upward to a dozen Matrona Police pointing guns at him.

The man in front nodded, his lips pursed, and his eyebrows drawn upward. It was an acquaintance, someone Shae had known for years. "Sergeant Frank Jones."

Frank lowered his eyes. It was a sign, a tell, and an easy one at that. "I'm sorry, Shae. I must follow orders."

It was clear Frank didn't like what he was doing. This was good. It may allow him, being the admiral, a little leeway on his way to lock up.

A loud, robotic beep reverberated against the walls, and a hovervid camera flew inside the doorway and floated near the top of the doorframe. Frank turned and aimed his weapon. "Get that hovervid out of here before I blow it to Guild and back."

The hovervid dipped and sped out and down the corridor.

Shae bowed his head, his mouth straight and his eyes steadfast. "Thank you, Frank."

Frank huffed. "I don't like this, Admiral, but please come with me." He turned and reached for Shae's arms, readying the handcuffs.

Shae stiffened. "Please allow me a little dignity as I leave my quarters and my ship. Don't embarrass me any more than I already am. What the Prime Director is saying about me isn't true, or he is gravely mistaken." Shae's eyes softened. "If I run, you have permission to shoot me."

Frank considered for a moment then gave a nod. He gestured for another guard. "Screen him."

A man walked forward and pulled out a thin wand. He moved it up and down Shae, then stepped back. "He's clean. No weapons."

Frank's eyes met Shae's for a moment and looked away. "Let's go."

Shae walked out of his office, following the police down the corridor. Frank was behind him, his hand on Shae's upper back.

Shae glanced over his shoulder. "I ask one more favor, my friend. I need to give instructions to my leading officer, Louise Stripe. She'll be around the corner. It won't be long."

Frank paused. "Shae, please tell me you'll be cleared of all charges. I'm not at all pleased with what I'm doing."

"I will."

Frank led Shae around the corner. Louise stood there, glaring at each passing police officer, seeming to burn imaginary holes into each of them.

She saluted Shae, her eyes unwavering.

"At ease." He brought his hands to meet hers, skillfully transferring the folded note into her palm. She curled her fingers around it and concealed it from view. "You run *Brigantia* until I get back, and Brigger steps into your command. She's your bird now."

Louise looked past Shae at Frank. "Yes, but it won't be long before I see you back on the ship."

"Aye, Louise, in times like these, the truth is all we have. Let's prove my innocence."

Shae turned on his heel and continued with the Matrona Police.

"Where are you taking me, Frank?"

"It's not good, Shae. I'm sorry."

Shae's insides burned, his heart wanting to sink into the boiling acid that had taken over his stomach.

"Explain to me what 'not good' means."

"I'm afraid they are deciding your execution. You'll be tried, and it doesn't look favorable."

23

ALI

Planet Eos, West of the Radiation Zone—Adarta System, Orion Spur

Blue lights beamed from Mount Gabriel.

Ali wanted to scream. She couldn't take it anymore. This blue light, *whatever,* wanted to grab her and take her to its source. It clawed at her very being.

She squeezed her eyes shut, doing her best to focus on the job at hand. They had to get to Starship *Sirona.*

Sweat dripped from her nose and off her chin, and her lips quivered like her father's had when he was trying to shake his drinking habit.

The habit always won.

Were those memories real? The image was a flash, not a movie like her most recent remembrances had been.

She shook her head. The blue light was taunting her as much as inviting her to its home. It had to be coming from that door inside the mountain, but the mountain had to be crawling with enemy soldiers trying to find the light source by now.

She turned her mech and began to walk away from Mount Gabriel.

"No," said William. "You're heading off course."

Ali reached forward and traced her finger over the holographic map in front of her. A black dot on the map pinpointed *Sirona*'s location. She saw a clear path away from the mountain and around a ridge, though it would take longer.

She let out a loud exhale. Once she got onto *Sirona*, they could send out more search parties to find others and then get off this planet.

"Excuse me, miss. You're—"

"I know what I'm doing," replied Ali. "Daf will follow my lead, and we'll be at *Sirona* in no time." And far from Mount Gabriel.

Ali twisted her torso to look behind her and wondered when the blue rays of light would turn off. She wanted to hiss at the mountain, to do anything for it to leave her alone.

William touched his ankle, now strapped in a splint. "She was looking for you."

Ali twisted her mech back around. She looked at her holodisplay. Twenty-two minutes to their destination. "Who's looking for me?"

"Your mom, Captain Johnson. She was worried."

Ali gave him a strange look. "How do you know who I am?"

"Everyone knows who you are." He leaned his head back against the cockpit window. "She wanted to find you more than she wanted to find anyone else on this planet."

Ali couldn't help but snort. "Yeah, I'm so grateful Mom was thinking about me." Her voice was full of sarcasm. The only time her mother ever worried about Ali was when she was first stationed on Starship *Hathor*. She hadn't wanted Ali to make her look dumb.

A crackle came over the comm. "Come on, slowpoke." It was Daf. They had left warehouse Twelve over forty minutes ago, and Daf was by her side.

Daf jerked forward, racing her mech faster.

"Daf, slow down. We're in a Guild-damn war zone. Do not get discovered."

A heavy sigh came over the commlink. "All right, Chief." Daf slowed her mech. "I just want to get there."

"We all do."

William cleared his throat. "How far have we deviated off course?"

Ali noted the ending coordinates were adjacent to warehouse Twenty-six. "We're fine." She furrowed her brow, looking more closely. "Did Mom land on top of a warehouse?"

He nodded. "Practically. She wanted to use the warehouse for strategic purposes and for whatever supplies they had on hand. She was willing to stay there as long as possible to save you, Ali."

That didn't sound like her mother.

"Why? That's Captain Johnson you're talking about, right?"

"Yes."

She hadn't talked to her mom in years. Other than her mom's pissy nature and her constantly looking down on Ali's life like she was a piece of shit, the biggest reason was that Captain Johnson didn't *feel* like her mother in the slightest.

There wasn't a bond. There had never been. It was odd. Just like her father, Ali didn't remember her mom much past four years ago other than pictures here and there, as if they'd been downloaded into her brain.

It didn't matter.

Ali walked forward and up an incline toward a high ridge. She wondered how much damage *Sirona* might have sustained after touching down on Eos, or if it had any damage at all.

"Has the enemy spotted *Sirona* yet?"

"Ali," shouted Daf.

Ali looked through her cockpit window. Daf's mech had already made it to the top of the ridge. She stood with its arm raised and a finger pointing at something in the distance.

"What is it?" asked Ali, reaching the ridge's peak. She looked where Daf pointed and didn't need a reply.

A battle was occurring in the distance, explosions erupting in all directions.

Ali's gut spasmed. Glancing at her HDC, she double-checked the coordinates. Her breathing hastened. "Daf, according to the doctor's coordinates, that's Starship *Sirona*."

24

SHAE

Starbase Matrona—Unknown Sector, Orion Spur

Shae sat on a small bed in a rectangular cell. A walled bathroom, complete with a door, stood in the corner of the room. Mounted on a column at the foot of his bed was a holovid, blaring the news.

The news was empty, devoid of truth, and today Shae was the focal point of their spin, broadcast to all twelve spheres on Starbase Matrona and most assuredly to Starship *Taranis* and *Brigantia*.

The admiral had been targeted with the latest batch of lies, and because so, hot rage boiled in his veins.

The citizens of the spheres, he thought, can't be this easily controlled and manipulated. Can they?

Matrona consisted of spheres, twelve large domains, each with their own governance and structure. All twelve were ruled by one Prime Director, Zim Noki, who acted as the face of the governance, an elected leader with the final say on anything and everything.

Each sphere's governance had political figureheads, but none trumped the Prime Director. Zim Noki oversaw even the news. Most people saw him as an open-hearted individual, someone dedicated to civilian interests and wellbeing.

Shae had perceived Zim in the same way until recently.

You sick bastard.

Shae shook his head in disgust and spat on the ebb-rock floor.

The news anchor smiled, his eyes beaming a fake bravado. He held a holopad in his hand, a holopad he never looked at or used except to hold during the newscast. A stupid prop. "According to all reports, there has been an attempted coup d'état, and the fleet admiral was the sole conspirator. He executed a nearly flawless overthrow of the governance."

"It was that simple, huh?" Shae frowned, scrunching the sheets under his fingers and wrinkling them. "I must have done it all in my sleep."

The news hadn't mentioned the triangular ships that were completely foreign to Star Guild. They did say, however, and several times over, that if it weren't for Prime Director Zim Noki blocking the admiral's efforts, "Fleet Admiral Shae Lutz would have been our new Prime Director, imposing a military regime over the entire starbase."

Shae thoughts raced to the real enemy, those who attacked. For one, where did they come from and where did they disappear to?

"We are receiving reports and conclusive evidence that Admiral Lutz did indeed attempt a coup," spoke a female voice over the holovid, her voice familiar.

The admiral looked up. The news had shifted to another scene, much like holomovies, panning to the same woman reporter he had ordered out of his office minutes before his arrest.

She had carrot-colored hair, thick lips, hazel eyes, and a smile worth every dime she had paid for it. The reporter was standing on the steps to the courthouse in Sphere Eight, the capital.

Her lips were downturned. "The evidence is, in fact, piling up according to Prime Director Zim Noki's office, and in a few moments we have…" she paused, staring into the camera. She tapped her earpiece, listening intently to someone. She nodded, then touched her cheek and pushed a strand of hair behind her ear. "Okay, it's ready. We have an exclusive interview with Captain Stanley Jenkyns."

Captain Jenkyns replaced her image with Lyle Geller, a news anchorman, sitting across from him.

Shae sat erect. "You better not be in on this, Jenkyns. You bet your ship I'll break every bone in your body if you are."

Maybe Louise showed Jenkyns the holovid of the two orbs and the Thunderbird, and he was on the vid channel to clear the good admiral's name.

Shae slumped. That couldn't happen, no matter how hard he wished. The orbs and the Thunderbird had been erased.

Jenkyns scratched his nose and pulled at his tie. The camera panned away from him and focused on another individual sitting next to Jenkyns.

"Louise?" Shae's heart sank, and he blinked several times as if doing so would take her off the news or vanish her altogether.

"No, no," said Shae. "You backstabbing, no-good traitor." Jenkyns might be a person who could do this to him, but he never thought Louise would turn her back on him and throw him under a hovertrain.

Words were coming from the holovid, but the admiral couldn't pay attention even when he saw Jenkyns' mouth move.

What was Zim's agenda? He had obviously been upset that Shae sent a distress call to the Space Templars, but why? Were the Templars real, and if so, why didn't Zim want others to find out? Did the Templars have the true story of humanity's origins?

What was he thinking? Shae knew most thought humanity's beginnings originated on Eos, and they had to leave due to resource and atmosphere failure brought on by his people eons before. They had orbited the planet in a starbase ever since. That's what the history books explained.

"I love Fleet Admiral Shae Lutz. He's like a brother to me."

Shae tilted his head.

Louise?

She forced a smile at the interviewer, Lyle, an older man, and a famous reporter, well known for getting the best interviews on the starbase.

Lyle leaned forward. "Now, Captain Stan Jenkyns, I—"

Jenkyns put his hand up. "Call me Captain Stanley Jenkyns, please."

"My apologies," replied Lyle. "Captain Stanley Jenkyns, when did you first suspect Admiral Lutz was attempting a coup?"

Jenkyns scratched the side of his face and looked away for a moment, his jaw muscles twitching. To Shae, Jenkyns looked like he was about to formulate a lie or an already formulated piece-of-crap tale. He could see it all over the man's face.

Jenkyns hesitated, then inhaled what looked like an uncomfortable breath. "I had intercepted infovids, and communications over a Star Guild commlink several months ago."

Lyle leaned against his chair's armrest and raised his brows. "Really? Can you tell us more?"

Jenkyns coughed into his hand as Louise shifted in her chair. She ran a finger over her pant leg, slow and deliberate.

She did it again, then drew a circle. A circle and a line through it?

She drew another line through the first and repeated the pattern. One line, circle around that line, and another line slashed through the first. A circle with a cross? What was she trying to say, or was it just a nervous tic?

Jenkyns looked down at Lyle's shoes. "I also found infovids showing a blueprint of a triangular-shaped craft that could move at very high speeds. As it turns out, they were the same craft that attacked us. They were approved by Admiral Lutz."

Shae's head jerked back and bared his teeth. "You lying sack of—"

Lyle's mouth formed an exaggerated 'o.' "You didn't tell anyone about the blueprints?"

Jenkyns shrugged. "I thought they were a new military design, something he and the Star Guild techs were creating. Little did I know the plan was sinister."

"You saw Admiral Lutz's signature on the blueprints?" asked Lyle.

Jenkyns, still staring at Lyle's shoes, nodded. "Yes."

"What? Are you mad, Jenkyns?" Shae pushed himself off the bed and began pacing back and forth.

"What did the intercepted commlink say?" asked Lyle.

Shae halted, watching the vid.

Jenkyns looked up, eyeing Lyle. "The commlink said...um...well...it was clearly his voice talking to a group we've come to know are the Space Templars. They, in fact, are real and have been planning this raid for a decade now. They were assuring Shae that he would continue as the head of Star Guild and the governance. This was to happen after the Templars seized command of Starbase Matrona and Star Guild."

Shae gasped and clenched his hands together. "This is absolutely insane."

Lyle turned to Louise. "And, Louise—"

Louise put up her hand. "Please, call me Executive Officer Louise Stripe."

Lyle paused, folding his hands in his lap. "Okay, Executive Officer Louise Stripe, do you have anything to add to Jenkyns' findings?"

Louise smiled, again drawing a circle with a cross, or was that an X?

"I'm sorry, Lyle. I changed my mind. Call me Louise." She batted her eyes and flicked her blond hair as she crossed one leg over the other, drawing the circle and X against her pant leg with her finger.

Lyle straightened his back. "Okay, Louise, do you have anything more to add about Jenkyns' findings?"

Louise turned to Jenkyns and gave him a long look, her lips tight and eyes narrowed. Jenkyns avoided eye contact. Turning and facing Lyle again, she spat in his face. "Fleet Admiral Shae Lutz is like a brother to me. He is honorable, and you're making a tyrant out of him. You and this man next to me are liars."

Lyle put his hand up, stopping someone from assisting him or maybe telling the guards not to throw Louise out of the room. "Don't worry. I got it." He wiped the spit off with his sleeve then eyed Louise intently. "Is that what you *really* want to say?"

She cocked her head to the side. "All right, Shae was with the Space Templars just before the attack occurred." She quickly squeezed her lips shut.

Shae unclenched his fists. Louise was doing her best to lie, but her heart definitely wasn't in the game.

Lyle tilted forward and grabbed Louise's hands. "Louise, do you have concrete, conclusive evidence he was with the Space Templars before the attack?"

Louise slowly squeezed Lyle's hand. He pulled back, unlocking from Louise's grip. Clutching his hand, he shook it back and forth, his lips forming a weak smile. "Strong grip."

Louise cracked her knuckles. "Yes, I know."

"What do you have to tell us, Louise?"

She glared into the camera. "That I do, indeed, have evidence. Evidence some higher-ups tried to erase."

Lyle scrunched up his nose, clearly confused with the answer. "What do you mean?"

"When Fleet Admiral Shae Lutz and I watched the replay of the attack—"

The screen quickly changed from the interview back to the carrot-topped reporter. She smiled brightly. "You can watch the rest of the interview tomorrow morning at nine."

"Shutdown," said Shae, turning the holovid off. This wasn't good, especially for Louise. She had clearly gone against Zim's desires, even to the point of dropping a seed of truth to the public and drawing some type of code.

"Dammit." Louise's life might now be at stake. They'd edit out what she said and show the masses a nicely cut holovid in the morning. Those who saw it again might forget the clues Louise had dropped, and anyone watching for the first time wouldn't see the clues at all.

A loud knock struck the door. Shae twisted around to see someone outside his cell, opening the door.

A chair came sliding through the doorway, moving smoothly across the ebb floor and stopped at Shae's feet.

"Hi, Shae." Prime Director Zim Noki, holding another chair by his side, walked into the cell. He gestured for the admiral to take a seat and nodded in greeting.

"The brilliance of politics," Shae mumbled. "Tell a lie long enough, often enough, and people will believe it."

He pursed his lips. He'd heard that before, but where? It was from some dictator. He frowned, not knowing where he had heard that term.

It didn't matter. The saying was true.

Zim plopped his chair down and sat, slouching and crossing his arms.

"What the hell are you doing to me?" The veins on Shae's neck bulged. "You set me up."

Zim looked over his shoulder and gestured for someone to close the cell door. When it closed, Zim turned back to the admiral. "So you say." He pointed to the empty chair. "Do me a favor and sit."

Shae shook his head. His pulse had elevated to twice the normal rate and pounded in his ears. "I'd rather sit on my own dung than do as you say."

Zim grinned. "It's not wise to piss off the Prime Director, Shae. Now, either do as I say, or I'll force you to sit. I'm fine with either option."

Shae remembered the last time they'd gotten into a scuffle. Shae hadn't fared too well when Zim's strong punch doubled him over. Just because Zim was a politician didn't mean he didn't possess incredible physical prowess.

Shae took a seat.

"Thank you, Admiral."

"When are you going to inform the public this is all a mistake, and I'm innocent?"

Zim uncrossed his muscular forearms and clasped his hands together. "I'm afraid I can't do that, Shae."

"You know I didn't do it, Zim."

"I don't know that at all. I'm trying to determine what's true. But, isn't it strange once you were captured, no more attacks occurred? It looks very suspicious to the public."

"You're fabricating everything." A rush of adrenaline took over, and Shae's chest swelled. "I'm here because of your lies. You're jeopardizing the safety of an entire population, and for what? What are you gaining here?"

"You called the Space Templars, Shae. What am I supposed to do?"

Shae blinked as he tried to decipher Zim's implication. "What do you mean? I did what my instincts told me to do. I felt I had no other option, even if that option was like throwing an arrow at a childhood fairy tale. And somehow, in some way, maybe that arrow is how we survived." He paused, catching his breath. "But what do the Templars have to do with this?" He pointed to his chest. "With me being under assault with lies of treason?"

Zim bolted out of his chair and grabbed Shae by his collar, his immense physique towering over him. "They have *everything* to do with this, Admiral."

Zim's outburst took Shae off guard, and he instinctively tried to stand. Zim pushed him back down and slammed him onto his seat, his immense strength keeping Shae locked into one position.

Shae felt Zim's hot breath on his cheek. "We had over a thousand years of peace with the Space Templars, and now you go and call them? Do you know how powerful they are? This was supposed to be a one-and-done deal; now everything has changed, and it's *my* ass on the line."

"What are you talking about? You said yourself they're just a myth."

Zim cocked his arm and sent a fast, right hook to Shae's jaw, knocking him to the floor.

Blood filled Shae's mouth, and he spat it out. He pushed off the floor, his chest heaving in and out. "What are you so afraid of, Zim? I don't understand what you're doing. Be transparent. That was one of your campaign slogans a quarter of a century ago. Now prove your words, because you're nothing but worthless to me."

"Afraid? Worthless?" He laughed softly. "No, not afraid...and far from worthless. I have to do a lot of clean up because of you, and the Monarch doesn't like that."

"The *Monarch*? What are you talking about?"

Zim nodded slowly. "Yes, the Monarch." He snatched both chairs, strode to the closed door, and kicked it with his boot for the police to open up. He glanced over his shoulder. "Don't think this is over for you, Shae. It's just begun, and no matter how it works out, you're dead. I just have to go through the slow channels to do it."

The door opened, and Zim walked through. It slammed shut and locked a moment later.

Shae sat on the bed, rubbing his chin.

An image of Louise drawing on her leg entered his mind, and he froze. The circle and the cross were from a fairy tale, in a book about the Space Templars that had seemed to mean nothing, but right now, meant everything.

In that book, the Space Templars' Grand Master Skye Vortek wrote that code on a piece of paper and handed it to an inmate in a prison cell. The inmate was Skye's brother, and the circle meant a wall. The X meant the wall would break.

Louise was going to attempt to break him out.

25

KODA

Sphere Nine, Starbase Matrona

Prime Overseer Koda Lutz stared at Shae's letter, a message asking him to do the unspeakable. To spy on Zim Noki and the governance.

Koda would gladly do it.

Koda wrung his hands together. Being a spy against a governance conspirator was his pleasure. Yes, it was for his uncle, but he'd be the champion of the people if he uncovered a lie the Prime Director was thrusting upon them.

Koda rested his elbows on his desk, his eyes on his uncle's letter.

He didn't know how the letter had made it to his desk or who had delivered it. It had been lying there when he entered his office that morning.

He shifted the desk lamp and turned it on, pointing it at the letter. He'd already read it a number of times, but each time it felt like he was missing something.

He wants me to uncover as much as I can on Zim? How? What am I supposed to look for, Uncle? He tapped his finger on the paper, then shot a leery glance over his shoulder, feeling like someone could be watching him.

Of course, no one was there. Only an empty wall that as of yet displayed no pictures, framed certificates, or the Sphere Nine's Prime Overseer plaque with his name on it.

Two weeks ago, Koda had achieved one of the highest positions in governance and won the election bid to become the Prime Overseer of Sphere Nine.

His plan was to eventually try and change the law to allow anyone under seven foot five to run for the next Prime Director position, a position he desperately wanted for himself.

He'd never trusted the governance, and it was why Koda joined the crooked political game in the first place, to clean it up. Now this, a way to help his uncle gifted like a Star Guild medal presented to him on a silver platter.

He looked at the office door. "Open."

It opened to display an office of busy workers shuffling papers, speaking over commlinks, or typing on their desk's holodisplay consoles. A woman frantically rushed past, papers in hand.

This was Sphere Nine's governance headquarters at its finest occupying all of level one in this twenty-story building.

He pressed a button on his HDC. "Bonnie?"

Bonnie's animated face, young and vibrant, came over the holodisplay. "Yes, Prime Overseer Lutz?"

Koda rolled his eyes and swatted at the air as if the title "Prime Overseer" was an irritating fly. "Just call me Koda."

"Pardon me, sir…Koda."

"Bonnie, can you get me Savanna Levens' office?"

"Yes, immediately, Prime Overse...I mean—Koda." Bonnie's image disappeared.

Koda opened his mouth wide and stretched his lips over his teeth, working his mouth muscles and relaxing them, then worked them into a smile, starting small and then wide, something he learned in acting school before he entered Star Guild Academy.

Politicians were always at their finest, and he had to act the part even if he didn't want to, the way politicians did it best.

He smiled again and relaxed. Again and relaxed.

An older woman's giggle came over the holovid. "How may I help you, Prime Overseer?"

Startled, Koda slammed his palms on his desk and stopped his smiling session. His eyes grew wide when he saw a woman smiling back at him.

Savanna Levens, other than himself, was one of the few allies his uncle had.

He cleared his throat. "Yes, this is Prime Overseer Koda Lutz. About my uncle."

Savanna put her finger up. "Listen, Koda. I have something I need you to see. It's important. Can you get here as soon as possible? It's more than urgent, and I think you can help us with a bit of your wisdom."

Koda furrowed his brow. He had expected to have to practically beg to sneak into her busy schedule and see her. "Gladly, Prime Overseer. N-now?"

Savanna frowned. "I'm afraid now is all we have. My tech and I have found something odd and...important."

Koda nodded. "I'll be on the first hovertrain. Expect me there in a half-hour."

"Excellent. I look forward to formally meeting you. Until then, be careful."

Koda hesitated. Did he need to be careful? He dipped his head. "Yes, until then."

Her hologram disappeared, and Koda brought his fingers to his chin. *Am I in danger?*

Standing, he slid his hands down his sleek suit, turned, and walked through the outer office, out of the building and onto the sidewalk of Sphere Nine's main street. The buildings were a long string of tall rectangles.

Above, the sky consisted of ebb walls with clear ebb-striated glass windows. They were nearly impossible to break, though some had in the attack. Emergency safeguards were in place, usually necessary when small space rocks cracked or broke the glass. Hoverbots, stationed at every nook and cranny in the starbase ceilings, could replace the glass in under a minute and sometimes mere seconds.

Koda peered through the glass above. A galaxy of stars was displayed before him, along with the strange green planet here when they had jumped.

A bell dinged loudly from the dome-shaped hoverstation up ahead, his destination. A quick half an hour hovertrain ride, and he'd be at Sphere Six's capitol building where Savanna worked.

"Welcome, Prime Overseer Koda Lutz."

He closed the capitol building door behind him and lifted his head, his mouth opening in surprise. It was Savanna, one of the longest-tenured politicians on Matrona.

He'd idolized her when he was a kid, and now here he was, in her presence, one on one.

Or, rather, she was an image on a holoscreen just above a vacant desk at the moment. "Come to my office."

He walked down a hallway and stopped at the door with her name on it. The door slid upward, and there sat Savanna.

She stepped around her desk and walked toward him, her long white dress billowing out at the knees with each step. Her gray hair bounced, and her blue eyes danced. She smiled and extended her hand. Even at her age, she could turn heads in a room. "Koda, we have a problem. A big problem."

The door shut behind him, and out of the corner of his eye, he saw a young man tapping away at a holopad, dots of sweat covering his forehead.

"What's the problem?"

"My tech here decoded something. And it's not good."

The tech raised his hand without looking up and dropped it a second later to continue tapping away on the holopad.

"What did he decode?"

"As you know, your uncle didn't set up a coup in order to overtake the governance." She rolled her eyes at the thought. "But what we found is worse than I could have ever imagined. The attack on us was an inside job by a group I still don't have a grasp of, but it's not over. The problem? They aren't coming for us in their ships during the next wave of attacks. That was Plan A, and it failed."

Koda scrunched his nose, the skin around his eyes wrinkling. "I'm not following."

"There is another attack coming. It's a Plan B, and it's a whole lot worse than Plan A."

26

ALI

Planet Eos, West of the Radiation Zone—Adarta System, Orion Spur

Ali edged around a boulder, her eyes on the bursting lights as heavy cannon from Starship *Sirona* pounded the dusky sky, targeting the enemy starfighters.

Explosions erupted around *Sirona*, its shield taking hit after hit, though it looked as if the gravitons were holding stable, keeping the attacking fire from penetrating.

Sweat dripped down her face, her body, and from places she didn't know sweat could leak. It wasn't from fear or nerves, but the immense heat inside the cockpit.

Ali took a sip of water and pulled back, spitting it out. "Hot."

Mechs weren't designed to walk over fifty or more kilometers at a time. They were designed to continually stop, mine, and mine more until the shift was over.

"Daf, how are you doing in there?"

"I'm in an oven. You?"

"Not faring any better."

Daf was behind her, and the battle was so close they could almost reach out and snag an enemy missile.

Sirona starfighter and enemy starfighter combat had extended behind them as well and was coming ever closer.

"*Sirona*'s getting the crap kicked out of her, Ali," yelled Daf.

"Not really." Ali spat out sweat that dripped into her mouth. "I'm telling you, she's dishing out more damage than she's taking. What I'm more worried about is getting spotted. It'll happen sooner or later, and from what I see on our six, the war is heading our way, surrounding us, and we'll be smack dab in the middle if we don't hurry."

"I see that too," replied Daf. "But I can't keep pushing my mech. It'll shut down any minute now."

A bright light flashed in the sky, and if Ali could hear anything outside the mech, she'd no doubt hear a sharp boom.

She closed her eyes for a moment, hoping it wasn't one of their own. She shook her head, her eyes like missiles targeting the attacking enemy starfighters over *Sirona*. "Keep following me, Daf. We're coming around the back of the ship."

Ali and Daf were on a plateau extending in a straight line for kilometers, and *Sirona* was at the base only a quarter of a kilometer away and thirty meters below.

"Daf, you see how the plateau takes a dip behind *Sirona*?"

"Sort of. I don't know if I can see that far."

"Well, when we get to that location, we're going to jump down from the plateau and land behind *Sirona*. Got it?"

"Uh…hell no, Chief. Not happening."

"Trust me on this, Daf. It's the lowest point of the plateau, and we can't walk all the way around, or we'll be in the middle of a damn war. Plus, we'll shut down from engine failure. This is the safest and closest route."

Silence hung in the air on the other end. Finally, Daf sighed loudly. "That's not something our mech's dampening system can handle, Chief. The shock absorbers' upper mounts will force compression into the tubes on impact so damn fast it'll blow the chambers like bombs. We'll be a pile of scrap metal seconds after we land."

"We slow ourselves with the air thrusters."

On both sides of a mech's lower legs were four air thrusters, used for small jumps to spring into the air and for slowing down the mech's descent when needed.

Ali knew they weren't designed for high-performance jumps, but the sheer power of the thrusters would slow them down easily.

A cough echoed in the cockpit, and Ali lurched back, startled. She dropped her eyes to the doctor. She'd almost forgotten he was there. It looked like he'd taken a dip in a biosphere lake. "I think she has a point, Ali."

"She doesn't. I've performed jumps like this before, and from the looks of the battle, it's the only way to Starship *Sirona*, and since we can't just stop, it's the only option we have."

He stared deeply into her eyes as if searching her soul for the truth. "Are you sure?"

Ali pursed her lips. "No, I just want to jump and die." She rolled her eyes. "Of course, I'm sure."

"Okay." He squeezed his arms around the HDC column and gave her a thumbs-up. "I trust you."

Ali cocked her lips into a half-smile and then quickly let it fall. She didn't have time for pleasantries or for being told what would work and what wouldn't. She was the chief, and she wouldn't purposely steer them wrong, but Daf was Daf, always whining, always second-guessing her and now this guy.

She shifted her mech around another boulder, pressed it forward, and glanced at her HDC, swiping her finger over it. "How much time until we reach Starship *Sirona*?"

Four minutes blinked on her HDC.

"Daf, we're almost there."

"Yes, but look who—"

Daf's commlink fizzled out.

"Daf?"

No reply.

Ali turned and gasped. "Daf," she yelled.

27

ALI

Planet Eos, West of the Radiation Zone—Adarta System, Orion Spur

A large humanoid in a green and gray suit was atop a boulder, its spear-looking gun pointed at Daf and shooting fiery slugs one after the other.

Daf took a step back as sparks flew at every impact. The giant shot into ebb armor, and with whatever rounds the giant used, they weren't doing any more damage than scratching Daf's mech and shoving her backward.

Another humanoid emerged to stand beside the first one, wearing the same outfit. These were grunts, perhaps scouting ahead of the line, and they had found something they probably thought was easy pickings.

Ali pushed her mech toward the attackers as the heat sensors blinked wildly on the HDC. She turned off the warning, sweat dripping from her fingers, and readied the jump sequence.

She crouched in her standing cockpit and jumped, her air thrusters pushing her mech off the ground like a rocket and targeted the men on the boulder. She didn't have weapons, but she'd make full use of her mech as one.

She reached peak jumping height and eyed the soldiers below. They shifted and aimed their weapons at Ali, sending hot projectiles her way.

Sparks flew out, almost blinding Ali's view out of the cockpit. Her mech's head faced down, as she calculated the perfect descent onto the boulder, the ebb-striated cockpit window taking shots that created small cracks on the outer lining.

On the descent, Ali activated the thrusters, slowing her down. She brought her arms up, and the grunts backed away, even as they continued to fire.

Ali landed hard and slammed her hands down as she did. The cockpit vibrated, and her mech's hands pounded a humanoid as they connected with its chest.

His hands went outward, and his spear flew off the boulder as Ali ground him into the large rock, breaking every bone in his chest cavity.

His body went limp.

Ali's mech slipped. The edge of the boulder cracked and gave way, and her mech's front legs and chest scraped against the side of the rock as she fell.

The mech jostled back and forth as its feet touched the ground. Ali took a step back, keeping her big metal lug upright as her sweat splattered the cockpit floor.

She took a few heavy breaths, glaring out her cockpit window. The other soldier was running away from them.

"We go now, Daf."

The grunts in response likely gave out Daf's and Ali's location to enemy reinforcements.

She twisted her mech and pushed it onward, heading toward the dip in the plateau just above Starship *Sirona*. "You okay, William?"

"That maneuver you just pulled wasn't so kind on my ankle, but we're alive."

"Ali, more are coming," shouted Daf over the comm. "Three of them."

Ali eyed the window. "I see them."

Ali rushed toward them. A wave of heat hit her, almost taking her to her knees as if someone had dropped a scolding bucket of water on her.

She didn't know how long her mech could take this abuse, but the oncoming trio of soldiers didn't give her much choice. The closer she got, the more the soldiers' weapons became visible.

Crap.

These spears were longer and wider.

She gulped hard as they aimed their weapons. A flurry of raging bullets exited the spears' tips, pounding Ali's mech.

Her cockpit rattled, and she was jostled backward. She pushed forward and leaned into the impacts, digging her mech's feet into the ground.

"Why are they rushing toward us? Don't they know better?" screamed Daf.

Good question.

Ali's mouth dropped when she saw a fourth and fifth man running behind the other soldiers, both carrying large discs. Were those bombs? Perhaps they were going to mount them on a mech as they rushed by?

"Daf, I think they are going to detonate something on us. Check out the soldiers in the rear."

"I see them."

"Fight, but don't let them get—"

An explosion near Ali rocked the cockpit, and William yelped in pain. She pulled up the rear camera view. "Oh, no."

Some type of military mech with turrets on its shoulders and cannons for arms was sprinting in their direction.

"A mech?" This one was larger than hers but similar in build except for the weapons. "Daf, do you see that mech?"

"I do. It's almost identical to one of ours."

"Guild dammit." Ali paused and looked at her holodisplay, bringing up her heat indicators. They didn't have a choice. They had to run for it.

"Daf, we have to forget about the soldiers and run to the edge of the plateau and jump." A slug hit Ali's mech, pushing her back a few steps.

She righted herself quickly.

"Yep, no other choice, Chief."

"Go."

An image came up on the display. A man smirked, his red beard and mustache curling upward. His eyes pierced her. "I'm on my way, Ali. I brought you here, and I'm going to take you out."

Ali's heart gave a thud, and she quickly swiped him off the holomonitor. He was the asshole in her dream, the guy who killed Hendricks and almost her.

"What was that?" William asked through gritted teeth, his face twisted in agony.

"I don't know."

She did know, but now wasn't the time for a lengthy story.

Her HDC blared an alert. Ali's eyes went wide. A dot on the screen was coming in fast. "Incoming starfighter, and it will be here in less than two minutes."

"I see it," said Daf, her voice strained and jerky as she pushed her mech to its limits, now running beside Ali's.

Ali pounded harder against the ground as the blinking light on the heat gauge turned solid. She tapped the control panel. "You can make it. Push through the heat."

One minute blinked on her HDC, indicating the time until the starfighter would be overhead.

"Move faster, Daf." Ali pointed at a boulder up ahead. "Get behind that."

"I see it."

The starfighter neared. If they didn't find cover quickly, they'd be strafed out in the open, and she knew those cannons had more power than the grunt's large spears.

"Once we get behind that boulder, we can only stop for a micro-second. We have the soldiers and that mech tailing us as well."

The starfighter opened fire, and from the rear cam view, rocks and dirt flew into the air in bursts, one after the other, closing the distance on Daf and Ali.

A cannon burst hit Daf's mech and sent her toppling forward, skidding across the ground on its chest. Thick dust curled into the air, but as quick as she had fallen, she was up. The starfighter zipped overhead and pivoted.

"Stop in front of the boulder," ordered Ali, sliding her mech to a halt and banging against the side of the big ebb rock.

William let out another yelp, his face gnarled in pain. The poor guy would have to deal with it until they made it to safety if they made it to safety.

"Daf, are you okay?"

Daf's breath came fast and shallow as she leaned her mech against the boulder next to Ali. "I'm all right."

Chunks of rocks poured on top of them, riddling their armored domes and shoulders as the starfighter flew on by, strafing yet again. It turned sharply and headed back in their direction.

Ali eyed the terrain in front of her. "Crap." The soldiers were on their way, and the mech wielding turrets full of missiles and guns for arms was now in the lead, its turrets rotating and aiming at Ali.

Ali rushed around the boulder. "Move to *Sirona* as fast as you can."

"On my way."

Shards of rock splayed against Ali from a missile blasting the ground next to her.

Daf reached the plateau's edge first and stopped, almost teetering over.

"Chief?"

The sweat stung Ali's eyes, blurring her vision. She wanted to wipe it away, but if she turned off the parrot switch, she'd be switching off her mech's joint controls. "Jump, Daf. Jump."

Daf hesitated.

"Jump and hit the air compressor, Daf."

"Um...no, I don't think so. You see how far down that is? We have to find another way."

"There is no other way."

Daf let out a loud exhale. “I don’t think we can survive that.”

“We either die on their account, or on ours, and we have more of a chance surviving the jump than we do surviving them.”

A concussion blast rocketed dirt into the air next to Daf.

“I’m jumping.” Daf leaped.

Ali reached the edge. “When you’re at ten meters—”

A cannon slug hammered the back of Ali’s mech, pushing her forward. She inhaled sharply. “We’re going over.”

A blur of dark-blue light spun through the cockpit window as they fell.

Ali reached a finger toward the air compression button but missed, feeling the dizzying spin grab hold of her, not allowing her to position her finger correctly on the holographic button.

She tried again but missed.

Push it, Ali...push the damn button.

She glanced at the HDC to see how many more meters she had until they hit the ground but couldn’t focus on the numbers.

In desperation, she reached her hand outward. If she didn’t press it, she and the doctor would be a bloody mess when they hit the ground.

28

ALI

Planet Eos, West of the Radiation Zone—Adarta System, Orion Spur

Ali extended her finger and wiggled it, making sure she hit something, any button.

The mech abruptly slowed as the air compressors switched on, automatically calculating the mech's center of gravity and mechanically moving the air thruster tubes where they needed to be, and successfully flipping Ali's mech upright.

Ali's body relaxed as her mech leveled, its feet now pointed to the ground. Numbers spun on the HDC and registered eleven meters until impact.

She gripped the cockpit safety restraints attached to her with all her strength. From this fall, the mech's dampening system couldn't keep the cockpit from feeling the landing hard.

"Brace yourself, doctor."

A crashing thud and a loud screech of metal against metal rang through the cockpit, and the mech shuddered violently.

A loud pop accompanied by a boom sounded, and the mech's torso swayed.

Ali moved her foot forward, and her mouth fell open when her mech did the same. The rocking halted, and her mech remained on its feet, dust wafting into the air all around it.

William leaned against the window behind the HDC column, his leg with the broken ankle stretched on the floor, his other knee pulled against his chest.

He pressed his hands against his eyes, rubbing them. Blood smeared his face, probably from banging against the wall and the HDC column, but miraculously he was conscious. "Oh, my Guild. I can't believe…oh, my Guild."

Ali peered through the window. Dusk's shadows covered Starship *Sirona,* but the ship was there, shooting myriads of cannon fire into the darkness.

"Ali."

Ali turned her head. "Daf? Where are you?"

"Inside *Sirona*. Bay Fifteen is open."

How did she get into Sirona so fast?

"Where is bay Fifteen?" She should know, but she was out of sorts.

"Starboard side, near the back of the ship."

William pointed to the right, then wiped blood from a cut above his eye. "Around the ship there."

Ali stepped to the right, the crunching of metal against the actuators echoing in her cockpit, screaming at her. "I see it. I'm on my way."

Orange lights flashed near the inside of the opening as Ali stepped up the ramp, her mech moving at a slow clip. She walked through the gravity field and entered the busy launch bay.

The bay door closed.

Crew members ran everywhere, and a few starfighters were parked, their cockpit windows raised, and ladders butted up against them.

She parked her mech near a wall, the heat inside practically melting her skin. She wanted nothing more than to pop the hatch open and let the heat escape.

She turned her mech off and unstrapped her belt harness. After reaching up and popping the hatch open, she sank to the cockpit floor, pulling her knees to her chest and wrapping her arms around them.

The heat rushed out, and cool air swept across her face. She rested her head on her knees and held in a cry. A cry for miraculously surviving, for all those that died, that she was on her mother's ship. A cry for her suspicion that Captain Diana Johnson was not her real mother.

"Your mom will be proud, Ali."

Ali glanced up. William sat wearing a serious expression, his face dotted with perspiration.

"She'll find a reason not to be proud. Trust me."

William nodded. "I'm not telling you what she'd say, just what she'd think."

Ali gave a curt affirmation, thinking he could believe what he wanted, and looked past him out the window, at the bay's tarmac.

Men and women in dark Star Guild uniforms were walking toward her mech.

"It's time for us to get out of here." She stood, moving up and over the hatch.

Daf was halfway up the ladder, climbing up to help her.

"Daf, tell them we have a wounded doctor in here. He needs a Sufi-cell Pod as soon as possible."

Her brows rose. "Is he okay?"

"He's seen better days."

An explosion slammed nearby outside, and the starship shuddered.

Daf lost her balance and slipped off the steps, falling to the floor and awkwardly on her side. She pushed to her feet and headed for the men and women hurrying in their direction.

Ali looked down at William. "People are coming to help you."

He dipped his head. "Thank you. You saved my life."

"No problem." Ali found a foothold on the side of the mech and climbed down.

A soft hand landed gently on her back. She twisted around to give Daf a thank you and a job well done but found herself staring into her mother's eyes.

She swallowed hard and took a step back. How could she face a woman who claimed to have raised her and be blood-related?

Diana grabbed her, choking back tears, and squeezed her arms around Ali in a hug. Ali's arms hung by her side.

Diana let go of her daughter, moving her hands to Ali's face and kissing her cheek. "I was so scared. I couldn't find you. We searched and searched."

Ali nodded and pointed at an approaching Daf. "You can thank her for my life." She tilted her head and looked her mother up and down. Ali was taller than her, with whiter skin, and didn't look that much like Diana, or her dead father, for that matter. "We need to talk, but right now I—"

Daf extended her hand. "I'm Daf."

Diana pushed her hand away, embracing her instead. "I owe you for saving my daughter's life."

Ali eyed a corridor leading out of the launch bay. "We need to save everyone on *Sirona* and get off this planet."

Diana's face hardened, all emotion draining away. "That isn't happening anytime soon. Expansion engines are offline, and we can't leave this planet with ion boosters, so we're stuck here until the expansion engines are repaired." Her mom shifted her gaze.

She was hiding something.

Ali folded her arms. They were weak, like the rest of her body. She just wanted to rest and perhaps wash up, get all this drying sweat off her. "That's not all that's damaged, is it?"

Diana shook her head, then turned and walked toward a corridor. "We're on our last reserves. I'm talking ammunition, aquaponics, you name it." She pointed over her shoulder without looking, her demeanor a captain now, something Ali knew too well. "Warehouse Twenty-six is over there. We've hooked into their water line."

Ali placed her hand on Diana's shoulder, not something she'd ever done before, but she wanted to shake Diana out of her captain mode. "Why hasn't the enemy targeted the warehouse if you're hooked up to it?"

Diana eyed Ali's hand on her shoulder, and Ali took it away.

Diana's eyebrows rose. "I think we have more pressing issues than your question."

"I know we're in some kind of war, but there is—" A Thunderbird caught Ali's eye, and an idea popped into her mind. "How many Thunderbirds are operational?"

"All of them," replied Diana, cocking her head to the side. "But we only have about a hundred left. Why?"

Ali studied her mech for a moment and saw the doctor being placed on a gurney. She blinked her tiredness away. She couldn't believe what she was about to ask. "How many Thunderbird cannons do you have lying around?"

Diana shrugged. "I don't know. What are you getting at?" She turned and walked toward the corridor.

Ali followed her with Daf by her side. "How many mechs are there in warehouse Twenty-six?"

Diana wagged her head as she marched down the corridor. "A couple dozen. Again, why?"

Ali yawned, rounding a corner lined with doors, gray walls, and dim lights, her body beyond tired. "I need to talk with tech. If they can find a way to hook a cannon onto some mechs, then we would have infantry—a powerful infantry. Is there any way to mount missile turrets on them and wire it to a mech's HDC?"

The ship vibrated as it fired a barrage of missiles.

Diana stopped and furrowed her brow. "Ali, I just got you back. I'm not letting you go out there again nor anyone else *except* the Thunderbirds. We stay on *Sirona* until I get her repaired enough to get off Eos."

Ali walked past Daf and Diana.

"Where do you think you're going?" asked Diana.

Ali rubbed her eyes, hurrying down the corridor. "To Tech Quarters."

"Stay here. That's an order."

Ali spun on her heels, facing Diana and placing her hands on her hips. "Since you're too busy to answer my questions, I might as well pose some questions to them."

"Stop now," demanded Diana. "If there's a question for Tech, it's a question for me."

"Other than trying to weaponize our mech," said Ali, as she moved quickly down the corridor, not bothering to look back. "I need to see our earliest specs. The enemy mechs are identical to ours, so someone has either given the enemy our mech blueprints, or we somehow got ours from them. And I'm going to find out which."

29

EDEN

Unknown

Eden walked beside Skye Vortek in a meadow surrounded by tall thin trees, with leaves that reminded her of large green teardrops.

Skye was barefoot and held his hands behind his back, deep in thought.

A bird's screech pierced the air, and a tree shook in the distance as a bird with a purple-feathered face, and a white-feathered body extended its wings and flew into the sky.

Eden watched in awe as the bird flapped to another tree and landed, shaking the limb.

She took a deep sniff and smelled the sweet fruit-like aroma in the air.

Everything around her was magical, more colorful, and brighter than the biosphere on Matrona. She had to remind herself she was on a planet, not a biosphere, which was something previously inconceivable to her.

She had only seen Eos' desert and had been told that most planets were plain and lifeless, devoid of an atmosphere.

A snake slithered in front of her, long and green, sporting a purple diamond-like design on its head. Eden stopped and gasped, her hand accidentally hitting Skye in the chest.

She'd seen small snakes in the biosphere, but nothing like this large and wide specimen.

It halted and turned, hissing, exposing its long fangs and forked tongue.

Skye moved his hand up and down in front of Eden.

The snake calmed and went on its way, moving under a bush.

Eden shot him a look. "How did you do that?"

"I dissipated energy. Snakes can smell and taste fear." He dipped his head. "Please, don't be afraid. There's nothing here that will harm you." He motioned with his hand for her to follow him. "Continue to walk with me."

"I haven't seen many people here, at least not with their hoods down."

Skye glanced at her, his blue eyes soft. Although his face looked young, his voice and his mind seemed much older and wiser. He radiated a sense of peace, something Eden hadn't experienced in a person before.

"May we sit, Eden?"

Fresh air breezed across her, ruffling her white robe. She took another deep inhale, tasting oxygen.

She let out a long exhale.

The air here felt alive, unlike the stale air in the starbase or on the ships. She gazed around, watching robed Beings in the distance, some smelling wildflowers in the field, and others walking into the dense forest and disappearing from view.

"Eden?" Skye sat cross-legged, his eyes practically touching her soul. "Please, sit."

"Sure." Eden sat down and leaned on her hip, the soft grass scrunching underneath.

Skye patted his thighs. "One day, you might like to sit like this. It stretches and strengthens your core, thus strengthening your solar plexus."

"Your what?"

"Your solar plexus is an energy center right here." He touched just above his stomach.

An energy center?

She'd never heard of the term and kept her mouth shut, crossing her legs like him. She gazed at the sky, observing the yellow sun's rays glistening upon the nearby trees.

"To answer your question," he cupped his hands in his lap and cleared his throat. "We call this planet Aurora, and there are many people living here. This world's population is about one hundred thousand in all, all of whom are initiates or members of the Eighth Order of the Melchizedek, an order of priests and priestesses who stem from the Magi of old and are now known to you and the galaxy as the Space Templars."

She gave a tentative smile and wistfully tilted her head to one side. "I can hardly believe you exist, that the Space Templars really exist." She shook her head. "I've never heard of the Melchizedek or the Magi, but as kids, we used to act like you guys, pretending we were using magic and flying around in our imaginary spacecraft."

Skye swept his long chestnut-brown hair behind his ears. "And did you create any magic?"

"Sure," she replied. "Sometimes, I'd act like I shot lasers out of my hands and at my friends, and they'd fall to the ground and fake like they were dead." She shrugged. "Well, that's about it. I don't know if that's the kind of magic you're referring to."

"A child's magic is very powerful. We call it *imagination*—knowledge from the Magi nation mixed with creativity. Just add the letter c to the word 'magi,' and you get 'magic.' It's a powerful creative force, and limitless."

Eden raised her brows. It was interesting information but as foreign to her as this planet. She couldn't believe it. She was sitting with the Space Templars' Grand Master. Until a few days ago, everything, including a breathable planet and these mystical knights, had been fiction.

Eden looked off in the distance, eyeing a white cottony cloud in the sky, different from the constant wispy clouds on Eos. "You know, all of our Prime Directors told us that throughout all the star systems that the first Star Guild aviators explored, they could never find a planet safe enough for us to inhabit after Eos' oxygen was used up." She brought her gaze to Skye. "It doesn't surprise me they were wrong. I wish I would have followed my own instincts. I could've been exploring space all this time and maybe found a place like this."

She sighed. It was a wish she'd had when she was little, a way to get away from her drugged mother. "They said we were created on Eos, and no other beings existed."

Skye nodded. "Do you accept that?"

She gave him a half-smile. "Well, obviously you're in front of me, so that's a negative. But the rest of my race thinks we're alone in the galaxy, well, until recently. You know, after the attack and all."

Skye placed a palm on his chest. "I have some news for you that you might not accept yourself. I live on this planet, Aurora, but that's not where I'm from or where we humans originate."

"I know," replied Eden. "We're from Eos, and you Space Templars left and came here and probably to other planets, I'm guessing."

Skye folded his hands in front of him. "We're from a planet known as Earth. And we didn't leave you. We've always been around, waiting for you to call upon us, for you to remember who we are. We can bend the laws of physics in a way you'd call magic, and we could help your race unshackle the chains that bind you. We've trained our entire lives, and those before us trained their entire lives as well, for several specific goals. To protect the innocent, to serve the light against the darkness, and to teach the truth by way of being an example to others."

"How do you train?"

"In many ways, and someday, we'll train you. But the ways are too many to describe here. Most of us train from birth. However, some are called to us later in their lives. We train in the art of hand to hand combat, flight combat, and weapons combat. We are faster and more skilled than any warrior you'll ever meet. Most importantly, we train our minds and hearts to meld into one, and in so doing, we operate on a high intuitive level and can do things many call magical. In short, we work on our inner being for the welfare of our outer being."

"And where do you originate? Who taught you?"

Skye smiled. "We're ancient, Eden. Very ancient. We can be traced back to Atlantis, an old nation on Earth, long lost into the sea. We made our way through the Egyptians and Mayans, and then rose up in Greece again, then became famous for a time as the Knights Templar, again on Earth. We expanded to the stars with technology unknown to Earth at the time thanks to the Anunnaki and other races that left ship plans and designs we found and expanded to other races as well. To make a long story short, we originated on Earth by way of the ancient light-bearers, those who wanted to shine light, truth, and protection to the people. It started with one light and expanded outward."

Eden froze. "No, can't be." She ran her hands through her hair. "What the myths say is that the Space Templar Order was born on Starbase Matrona until they flew off and left us."

"Is there more to that myth?" asked Skye.

Eden took a deep breath, thinking. "No, not really, except that you used magic, were defenders of the galaxy, and ran away because of a difference of opinion with the Prime Director at that time. There really isn't much else but the children's stories about you guys and gals fighting bandits, pirates, and evil, of course."

Skye rolled his eyes and tapped her knee. "Can we put these stories to rest and stick to the truth?"

She looked down at her knee to see a smooth, dark-blue egg-shaped crystal. She touched it and looked at Skye. "What's this?"

"It's for you. It's called a crystal egg. It's charged with what you call magic. It helps to raise one's vibration and assist in thinking from a higher perspective. It tunes your natural antenna to receive inspiration and quickens thought receptivity." He leaned forward, running his hand along his arm. "Our body has a skeleton made up of calcium phosphate crystals. We keep our balance thanks to calcite crystals that are found in the inner ear, and we chew with teeth made with apatite microcrystals. All of these also act as a natural antenna to the energy all around us. Carry this crystal, and you'll be able to think more clearly, understanding concepts much faster."

She curled her fingers around the warm and smooth crystal egg, her brows rising high. She had no idea what he was blathering about. Yes, this guy was handsome, calm, and polite, but he wasn't making much sense with all the mumbo-jumbo talk.

Eden opened her hand and ran her finger over the crystal's surface. She held it up. "I can have this?"

"Consider it yours."

"Thank you." She slipped the crystal into her pocket, smiling. "I'll cherish this."

"That is my hope." He grinned. "Now, let's talk about truth."

A shot of adrenaline hit her in her heart, a sudden memory of the battle that brought her here. "How did I survive the torpedoes?"

"Our technology is more advanced than yours and even more advanced than the Beings who attacked you, though their military numbers more than quadruple ours. To answer your question, we jumped to your location, attached your energy signature to our drives, and jumped to another portion of the sector, taking you with us."

He grinned. "In the process, and what you'd consider in the blink of an eye, we drew the two torpedoes together using similar technology, and they collided far from Starbase Matrona." He winked. "And to answer your next question, we destroyed the enemy pyramids as well. Your Star Guild friends are still alive."

Eden bolted upright, her eyes tearing up. "They are? Take me to them."

"It's too dangerous now, but you will find your way to them soon."

She narrowed her eyes. "No, they need my help."

"You can't help them if you don't help yourself first."

She scrunched her nose. "What?"

"You have a lot to learn about yourself, but you must learn something otherworldly first, and it will change a bit of you from the inside as you process it."

Eden stood. This guy talked in riddles. "Okay, enough of that. How do I get back to my people?" She placed her hands on her hips. "And now."

Skye ignored her. "Starbase Matrona was originally assembled by a race named the Anunnaki who had many of their own kind living on Earth eons ago. When Matrona was transported to the Adarta System to orbit planet Eos, the Space Templars from Earth followed it in an attempt to change its course back to its home planet."

Eden fidgeted with her arm as her brows creased. "What?"

"Furthermore, your race has never lived on Eos. You've always lived on a starbase orbiting Eos."

Eden looked off, her mind spinning. "That's not true."

"Before you met me, the Space Templars were considered 'not true' as well." He put his hands up. "There's a lot to explain, more than what can be absorbed in one sitting. Just know that a small percentage of your race was highjacked physically, emotionally, and spiritually when they were taken to Eos for a specific purpose that was not to your benefit."

Eden furrowed her brow even more. "What purpose? I don't understand."

He lowered his head and picked at some grass. "I'm sorry. This is a lot to hear, I know." He gazed into her eyes. "In order to understand, you must first realize there is much to question about your Prime Director. Prime Directors, in general, aren't on Matrona for the well-being of its citizens."

He cleared his throat. "They're there for the benefit of their *own* race. My band of knights tried to stop them almost a thousand years ago. We made a costly mistake and lost thousands of us, almost wiping the Space Templars out of existence. That's when we fled and came here to Aurora—a stronghold."

Eden scratched her jaw. "Wait. Back up. What are you talking about?"

Skye stood. "Come. I have something extremely important to show you. It's going to tell you more about who you are and why you are here."

30

KODA

Starbase Matrona

Sphere Six Overseer, Savanna Levens, sat in an office chair behind her desk, gazing through a large observation window overlooking Matrona's biosphere. Teary-eyed, she appeared to be watching a waterfall cascading down a rocky precipice.

"What exactly are you saying, Savanna?" Koda stood at the foot of her desk, his arms crossed, his mind numb. What Plan A and Plan B was she talking about? She had just told him it would be worse than the attack they had just experienced.

She held papers in her hand, looking as if sorrow had gripped her heart.

She squeezed her hand, crinkling the papers, then easing up.

A young man sat in a chair near Savanna's desk. "It's called *The Kill-Off*. It's a fitting title."

Savanna turned and eyed the young man.

Koda held out his hand at the young man. He saw him when he first walked in, but nearly forgot he was there. "I'm Prime Overseer Koda Lutz."

The young kid took his hand, squeezing gently and shook it. "Devon Gray, Prime Overseer Savanna Levens' assistant." He had dark brown skin, and was probably in his early twenties but looked like a teenager entering puberty. He had large glasses and untidy black hair.

Savanna set the papers down on her desk. "Devon is a savvy technician who knows the ins and outs of HDC mainframes like no one else."

Koda let go of Devon's hand and faced Savanna. "Give me the details. What do you have there?" He pointed to the papers, wondering why she had papers instead of a holopad with holographic documents.

"We have to print these out to be a back up to a backup." She tapped on a holopad on the side of the desk. "We also have backups on several holopads and on two HDC's. But, like I said, we have it on paper just in case our information is found and wiped."

Koda crossed his arms at his stomach. "I'm not following. What is it that could be wiped?"

"Last night, I gave Devon the task of intercepting all messages to and from Zim's HDC, with the sole purpose of helping Shae by finding anything we could on the Prime Director."

She paused and let out an exhale, her face twisting in disgust. "At first, the messages were hack-proof, meaning hard encrypted through the holonet." She looked at Devon as if asking him what she had said was accurate. He gave her thumbs up.

Savanna continued, "Within two hours, Devon, my tech genius here, had broken into the holographic mainframes, deciphered the encryptions, and translated them. The codes weren't just a bunch of random messages like we first thought. They were correspondence labeled *The Kill-Off* related to a series of events already set in motion and were to finish playing out over the next two weeks."

Savanna twisted around in her chair, eyeing the beautiful biosphere again, the trees, green grasses, and wildflowers poking up out of the soil.

She pressed her hands against the window, her palms open and fingers splayed flat on its cold surface. "Only two weeks."

She turned and pulled a handkerchief out of her pocket, wiping her tears and blowing her nose. "I'm sorry. I'm having a hard time with this."

Koda dipped his head. "I understand. So, what's this Kill-Off exactly?"

She returned the soggy cloth to her pocket and rested her hand along the windowsill, again staring at the waterfall. "It's heartbreaking to think that this place—our starbase—won't be here much longer." She faced Koda. "The animals, the plants, the people. Who would want to end all of this? And why?"

Koda bit his bottom lip, doing his best to not explode. "Savanna, I understand you're sad, but I need to understand exactly why you're sad."

"Yes," she responded. "The Kill-Off is a genocide event like the first attack. Plan A was genocide event one. If that failed, Plan B would be enacted. Plan A failed and was created by our Prime Director, and *they*, whoever *they* are, have Plan B in effect as we speak. It's evil and insidious. It's a massive killing of the starbase, but by what means, we don't yet know."

Koda's mouth opened wide. "Are you sure?"

"One-hundred percent positive," said Savanna.

With both hands, Devon curled his fingers around the base of his neck. "Let me display these papers all over the vid channels. I can hack in and do that, plus send the holodocs out to as many politicians as I can. We may even get a minute of airtime before they pull the plug. If some of the population believes us, maybe we can escape Matrona somehow."

Savanna let out an exasperated breath. "Devon, we don't have an escape plan. How are we going to get hundreds of thousands of people off Matrona, let alone millions? We don't have enough transports for all of those people, and where would we go if we did? We don't know of any planet capable of sustaining human life."

Devon shook his head. "At least we can save some people."

Koda nodded. "Savanna is right. We'd just cause panic and gridlock."

Devon threw his hands up in the air. "Isn't that the point? Don't we want to stir the pot and get this information out to as many people as we can? If some of us can survive, then why not do it?"

Koda looked into Devon's dark-brown innocent eyes. He was young, not yet old enough to enter the Suficell Pods. Koda had been in the pods once, and Savanna had probably been through five age-reversals in the pods. She had nearly a hundred and seventy-five years on them.

Savanna sat straighter in her chair. "Look, Devon. You understand how a micro impulse travels through one holographic synapse to another. You can completely disassemble a mainframe and rebuild a better one. But," her eyes went from Devon to Koda, "You both are too young to understand the intricacies of life, how society functions, how politics cheat, lie, and move walls that don't exist, fabricating *truths* that aren't even there."

It was a punch to Koda's system. She was probably right, but Koda felt he knew something about people and life. Not to the extent she knew, but he was a politician who had gone into the game to stop the lying, cheating and fabricating.

What Koda had always known about Savanna was that she had mastered the technique of being able to convince her fellow politicians and business associates to pass something even when there was no proof. She always seemed to be correct after a bill she created and sponsored went through successfully, helping the public in some way or another.

She knew people and could predict their actions and reactions. It was uncanny.

Devon stood, tapping his index finger on the desk. "We have to tell the public."

Savanna shrugged. "And if we tell the inhabitants of Matrona, then what?"

Devon's face went stern, and he pushed his chest out. "They will know, maybe even riot. We'd stop the Kill-Off."

Savanna tilted her head as if she was speaking to a toddler. "Zim and his...whoever they are...would just let this happen?"

"It doesn't matter what they—"

Savanna raised her hand, interrupting Devon. "Look." She touched the crinkled papers on her desk, counting them. "There are over twenty pages of this Kill-Off, and there are hundreds of pages going over the HDC waves that we haven't translated yet. They've probably had this planned for years, Devon. It's *their plan,* whoever *they* are, and that's why *we* need a plan. If we do as you suggest and broadcast our findings to everyone on Matrona, who's to say they couldn't simply flip a switch and kill us all, just like that." She snapped her fingers.

"But," said Koda, "if they had that capability, don't you think they would have done it already?"

"I don't know why they're waiting for two more weeks, but they are. Let's not entice them to speed up the process."

Devon stared at his shoes and bit his fingernail. "I don't know what to do." Tears welled in his eyes. "My parents. My sister. I just want to get them out of here. At least give them a chance. Give you a chance—give everyone a chance."

Koda rubbed Savanna's desk, trying to erase a smudge that wasn't there as he thought. "Then, let's come up with a plan. We bring the papers to Louise Stripe. She's the only one I know who isn't on board with the witch hunt being perpetrated on my uncle. Everyone knows *that* after watching her interview, and she probably doesn't know about the Kill-Off. In the meantime, we uncover everything we can. We decode as much as we can. If we can understand their plan, we can use it against them, or at least gain enough information in order to stop them. Whoever *they* are."

"But how?" asked Devon.

Savanna stood. "We won't know that until we have more information. We have to know why they're waiting two more weeks to kill us. If we can extend that time further out by understanding why they're waiting, then that would be critical information to have, don't you think?"

Devon sighed. "I don't know if I can stay awake much longer."

Koda rubbed his hands together. Devon and Savanna probably hadn't slept since they uncovered the plan. "Whatever you need, I can help."

"Koda, I'm going to take you up on that." Savanna walked toward the door exiting her office. "Right now, I have to find Louise. You stay here and help Devon with whatever he needs."

Devon dipped his head a few times. "No, I'm going to go home. I need sleep. I can pick this up again tomorrow."

Koda sighed. They had vital information that no one else had on Matrona, and he wanted to understand it all. This wasn't a time to rest or to do things out of convenience. This was a time for action, and right now, sleep wasn't an option.

"I'm almost two hundred years old," said Savanna. "If I can stay up this long, then you can, too." She touched the control panel, and the door slid open. She looked over her shoulder. "I'm going to the executive officer's quarters. I know this is a trying time, but you two are all I have. You're all the human race has right now. Don't let them down."

31

KODA

Starbase Matrona

The door shut behind Savanna, and silence filled the room. Koda eyed Devon.

The young man yawned, rubbed his eyes, and then gently slapped his face a few times. "I guess we do what she says."

"She's right, though. We do this for the people. We save humanity." Part of him wanted to cheer. He was doing what he set out to do while running for his current position, to end the corruption, and it started today.

Devon stood and walked around Savanna's desk and sat in her chair. "Okay, back to decoding." He let out a nervous laugh. "If anyone told me a couple of days ago I'd be sitting in an overseer's chair, I would have laughed in their faces, thinking how stupid they were. Now, here I am decoding the fate of our race in an overseer's chair."

He cracked his knuckles and stared at the desk's HDC.

Koda walked around the desk and placed his palms on the desktop, eyeing the holoscreen. "Let's save our species."

"On it." Devon pressed a holographic button, his finger turning the many colors the hologram was projecting as it dipped slightly through the image. "HDC, enter code eleven-seven-nine-four-delta-bravo-papa-papa, complete. Send to Zim Noki's back-end mainframe for holographic dialogue interface."

The HDC computed the numbers and displayed a line connecting Savanna's HDC to Zim's. "What takes seconds to complete now, had taken me almost a day to hack to create this five-second connection between the Prime Director's office and Savanna's."

Koda lifted his brows. This kid was doing things Koda didn't know were possible with an HDC. Illegal, yes, but Koda would keep his lips shut.

A graphic bubble materialized on the screen. A line formed and moved from Savanna's HDC to Zim's, then back to Savanna's.

COMPLETE blinked.

Devon slapped his hands together, "I'm back...and badder than ever."

Koda snorted. "It's better than ever." He shook his head. Why did it matter, especially at a time like this?

Devon stared at him like Koda was a mother correcting his verbiage.

Koda pointed at the screen. "Sorry. Commence."

"It's commencing." Devon brought his eyes back to the screen.

In front of them, the HDC computed dialogue Koda didn't understand. "I have no clue what we're looking at.

Devon leaned back in the chair, watching the holomonitor. "That's the point. To the laymen, it looks like inconsequential junk data streaming across the interface. That's how me and the other techs were trained to interpret it in college, to think of it as incoherent information traveling from one interface to another, unreadable specks of holonet trash en route to deletion by the servers to grant more space for new, more important data streams." Devon's eyes widened. "We have been lied to."

Devon leaned forward, frowning. "The night before, while hacking into Zim's back-end mainframe, I came across a gigantic slew of this junk data, and that's all there was, which in itself struck me as odd." Devon shook his head. "No personal messages, no top-secret notes, nothing, just an enormous amount of junk data. Since there was nothing else to examine and I could tell Savanna was desperate enough to grasp at straws, I broke the junk data down. That's how we discovered it meant much more than what anyone had been led to believe."

Koda nodded, his voice soft and low. "And, within it, you discovered the most unimaginable, worst possible information ever to be concealed from a population."

Devon sunk in his chair slightly. "Yes. I-I still can't believe it. But it's right here in front of us." He took in a deep breath and pressed several holographic buttons. "Okay, junk data, time to translate."

He highlighted dialogue coming in and out of Zim's office. In seconds, letters appeared out of the dialogue stream, forming thousands of discombobulated sentences.

He waved his hand in front of the sentences—a command that also highlighted everything. "Program Decode software into HDC, now."

"Program decode?" asked Koda.

Devon nodded. "Yeah, we needed a way to take all the discombobulated words and successfully convert them into readable sentences. So, I created Program Decode to do this in a matter of seconds, compiling pages and pages of endless words, sentences, and paragraphs."

Koda stepped back as a paper materialized on the desk, and then another and another. In less than five minutes, they had dozens of pages of information on paper exiting from a materializing spool on the desk connected to the HDC.

Koda grabbed the papers as more materialized. The first page was titled *Kill-Off*.

He skimmed the next few pages and added them to the rest to make a tidy stack he tapped neatly into place on the desktop.

Putting the papers down, he picked up where he'd left off. He bit down on his thumb about halfway down a page and froze.

"What is that?"

He placed his index finger on a single word, not knowing what it meant. "Batrachotoxin?" He furrowed his brows, pushing his lower lip out. "What is batrachotoxin?"

Devon eyed it. "That doesn't look good." He read where Koda was looking. "They're going to use Batrachotoxin to kill us?"

"It's a poison?" said Koda.

"A toxin of some sort." He waved his hand for Koda to move away from the desk. "I'm going to call someone. If she knows you're here, she'll get shy. Stay out of vid shot, okay?

Koda backed up. "Is this far enough?"

"Yes." Devon clicked the comm. "Sally Gray in Chem Lab, Sphere Nine, commlink."

A pause, then Sally popped up on the screen, overlapping Program Decode's translations. The spool continued materializing papers in the background.

"This is Sally." Her face brightened, and she smiled wide. "Well, long time no chatty, little brother."

Devon smiled in return but then bit a fingernail again. "Hey, Sis, I have a question."

Sally's lips downturned. "What's the matter? You're biting your nails again. And are you perspiring?"

He touched his forehead and looked at his fingertips. He nodded but didn't comment, getting down to business. "Can you tell me what batrachotoxin is?"

Sally stared into Devon's eyes, examining them. "Are you all right?"

He nodded. "I'm fine." A door slammed somewhere outside Savanna's office, one of the few that actually opened by hand instead of by command, and he bolted up, his eyes darting left and right. "Just a second, Sis."

Koda jerked forward and hurried to the door. "Open." It whooshed open, and he peeked down the hallway, looking past the plants in the pots and the natural paintings lining the walls.

There wasn't anyone there. Perhaps someone had just left, but who? It was getting late, and everyone had gone home long ago. No one should be in the office, unless...

"Savanna? Is that you?"

No answer.

"Hello? Savanna?"

Silence hung in the air.

He shook his head and backed away, uttering, "Close."

The door slid shut. "Lock and only open on my voice command."

The door clicked and locked. No command, not even Savanna's, could gain access. He walked to the desk.

Devon's eyes were locked on his. Koda gestured at the HDC, telling Devon to continued.

"Okay, Devon, you're acting a little strange," said his sister. "Is someone there with you?"

"I'm fine, Sis. Can you ask someone in your lab what that stuff is?"

She shook her head. "I'm the only one here." She tilted her head, grinning. "Are we our father's children or what? Workaholics. That's why we're still single, you know?"

"Yeah."

Koda glanced at the door, hearing something beyond it. Did someone drop something? He couldn't quite tell.

Devon looked at him. He'd heard it as well. He went back to his sister. "Any idea what batrachotoxin is?"

"Well, it's obviously a toxin. I don't know what it does, though." She put her finger up. "Just a second, I'm going to type it in and see how bad it—" She pushed back into her chair, her mouth forming an 'o.' "It's classified as one of the worst toxins."

Koda opened his mouth. "If it gets into the air or water supplies, how bad could it be?" He shut it quickly, realizing he wasn't supposed to talk.

"Who was that?"

"No one, sis. It's not important. Can you answer that question, though?"

Sally gave Devon an odd look. "Okay, this is so weird. You're acting weird. I'm hearing voices in your room—"

Devon thrust his hands out to the side. "Just answer the question, please. I'm in a hurry."

"All right, all right. You're always so impatient. I'm not an expert, Devon, but it wouldn't be good if it gets into the air or water supplies, that's for sure. It depends upon what type of toxin and how much is released and or consumed. Some toxins, like tetrodotoxin, can kill a person within four to six hours. You'd feel paralysis creeping throughout your body while releasing bodily fluids, and even though you'd be fully aware of it, you'd be unable to do anything about it, except die. It's not the nicest of toxins. Or, there's cyanide, it does—"

Devon held up his hands in surrender. "Best guess what batrachotoxin could do?"

Sally leaned in closer. "You're scaring me. What's going on?"

A heavy bang against the door jarred Devon out of his seat. Koda froze, eyeing the door.

"Devon, what's happening in there? Where are you?"

"Uh...I gotta go, Sis."

Devon switched off the HDC and desperately looked to Koda for help. "What do we do?"

Koda turned, his eyes scanning the biosphere through the window. He didn't know, but he'd have to figure it out in a hurry.

Another loud pound echoed, and they both jumped.

32

KODA

Starbase Matrona

Devon slid under the desk. Koda hurried toward him, about to get under the desk as well. Instead, he crouched, staring at a freaked out Devon.

In truth, Koda's insides were a bundle of nerves, and he couldn't blame the kid.

Zim had no doubt found out that someone from this location was hacking his system.

Devon's lips straightened. "I should have left the office and gone home like I wanted. I should have followed my intuition, but Savanna wouldn't allow it, pushing the responsibility for all of humanity onto my shoulders, our shoulders, and for what?"

"If we die today, right here and right now, Devon, everything you found will be for nothing. Everything would be lost with us. We have to do something."

"We show the entire starbase what we found."

"Exactly." Even though Savanna advised against it, right now, they had no other option if they wanted to let the starbase know the truth.

Koda extended his hand, and Devon took it. Koda pulled, helping Devon out from under the desk.

Devon powered on the HDC, and touched a few holographic buttons.

A third pound, and this time the door shook.

"Patch me into the Matrona Network News mainframe," commanded Devon to the holoscreen.

ACCESS DENIED blinked across the screen.

Koda's insides tightened. "Damn."

"No, that's what we want and what I expected. I've moved in and out of the network's mainframe so many times before, this is normal and a breeze." He cleared his throat. "Program Decode."

A small rectangle appeared below the blinking **ACCESS DENIED** with **TYPE PASSWORD** next to it.

"Superhero," he said and watched as the word appeared in the password box and was accepted, allowing them to view every code and link inside of the network's mainframe.

Thirteen icons came into view, one for each of the twelve spheres and one icon that said All, which was the one Devon apparently wanted. He pressed it.

Another pound hammered the door, creating a crack across the top.

Koda's heart skipped a beat, and Devon gasped.

"Hurry," whispered Koda.

"I am." Devon's fingers picked up speed as he typed.

Two more icons materialized on the HDC, one asking for a specific time and the other that said LIVE.

Devon pressed LIVE. "Tie all broadcast streams into one and reroute to Savanna Leven's office."

Devon's face holographically appeared in front of him. He pulled Koda into view. The HDC was recording them now and was fully online. The top of the screen said they were being streamed across all news channels at this very moment.

Koda swallowed, his eyes going wide. The only problem was it was getting late, and not enough people would be watching the streams.

Koda held up some papers and saw himself do so on the holodisplay. He moved the papers in closer to the HDC, and pointed with his index finger at the words, Kill-Off.

"I'm Prime Overseer Koda Lutz—" Another bang echoed across the office. Koda's and Devon's heads jerked back.

Koda would have to ignore it.

"My name is Koda Lutz, and if you're watching this right now, my friend right here and I may be dead in a minute or two, so pay close attention. This isn't a movie or a TV show. Tomorrow, we may be found dead in Savanna Levens' office, or we will have gone missing."

Koda shook his head. "We've found critical documents that my tech friend here intercepted from Prime Director Zim Noki's office stating that we are all going to be killed in two weeks with a toxin known as batrachotoxin."

Devon cut in. "Listen to us now. This is not a joke. This toxin will be released into our water supply, and into the air we breathe through the filtration systems. I don't know how quickly it kills, but I do know that it does kill."

Koda shook the paper in front of the screen. "We must, and I repeat, *must,* revolt against the Prime Director. He is the one responsible for the attack, not Fleet Admiral Shae Lutz

Devon spoke. "Zim is part of some type of overall plan that failed, and we were supposed to be wiped out several days ago during the attack, but something backfired. What it was that backfired, I don't know. Plan B is now in effect, and they are going to poison us all with this batrachotoxin." He put his hands out, pleading. "Please, this is not a joke. I'm risking my life. The documents also state that—"

The door crumpled and shattered with bits and slabs of ebb splattering all over the floor, dust and small pieces smacking into Koda's chest and face. A cloud of dust formed in front of the doorway, concealing whoever it was on the other side.

Koda dove under the desk and held his breath. He pulled Devon with him.

Bullets riddled the room, penetrating walls and shattering the large biosphere window.

The window.

It was only three steps away from the desk, and then it was only two stories down to the biosphere's forest floor. If they moved fast, they could jump out the window and land on the grass, then run and hide in the forest twenty meters away.

Koda looked down at his hands. They were still holding some papers. He looked behind him, wondering why he hadn't been hit. The desk's back panel concealed them not only from the perpetrators but had blocked the bullets as well.

Was this desk made out of ebb? He touched it, nodding. It had to be. It would take a bomb to blow through it.

"Did we get them?" asked a gruff voice.

Boots crunched over the debris. Someone was walking toward them.

Koda shoved the papers down his pants.

"Did you hear that? They're still alive," someone shouted. "This is the Matrona Guard. Do not move."

The Matrona Guard? That was the starbase's military marines. Each starship had their own, and Matrona's was rarely used, except for some terrorist activities years ago and the occasional riot on the streets.

Other than that, they stayed out of everyone's hair.

Koda heard more crunching as several people entered the room. "I don't see anything but dust, Sergeant." There was a pause as if waiting to hear the sergeant's reply on a comm device. "Proceed? Yes, sir."

Koda closed his eyes, feeling Devon shaking uncontrollably next to him. There was only one way out and one way to survive, if possible.

He grabbed Devon and dashed forward. They leaped through the now windowless frame, Koda's legs and arms windmilling and the air rushing at him as he fell to the ground hard, his feet landing on the grass, and a loud pop crippling his knee.

Devon yelped loudly when he landed and rolled. He limped up and grasped Koda by the back collar.

Koda stood and fell back down as intense pain pierced through his kneecap. He let out a loud grunt, grabbing at his knee, cringing.

A crack echoed above, and a bullet sunk into the earth next to Koda's hand.

He gasped and pushed into a hobbling run, adrenaline coursing through him as he rushed toward the forest, Devon by his side.

More shots rained down, and Koda lifted off the ground as a sharp sting took hold of his hip and another on the back of his leg, blood splattering outward.

He twisted in the air and landed, falling face down, his nose buried in the grass. He looked up and reached for a tree, crying out in agony, and through sheer willpower and the adrenaline saturating him, he got to his feet and staggered onward.

"Come on, Koda," yelled Devon.

A bullet sunk into Devon's thigh, and blood sprayed out everywhere. He twirled and fell, holding his leg and screaming loudly.

"Ow," Koda yelled out as another bullet dug into his calf. Blood quickly drenched the back of his sock.

He fell and grasped Devon's arm. "Get up."

Devon pushed up, his eyes displaying burning pain. They hopped, moving toward a wide tree until they reached it, then moved behind it.

Koda's chest heaved up and down, taking in air and pushing it out just as fast.

He leaned his back against the trunk, red bullet tracers zipping past him, sinking into the ground. "Are you okay?"

"I'm shot," said Devon, looking Koda up and down. "You've been hit a couple of times too."

"Yeah, and—"

Loud footsteps approached, heading right for them.

Wracked with pain, Koda peeked around the tree. He counted a dozen guards on the ground, firing weapons up at the guards in the office they had just jumped from.

What was going on? That didn't make sense. Why were guards shooting at guards?

Footsteps came closer, and he ducked back around, closing his eyes. His days were over, gone. Maybe they'd keep Devon alive.

He doubted it.

He glanced down at his leg, watching blood drip to the grass, then reached into his pants and pulled out the papers, holding them feebly like a white flag of surrender. Maybe after he was shot to death, one of the guards would read these and believe what was printed. Maybe then the human race could somehow survive.

"Put down your arm," shouted a man wearing guard fatigues. He crouched next to the tree Devon and Koda hid behind, his rifle pointed toward Savanna's office.

The guard inched back and pushed Koda's arm down. He placed his hand on Koda's head, patting it like his uncle Shae used to do. "We got here in the nick of time. I'm Sergeant Major Manning Jones of the *Brigantia* Guard."

Koda's body began to shut down, and his eyes wavered between open and closed. "What?"

Ten more guards ran past Koda and Devon, hiding behind trees and shooting at the office.

"Able's down, Sergeant," said a voice through Manning's comm device.

Manning brought his mouth closer to his shoulder, speaking into the comm. "Where is the damn med tech?"

"Dead," the voice said over the comm.

"Son of a Guild." Manning slapped his rifle and aimed, pulling the trigger. Round after round expelled, and the butt of his weapon recoiled against his shoulder after every shot.

Manning halted and flicked his head toward Koda and Devon. "Get them to the infirmary now."

A guard grabbed Koda and threw him over his shoulder, shouting, "I'm going. Cover me."

The guy ran fast, and Koda bounced up and down, watching the man's boots clomping on dirt and ferns, stomping through shrubs and dodging small brush.

"They have reinforcements. More are coming," yelled the man as they passed more guards.

Koda glanced at his hand, and the papers were still there, locked by his grip while his brain spun in confusion. Why was he still alive? Who were these guards, and why were they helping him?

Several more guards ran by toward the gunfire until it seemed like an endless stream of guards.

Koda caught a glimpse of another guard carrying Devon several paces behind. He caught a small yellow insignia on the back of the armored vests worn by a guard rushing toward the battle. It was a yellow thunderbolt inside of a wheel, the insignia of the Starship *Taranis* Guard.

The *Taranis* Guard and the *Brigantia* Guard were fighting the Matrona Guard?

None of this made sense.

He glanced down at the vest of the guard carrying him. An insignia of a white spear inside the globe of Eos. The guy was a *Brigantia* Guard just like that Sergeant Manning back there.

A few days ago, an unknown enemy attacked, and today he found out Zim was probably behind it, and even though it failed, Zim had a Plan B in place. Now Koda was in the middle of a civil war?

33

SHAE

Unknown Sector, Starbase Matrona

"Koda is where?" Shae pounded his fist on the wall beside his bed. The admiral looked at the clock on the HDC screen that read 1:17 a.m.

Louise stood near the door, arms crossed with one leg extended in front of the other. "He's in the biosphere's infirmary receiving medical care."

Shae's nostrils flared. "Get him to our ship." Shae stood and slowly walked toward Louise. "He almost got assassinated."

A buzz pierced the room. "Admiral, you're forbidden to leave your bed when a visitor is here. Sit back down, sir."

Shae moved backward until he felt the hard cushion on the back of his legs, and plopped on the bed, his breaths coming shallow and fast.

"I assure you, Shae, I tried everything to get him out. He is—" she paused and looked over her shoulder at the police through the small window on the closed cell door. "Stan and I are trying to figure out what to do." She drew a circle and an X on her leg and tapped it once.

The plan was about to begin, whatever plan that was.

He needed to play it off, but at the same time, he had reservations about the bastard who used to be his friend, Captain Jenkyns. "Stan is a weasel. Don't trust him, Louise. You know better than that. I saw you on the—"

He cut himself off, not wanting to give too much away. The police no doubt had this room set up with recording devices, and he'd be surprised if Zim wasn't listening. If he was, the fact Louise was more on Shae's side than Zim's might put Louise in the brig sooner than later.

Louise huffed. "I know what you think. But I believe Captain Jenkyns is on our side. I think he was given some misinformation—"

Shae threw his hands up. "By whom? Who gave him this misinformation, and why? Who is directing this entire shitshow on me, and again, why?"

He figured Zim, but Zim apparently had some higher-ups Shae had no idea about.

"I don't know," Louise said calmly, her voice low. "I think he was being misled."

"Jenkyns doesn't know what side he's on, Louise." Shae sat straight and took a deep breath. "He said outright lies about me."

Was Louise full of crap right now, acting the part but thinking otherwise? How could she actually believe Stan was on their side?

She drew a circle and an X again and took a step closer to the door handle.

Shae caught the signal, happy to oblige in his part of this makeshift play. "I'm sorry, Louise. You must go." He turned and swiped the air with his hand, indicating the conversation over. "Leave. What's done is done." He averted his eyes. "I said to leave." He scooted toward the wall and rested against it, sighing heavily.

Louise turned and knocked on the cell door. Before it opened, she glanced over her shoulder. "By the way, when the governance finds you innocent, it would be smart for you to see Koda."

Shae merely nodded and folded his arms, holding his breath until Louise had walked halfway down the hall.

The door shut, buzzing and clicking locked.

Was Louise acting or playing a part or being truthful? Did she really trust Stan? Did the circle and the X actually have anything to do with breaking him out, or was that wishful thinking?

He threw a palm to his forehead. "I'm an idiot."

Even though the circle and the X were in that mythological tale with the Space Templars, it was also a sign for a kiss and a hug, something he used to do with his daughter. Louise had been telling him she loved him, in her own way, like a brother to a sister.

That was all it meant.

He should have known because of his daughter.

He coughed and pounded his chest, coughing more. "A daughter I don't even have." He whacked his head with his palm again. "Why do I keep thinking about this make-believe girl?"

He lay on the bed and stared at the gray ebb ceiling, counting the little nuggets of red and black inside the rock.

A memory came to the forefront and invaded his mind like the enemy had invaded Star Guild space.

He was crouched at a train station with his arms around a little girl, holding her in a hug. "I love you."

He let go, and she straightened her white hat, her blue eyes shining back at his. "I love you too, father." Her eyes welled with tears.

His heart longed for her, wanting to take her with him. He didn't want to leave her, but military orders had dictated otherwise, and country came first, then family.

Or so he had been told his entire life.

This girl, however, couldn't have been more than twelve years old. A woman stood proudly behind her with her hands behind her back. Was that this little girl's mother? His wife?

"Why do you have to go, daddy?" His daughter lowered her chin, her lips quivering.

"I've gone over this. I'm being sent to Haiti. They need our help." He pushed her chin up. "Look at me. I'll be safe, and I'll be home soon." He stood back, boarded the train, and waved—the last wave he'd ever have with her.

He lurched back, coming to the present. "What the hell?" He sighed and stretched his neck from side to side. “Haiti? My daughter? I’m going insane. The stress is creating memories I never experienced.”

He glanced at his hands. Had he nodded off and had a dream? He shook his head. It was far from a dream.

Koda entered his mind, and he sat straighter. Koda wasn’t like Shae’s strange, made-up daughter, something his mind was creating to cope with all the chaos happening to him.

No, but the loving feelings he had for Koda were close enough. Shae cared deeply for his nephew, the only kin Shae had left. Now the poor guy was in the infirmary, seriously injured, and Shae couldn’t do anything about it.

He twisted toward the holovid, needing to take his mind to someplace else.

“On.” The holoscreen blipped on, flashing the nightly news and showing a vid of the morning after he was named the Fleet Admiral, smiling at the camera all those years ago and wearing his full regulation uniform with all of its bells and whistles.

What other lies are they going to tell now?

“…had a dark side. His great-grandfather, renowned for his undefeated record as a starfighter pilot in the annual Star Guild Academy Games, was Admiral Mort Lutz. His grandfather, Admiral Ronald Lutz, was the longest-tenured admiral in the history of Star Guild. The son of Admiral Bud Lutz and Doris, Admiral Shae Lutz is descended from a prestigious line of Star Guild admirals, all passed long ago, never to know what treachery their own blood would later perpetrate against the entire human race.”

A picture of Louise appeared. “If not for Executive Officer Louise Stripe, in addition to the efforts of Captain Stanley Jenkyns, what we now know about Star Guild and Starbase Matrona would have been lost forever.”

The admiral rolled his eyes. This spectacle was propaganda, and he was just the scapegoat they needed, but for what? Why were they going to such great lengths to discredit him?

He sighed, thinking of his time in the academy and his friends.

“Admiral Shae Lutz has lost the case. His—”

Shae stood. "I lost the case? What case?"

On the vid, a man, nicely dressed in a suit, obviously a lesser political figure of some type, spoke: "Admiral Lutz has pled guilty on all counts."

Shae clenched his jaw, his face turning bright red, his neck veins popping out. "I what?"

The man continued, "He has since apologized and accepts all punishment."

A news reporter came into view, holding a mic up to the politician's face. "What is the punishment?"

The nicely dressed man straightened his suit. "The penalty for treason is death."

Shae's face turned ashen, and he sat down slowly.

He had already used all five of the allowable Suficell Pod anti-aging sessions, or so he had been told because he only remembered one of them, but given his current age, he could only expect to live another thirty years or so, and he was okay with that.

Being killed over a lie, and knowing death was knocking on his door, ready to barge in and take him at any minute, was a game-changer.

His hope, his life, and his wishes for a better outcome faded, and he eyed his hands, observing the rough skin. He'd spent years with these hands helping his fellow military officers all the way down to cadets, teaching them how to better their lives, and in the process, better those around them.

This was what he got for skipping a beat with Prime Director Zim Noki, the benefactor of Shae's soon-to-be execution.

"...he will be terminated by this time tomorrow," blared a media personality on the news screen.

Shae bit his lip and stood proudly. He was an admiral, and even death wasn't going to kick the honor out of him. This was yesterday's broadcast, so tomorrow was today.

Footsteps clanked down the hall.

The executioners are coming.

The cell buzzed, and the door opened. He turned and faced them, the Matrona police, there to escort him to a windowless room where they'd gas him until he couldn't breathe anymore, or until he choked to death on his vomit.

Whatever came first.

It had been a good life, he thought. His first and only admiral assignment had been Starship *Brigantia*.

Fingers curled around Shae's wrist and yanked, jerking his arm behind his back, and then the other. "Come with me, Admiral." A handcuff snapped snugly around each wrist. "We have a long walk to the gas chamber."

Shae lifted his eyes and gazed upon the executioner. Out of the corner of his eye stood two more policemen, waiting to help escort the admiral to his death.

Shae nodded, accepting his place in life. "I know you think you're doing the right thing, but after my death, please look into everything that happened before and after the attack. I guarantee you will find a lot of discrepancies with—"

Wait.

Shae stopped mid-sentence, thinking how oddly the policeman had spoken. The voice was familiar and had a strange rhythm, a distinct cadence after each word.

The man wore a police uniform, with its boldly displayed insignia of a mother and child with a star drawn through the image, Matrona's insignia.

The police officer winked and whispered, "It's time to take you back to your ship, Fleet Admiral."

Brigger?

34

EDEN

Planet Aurora

A robed figure, its hood covering its face, walked past Eden. Apparently, the ones who covered their faces weren't human. Humans on this planet let their hoods down. Did they have tentacles on their faces or something?

She sat barefoot on a thick pillow, wearing a white robe, on the porch of a domed house, and held the crystal in her hand.

Eden wanted to get back to her family, Star Guild, and her home, Starbase Matrona. There, she'd help defend them, and blow the crap out of the enemy.

A fire erupted in her belly and slowly faded as she stared at the robed figures doing their business and walking here to there.

These people saved her, but they were peaceful and less warrior-like than one would think. They gave her a place to sleep, food, and clothing, and they were polite and happy.

She watched people walk by on a wide path in front of her, and then the flowing, colorful leaves on the trees that sprinkled the hills beyond, the sun shining down, brightening the hilltops like beautifully lit lamps.

She looked back to the robed Beings. She wanted to introduce herself, and perhaps make them tea as she had with her guests back on Matrona.

Her gut wrenched again.

Matrona. My home. I have to get home.

Skye told her it survived, but how much damage, how many killed? She buried the thought, swallowing it down whole.

"Hey, Eden."

"Skye?"

He walked up and sat next to her.

Eden waved her hand toward the path in front of her. "Why do they hide?"

"For your well-being."

Her lower lip puffed out. "I'm a big girl. I can handle it."

"You've led a sheltered life in the sense that you've never seen races other than your own."

She frowned. "Like I said, I think I can handle it." She rolled her eyes. "I'm sure they're not horrendous-looking with eyes popping out of their heads, daggers for teeth, and noses hanging off."

"They're beautiful, so very beautiful. But to you, they're foreign. You'll be introduced to them soon enough, but not until we feel you're ready." He stood. "Come with me. We got sidetracked the last time I wanted to show you this. But now it's time for you to see." He extended his hand.

She took it and allowed him to pull her up. "Where are we going?"

For the last few days, Skye had been showing her around, visiting places like Eden Fountain, a statue of a man named Atlas who held a trident. Near Atlas stood a building-sized crystal which emitted the energy that powered the entire village. He mentioned it was Atlantis technology, but the name was as foreign to her as this world.

Skye bowed. "Today, we're going straight up the hill." He turned. "Follow me."

She followed him across the path to the base of the hill she'd been staring at for hours, walking on what looked to be soft moss, but healthier and more vibrant.

They started up the hill, the path zigzagging. The moss grew thinner and the ground rockier, yet soft. Trees lined the path, shading them from the sun's rays, and ferns and other greenery grew between the trunks.

Eden halted and grabbed Skye's arm, stiffening, and taking a step backward. "What's that?"

A sleek animal as big as her sat with two smaller versions of itself in the middle of the path. It intermittently licked what had to be its children, while the small creatures played, tackling and throwing themselves around in their mother's lap.

The animal eyed Eden. It sniffed the air and let out a sharp, low growl.

Skye stood still. "She won't harm you, but she senses your fear. She doesn't like it, and she doesn't like it near her cubs."

Eden put her hand to her mouth. "I'm sorry."

"It's called a purple panther. Earth has several types of this particular creature's descendants, though many of a mixed nature and not as large as this one."

"I've never seen a creature so gorgeous."

Skye nodded. "They're part of the big cat family." He clacked his tongue against the roof of his mouth at the panther and dipped his head to the side. The cat let out a high pitched grunt, stood, and walked away. Its cubs trailed after her.

Eden shot a look at Skye. "How did you do that?"

"She trusts me and knows I respect her, and she respects me." He motioned to continue up the hill.

Shortly, they crossed a small footbridge arched over a gurgling creek. They moved farther up the path, passing a massive tree with branches full of needles that seemed to grow into the sky for kilometers.

They walked in silence until they finally stopped at the top of the hill, overlooking an amazing vista, a panoramic view of a boundless landscape of rolling hills, lush forests, and varying types of foliage that extended well beyond the village, with several more crystal domed structures popping up throughout the vastness before her.

"Take a look over there." Skye pointed.

"Wow. Is this what you wanted to show me?"

An enormous city with giant domed structures littered a thick forest. Orbs, some gold, and some silver flew from dome to dome, like the hovercars on Matrona flew from street to street.

"It's not what you are up here to see, but that city is named Lux. We're less than a two-hour walk away. Yet, I haven't been there in..." he shook his head, "I don't know how long." Skye shrugged, then sat on the ground cross-legged, inviting Eden to do the same. "Now, the reason why I led you up here. Please sit."

She nodded and sat facing him.

"Hold on to the grass," he said.

"Why?"

He pressed down on a perfectly round rock next to him. A holographic image of Aurora materialized in front of her.

"Village Onyx, Templar Hill," he said.

The holographic world lit up, then spun around and stopped at their current location. It zoomed in, and Eden could see the small figures of Skye and herself sitting cross-legged within the hologram. A red glowing dot pulsed on the figures and Skye touched the dot, turning it blue. The hologram disappeared.

The ground shook and began to sink, taking Eden's breath away, her hands gripping the grass instinctively.

A glass dome materialized and enclosed them.

"What's happening?"

She glanced across at Skye. He dipped his head and smiled. "Patience. You'll like what you see when you see it."

Like an elevator, they descended, but unlike an elevator, they lowered past dirt and roots, solid rock, and more dirt.

"Be calm," said Skye. "What I want to show you is beneath this hill."

They entered an enormous underground cavern, illuminated by an immense rock crystal jutting three or four meters upward from ground level.

Two extremely large craft were parked beside the giant crystal.

The ships were as large as Starship *Brigantia*.

Skye stood, and the glass dome dematerialized. He pulled her to a standing position. "I want to introduce you to our small Space Templar fleet."

He walked down a rocky incline toward the two enormous starships. Several smaller craft dotted the area, but none were as brilliant and grand as the two giant ships.

Eden followed him, all the while admiring all the glowing crafts.

The two starships were massive, translucent, and seemed to fade back and forth between a silver shine to a golden luster, their sleek design indicating they were built for speed.

They were sphere-like in the front, which merged into an orb-shaped midsection that thinned out toward the stern consisting of two large, thick wings that looked long and wide enough to hold a thousand or so people. A large booster was fixed on the underbelly, where the wings would have met in the middle. The craft's landing gear had four sleds, two in the front, two in the back.

Now close enough to touch, she ran her fingers on a sled. It was cool, much like metal, though a metal she'd never felt or seen before.

She put both hands on it, wanting to hug the sled, let alone the entire craft. She gazed at the belly. "I'd give anything to fly this puppy."

Skye walked beside her and placed his hand on the sled. "There is nothing like these ships in the entire galaxy." He shrugged. "Well, the third one is on Eos, but that's a different story."

Eden furrowed her brow. "On Eos?"

"Yes. It was left there in hopes your people would find it someday, but we made sure it wouldn't be found until your people woke up to the truth of what was happening to you."

"Where on Eos?"

Skye lifted an eyebrow. "Wouldn't you like to know." He winked.

Eden, realizing he wasn't going to spill the beans, looked at the crafts. Her eyes abruptly widened, remembering something. "When I was about to make contact with those torpedoes, two orbs about the size of my Thunderbird jumped in next to me. Was that...no, it couldn't have been one of these?" She looked around the immense cavern, gazing at a small, orbed ship. "Were they one of those class types?"

Skye shook his head. "Those are much too big. The ships you describe were our Avens. There are hundreds of them docked within each one of these starships."

He smiled, then waved his hands in the air expansively, introducing Eden to the starship in front of her. "If you're of the bloodline, as I suspect you are, then you'll pilot one of these. I would surmise your main mission in life has just begun. The first time you fly your starship, she'll give you her name."

"She'll give me her name?"

"Oh, she'll give you more than just that. She'll give you a new life. You, my friend, are now this bird's captain. And here she is, waiting for you to board."

Eden moved away from Skye. "Excuse me? A captain?"

"Yes."

"What the Guild am I going to do with a ship like this?" She always wanted to be a captain, but right here, right now? She needed more training, more experience under her belt, more mentoring. More importantly, she wanted to get back home and be a captain for Star Guild, not the Space Templars.

"What are you going to do with a ship like this?" He shook his head like she should know. "You're going to save your people from the tyranny that's shackled them for centuries. You're one of their liberators, Eden. You're one of the three."

35

ZIM

Planet Eos, East Radiation Zone

Prime Director Zim Noki glided his starjumper in for another pass at a landing pad, staring out through the cockpit windshield.

This side of Eos, known as Eos Two, was filled with tree-covered hills, red rock, and ebb factories expelling massive amounts of steam through huge stacks.

A tall man was seated next to Zim, Chan-Ru, eyeing the view below and scratching his chin, lost in thought. Like Zim, he had a reddish hue to his hair, though he was much thinner and nearly three feet taller.

Zim gave Chan-Ru a nod. He twisted in his chair to look at the two men in the rear, both wearing the same strange robes as his guest in the front. "We're clear to land, gentlemen."

Several hours prior, Zim had been ordered to pick these men up from a larger transport ship for unexplained reasons. He had assumed two of the men were interviewing for the next Prime Director position since their height exceeded the seven-foot five-inch requirement.

The new human cycle was about to begin, the current one ending by gen-term, or genocidal termination in less than two weeks, which meant Zim's job would be coming to an end.

Zim pulled back on the stick, hovered, then descended onto the landing pad. He switched off the engine, and the door opened like a bird's wing, flipping up and extending outward.

He stepped out first, followed by the others. He grinned and took a deep breath, taking in cool oxygen. "Fresh air, fellas. Get it while it's good."

The other men took deep breaths and nodded in approval.

Zim pointed toward a red mountain range riddled with jutting yellow and white rocks at its base. "Over there, more than a thousand kilometers away, our forces are in combat with Starship *Sirona,* one of the human ships that tried to escape." He touched his belly and laughed. "All the troops and pilots we sent are recruits. They've never fought a live battle in their lives. Practice makes perfect, and they're in training, so to speak. Our elite fighters would have squashed them by now."

He slapped the back of his nearest companion, then uncomfortably gripped his own collar and straightened his nice shirt. "Welcome to the other side of Eos, boys, where we play, and humans are forbidden."

Chan-Ru gave Zim an odd look, his hands within the long sleeves of his brown robe. "You mean to say that no human has ever been to this side of the planet?" He eyed the spectacular view. "It's quite breathtaking."

"They're not allowed on this side of the planet. We've starved the other side to create a desert. All they know is ebb mining over there, and they suspect the rest of the planet looks the same, which is why we've kept Starbase Matrona in constant orbit on the same side of the planet since its conception. So, over here, humans are forbidden."

Chan-Ru crinkled his brow. "That's peculiar."

Zim clapped his hands together and then kept them clasped. He held them out in front of him. "We've set up two separate civilizations. Of course, as I said, they don't know they occupy one side of the planet while we occupy the other. In some ways, it makes things a bit more difficult, but in other ways, it makes things a lot easier. It's a give and take kind of thing, you know? We have them believing that no other races exist. Therefore, *we* don't exist."

Zim chuckled, rolling his eyes at the stupidity of the human creatures. "They think this side of Eos is exothermically radioactive, and they can come no closer than fifty kilometers to the prohibited line or they'll die a hideous radioactive death. The Prime Directors of the present," he jabbed a thumb at himself, "and the past have *informed* the humans through the centuries that the radiation is somewhat under control yet unable to cross the boundary. They believe it's well contained."

He smiled heartily and slapped the back of Chan-Ru's shoulder. "So naive." He walked toward an elevator at the edge of the landing platform. "Follow me, fellas."

Chan-Ru watched the ground as he walked as if deep in thought.

Zim stepped inside the elevator and motioned at the men, inviting them inside. "Ground level," Zim ordered the elevator.

The elevator began to move, smoothly slipping into high speed. Clear ebb windows encased the compartment, allowing a topographical view of the surrounding area.

A massive rock-face stood in the distance, bordered by sloping red rock hills and boulders. Trees, although small and spindly, were many, hugging the base of the hills and flowing up them.

Large dome buildings and palace-like structures littered the ground like small figurines, and a gigantic lake lay ten kilometers east with a few islands in the middle.

Chan-Ru remained quiet.

Zim didn't like quiet. It was a sign of distrust. People thinking too much were judging too much, looking for weaknesses, perhaps thinking of ways to get the upper hand.

Zim put his arm around Chan-Ru's shoulders in a friendly manner. Surely his charm would cheer him up. "What seems to be your worry, Chan-Ru?"

"It's difficult for me to understand lying to the human race, especially if it's not benefiting that race." Chan-Ru pinched the skin at his own throat, looking to Zim as if *lying* was an idea difficult to fathom.

Zim paused and frowned. He needed to act the part to show this Chan-Ru sucker that the policy, though effective, was foreign to him as well. "It's what we must do in order to keep our home planet Nibiru alive. We do so out of the love we hold for our race."

The elevator gently shuddered as it slowed and jostled as it touched the ground. The door opened, and Zim escorted his companions to the steps of a large white palace with giant columns supporting the roof of the palace's entryway.

Chan-Ru rested his hand on Zim's back. It was warm and conveyed a sense of calm to Zim, a calm he wasn't used to feeling. "Nibiru will survive without us. It is we, not Nibiru, that need saving. Please bear that in mind, Zim, for the sake of another race."

Zim nodded and smiled brightly, showing his perfect teeth. "I'm just doing my job, buddy. If you have an issue, you know who to take it up with." He gestured to the doors.

Chan-Ru dipped his head. "That's why we're here. It should be our race that sweats, digs, and provides ebb gold and crystal for our own people, not a slave race."

Zim stepped ahead to open the palace doors but stopped and looked at Chan-Ru and his two companions standing by his side. "I thought you were here as an adviser to your two friends, no?" He folded his arms across his chest and leaned back. "I thought they were auditioning for the next Prime Director's position."

Chan-Ru peered into Zim's eyes. Expressionless, he didn't reply and stood waiting for Zim to kindly move out of the way.

Zim cocked his head, his breathing shallow and his nostrils flaring. "Is Enlil keeping me as the Prime Director for the next human cycle? If so, I refuse."

Chan-Ru raised his hand. "My friend, don't worry. You are not going to be the next Prime Director. There will be no more Prime Directors. I am here to stop the cycle. To end it forever."

Zim widened his stance, standing boldly in front of them. "Then you may not enter."

The doors swung open, and Zim jumped and turned. In the

entryway stood Enlil, with his dark-red hair and blue eyes, the mainstay combination of his race, the Anunnaki.

"Zim, dammit. Let them enter."

Zim quickly moved out of the way. He didn't want to piss off the Monarch.

Enlil slapped Zim's shoulder and squeezed. "Zim, come join us."

Zim pushed out his lips, keeping down a smile. The palace was for the higher-ups, and he had never entered before.

All Zim knew himself to be, at least in the eyes of those with a larger pay grade, was a puppet, treated well enough and given many luxuries for his service as the Prime Director, yet without ranking high enough to enter most of the buildings on this side of Eos.

He was small in height and stature compared to the rest of his race, as were all Prime Directors, and that was looked down upon. Yet, his reward for being the Prime Director at the grueling end of a human cycle was riches beyond anything he could ever fathom, or so he'd been told. He'd do anything to keep his position until the finish line, and anything not to carry his position on to the beginning of the next human cycle after they killed the current one.

Enlil led them through a large hall with columns and marble floors and finally to a large office. He sat down behind a desk, asking for his guests, including Zim, to take a seat.

Enlil folded his hands in front of him and stared at Chan-Ru, his brows lowering. "Speak."

"I'm here on behalf of Enki—"

"Ha!" Enlil slapped his desk. "Yes, Enki, my dear brother. He will kill his race to save the universe just so these damned humans can have some," he touched his heart with folded hands, mocking a friendly gesture, "freedom."

Chan-Ru stood. "I will be heard, or we shall leave." He waved his hand at his companions. "You interrupt me again, and you'll have a lot more than disgruntled human slaves on your hands. Your father grows impatient with you and your little project here."

Enlil placed his palms on the desk. "I apologize." He spoke in a calm voice, his demeanor changing. Zim knew Enlil's dad had a lot of clout.

Enlil continued, "If my father wishes to keep the Kingship of Nibiru, then he will allow me to continue this operation. The Anunnaki will not stand to see their way of life decline. Here on Eos, we mine and create what is needed for Nibiru's atmosphere, and without us, you'd all be dead. Tell him not to forget that. Tell all Anunnaki not to forget that."

Chan-Ru and Enlil glared at each other for several seconds. "There are other ways, young man."

"Like what? Amuse me, Chan-Ru."

He pointed at his companions. "These two with me are scientists, half-human, half us. They have created an easier way to mine and manufacture mono-atomic gold, so you won't need humans anymore. You can let the humans go free."

Zim straightened in his seat. *Half-human, half-Anunnaki?* A hefty punch, like a hammer to his stomach, hit him.

He held it in. He didn't want to show anything other than a straight face.

This was the first he had ever heard of such a thing. Was he half-human as well? If so, why hadn't he been told? He looked at Chan-Ru's companions. They were his size, no mistaking that, but it would make sense as to why there were so few of his size among his race.

Zim bit his cheek. Is that why he was never invited to Nibiru? Why he had never seen his home planet?

Enlil waved his hand in the air. "Look, we've tried using Anunnaki to mine ebb and gold many times before, and what were the results? War, mutiny, revolt, and—"

An alarm sounded, interrupting Enlil. He bolted up. The alarm turned off as quickly as it blared, and Enlil plopped in his seat, tapping the corner of his desk. A red circle glowed, and he leaned in. "Paislee, my dear, what was that?"

"I'm sorry. We've received an urgent communication, and the network stamped it as an immediate threat," replied a woman.

"Send it over."

"Yes."

A holographic message flowed upward from his desk, visible to Enlil, but white from Zim's point of view.

Enlil swiped his hand over the paper, and it vanished. He glanced at Chan-Ru. "Leave now. I will send you a transport back to your ship. Give my brother Enki my best."

Chan-Ru shook his head. "Our discussion is not over."

Enlil tilted his head and eyed Chan-Ru, his lips twitching slightly as he obviously held back a barking order. He breathed out slowly and closed his eyes. "I'll say this one more time. Leave. Now."

Chan-Ru and his companions stood. "As you wish. But your brother and father won't be happy you gave us only a brief moment of your time."

"Other *things* got in the way, Chan-Ru. They'll understand." He smiled and ran his finger along the edge of his desk. "You know, politics." He lifted his finger and pointed it like a gun, his eyes like daggers. To Zim, it looked like Enlil's last warning.

"I will give them your best." Chan-Ru bowed, and he and his friends exited the office, their footsteps echoing down the hall.

"Door, close," said Enlil, and the door shut. He cleared his throat and set his elbows on his desk, resting his chin on his steepled hands. "A war is going on inside of Matrona, and yet you're here sitting on your ass?"

Zim ran his fingers through his hair, confused. "What do you mean?"

"I have just received communication that the *Taranis* and *Brigantia* Guard have commandeered the biosphere. Your Matrona Guard doesn't have a handle on it, nor do you."

Zim stood his hands in fists. "What? Impossible."

"Sit down until I tell you to stand, Zim." Spittle came out of Enlil's mouth when he spoke, and his eyes were full of fire.

Zim sat, shaking his head, wondering how something like this could have happened. The last he heard, Fleet Admiral Shae Lutz was going to be executed today, and it should have already happened.

More importantly, in less than two weeks would be the eradication. In less than two weeks, all inhabitants on Starbase Matrona and in Star Guild would be good and dead.

Everything *should* be running smoothly.

"I gave you one order, and one order only, then I would do the rest. You were to kill Admiral Lutz while he was on vacation, that was it. I had everything else set up. We've seen from pirate attacks Shae has an uncanny way of getting out of the most precarious situations. And he's done so again."

Zim went to speak, but nothing came out. He had given the admiral a vacation, and on the first day of that vacation, he had the admiral's lemonade spiked with a deadly poison, but somehow Shae lived.

The admiral had been given the wrong lemonade, or he didn't drink it at all.

It wasn't Zim's fault. Was Shae somehow poison-proof? The guy wasn't supposed to lead Star Guild to safety, and more importantly, he wasn't supposed to call the damn Space Templars.

Enlil sighed. "Tell me this, Zim? Why hasn't Plan B been implemented? Why are they still alive? We need to start the next cycle, and you're slowing things down. I could send in our elite pilots to finish the job, but my father forbids it. All I have are my own self-made military from my father's newest recruits. He thinks they're here for training purposes, not to kill an entire race. Do you know how hard it is to get weapons, battleships, and personnel from my father? He gives us these lackluster, petty weapons the humans use. I mean, bullets? Missiles? Cannons? It's embarrassing. Get Plan B done, do you understand?"

Zim looked away. "The attack destroyed a majority of the filtration and hydro system, slowing Plan B to a halt. It's all being fixed as we speak. Due to the now faulty systems, the other issue we're having is that the mind-dumbing chemical pack we've been using for the last thousand or so years isn't flowing. The people are starting to wake up and see through the illusion we created for them."

"How much longer will it take to repair?"

"Right now, we're looking at a week and a half."

"Speed it up."

Zim bowed his head, pressing the palm of his hand over his heart. "Yes, at your command."

"My command was to destroy Starbase Matrona and Star Guild, not bring the Space Templars to our doorstep. You have failed, Zim. Make it up to me, or your head will roll from the chopping block, understood?" He sighed and shook his head. "We gave this cycle of humans too much freedom. Our scientists here on Eos Two wanted to know what it would be like to allow them to create a military."

"Yes."

"Sabra," called Enlil, staring at the door until a ten and a half foot woman walked into the room, her aqua-blue eyes shining, and her red hair flowing past her shoulders and down her back. "This is my bio-technician. Her IQ doubles most of our own. You're to bring her with you to speed up the process."

Zim nodded and stood. "At your command."

Enlil tapped his desk again and leaned into the red glowing light. "Paislee, my dear, could you do me a favor?"

"Yes?"

"Don't let Chan-Ru and his companions leave the planet. Send a handful of troops their way and kill them."

"As you command."

Zim smiled, liking the sound of that. After meeting Chan-Ru, it was easy to tell he had no loyalty to his own people.

Zim exited the room, followed by Sabra, her long, athletic strides reminding him of a cat. Her beauty was unique because it wasn't only her looks that would turn heads, it was an inner glow and the way she held herself. She was confident, more so than any woman he'd ever met, and that drew him in more than anything else.

He dipped his head at her, and she grinned, extending her hand.

"I'm Sabra."

He took her hand and pulled it close to his lips, kissing it, her smooth skin like silk. "I'm Zim, and it's *all* my pleasure."

She pulled her hand away, halting in front of the palace's exit. "Gentlemen first."

He walked out of the palace and down the stairs, heading to the elevator that would lead them to the landing pad. "We should just blow up the starbase from the inside, and then we can be through with this. It would have been more efficient and easier. We could train our new military pilots elsewhere and not use them up on useless missions like taking out Star Guild and Starbase Matrona."

He pointed to his chest. "I get blamed, and here these pilots were, not doing their job and not taking out that starbase." He stopped and looked up at Sabra. "What do you think?" He gave a sideways smile like his plan was the ace of all plans.

Sabra lifted a brow. "We've already attempted such. Each weapon's transport carrying explosives to the starbase has been intercepted and neutralized."

Zim stood straighter, his back arching. "By who?"

"The Space Templars."

Zim grimaced. He knew the Templars would be an issue.

Sabra's lips sneered over a toothy smile. "By the way," she added, "that Admiral Shae Lutz of yours?"

"Yeah?"

"He didn't die today. In fact, he escaped the brig."

Zim bared his teeth. "What?"

36

KODA

Starbase Matrona

Koda opened his eyes to see a dark-gray ebb ceiling dotted with red and black rock. *The usual,* he thought. What wasn't usual was the room. It wasn't his, and he was lying in a bed with the sheets tucked tightly against his feet.

Where am I?

He moved his eyes. They stung, and his eye muscles cramped, if that was possible.

He tried to sit up but grunted and fell back as pain shot through his head, then down to his chest and arms.

What happened to me?

Papers shuffled somewhere in the background. He turned his head, and a sensation like someone squeezing his skull in a vice overtook him. He moaned and squinted.

"Hello?" His voice cracked, pushing out a whisper.

"Wow, bud. Welcome back," said a young, male voice.

"Who are you?"

"It's me, Devon Gray, the tech assistant for Savanna Levens. Remember me?"

Koda gave a nod and was glad the movement didn't hurt. "Where am I?"

"You're in the infirmary."

Koda rubbed his eyes again. "Why am I here?"

Devon chuckled. "You don't know?"

Koda moved his head to look at Devon, and a jolt of pain cracked across his skull. He massaged the back of his head. "Please answer the question with an answer."

Devon was plopped on a small bed set against a wall. He had a bandaged leg, the bulk of the bandage around his knee. He moved his knee back and forth. "I was shot, and these Suficell Pods fixed me up pretty well. I mean, not completely, but look, my leg is almost healed and has little pain. I'm telling you that technology is amazing."

Koda gave him a blank expression. He didn't know what the kid was blathering about. Being shot? Why had Devon been shot? He was a harmless young man who probably spent most of his time on HDC's doing nerdy stuff.

Far different from what Koda had done at his age—an athlete, one of the best jocks in the Star Guild Academy Games, and going after women when not winning awards.

"Someone tried to kill us, Koda. You were shot several times like me. But it looks like the Suficell Pods also patched you up okay."

Koda turned his head and shook it, even through his headache. "What do you mean I've been shot?"

A memory came to him of jumping out of a window, landing two stories down, and weapon's fire going off everywhere.

He sucked in a quick breath of air. He *had* been shot and multiple times. That was the last thing he remembered.

Koda's heartbeat picked up. "How long have I been out?" A stabbing needle-like sensation stung his shoulder and went down to his hand.

He flinched.

Whatever the Suficell Pods did to Devon to heal him, Koda figured it must have skipped him.

"Two days," said Devon.

Koda wanted to jump out of bed. *Two days?* "Wait." He went rigid. "The papers. Where are the papers?"

"In my hands."

He let out a breath of relief. "Thank Guild." He peered at the ceiling. He was in a hospital room surrounded by ebb walls. An HDC beeped in the background. "Why are we in the same room together?"

"Well, I can't be in any other room. The *Brigantia* and *Taranis* Guard are occupying all of them."

Koda narrowed his eyes. "Why?"

"I don't know yet. A civil war is going on, I think. All I know is that the *Brigantia* and *Taranis* Guard have taken over this infirmary."

Koda pursed his lips. "Dammit." He remembered seeing the *Brigantia* and *Taranis* Guard firing at the Matrona guards before he blacked out. Civil war during this time was a bad idea. Along with fighting an unknown enemy, they shouldn't be fighting themselves.

Idiots.

"Yeah, I figure if we find an antidote, we can blast it through the water supply and air channels," said Devon.

Koda turned his head to face Devon, pushing through the ache gripping his temples. "Antidote? What are you talking about?"

Devon's eyebrows rose as if surprised that Koda didn't know what he was saying, then he nodded. "Oh, yeah, you probably don't remember what's on these papers. Stress can do that." He eyed the papers in his hand. "I cracked Zim's code and printed a lot of the information out, you know. We're piecing everything together and coming up with a plan, but there has to be an antidote."

"Again, the antidote to what?"

"The batrachotoxin?" He paused, waiting for Koda to remember.

Koda went to bolt up, but the pain restrained him. "The toxin. We have to stop it."

"We also found some other weird stuff in the papers. Something about an extraction process with the ebb we mine. Apparently, before the final mining product gets to us, it's cleared of a gold element, but I don't know why gold is supposed to be so important that it's taken.

And, they also remove a mineral crystal." Devon hesitated as if waiting for another reaction.

Koda remained still, thinking. "Why…who?"

"We're trying to find out who is doing *all* of this to our race." Devon paused. "Anyway, they take the gold and crystal out of the ebb, store them in some facility on the other side of Eos and then transport it all off Eos to another planet. Once it's there, they leave the crystal alone and heat the gold to a certain temperature, then it's cooled into a powder and blasted into that *unknown* planet's atmosphere, where—"

"Whoa," interrupted Koda. "Hold on and back up. You mentioned the other side of Eos? No one can go to that side of the planet. It's full of radiation."

"Yeah, about that. It seems that we've been lied to for, I dunno...our whole lives. And now they're going to kill us off soon. They're assholes, really."

"Wait, we—" Koda sighed in frustration. "Again, back up. The ebb quarries contain gold and crystal? Wouldn't the mechs see it when they're mining the ebb?"

Devon shrugged. "We wondered about that and don't know how we've missed it for as long as we've mined ebb. We think there's more to the cover-up, and I think the view screens on the mechs have been tinkered with, perhaps not displaying the gold and—"

A tall woman walked into the room, the sound of her footsteps cutting Devon off mid-sentence.

Koda winced, not able to look up.

"Hello, Koda. Glad you're awake."

Koda relaxed and forced a smile. It was Executive Officer Louise Stripe. He liked Louise. "What's going on, Louise?"

Louise puffed out her lips in thought and leaned on one leg, crossing her arms and standing over Koda. "Your uncle is—"

A nearby blast rocked the building, and shots fired, echoing down the outside hallway.

Koda stiffened, and Louise gasped, her hand moving quickly to her holster and unclipping her gun. She pulled it out and turned, rushing out of the door. "I'll be back, Koda."

Another explosion shook the building, and Koda pushed off the bed with his hands, wanting to sit up, but dropped onto the mattress a moment later. The pain wouldn't let him move, let alone walk out of here.

Devon bolted off his bed. "Naveya," he yelled. "I almost forgot about her." His eyes were like saucers. He limped toward the door.

Koda reached for him. "Get us both out of here."

"No, I mean...I have to let Naveya into the biosphere, or she and her dog might die of thirst."

"Who?"

A tall, bulky man dashed into the room, his biceps the size of Koda's thighs. His stubbled chin and sunken eyes told Koda the guy was either overstressed or hadn't slept in days or both. The soldier wore *Brigantia* Guard fatigues and a rifle strapped over his shoulder, and sweat rolled down his face.

He pushed Devon onto his bed. "Get back."

Devon threw his arms up. "Manning, what's going on?"

Manning looked at Koda and then at Devon, his breath coming quick and heavy. "I've got to get the two of you out of here. We're being attacked." He pointed at the doorway as a guardsman wearing the same outfit as Manning burst into the room. "Help, now."

"Aye, Sarge," said the soldier.

"Lance, grab a bed. We'll wheel them to the basement."

Koda's eyes darted back and forth between the two muscle heads. "What's happening?"

"Sorry, Overseer." Manning straightened. "A special unit of the Matrona Guard is inside the facility and causing a shitload of problems. I don't know how they got in, but they're here."

A blast and then yelling broke out in the hallway, along with a myriad of bangs clanking loudly, signaling exchange of gunfire.

"Go, go," said Manning, gesturing for Lance to grab Devon's bed.

Manning rushed to Koda, gripping the head railing and pushing him toward the door, following Lance, who was pushing Devon.

Manning halted. "Stop."

Heavy tracer fire zipped past their door, followed by an explosion further down the hall.

Koda's body tensed, adrenaline surging. Fighting his sore muscles, he lifted his head. Watching the tracer fire, he figured if they went out into the corridor now, they'd be a pile of blood and guts.

Another guard dove into the room, ducking just inside the doorway. He aimed his rifle around the corner and fired down the hall. He wore a *Taranis* Guard uniform and glanced at Manning and Lance. "Hey, guys. Looks like we're having a little issue here."

Manning went to a knee, eyeing down the barrel of his gun at the doorway. "What's the status out there?"

"Bad." He pulled back from the entrance, his face slackening when he saw Koda and Devon. "No way those two can go out in the hallway right now."

Manning nodded to Lance. "Wheel them back where they were. We'll have to protect them in here."

Koda's stomach churned. Protect them in here? With all the firepower he was hearing, they'd need more than three guards.

"Give me a gun," ordered Koda as Lance wheeled him back in place. "I've been trained half my life."

"Here." Lance handed him the magazine end of a pistol. "Pull the trigger on any guards wearing Matrona's red insignia. Remember that. They might be on us in minutes, if not seconds."

Koda held the pistol in his hand and looked at Devon, who also held a gun, probably from Manning. It was obvious Devon hadn't a clue how to use it.

"Just aim and pull the trigger, Devon," said Koda.

Devon nodded quickly. "Yeah, yeah. Okay."

Lance crouched into position, his shoulder against a partition in the room.

Manning told the guard near the entrance, "Shut the door. It will buy us some time while the Matrona Guard tries to break in."

The guard quickly pressed buttons on the wall panel, and the door shut.

Lance studied the door like a carpenter. "It's not entirely the Matrona Guard attacking us, Sergeant."

The other guard shifted on his feet. "Yeah, I don't know who exactly is out there, but they are like the elite of the elite."

"I don't know who they are either," said Lance. "But I noticed Zim's last campaign slogan printed on a dead insurgents jacket. It said, Taking Action, Getting Results."

Manning's face went ashen. "That's a slap in the face. So Zim must have a personal guard. When did that happen?"

"Zim always had a few guards around him but not a platoon." Lance spit on the floor as if he didn't like the taste of Zim's name on his tongue. "But we might as well call them super soldiers because with what they're doing out there, they must be cybernetically enhanced."

Koda switched the gun's safety off. Even though he couldn't move too well, he wasn't going down without a few of his bullets flying toward anyone wanting to kill him.

37

SHAE

Starbase Matrona

Shae held several papers in his hand, astonished by what he was reading. He was sitting in an administrative room on the second floor of the infirmary. Large tree branches sheltered the window, more or less preventing anyone from seeing inside.

"Why do I have papers and not a holodoc?" he asked.

Captain Stan Jenkyns sat on a couch in front of him, smoking a cigar, his gun holstered at his hip. His round cheeks hollowed as he sucked in a puff, and smoke dribbled out of his mouth. "I don't know, and I also don't know how accurate those papers are."

Brigger stood next to the window, watching the branches. He held more documents, waiting to hand them to Shae.

Shae placed the papers on a table next to his chair and rested his feet on a footstool, leaning back. "They're from Prime Director Zim's holocomp. They are legitimate, Stan."

Jenkyns pulled another puff. "I hope your escape went without difficulty?"

"It was without difficulty, thank you."

"So, you *really* think Zim wants to destroy this entire starbase, with all of us inside of it? How would that help his efforts for his next campaign run for the Prime Director position?"

Shae could tell Stan held back a smirk. He didn't believe one iota of the document's claims.

"I don't know Zim's motivations, but I do know he was intimidated by what I did. He mentioned my calling the Space Templars was the biggest mistake I could have made, and I could see it scared him. He also commented about his higher-ups. Now, I don't know who they are, but I do know they aren't here for our benefit. They want us all dead, and if we don't find a way out of this, according to Devon Gray's translated papers here, we'll all soon meet our maker."

Smoke trailed out of Jenkyns' mouth. "What do you think we should do?"

"We're coming up with a plan, rest assured. I don't yet know how we'll stop the batrachotoxin, but my guess is someone may have some insights."

"Who do you have in mind?"

Shae paused, looking Jenkyns up and down. Something was amiss. "I don't have anyone yet. Is anyone on your staff experienced with deadly toxins?"

Jenkyns reached over to a side table next to the couch and tapped his cigar in an ashtray. "I have someone, yes. Her name is Sally Gray. She's the sister of the kid who translated the *Kill-Off* documents."

"She's part of your staff?"

"Not exactly. I plan on grabbing her from Chem Lab in Sphere Nine when there's a chance."

Shae paused again, glaring deeply into Stan's eyes. The guy was playing it cool and almost too nonchalant. This type of news—the Kill-Off—should warrant some nerves, some anxiety, even in a captain. No one was perfect, and of all people, Jenkyns was far from it. "How are you planning to do that?"

Jenkyns blinked a few times before answering. "I have people on the inside searching for her now." He looked off to his right.

Jenkyns just lied.

Shae rubbed his hands together, his eyes shifting to Jenkyns' right ear, the side Jenkyns had looked. Was he wearing an earpiece? From this angle, it'd be impossible to see a small device lodged in his ear, but an eerie sensation creeping up Shae's neck told him that someone had just spoken to Stan.

Shae leaned forward, pressing his fingers against his boots, attempting to distract Jenkyns. "I like these boots." He wiggled his toes, making the boot's toe box move up and down. "But they seem a little too big."

"I can get you some new ones, sir," responded Brigger.

Shae twisted, staring at Brigger. The man held a pleasing smile, ready to help at a moment's notice. Yet, Brigger had drawn Jenkyns' attention as well, like a loud bang in a silent room.

It was a good move on Brigger's part.

"That's not necessary, but thank you, son."

"And, Admiral Jenkyns," said Brigger. "Do you want me to get you another cigar?"

Shae slowly moved his fingers up his hip, feeling the tip of his concealed pistol.

"I think I'm fine, Brigger," replied Stan, grabbing the cigar between two fingers. "I haven't used this one up yet. But, if you wouldn't mind getting me something to drink?"

Shae silently unclipped his pistol and slid his finger through the trigger guard, touching the cold metal.

"Shae?" asked Jenkyns, placing the cigar back in his mouth. "What's your plan to expose Zim? I want to help, so I'll need to know details, points of attack, everything."

"I don't plan on exposing him, Stan. I plan on killing him." He lifted his pistol, pointing the muzzle at Stan's forehead.

Jenkyns pulled the cigar out of his mouth, his lips downturned, and stared at the gun and then at Shae. He looked over his shoulder, most likely about to yell for his personal guards.

Shae moved off the couch swiftly and pressed the muzzle against Stan's temple. "That wouldn't be wise, Captain Stan Jenkyns of Starship *Taranis,* sworn to protect the people of Star Guild." Shae kept the tip of his gun against his old friend's head. "Stand up."

Stan dropped the cigar from his fingers. He raised his arms in the air and stood up slowly. "What are you doing, Shae?"

"You're a traitor, Stan."

Jenkyns stiffened. "I'm a what?"

"Don't move." Shae reached for Jenkyns' ear.

Jenkyns flinched and moved back.

Shae stepped forward and brought his knee up, landing it hard into Stan's gut.

Stan bent forward as he let out a yelp and dropped to the couch, his hands on his stomach, gasping for air.

Shae snatched a metallic piece out of Jenkyns' ear and examined it. It was an audio device. Someone was feeding information to Stan and listening to Shae's responses.

He dropped the device on the floor and crushed it with his boot. "Who's been listening to our conversation?"

Stan lifted a hand, trying to catch his breath, his face ashen.

Shae eyed Brigger. "Close the door and change the code."

"Yes, sir."

Brigger moved quickly to the control panel on the wall, typed in a code, shutting the ebb door.

"Voice lock on my command, and open and close only on my command," Shae ordered, and a beep responded from the panel.

"Please, Admiral," said Jenkyns, his voice gruff and winded. "This was not my idea."

"Yes, I know. It was Zim's or a higher-up's, or whoever, but you went through with it."

Jenkyns shook his head. "Shae, you don't know what you're doing. Put down the gun."

Shae dipped his head toward Brigger. "Get Executive Officer Louise Stripe on the comm."

Brigger tapped a small silver band on his shoulder. "XO Stripe, Brigger here."

Shae pressed his gun against Jenkyns' skull, putting a little more pressure this time. "Move in front of the door."

Jenkyns stood strong and tall, gritting his teeth. "No."

He thrust his hand at Jenkyns' chest, pushing him hard over the couch. Jenkyns landed with a thud. "Why are you scared to stand in front of the door?"

Shae knew why.

Jenkyns pushed off the ground and held his arms up. "Don't do this, Shae. They took me, they made me by Guild damn gunpoint spy on you."

Shae rushed at Jenkyns, his hand and gun out, pushing him toward the door. Another loud thud and Jenkyns was pressed against the door, his eyes wild, his face flushing red.

"Who?" demanded Shae.

"I…I don't know. I've never seen them before. They claimed to be Zim's personal Guard. I can't be sure if Zim ordered these guys to kidnap me or not, but—"

"Stan, let Zim's guard know that if they decide to come in here, one way or another, you'll be the first dead, either by their blast or by mine."

This wasn't a tactic Shae preferred, but it would keep him safe, and in the process, keep the rest on Starbase Matrona safe, especially those in Star Guild still on his side.

If push came to shove, Shae only trusted a few people wholeheartedly. Except for Eden, he figured no one would risk their lives to save humanity more so than him, and no one was more fit for the job to lead whatever revolt needed to be led except him.

"What have *they* told you, Stan?"

Jenkyns' eyes began to well, and his voice cracked. "By now, Shae, they're on their way. They've heard the entire conversation and most assuredly realize that the ear device was destroyed. They couldn't care less if I lived or not."

"Who are *they*?"

"Like I said, Zim's personal Guard. I smuggled them in here as my own personal Guardsmen. They're highly skilled warriors, experienced, and better trained than any of us, by far."

Jenkyns' lips quivered. He had to have known what he'd done—

created another obstacle against his own damn race. He wasn't just a traitor. He was a coward, only out to save his own skin.

Shae wanted to slam the butt end of his gun into Jenkyns' face and then push the muzzle in Jenkyns' mouth and pull the trigger, but he needed more information. He had to figure out more about this conspiracy, so he refrained from committing an act that wasn't like him, an act that would haunt him for the rest of his days. "You're a traitor of the worst sort, Stan."

Jenkyns swallowed hard.

Brigger tapped his silver band. "Louise Stripe isn't responding to my call, Admiral. It seems my comm is jammed for some reason. It's not making—"

A bang against the door shot through the room and Jenkyns flinched.

Brigger and Shae both took a step backward, Shae steadying his gun on Jenkyns.

A shot rang in the hallway and then more shots.

Shae stayed his ground, keeping his eyes on Jenkyns, who was looking left and right, sweat dripping from his temples and down his cheeks.

An explosion nearby rocked the room, and holopads fell off a shelf, pounding loudly against the floor.

Shae moved further away and toward an ebb desk.

Jenkyns let out a gush of air, his arms still raised. "Let them in, Shae, and there will be no more of this bloodshed."

"Zim is going to kill us all. Even you, Stan. Order them to stand down."

"Again, I'm not in charge here. Plus, I have my own plan in place. By the time they release the toxin, my people and I will already be gone."

Shae jerked his head back at Jenkyns' words. "So, you *knew* it was going to happen all along?"

"I knew about Plan A and Plan B long before the attack. You weren't supposed to survive, but you did, and I'm sincerely glad for it. My plan now is to take you and," he gestured toward Brigger, "Brigger onto my ship. We'll leave for another star system in a day or two, away from all of this. I can save some of our race, Shae, enabling our species to survive."

"Really?" replied Shae. "We would leave Starbase Matrona just like that?" He snapped his fingers. "Just fly on out of here and say, 'we have a noble cause, so long, kids.' Is that how we serve and protect?"

Jenkyns snarled, his lips curling, and his eyes narrowed. "You've always been inflexible."

"I may be inflexible, but I don't sell out my people."

Gunfire echoed just past the door and clanks reverberated as bullets sank into the hallway walls.

Shae did his best to ignore it, keeping his gun trained on the traitor.

Jenkyns shook his head. "The entire human race rests upon your shoulders, and you're going to let us fall into extinction because you have some stupid oath to follow? You'll be the downfall of our race, Shae." He lowered his arms but kept his palms up in supplication. "Just think about what you're doing."

Shae glanced at Brigger. "Do what you can to get the comm working, and get Louise—"

Jenkyns went for his gun.

Shae pulled the trigger, and a loud crack boomed in the room.

A bullet sunk into Jenkyns' chest, and he fell back against the door, his mouth open, eyes wide as he gazed into Shae's.

A thread of smoke rose from Shae's barrel, and blood oozed from Jenkyns' chest as he slid down the door and onto his rear, his gun clattering on the floor. He went limp and slumped forward, his lungs deflating with one last exhale.

Shae went on one knee and bowed his head. "You idiot, Stan. Why did you have to pull your gun?"

He refused to cry, something he didn't want to waste on the man he had just killed, an old friend, someone he thought was a lifelong ally and a trusted brother-at-arms.

He walked toward Jenkyns and checked his friend's pulse, a piece of him hoping he was still alive.

No pulse.

A clang rang against the door, and Shae jerked his head up. He stood and backed up behind the desk and knelt, aiming his weapon at the door.

Shae waved his hand in the air. "Brigger, grab Stan's gun and kneel over there next to the wall and away from the door. The doorway is narrow, and they'll have to enter one by one. They won't see you until it's too late."

Brigger nodded. "Aye, sir."

Something smashed against the door, budging it and cracking the middle portion. One more hit, and the admiral expected it to give. "Get ready, Brigger."

"Yes, sir."

A thunderous roar and the door blew apart, flinging chunks of ebb and dust in all directions.

"Fire, Brigger, fire," yelled Shae as he pulled the trigger, blasting at the doorway.

"I can't see anything," responded Brigger.

"I don't care," shouted Shae. "Fire."

Brigger fired, singeing the hip of a guard trying to sneak into the room through the dust cloud. The man fell, curling into a ball and shouting, "Cease-fire, cease-fire."

Shae continued to shoot as the dust expanded, thinning enough to allow him to see the outlines of guardsmen backing away from the doorway and ducking and jumping out of the way.

"Hold your fire, hold your fire," hollered a woman.

A hand gripped Shae's shoulder, shoving his shooting arm toward the ground. Another hand came down hard on Shae's gun, flinging it out of his hands.

Shae yanked the person's arm and dipped his shoulder, throwing the assailant to the floor. He reared his arm back for a punch, then halted in mid-motion.

"Brigger?"

Brigger was on his back, his arms in front of him, ready to block

Shae's flying fists. "Hold your fire, Admiral. These are friendlies and—"

A hand touched Shae's back, and he turned, swinging hard, only to be pulled forward and flipped onto his own back.

Legs wrapped around his neck, trapping his arms in a raised position and pinning him in a submissive hold.

Shae couldn't move anything except his head.

It was Louise, her mouth tight. "Guild dammit, Shae. Why didn't you answer your commlink? You almost killed your own men." Louise narrowed her eyes.

"I didn't receive a call."

Louise bit her bottom lip, her brow deeply furrowed. "Someone scrambled your commlink in here?" She looked at a dead Jenkyns on the floor. "Right now, it doesn't matter. We have to get you to safety and now."

38

ALI

Planet Eos, Starship Sirona—Adarta System, Orion Spur

Ali examined a mech blueprint and pointed a finger at the specs. "This was created two hundred years ago," she said to herself.

She was in Tech Quarters, her eyes straining against the dozens of holoimages she'd been perusing since she'd arrived on Starship *Sirona*.

It had been several days since the battle had ceased. No one knew, especially her, when the enemy would be back.

She glanced at Hank, a tech sitting at his desk. He was slurping a beverage as he leaned back in his chair, staring at the HDC screen in front of him.

Obviously bored by what he was viewing, he released an obnoxious belch and slapped his huge belly, sending ripples throughout the gelatinous mass that he contentedly massaged.

Ali kept her eyes on the screen. "Yo, Hank. What percentage are the shields?"

Keeping his face snug to the holodisplay, Hank let the straw drop out of his mouth. "What?"

Ali reached over and slapped his desk to get his full attention. "Percentage of shields?"

He sat straighter. "Oh, yeah. Forty-two percent and shrinking." Hank shrugged. "It ain't nothing to worry about, sweet thang."

Ali wrinkled her nose at the comment, not knowing why the crude tech thought his continuous stream of comments was attractive. She shook it off. "How long can this ship take the pounding it's been taking?"

Hank set his drink on top of his HDC and folded his arms. He sighed. "Truthfully, I'm surprised our shields are still holding. Most of our cannons are undamaged, which is baffling the Guild-jeebies out of me."

He leaned back in his chair, tipping it with him. He looked left and right and leaned toward Ali, his voice quiet. "It's almost like they're toying with us, using their lackeys to train against us. I mean, *we're* not that good with our cannon fire, and if I were them, I'd target our cannons one by one, leaving us defenseless."

He pivoted his chair to face her, his gut hanging lower than his seat. He winked. "You know, we may not have long." He flicked his head toward the bathroom. "Why don't you and I just head in there and...you know?"

You don't know how badly I could kick your ass, she thought, keeping her mouth shut. She couldn't believe she needed this low-life's help. "You're kidding, right?"

He didn't bat an eye.

She did her best to stay calm. This guy was an asshole.

She returned her attention to the holoscreen. "Next blueprint." The HDC softly clicked, pulling up a schematic.

This particular one indicated that a little over a hundred different mechs had been designed with this spec in the past. With what Ali was finding, design was the keyword here. There were many designs but very few actual creations. Only a few of the mech specs had ever been built, and the current design being used today was the Mech S101 series. The last mechs, decommissioned over a hundred years ago, were labeled Mech S100.

She clicked back and forth between the Mech S101 and the first blueprint that had caught her eye a few hours ago, the Mech S12, a design built in the earlier days of Star Guild. The S101 and S12 were almost identical, although the Mech S12 stood four meters in diameter larger than the ones currently being used. It was nearly the same width and height of the enemy mech she had seen on the battlefield a few days ago. Could this be *that* mech's blueprint?

She wiped a sweaty palm on her pant leg. She was getting close to the truth. Whoever had created the Star Guild mechs had used the same design for the enemy mechs, but how and why?

"Inventor of Mech S101's design," she told the HDC.

ARBAS ONE blinked on the screen.

The smell of grease and onion wafted to her nose. She felt heavy breathing on her neck and turned. Hank was looking over her shoulder, his chin nearly resting on her upper back.

"Hank." She swatted him away. "Get away from me."

Hank stepped away. "Ali, why so serious?" He smirked and sat in his chair, leaning back again. "Sorry about that. You're so beautiful, I just can't help myself. I had to see what those gorgeous eyes of yours were looking at."

What she wouldn't give to knee him where it counted. She shook her head and eyed the screen, pointing at the blueprint in front of her. "Who is Arbas One?" It was a strange name, not one she'd heard before.

Hank leaned forward, shrugging. "Uh, he's obviously the guy who designed those walking tin cans used at the ebb quarries."

"Have you ever met him?" Arbas was no doubt old, but with the Suficell Pod age-reversals, he could still be alive.

"No, but I know who has some information on the guy." Hank twisted in his chair, calling to the other side of Tech Quarters. "Sleuth, we need you here."

"Leave me alone, Hank," replied a high voice, similar to a squeaky biosphere mouse.

"Get over here," Hank bellowed. "We need you."

"Nope," replied Sleuth. "I'm recalibrating cannons on the starboard side. I'm a little busy here, all right?"

"Ali wants to know who Arbas One is."

Silence.

Footsteps came around a partition, and a small, skinny man, wearing large wire-framed glasses, came into view. His hair was disheveled like most techs, yet this tech held a larger than normal frown. "Why do you want to know about Arbas One?" He put a hand up, withdrawing his question for a better one. "Actually, where did you find that name?"

Ali waved her hand over the screen in front of her. "It's all right here. I have the inventor of several mech designs in front of me."

Sleuth wagged his index finger. "Don't be too quick with that name."

Ali wanted to roll her eyes. "Look, relax. It's a name that anyone can find. See?" She motioned toward Arbas One's name, blinking next to the Mech Series S101 blueprint.

Sleuth slowly moved closer, his eyes fixed on Ali. "Yes, but nobody looks, do you understand?"

Ali glanced at the man's badge. He was the lead tech. Great, a guy with a flair for either exaggeration or mystery, and he's the one in charge? Of course. "Do you know who Arbas One is or not?"

Sleuth stiffened, his lips forming a straight line. He turned and walked back to his station.

Ali shook her head. "What the Guild was that about?"

Hank rolled his eyes. "He uncovered some things about that Arbas guy a couple of weeks ago. I overheard him talking to someone on the coms, and he said something about that name is too easy to find, or some shit like that."

"That's odd." Was Sleuth hiding something? Or maybe he wanted that Arbas name hidden from prying eyes. If so, why?

Hank raised his shoulders and let them drop. "Who knows? Sleuth has turned weird recently, even before the attack. 'Odd' isn't even close to how he's been acting."

Ali nodded. "Well, he's not going to stop me from digging for more."

Hank chuckled. "Good luck with that. Sleuth's our best technician. He was able to break through the cryptography hiding behind that name, and I doubt he'll tell you how. I also think he put some more safeguards preventing anyone else from searching further past the name. My guess is the Arbas One name is all you'll discover."

"Is there something I should know?" Ali pushed her chair out from the desk and stared past Hank's shoulder. Sleuth was in the far corner of the room, moving his hands in front of a holoscreen, probably recalibrating the cannons again.

Sleuth yawned and rubbed his eyes. She imagined the techs had been on the job nonstop for many days now, keeping Starship *Sirona* safe. Perhaps this guy wasn't weird or paranoid but tired as all hell.

"Hank," said Ali. "Is there anyone else who can help me break through the cryptography?"

Hank made a sucking noise through his teeth, thinking. He shook his head. "I'm afraid not. Sleuth changed the codes and password, making the schematic software pretty much hack-proof. All you can see now is what you have seen. You know, basic information."

She let out an exasperated breath and placed her hand on Mech S101's blueprint. She moved it aside and pulled up Mech S12. "Mech S12's inventor, please."

ARBAS ONE blinked on the screen.

She moaned and threw her hands in the air, letting them drop on her thighs a moment later. "This is frustrating. It's the same inventor for both designs? How is that? Each design is a thousand years apart."

Hank idly twisted strands of his shaggy beard around his index finger. "Must be a mistake. Maybe Sleuth did that to make curious people think there was a problem with the schematic. Or, it might simply be whoever entered the information could have accidentally duplicated the same name. There are many possibilities."

Ali brought her attention back to the holodisplay and asked it a question, "Are there any mechs that aren't designed by Arbas One?"

NO blinked on the HDC.

"More information on Arbas One," she told the screen.

AUTHORIZED ACCESS ONLY appeared, and an empty rectangle with **PASSWORD** underneath materialized.

She pressed on the rectangle.

"Ali?" whispered Hank, his hot breath against her ear.

Ali bit her bottom lip and lunged toward him. Hank jerked back, and the chair tipped over, slamming against the ground, his body going with it.

She stomped on his chest hard, digging her boot into him. "I warned you. Next time you try something like that, I'll give you a broken nose. Now, get up and go away, Hank."

She slumped back into her seat and concentrated on the screen in front of her. "Bypass authorization," she said, through gritted teeth, her adrenaline still spiking.

DENIED flashed on the screen.

Her shoulders drooped. "What would Sleuth use as a password?" she asked under her breath, more to herself than Hank.

Hank picked himself off the ground and stood, rubbing his chest and grimacing. "I don't know what Sleuth would use as a password, but maybe I can find it for you."

She glared at him. "You might want to leave or go to another station."

"Please, I can probably help. I mean, breaking Sleuth's encryption may be impossible, but I have some skills." He craned his neck to look at Sleuth. "Plus, I like screwing with him, and this would piss him off. It'd give me something to do."

Ali stared at him for several seconds, looking him up and down. She dipped her head and stood, gesturing toward her chair. "Fine." Maybe this was Hank's way of apologizing.

"You won't regret it." He sank into her seat and gave a thumbs-up. He dove into the keypad, typing furiously.

Ali stretched. "I'll be back in ten minutes."

Hank's eyes remained fixed on the HDC. "Where are you going?"

"To find Wrench."

Hank continued typing. "My guess is he's still working on that project of yours."

"That's why he needs a quick visit." Ali twisted on her heels and marched out of Tech Quarters, the door automatically opening in front of her and shutting behind her.

If Ali was correct, Wrench was mounting cannons or missile turrets onto Ali's mech right now. Hopefully, he'd already rewired her HDC so she could fire weapons from inside her cockpit.

Her mom wouldn't be happy when she found out.

She rounded the corridor, passing several crew members rushing down the hall.

"Calling Ali to Tech Quarters," blared over the ship's intercom.

Ali halted, her eyebrows high. There was no possible way Hank had hacked through already.

Ali twisted around quickly and ran toward Tech Quarters. The door whooshed open, and she rushed to the station she'd been working at for hours.

And there was Hank wearing a satisfied grin and stroking his beard.

"What did you find?"

"Yep," he said, throwing off an air of ease as if everything he did on an HDC was easy for him. "We're in."

She moved around his chair and gazed into the HDC. A blueprint of the human anatomy displayed on the screen. Her shoulders drooped. "Why do you do this to me, Hank? This isn't funny."

"It's not a joke. This is what came up."

Ali studied him. From his expression, he spoke the truth.

Ali pointed to a DNA strand next to the anatomy blueprint. With her limited knowledge, she at least knew what that was. "This is the DNA of the human genome, but I don't know why most of it is X-d out." She tapped her finger on the bridge of her nose, thinking out loud. "Why are we seeing a human genome?" She touched an X-d portion, and words appeared next to it: **Limit Memory**.

She pursed her lips. "What does that mean?" She pressed on another X-d area.

Lower Willpower. Manipulate. Control Function.

Her hand came to her mouth. "Junk DNA isn't just junk DNA?" She looked at Hank, her mouth agape. "Do you think?" She shook her head. "No. It couldn't be."

"What?"

She bit her fingernail, and blinked, her mind spinning. She wasn't a genius by any means, but perchance her first thought was correct. "Maybe we've been dumbed-down, and these areas in our genome have been limited to control us better."

Hank rolled his eyes. "It's just a picture. Don't take it so seriously. Who knows who put that in there in the first place or why. Maybe Sleuth did it to screw with anyone who broke through his encryptions?"

"Ali to launch bay," blasted over the comm. It was Wrench.

She walked toward the exit. "Hank, do me a favor? Keep doing your *stuff* and find more information like this for me, okay? I want to come back to this later. But I'll need the password for when you're not here. You know, the way to bypass the passcodes."

Hank pulled out a small holopad and jotted something down with his finger and handed it to her. "You won't believe the password that allowed me access, but that's what it is."

She looked at the holopad and gasped, then dropped the pad in Hank's lap. "Haha, very funny. Now, give me the correct password."

"That's the password. I'm not making it up. I didn't decipher it, either. It blinked up on the screen when you left. I don't know who hacked the HDC, but whoever it was provided *that* password."

She picked up the pad and looked at it, then back at Hank. "The password is my full name, Alison Johnson?"

39

SHAE

Starbase Matrona

Shae stood in front of a line of prisoners and glared into a holopad Louise gave him.

"This is from the infirmary security cameras." She tapped on the pad, turning it on. "Look what they can do."

Shae almost fell over at what he saw.

A man, a super soldier in his eyes, jumped against a wall, somehow perfectly timing gunfire streaking past him, and kicked off the wall, flipping to his feet.

He sent return fire, hitting several *Brigantia* and *Taranis* Guards, then dove into a room, avoiding more gunshots.

The vid switched to another super soldier moving at incredible speeds, rushing forward, dodging a few bullets, and sliding toward a *Brigantia* guard's feet, and then swiping the guy's feet out from under him. Just as quickly, he placed the guard in a chokehold, then snapped his neck, only to move on to join another fight down the hallway.

Shae handed the holopad to Louise.

These men, standing in front of him, wearing fake fatigues with Zim's old campaign slogan, Taking Action, Getting Results, printed on the back of their garments, were cuffed, now prisoners under Shae's watch.

They were the Prime Director's personal guards, almost two dozen troops no one in Star Guild had ever seen until today.

Their eyes were numb, and their faces like statues, and as Shae stared into their eyes, he noticed one particular pattern: they had no fear, no pain, no sorrow.

Bred to kill, he mused.

Shae paced down the line. "So, they won't talk?"

Louise wiped dried blood off of her face that wasn't hers. "No."

Shae glanced at one of his Guard leaning against the wall. The man held a weapon, not of Star Guild military design. It was a black rifle with a short saber fashioned on top of the barrel. "Is that one of theirs?"

Louise nodded. "Yes, and the saber thrusts forward by a press of a button. It sends electricity into its victim. They were using it effectively in close combat." She looked away, remembering a fallen friend, a soldier.

Shae stopped and narrowed his eyes. "They were advancing and gaining a foothold on the battle before they knelt and surrendered?"

"Yes, and we have no idea why. They were slaughtering our forces, then they just put down their weapons and put their hands in the air."

Who gives up so easily?

Louise walked to a prisoner. He looked past her. She put a finger to his cheek and swiped the bootblack that covered his skin. She eyed the smeary mix on her finger, then wiped it across the man's lips and spat in his face. "You disgust me." He didn't flinch or twitch a muscle. She stepped away, scanning the murderers standing before her.

"How many were there?" asked Shae.

"Including their dead, we count thirty."

"Thirty?" With all the killed and wounded from his own Guard, he thought there were hundreds of these soldiers slicing up his men and women and shooting in the infirmary.

He studied them, stroking his fingers on his stubbled chin. They were big men, all with square chins, black hair, and pale white skin. It was as if they were cloned similarly, but not identically.

He gritted his teeth, wanting to lash out at one of them, all of them, but he refrained. As with Stan, he needed information.

He turned and faced Louise. "How'd they get past our guards and into the infirmary?"

Louise turned her gaze through a busted door and into the room where Admiral Jenkyns was lying dead in a pool of blood.

She pointed at the lifeless man. "Most likely him. They came in with disguises, some wearing *Taranis* fatigues, others wearing janitor uniforms or medical robes. I think Stan gave them access codes. We found a bundle of their disguises in a few infirmary closets."

Shae frowned and glanced at a group of his *Brigantia* Guard. "Take the prisoners down to the basement. Lock them under heavy guard, gentlemen. These are the elite of the elite. They may have more tricks up their sleeves."

"Aye, Admiral," replied a Guard.

They marched the prisoners down the hallway. Shae grabbed the last prisoner's arm. "Come with me."

The man stiffened and looked down at the admiral's fingers, then coldly into the admiral's eyes. The guy was young, too young to be so confident.

The prisoner glanced at his friends as they moved down the hallway without him.

"Come with me." Shae pulled the prisoner into the next room, not giving him a choice.

He pushed the soldier into a chair in front of a table. Shae sat on the other side, maintaining a safe distance from the lethal killer.

Louise and a handful of *Brigantia* Guard followed Shae into the room. Louise gave Shae an inquisitive look.

Shae folded his hands. "Bear with me."

He returned his focus to the prisoner. "What's your name?" He sat back in his chair and folded his arms across his chest, waiting. He had all night, and he knew this would take time.

Silence.

"I can get your name the easy way," the admiral pulled out his gun, "or the hard way. Which do you prefer?"

The soldier looked at Shae's gun. The skin around his eyes wrinkled a tad, yet he held his tongue, not saying a word.

Shae stood and stepped around the table, pressing the gun against the man's temple. "I'm going to ask again. What is your name?"

The man turned his head, pressing his forehead into the weapon.

Shae pushed into the gun harder, moving the man's head in the opposite direction. "Do you have a death wish, son?"

The soldier blinked slowly. "Why don't you uncuff me and find out?"

Louise's footsteps echoed across the room as she moved quickly toward the man and clutched the back of his hair, pulling his head back.

His neck strained, and his veins popped out, his muscles flexing against Louise's strength.

"What are you?" she said, spittle flying from her lips. "Why are you emotionless?"

The prisoner gazed at the ceiling against his will. "Emotions are useless."

"Useless?" She released his hair, returning his head to a neutral position. She then slapped her palm against the back of the captive's head.

He smiled.

"You piece of Guild." She punched him hard across the face.

"Enough." Shae holstered his gun. "He doesn't care if he dies. He's of no use to us."

"Then let's kill him. Just one less worry."

Shae glared into the prisoner's eyes, searching his soul. Did he have children? A wife? A mother, a father? Probably not. The guy acted like nothing was important in life, even his own mortality.

Shae released a heavy sigh. "Do what you must, Louise."

She was right. He'd be one less enhanced cybernetic killer—or whatever these soldiers were—to worry about. He hated the idea of killing prisoners as it was against many war laws, but perhaps this guy and his troops should be the exception.

The man's lips straightened into a thin line. "Please forgive me, I—"

Louise kicked him in the side. He tripped and fell, smacking his head against the ebb flooring.

Louise glared down at him, heaving. "Oh, I apologize. Please forgive me."

He twisted on his back and looked at Louise, then at Shae. "You want me to talk? Then stop this female snake from preventing me."

"Then talk." Shae motioned toward a *Brigantia* Guardsmen. "Lift him."

A hefty man walked over and set the guy upright, purposely elbowing him in the side of the head before he walked away.

The captive shook it off and eyed Louise. "You're forgiven." He turned his gaze to Shae. "I will answer your questions if you and I are alone."

Shae gave the man a long, hard look. He then nodded at Louise and tipped his head to the side and toward the door. "Take the Guard and leave the room."

"Admiral, are you sure?"

"It's okay, Louise. I'll be fine."

"Yes, Sir." Louise tightened her lips and turned, exiting the room. The door hissed shut when the last of the *Brigantia* Guard exited, leaving Shae and the prisoner alone.

The room was silent. A bird chirped outside, reverberating through the lone window in the room. On the other side of the window was a portion of the biosphere, a picturesque scene of a small pond set behind a long and wide green yard.

Shae leaned back in his chair. "What is your name?"

The man looked at his lap. "Payson Cole."

"Are you an enhanced human being?"

"No."

"Then what are you? I've not heard of anyone, besides the myths of the Space Templars, that can fight the way you and the rest of your outfit did."

Payson shifted in his seat. "You don't know what you're getting yourselves into, Admiral. This is far beyond your ranking."

Shae put his hands out. "Elaborate for me."

"I'm not a murderer like you think. I'm here..." He paused. "We're here to help you, not hurt you."

"Eighty-two of my dead *Brigantia* and *Taranis* Guard would say otherwise, Payson." Shae leaned in. "Now, tell me. How does that help me?"

"I am human." Payson's voice was low, and his lips curled. Shae could tell the guy had been accused of not being human before and hadn't liked it.

Good.

Shae could use it to his advantage. He could piss him off, and maybe the guy would accidentally spill more than he wanted.

"I don't think you're human. I saw what you guys could do."

Payson's nostrils flared. "I *am* human."

Shae ignored him. "You've done this work before, and you're trained well beyond any soldier I have ever seen. You're bigger, faster, and more skilled. Are you a cyborg, perhaps?"

Payson lifted his knee quickly, slamming it into the bottom of the table. "We could have killed double of your Guard, Admiral, but we chose not to."

Shae shrugged. "I'll tell their families about your compassion. Just don't expect a thank you over the commlink any time soon."

"We came here to kill Captain Stan Jenkyns."

Shae shook his head. "That's not why you came."

"It was. You see, good admiral, Captain Stan Jenkyns was a kink in our plan."

"A kink in your plan?" Shae let out a forced chuckle. "Forgive me if I have a hard time accepting that. He's the one who let you in here in the first place."

"Yes, he did. We needed him in order to see you and speak with you. As we changed out of our outfits, he disappeared from our sight, eventually finding you. We were on our way to eliminate him, but your guard was in the way, some questioning us. They died, thinking they were defending you." He let out a giggle. "We have no want or plan to kill you."

"You lie."

"Did we not surrender when you killed Stan? That should be proof enough."

"How would you know when I killed Captain Jenkyns?"

"We all felt his soul leave his body, thus knew our mission was complete. We were to give ourselves up the moment Captain Jenkyns of Starship *Taranis* was dead." He lifted his chin. "We gave ourselves up in order to meet with you."

Shae stood and placed his palms on the table. He leaned forward. "Nonsense."

"Just listen to me, Admiral. I was created, along with my comrades, as Zim's personal guard when he needed us. But I, and the other prisoners, are human, just not exactly like you. We've been designed with fewer limitations in our DNA structure, unlike your design. You have been dumbed down. We didn't like that, so we decided to help the human race overcome their limitations and beat the attackers, the evil-doers."

Payson continued, "To understand me more fully, understand that over ninety-six percent of your DNA is considered *junk* DNA. Not because it *is* junk, but because it is turned off. You and your scientists don't know what that *junk* is, so you label it as trash. I, on the other hand, have twenty-two percent more active DNA channels than you and the rest of your race on Starbase Matrona."

He pursed his lips. "In other words, my body's antenna is more tuned into life's subtle vibrations than your body's antenna. That is why we seem elite to you when what we do in actuality comes very naturally to us. We think faster and act faster than the rest of the human race."

Shae had no idea what Payson was trying to explain. "You are saying *design*. What do you mean by that?"

Payson frowned. "You don't know?"

Shae scratched his chin. He didn't know if he was getting somewhere or going nowhere. He let out an exasperated breath. "Tell me what you want me to know."

"You've been designed by other sentient Beings who are more advanced than you in technology and IQ, but not in heart or DNA."

"We've been designed?" He looked around the room. "By whom? I've never seen anyone other than humans walking around this starbase."

"They aren't on the starbase. They remain near your starbase, monitoring everything your race does. They keep you in line when needed, allowing you to create a nice sized military to defend yourselves against the pirates they created. It's a fun game for them, you know, like entertainment. They use you for other purposes as well, such as mining. They won't, ever, allow you to grow your military or technology to an advancement higher than their own." He folded his hands on the desk. "Listen, Admiral, you are their slaves without knowing it." Payson's eyes didn't waver from Shae's.

Shae had read the information on ebb quarries and the toxin that would be unleashed on the population if he didn't stop it first. None of it mentioned human slaves, but reading between the lines said as much. "We are their slaves by mining ebb, right?"

"Yes."

"You aren't telling me what I don't already know."

Payson shook his head. "You don't understand. You've been enslaved by your limitations as well. I am human. I am your potential. I am what you can be."

"You aren't a human, Payson. I'm sorry, but you're something more, something advanced."

Payson shook his head, his brows V-ing. "I am human. Pay very close attention to what I'm about to say, Admiral. If you don't listen to me and do what I say, these people who have enslaved you are about to kill you off. One. By. One."

Shae raised one brow. "The toxin."

"It's worse than just mere toxin."

Shae leaned forward. "Do you know the antidote?" If there was anything important to get from this guy, this was it. If there was an antidote, he needed it and now. "I can set you free if you tell me the anti-toxin to this toxin."

Letting him go free was the last thing Shae would do.

"There is a cure. There is always a cure, just in case the toxin infects some of the wrong people, the ones who have enslaved you."

"What is it?" Shae sat straighter, ready to receive the answer he needed to save his people, his entire race.

Payson shifted in his seat. "Not yet."

Shae leaned back, his shoulders lowering. "Bad move."

"I need some things from you before I give you the cure."

Shae would give him almost anything to save his people. "What is it?"

"You let me lead your people, your starbase, and I will not only give you the cure, but I will also teach you how to reach your highest potential, and never again will our race be taken hostage. We will never again be forced to do things against our will. Never. Again. Then we kill the race that enslaved humankind. All-out war. They'll never know what hit them."

This was getting out of hand, but Shae needed more information. "Listen, you and your team will be set free when you give me the antidote." He put his hands out. "Please, for the sake of *our* race's survival, what is the cure?"

"That is above your ranking."

Shae stood. "Isn't everything else you told me above my ranking? I don't care if it's above or below. You answer my questions and stop playing with me, or I'll—"

Shae sat, and took a deep breath, relaxing his muscles. A memory entered his mind like a vid on a holoscreen. It was a time when he was in academy training. In fact, it had been Shae's final day being lectured, but this time it was a surprise lecture from the one and only, Admiral Revel Sun. Revel ended his speech by saying, "Remember class, the greatest weapon against stress is the ability to remain calm and to choose one word over another, one emotion over another. If you don't choose wisely, you lose the upper hand. The alpha in the room is always the calmest."

Shae cleared his throat and cupped his hands. "I know I won't be able to beat answers out of you, Payson. But I'll try."

Payson leaned forward. "Let's do one better, shall we?" He glanced down at the desk, looking like he was trying to find the right words. "I will kill Zim and get rid of the toxin. It will no longer be released if you set my men and me free, and allow us without restraint to govern the starbase."

"First, the antidote, and then you'll be set free. We'll negotiate the other *stuff* later."

Payson closed his eyes and let out a hefty breath. "Well, I tried."

A clank echoed in the room, and Payson lifted his hands, the chains from the cuffs dangling, broken apart.

A smile slowly formed on his face. "You know I don't have to go through you to take over the human race, but I was trying to negotiate. I was trying to be kind. I was giving you and your soldiers a chance."

Shae's eyes went wide. "Guards," he yelled.

Too late.

Payson lunged toward Shae, jumping over the desk like it was a mere pebble, and landing beside the admiral.

Shae unholstered his gun and slipped his finger through the trigger guard.

Payson's knee came up hard, slamming against Shae's pistol and sending it flying across the room. He curled his hands around Shae's neck, squeezing and lifting him off the ground.

The door opened, and Louise, wild-eyed, rushed into the room with *Brigantia* Guards behind her.

Payson shoved Shae against the wall and sent a sidekick Louise's way, connecting with her chest. She stumbled back and fell against a guard.

Payson lifted Shae higher and glared into his eyes. "I now see that it's not only Stan that needed to die. You, as well, Fleet Admiral Shae Lutz, need to die."

40

ALI

Planet Eos, Starship Sirona—Adarta System, Orion Spur

Ali rolled out of bed, her thoughts dizzying. The attack, the blue light from Mount Gabriel, the mesmerizing door inside the mountain tunnel, and now her full name as the password?

Very strange.

She pressed the comm next to her bed and typed in her mom's personal comm line.

"What is it, Ali?" her mom answered. "It's late."

Ali rubbed her eyes. "I can't sleep."

"Well, join the crowd. None of us can."

"When can we jet off of this planet? The *bad guys,* whoever they are, haven't attacked in more than a day. At the moment, we are in the clear."

There was a pause over the line. "Tell that to the engineers. They are fixing the core reactor. Now, get some sleep."

"I'm getting up."

"Suit yourself. Also, stay out of Tech Quarters. Sleuth said you were in there snooping around and creating problems. He's my right-hand man. I don't want you in there, distracting them. Out."

The line clicked off.

Ali stood. "Yeah, love you too, mom."

She walked out of her room and down the empty, dimly lit corridor and turned a corner. She walked to Tech Quarters and stepped inside, the door shutting behind her.

A bright light blared in the corner behind a partition in the large room. Probably some techs on night watch, ready to man the cannons and warn the ship if another attack was in the makings.

A sharp clang reverberated through the air. Someone cursed, and another person laughed.

The one who cursed sounded like Sleuth. Ali needed to be quiet.

Ali softly sat in a desk chair, yawning widely. "HDC seventy-nine, on."

The HDC powered up, and within seconds she went through several commands pulling up the blueprints she had viewed earlier in the day.

She came to the Mech Series S101, and **ARBAS ONE** blinked onto the screen next to the schematic.

"Access Arbas One."

AUTHORIZED ACCESS ONLY appeared on display.

She waved her hand in front of it, and a blank password box appeared.

How in the Guild could my name be the password?

She spoke it out loud, though in a whisper. "Alison Johnson."

Someone touched her shoulder. She leaped out of her seat and twisted around, her hands in fists, ready to strike.

"Whoa, Chief."

Ali lowered her arms. So much for being quiet. "Daf, what are you doing here?"

Daf had her hands up, clearly ready to block whatever tired jab Ali threw at her.

"I thought you'd need some company." Daf grabbed Hank's chair and wheeled it next to Ali's. She sat.

Ali shot Daf a weary look. "You mean, *you* needed company."

"Yeah, that's about it. I went to your bunk, hoping you were still up, but when you weren't there, I went to Wrench, thinking he was building *my* mech alongside yours." She bit the inside of her cheek and raised one eyebrow.

"He's making changes to *my* mech, and no one else's. Not yet, at least. You know, until he gets it right."

Daf threw a dismissive hand. "Yeah, so when Wrench was nowhere to be found, I had a crazy feeling you'd be in here."

Ali nodded, her eyes blurry from lack of sleep. "Congratulations, you found me." She tapped on the holodisplay and swiped her finger across it. "And there it is." The human genome glared back at them. She eyed Daf. "That's why I came here tonight, to somehow figure *that* out."

Daf rested her elbow on the desk and her chin on her hand. "What are all of those Xs on the DNA strand?" Daf's eyes widened, and she grabbed Ali's wrist, squeezing it hard.

"Ow, what the Guild?" Ali pulled her arm away.

"Look." Daf pointed at the screen.

Something or someone had typed a sentence.

Hi, Ali. You're up late.

Ali pushed her hair away from her eyes. "Huh?"

It hadn't been there a minute ago.

I'm happy to finally meet you.

Ali scratched her jaw and shrugged. She lowered her voice to a hushed tone. "Uh...HDC, commence dialogue." She shot Daf a confused look and then brought her eyes back to the holodisplay. "It's nice to meet you, too."

The HDC spelled out Ali's reply.

I'm glad you're here.

"Who are you?" asked Ali.

You can call me S for now. Or know me as the one who kept you and your friend alive while you were fleeing for your lives in your mechs. You wouldn't have made it to your starship without the things I did to get you there. But, that's all you need to know of

my name for now. If someone is spying in on my conversation with you, I would be considered a traitor to my race for helping you and helping those of your race still surviving on Eos. I do all of this in secrecy.

"Are you of the race that is trying to kill us?"

Yes, but many of us disagree with that approach. We wish for you to live, to be free.

"Why is my name the password?"

To intrigue you. To heighten your curiosity. You see, you are of my blood, and I am of your blood. I've watched you for many years, and before that, I watched your father. You descend from a long and ancient line. I chose you because you are one of the strongest in our bloodline.

"My father?" The guy was a drunk, a bastard, and dead. Why would S follow him?

Deep down, you know what I know about your father. The man who posed as your father, the man who was married to Captain Diana Johnson, the man who you think raised you on Starbase Matrona, was not your real father. In fact, you weren't raised on Starbase Matrona at all.

Ali touched her hand to her throat. "How did you know I was feeling that about my dad?" Ali paused, and all sound appeared to shut off around her. How could anyone know what Ali had been feeling and experiencing lately?

Like I said, I've been watching you. You were kidnapped from another planet. In a way, you were lucky because if you didn't have the bloodline, the man who took you would have killed you instead.

"What's the bloodline?" asked Ali.

It's a royalty line. Your particular human ancestry has it from an intermixing long ago. I have it. And my brothers have it. And, as you have most likely surmised, my father and mother have it as well. My older brother was the one who found you and also observed you while you were on Eos and Starbase Matrona until he tried to kill you in your mech.

Was he the one in her dreams? "He was the one who tried to kill me?"

He frequents a mech on Eos, usually piloting it away from your mining operations. I interrupted his operating system when he pursued you and attacked you with his soldiers. I did the same thing when he tried to kill you when he was in a starfighter...after he killed your friend, Hendricks.

Pain shot into Ali's heart when she read Hendricks. He had been such a good man, loyal to his wife and kids, always on time and mined hard.

My brother wanted you dead because he didn't like what he was starting to see with you. You have a strong will, and that will was pushing through, showing you memories my brother tried to erase from your mind four years ago.

"Who is my father?" Ali shook her head, squeezing her eyes shut. "I mean, my real father. I have memories and dreams. In my dreams, I'm with someone who is kind, sometimes. He acts like my father. I have a memory of an older gentleman reading to me on a farm somewhere... with...with long wheat in the background. He's teaching me what particular words mean. I'm like eight years old or something?" She leaned forward. "Is that him? Is that my dad?"

Yes, Ali. Tell me more as it will awaken many dormant, hidden memories my brother tried to block.

Ali's heart beat faster, and she glanced at Daf, who was biting her fingernails, most likely wondering what the heck was happening here. Ali didn't care. She could discuss it with her later.

Right now, Ali needed answers.

"I have a strange memory of a guy who seems like he'd be my dad going off to war and never returning. I remember he used to take me on long walks by a river, showing me the rocks, and practicing throwing them in the water. I was good at it. He always gave me hugs, which was apparently strange for that time, that era on Earth." She hesitated, seeing a globe of a mostly blue planet coming to mind. "Earth? I was born on a planet called Earth, correct?"

Yes, Earth.

Ali gulped. This was all too much, but she couldn't stop, she couldn't choke down the insane memories swirling in her mind. The man, the nice, wonderful man. "Who is my father?"

Ali, understand that I can't give you that information. It's for your own good.

Ali's eyes welled up. "Please?"

I'm sorry.

"Then who is my mother?"

A picture appeared on the screen. It was black and white and had two women leaning against a vehicle with wheels. An older woman had her arm around a younger one. They wore dresses with puffed sleeves.

Both women were smiling.

"Helen?" Ali pointed at the older woman. She cupped her mouth, a tear sliding down her cheek. "How do I know that name? It just popped in my mind. That's…that's her name, right?" She eyed Daf, who was clearly dumbfounded about what was going on.

That's your real mother. And, yes, her name is Helen.

"Where is she?"

She's still alive and on Earth.

Ali leaned in, her eyes narrowed. "When can I see her? When can I go to Earth? Will my dad be there too?"

I will answer that in a moment. I contacted you to tell you this: Your time in physicality and that of your race is going to be immediately shorter if you don't do exactly as I say.

Ali drew back and wiped her eyes. "Okay…"

I need you to go to Mount Gabriel.

"What?" The last thing she wanted to do was go back to the mountain. She wanted to fly off this damn planet and live.

If you don't, you will die, along with the rest of Starship Sirona's crew. I can hold my race off and mess with their instrumentation only for so long. In the next few days, an experimental weapon will be used on your ship. There is a group of Beings inside Mount Gabriel who can help you. Reach them, and save the starship's crew.

Daf jabbed Ali in the shoulder, whispering, "Get my mech weaponized, and take me. You'll have a better chance."

And Ali, you can find your way back to Earth via a sarcophagus deep in Mount Gabriel's tunnels. Like you were taken to Eos, it will take you back to Earth by a portal connection. It—

The Tech Quarters' door opened and the HDC shut off.

Ali spun in her chair, wiping her tears, and faced Diana, whose chin was high. Her eyes were like missiles ready to launch and explode.

Diana put her hands on her hips. "I gave you a direct order to stay out of Tech Quarters, did I not?"

Ali stood and walked hastily toward Diana, shoving her finger in her chest. "What's the truth, mom? Huh?"

Diana took a step back, her lips flattening. "What are you saying?"

Ali thrust her chest out. "I have some good information that you're—"

Daf's hand came down on Ali's shoulder, pulling her away. "Ali…" She shook her head.

Ali caught her misstep. If anything was awry and if by chance this S character was telling the truth, Diana was in on the lie that had been perpetrated on Ali for years.

Diana thumbed over her shoulder. "Get out. Never come back in here again. If I see you in here, it's off to the brig for both of you."

Ali tilted her head and leaned on one leg, her nostrils flared. "Why?"

"Because you are interfering with Tech—"

Ali cut her off mid-sentence. "No, really. Why? Is there another reason?"

Daf grabbed her shoulder again. "Ali, this isn't the way you talk to a—"

Ali threw her palm in Daf's face, keeping her eyes on Diana. "Why aren't you getting us off this planet?"

Diana flinched, and the skin around her eyes tightened. Was she part of this entire conspiracy, whatever the entire conspiracy was?

"Ali," interjected Daf. "We should get going."

Ali crossed her arms. "No, I want to know."

"You're walking a tight line, daughter. I wouldn't allow anyone to speak to me, a Star Guild superior, in this way. They'd be locked up by now, the key thrown in a river of lava."

Ali stood her ground, knowing the consequences, but not caring. "Answer my questions."

Diana touched a silver band above a pocket on her shirt. "I need guards in Tech Quarters immediately."

Ali let out a gush of air. "You've never cared a lick about me." She quickly stepped around her mother and marched out of the room with Daf hot on her tail.

The door shut, leaving Diana inside, probably frothing with rage.

Ali hurried down the corridor.

"Where are you going?" asked Daf.

Ali's chest burned, her muscles tight. "I'm waking up Wrench. We've just been warned, and if it's a real warning, then you get what you want, a weaponized mech along with mine."

"But we don't know if this person on the HDC was telling the truth."

"Did you see my mother's eyes? Did you see her flinch? She's holding back something. She's not playing for the right team."

Daf stopped. "You're kidding me, right? She came down to Eos during the worst time in human history to save you, not kill you."

Ali halted and spun on her heels, eyeing Daf. "You don't know my mother. What she showed me during the time I *remember* being with her was nothing but a black heart."

"Ali—"

Ali took a step closer to Daf. "Listen. We make sure to keep this weaponizing-our-mechs business between Wrench, you, and me."

Daf touched her chest. "Seriously? You're definitely going to include me?"

"Yes, so keep your mouth shut because once we slap your mech and my mech together with the new specs, you're going to get your wish. You'll accompany me to Mount Gabriel. Once we get help from those *Beings,* I'm finding the sarcophagus and sending my ass back home."

To be with her *real* mother and father again.

41

EDEN

Planet Aurora, Starship *Swift*

It was dark, and no matter where she searched, Eden couldn't find the path.

Brush scraped at her bare feet as she tripped on roots and stumbled over rocks trying to find what she and Skye had hiked up on the day before, a path that led her to the top of Star Guild Hill and eventually to those orb-like starships.

The wind blew, and Eden's dark hair whipped at her eyes, her robe wrapping around her legs. She clutched at the cloth and pulled the hem past her knees.

Where's the path?

She'd never experienced more than a breeze during her entire lifetime, and now this?

A drop of rain splatted on her hand, then another landed on her cheek. Thunder clapped, and rain dumped, showering down upon her.

In minutes, the hill became soggy. She trudged forward, her feet pressing on wet moss. She slipped and fell, her feet in the air and her hands coming down to meet the ground at the same time as her chest.

She yelped and laid on her belly, wiping muck off of her face.

She pushed off the ground and noticed her fingers were curled around something bulbous and dense. She brought her hand to her face and opened it. Before her glowed a rock.

The crystal.

She stiffened, not knowing when or why she had grabbed it.

Swift.

A voice in her head called her like a moth to a flame, compelling her to hurry, to climb, to stumble over brush.

She tripped over a rock and landed on her knees in a puddle of slop.

"I can't see a thing."

She raised the crystal, hoping it would shed enough light to guide her way.

Its light barely outlined the shape of her hand.

She let out a puff of air. "Dammit."

She stepped on something sharp, and hobbled, smacked into a branch, and fell on her back.

She grunted loudly, accidentally dropping the crystal.

Oh, no.

She rolled to her knees and began searching. She didn't know why she needed the thing, but she did.

She frantically scrummaged around until she saw its glow beneath a leafy plant. She grabbed it with a sigh of relief.

She stood and continued up the hill at a faster clip, the rain dripping down her hair and face.

Swift!

She pushed forward, clutching the crystal as she thrashed through the foliage, stepping over more roots and rocks littering the hill.

"Where the Guild is the path?"

She felt grass between her toes and eyed the bridge's shadow up ahead, the sound of rain washing out the babbling creek.

Swift rang in her ears, this time so loudly she went to her knees, covering both ears with her hands, and dropping the crystal yet again.

She cringed and bent over, pressing her forehead to the ground. "Stop it. Please, stop."

The sound and the rain ceased, and the crystal pulsated with a white glow by her knees. She grasped it tightly and squeezed hard.

She rushed over the bridge and continued to the elevator on top of the hill.

Reaching the hill's crest, she sat crossed legged and pressed the rock Skye had pressed when they were here last.

A holographic globe of Aurora materialized, hovering in front of her. She touched **Village Onyx** and the globe disappeared, a glass dome silently forming around her.

She dropped, the grassy elevator taking her into the depths of the hill.

Swift.

"Stop. That. Voice." She clutched her hair, squeezing her eyes shut. The voice echoed in her ears again, violently vibrating through her body.

The elevator stopped, and light peeked past her eyelids. She opened them, and the glass dome dematerialized.

She was in the endless cavern she had visited yesterday. Her mouth gaped as she eyed the starships amid the many ships parked, their golden light slowly transforming into a silvery luminescence and back again.

Their beauty called to her.

She stepped off the elevator platform and walked slowly toward the starships.

Approaching the first ship, she reached her hand out and touched the side of the landing sled.

She cocked her head to the side, her lips turning down. Her stomach ached, and her muscles spasmed.

She dropped her hand. It wasn't the right ship. It wasn't for her. Somehow, she knew this, the sensation rising up her spine and tingling the back of her head.

She walked under the behemoth starship for nearly ten minutes, passing under the width of it, until she came upon the second, its golden underside glowing brighter than the previous ship.

She reached up, touching the landing sled. A zap of energy

streaked down her arm, and the starship's engine hummed, the underbelly vibrating.

She closed her eyes and listened.

Silence.

The humming had stopped.

You're the ignition.

She stepped back, flinging her hand to her heart. "What? Who said that?"

She wrinkled her brow and reached toward the skid again, planting her palm against it. Cool energy ran through her, and the ship hummed, gently vibrating against her touch.

"Oh my word, this is weird."

A sharp hissing sound echoed through the cavern. She twisted to face an open ramp descending from the starship's midsection. It clanked when it hit the rocky ground.

She walked toward the ramp, her adrenaline picking up almost as quickly as her curiosity.

What was in a ship like this? How did it operate? Who the Guild created it? Questions she figured she should have asked Skye yesterday, but in her amazement, it slipped her mind.

She placed a foot on the ramp.

I am Swift of Space Templars and am at your service.

She took a step off the ramp, her bare feet against the cold ground.

I will not harm you.

She ran her hands through her hair. Was she really hearing a ship talk to her?

Yes, you are.

Eden gasped, tilting her head, her mouth slightly agape. "Can you hear my thoughts?"

As you can hear mine.

"Uh...how?"

Step inside, and you'll learn more. I'm in no hurry. I've waited a long time for your bloodline to regain its power and enter my bridge. I can wait longer if you wish.

"Bloodline?" She shrugged and moved forward. The pull this ship had over her was like a negative to a positive magnet snapping together.

Something in her, something deep inside, told her it was meant to be. This was her ship to captain.

Eden headed up the ramp and inside the ship, stopping just beyond the top.

The walls emitted a golden light that illuminated the interior in a soft glow, soothing to her eyes.

Welcome home, Eden.

"Home?"

In a way, yes.

Of all things she'd experience lately, talking telepathically to a ship was the weirdest. She didn't know if she was going insane or if this was real.

She shook the thought away, her eyes widening as she spun in a circle, taking it all in.

Inside mirrored the craft's exterior, oval, like a giant egg, but that's all it mirrored. The walls tiered, consisting of twenty or so landings, each one high above the other. Walkways led to doors built into a massive wall separating the front of the ship from the midsection.

She didn't want to see the midsection. She wanted to hurry to the bridge, look at its instrumentation, it's vidscreen, its stations, and whatever else this massive beauty might have.

She turned and headed toward the ship's bow and then halted quickly, letting out a breathy, "Whoa."

How did she miss this a second ago?

The tiers extended to the ship's side walls as well, but built on top of the landings were thousands upon thousands of crystal dome-like quarters, surrounded by foliage.

"Bushes and trees?" She shook her head. It was too much. It was as if those stationed on this ship had their own yard, their own garden.

My divinely inspired architects and engineers utilized the perfection of the Divine's genius and created everything you see. A happy and healthy crew is an effective ship. Keep walking, Eden.

The Divine? She shook her head, not knowing what that meant and continued on.

She reached another large wall with several corridors and strolled down the center one. Its walls pulsed slightly, sending off a golden light that somehow energized her with each step.

She slowed when she entered the bridge. It looked like *Brigantia's* with the many stations, the chairs, and the vidscreen.

A door whooshed shut behind her, and she spun around to the gold and silver glistening door.

She took in the quiet, something she'd never experienced on a bridge before, this being the first time she'd been alone on a starship.

She spun on her heels and eyed the large view screen, which displayed everything in front of the ship—the damp, dark cavernous walls, the rocky terrain, and smaller parked ships.

She walked to the ship's helm where the captain and XO chairs were set two or so meters apart. She frowned. There weren't any HDCs on them or anything similar.

"How do you communicate with the ship or the rest of the crew outside the bridge?" she said under her breath.

No answer.

She took a step around the captain's chair and paused, her eyes resting on a necklace lying on the seat.

It's yours, Eden.

"Mine?"

She bent and picked it up, examining it. Etched on it were two knights riding a single horse, each knight carrying a shield. She dropped it back on the seat.

Place the crystal on top of the necklace, said Swift.

"Why?"

They will meld.

"Meld?" She puffed out her bottom lip and leaned forward to place the crystal in her hand on top of the pendant.

"Whoa." She stepped back. The crystal quickly melded around the pendant and encased it.

A hiss of air released into the room. She gasped and turned, her hand coming to her neck.

Hooded figures wearing violet robes entered the bridge, one by one and fanned out, their arms folded at the midriff, their long sleeves concealing their hands.

Another figure entered and pushed off his hood like running his hand through his hair.

Eden bit her lower lip, her heart sinking. Back on *Brigantia*, if she was the only one on the ship without the admiral's permission, she'd be written up for not following guidelines. A Star Guild admiral always stepped on a ship first.

"I'm so sorry, Skye. I was just looking around. I didn't tamper with anything. I'll leave right now and go—"

Skye dipped his head and smiled. "You followed your heart, Eden. There's nothing to be sorry about. It was your intuition and *Swift's* pull that brought you here."

A hooded individual walked in her direction and took a seat in the XO's chair, shifting around and getting comfortable. It faced the vidscreen, its arms resting on the armrest.

Its hands, however, were human. White skin. And female? Her fingers were definitely feminine.

"Welcome to *Swift*." Skye walked toward Eden and placed his hand on her shoulder. "This is your ship. We're each Space Templar members."

He took the necklace from the seat and held it up. "Lower your head."

Eden glanced left and right. The hooded individuals, besides the one now seated in the XO's seat, remained standing. "This is weird, Skye."

"Trust me."

She lowered her head.

"This is yours to keep, forever and always." He slipped the necklace over her head and pulled it down to her neck, where it hung. "You are a part of our Order and destined by blood to captain *Swift*. You are a Space Templar and Starship *Swift's* captain."

Eden lifted her head and took a step back. "Captain?" She had been told this before, but being told again didn't lessen the shock.

Skye nodded and extended his arms, gesturing to every robed figure in the room. "We're honored by your presence."

Eden touched the pendant and lifted it, wanting to take it off and hand it back to Skye. "No, no. I can't be a captain. You take it. You're more inclined to lead than I am."

This was nuts. She wasn't experienced. She wasn't ready to lead. It was a dream to run a starship one day, but it was a dream that needed a mentor to train her. She was a starfighter pilot, and sure, she'd led some squadrons, but leading tens of thousands of people on a ship was a completely different matter.

Skye put his hands over hers, stopping her from taking the necklace off. "It is yours by blood. You and a few others with your particular DNA type, which is coded in every millimeter of this ship, are the only ones who can run this ship."

Skye touched his chest. "I can't fly this." He motioned toward the row of robed people. "They can't." He jabbed his finger into her chest, pressing against the pendant. "You can."

The robed individuals removed their hoods, and Eden jumped back, her eyes wide and her hand over her mouth.

Many of them looked like her race but had an inner glow emanating from them. They were all unusually attractive, both men and women.

The other race, however, was shocking, and unlike anything she'd ever seen, not even in the old Space Templar mythology books she used to read as a kid.

Skye touched her arm. "Those that resemble us are human. Those who don't look like us are Sirians."

The Sirians were tall and ravishingly beautiful. They had strong, sleek physiques covered with fur. Some were gray with a bluish tint, some were a mixture of calico browns, or white and black.

They had human-like facial features, yet they were more similar to the panther Eden had seen a couple of days earlier. Their eyes were yellow and catlike.

Skye clapped, breaking the silence. "We are in service to others, Eden. *Swift*, your ship, has summoned you here and confirmed your blood contains the energies of light. We are in service to the light, truth, and love, and if need be, we will follow you into the depths of hell and back."

Fingers touched the top of her hand. She turned to see a beautiful young woman, hair the color of corn silk, sitting in the XO's chair. She seemed about the same age as Eden, somewhere in her early thirties.

The woman's twinkling blue eyes drew Eden in, making her almost dismiss the strange scar that swept over this woman's cheek. "I'm Nyx."

Eden searched her features. She forced a smile past the insane sensations flowing through her, like a windstorm inside a beautiful, calm painting. Everything felt wonderful and chaotic at the same time. "Are you human?"

Nyx furrowed her brow and glanced at Skye as if he made the wrong decision to make Eden a captain. She shifted her focus back to Eden, huffing. "Yes, of course."

"Where are you taking us?" said a gruff voice.

Eden turned to look up at a very tall, blue-colored Sirian. He bowed his head, his demeanor serious.

"What do you mean?"

He slowly closed his eyes and opened them. "We haven't gathered together to stand about and chat. We're here to join you on your first journey with *Swift*."

"What?" Eden looked around, her eyes sweeping across the Sirians and humans. "Right now?"

Skye smiled. "Yes, *now* is the time. Please close your eyes, press the crystal pendant hanging from your neck against your chest, and ask your heart where we are most needed. Listen quietly, and you will feel your heart's response, then you will see our destination in your mind. That's where you will take us."

Eden forced a laugh. "You're joking, right?" She put her hands out. "This is a joke? It has to be."

Skye shook his head. “No joke. Follow your heart.”

Eos jumped to her consciousness, an image of the old mining planet, its gold aura highlighting space, pulling at the forefront of her mind and tugging at her heart. She wanted to go back home, to see her people again and help them in their plight.

Starbase Matrona had jumped out of Eos’ sector, so her people wouldn’t be there, but perhaps there were some stragglers who need saving in the Eos warehouses?

Skye took a deep breath and grinned. “What did you hear?”

She stared into his eyes. “Eos.”

Skye barked an order, loud and clear. “Open cavern. We're going to planet Eos.”

42

ZIM

Starbase Matrona

Zim patted his slick black suit just before entering the capitol building. He cleared his throat and rubbed his tired eyes.

"Three hours of sleep."

It had been a long night giving orders to his Matrona Guard, and he was tired of all the bullshit. These humans should be dead by now, and the beginning stages of creating a new cycle should have begun.

He pushed the glass door open, a door designed by Enlil himself, far different from the automatic doors throughout the rest of Starbase Matrona.

"This door subconsciously ingrains into the human psyche that Prime Directors work hard. Thus they'll trust Prime Directors more," Enlil insisted.

How stupid.

"Hello, Jeremy," uttered Zim as he stepped into the foyer.

Jeremy Cumming's pointy nose perched on his thin face above a twisted smile. Not the most attractive human, but obedient nonetheless, all that Zim needed in an assistant.

Jeremy stood and bowed, paler than usual. "Welcome...Prime Director."

Zim stopped in front of Jeremy's desk and sniffed. "Why are you perspiring? You smell like you've been working out an hour too long, and Jeremy, I know you don't work out." He looked down upon his assistant, his lips curling into a frown.

Jeremy glanced over his shoulder and down the hallway to Zim's office door. "I tried to stop her, but she forced her way in." He looked away from Zim and stared blankly at his desk.

Zim eyed his door. "What's going on?" Without waiting for a reply, Zim gritted his teeth and stormed down the hallway. He opened his door and paused. Someone was sitting in his chair.

"What are you doing, Sabra?"

Sabra's back was to him, a cup of tea on his desk. Zim hated tea.

She slowly dipped her head. "I'm doing nothing and everything."

Zim scowled. "How is it possible to do nothing and everything at the same time?"

She inhaled deeply. "Clearing one's mind and thinking of nothing opens a path for an answer to any question you might have. The universe will dance at your feet when your mind is still. You should try it sometime." She twisted the chair around to face Zim. "Hello, Zim."

Zim shook his head. "Riddles. You speak in irritating riddles." He walked to the bar in the corner of the room and poured himself a glass of mead. He took a sip, swishing the contents in his mouth, savoring the taste on his tongue.

He swallowed. "Riddles are always washed down better with mead. Drink enough of this, and you'll see more than just the universe dancing at your feet." Zim put the glass down. "What do you want?"

Sabra stood and walked toward the bar, eyeing the pitcher. She picked it up, brought it to her nose and sniffed. She pushed it away and gave Zim a sickened look. "Like I suspected, your thoughts don't range far. You should give *this* to your population. Put this in the water, and they'll be dead by evening." She set the pitcher down and leaned against the bar.

"How is it that a biotechnician such as you can hasten repairs on the water and filtration systems? That's not your expertise." Zim raised an eyebrow. "Or, does Enlil have you here for another purpose?" His expression went flat. Maybe Enlil didn't trust him? "Perhaps to spy on me?"

Sabra looked down, scuffing the ebb flooring with her foot. "I have a high IQ, Zim. That's why I'm here. Finding a solution to any problem is one of my specialties. I'm not a biotechnician because I'm an idiot." She shot him an austere look, then looked off, as if in thought. "I've always wondered what it feels like to be a killer. It must be a heavy weight…from time to time."

Zim stood firm. "I do what I'm told. Enlil gives me orders, and I deliver."

"I'm not talking about *you*, Zim. I'm talking about Enlil."

"Are you calling him a killer?"

"Is there another word for him? Should I call him a human slayer? How about a mass-murdering coward? Do you like that one?" She went back to Zim's desk and sat, crossing one leg over the other.

Zim snorted. "You'd be executed if he heard you say that."

She casually shrugged. "Yes, my brother would shoot me, kill me, or butcher me alive like he does anyone who disagrees with him for too long. He was never much of a diplomat. Killers do what they do best and yearn for the kill like a starving beast. But, if he made an attempt on me, our father would have his head, and our father has the entire Nibiru military on his side, you know, being king and all." She gave him a wink. "I'm lucky that Enlil knows this. So please tell Enlil all I have to say and make up a few more ditties for all I care. I'd like him to think about the web of life and what he does to it."

Zim's eyes went wide. "Enlil is your brother?"

"Sadly, yes."

Zim shook his head. She spoke the truth. "You don't want to be here, do you?"

Sabra chortled. "This is the last place I'd like to be, so the sooner we get moving with this, the better."

Zim grinned, happy for her drive, something sorely missing with the chemically dumbed down humans.

He took another sip of mead, swallowing it down hard. "All right, what's our first course of action?" He couldn't wait for the slaughter to begin.

He took another drink.

"To tell the little bastards the truth."

Zim choked on the liquid and went into a coughing fit. He bent over and hit his chest a few times with his fist until it passed, then wiped his lips with his sleeve. "You're joking. That's not going to happen. Not now, not ever."

"It's no joke, Prime Director."

"You want me to tell these little shits they're slaves? That they're actually much smarter and more powerful than they think? Shall I tell them their home race is from a different planet? Oh, and how about that we kill them off every few thousand years or so, and this is the ninety-ninth kill-off cycle?"

"That and more."

Zim slammed his fist down on the bar. "We'd have riots on our hands. The filtration and water systems would never get fixed." He drew a deep breath. "You're supposed to find a way to fix the filtration and water systems faster. That's why you're here."

Sabra stood. "I'm here to convince you to tell humans the truth."

"That's not Enlil's orders."

She widened her stance. "Those are my orders. Enlil thinks I have his back regarding killing the human race." She touched her finger to her lips. "I'm good at lying to him, but only to him because I lie to no one else."

"You can't make me do anything."

"I can, and I will." She walked a couple of paces toward the door.

"You're mad."

"I have informants in place already. When I give the word, the population will be given the truth from you or from my informants."

He pointed at his door. "Every single one of the damned humans will want to kill me if I tell them everything. You're crazy, woman."

"If you tell them the truth yourself, you'll be their savior. They'll honor your courage in your service to them, and your ability to stand up to your own leaders in order to keep the humans alive."

He shook his head. "Never. Enlil would have my head." He couldn't believe his own ears. Tell the human population the truth? Not with his last dying breath. "There's no need to tell them anything. They'll all be dead soon."

"And...if they don't die soon?"

Zim jerked back, then stared at her, looking for a trick, or something that would tell him she was pulling his leg. "What are you saying?"

"I'm saying that if you don't do as I bid, *you'll* be the one who is soon dead." She waited for a reply. Neither moved their eyes away from the other.

Zim released a breath. For all he knew, she could have her father and his armies backing her. All he had was Enlil if he had him at all. He lifted his hands in surrender. "So, what will you have me do, then?"

"If you want human cooperation, tell them the truth. You tell them Admiral Lutz is not a liar or a traitor. You tell them about the oxygen on Eos and why they're mining ebb. I can make a list if you like." She mimicked writing something in the air.

"What's happening here, Sabra? Why tell them anything? I don't understand your motivation."

Sabra dipped her head. "When you tell them all they need to hear, then, and only then, will you have the people's undivided attention. They'll grasp at every word you say, and henceforth, you'll be a hero. The riches my brother promised you will pale in comparison to what they'll shower upon you."

Zim blinked a couple of times, not believing for a second what he was hearing. He chuckled. "So, what do you get out of this?"

"Nothing."

"You want me to believe that you get *nothing* out of this?"

"Actually, yes. I do get something out of this. My other brother Enki and I will be happy. We'll be content, like a mother and father watching their healthy children."

"Well, you can get your jollies any way you please, I guess. To each his own, they say." He wiggled his index finger in front of her. "But you forget, I already have control of the people. There's no need to do what you're suggesting."

"Of course you have them under control," Sabra said in a sarcastic tone. "Especially the *Brigantia* and *Taranis* Guard. Taking over the biosphere and fighting the Matrona Guard must be their way of liking your ideas."

"I have them where I want them. They're scared and pissing in their pants. That's control."

"That's not control, Zim, that's failure. You've created havoc in the streets all over this starbase, and most of the humans are starting to question you and their history, and rightfully so. They're starting to see through the lies."

Zim rolled his eyes, wanting to slap her. "That's because the water system isn't fully operational at the moment. The drugs aren't going through the system, and the humans are waking up. That's not my fault. Once you get the systems back up and running, we'll be fine, and our jobs will soon be over. Like you said, the sooner, the better."

"I'm afraid it's not going to be anytime soon."

Zim made a fist. "You're supposed to hasten the process, not stop it."

"That's not why I'm here. I'm here to stop it, by orders of Enki."

"So, you indeed tricked Enlil. He'll have a shit fit."

"I told Enlil that I would use my genius to help the cause, but for which cause I didn't say."

Zim turned and pressed a button on his desk's HDC. He'd had enough. "I need Enlil on the commlink, now."

Jeremy's voice came over the comm. "I'm sorry, sir. I can't do that."

"What?"

"Uh..." responded Jeremy. "I...uh...don't know—"

Zim bolted to the door and swung it open, slamming it against the wall. He marched down the hallway toward the front desk. "What do you mean you can't get Enlil on the commlink?"

The front desk came into view, and Zim abruptly stopped and raised his hands into the air. "What the hell is going on here?"

Six gunmen dressed in black pointed rifles at Zim.

"There will be no calling Enlil," said Sabra, walking down the hallway. "You have no other choice than to cooperate with us. If you don't, you will die."

43

ALI

Planet Eos, Starship Sirona—Adarta System, Orion Spur

Ali peered through a corridor window, moving every which way to see if she could catch a glimpse of any enemy: soldiers, mechs, or starfighters.

There was nothing. Was this the calm before the storm?

It had been almost thirty-six hours since the enemy had last attacked. To her, that meant something was wrong, and if S was correct, a new, powerful weapon was on its way to end the starship once and for all.

Perhaps that's why *Sirona* hadn't been turned into a ball of flames, and the enemy hadn't thrown everything they could at this ship.

These giants had been toying with *Sirona,* maybe waiting for the weapon to be ready. It was the only explanation Ali had for why *Sirona* and her people were still in one piece.

Mount Gabriel loomed in the distance, calling to her and pulling her to get her ass moving to enter its tunnels.

She was glad the mountain beckoned. It made it easier for her to leave on the long, dangerous journey. Staring at its giant peak, a burst of energy rose from her feet to her heart, and she took a deep breath, keeping it in until she couldn't hold it anymore.

She exhaled with a smile, tapping at the mountain on the window. "I'll be there soon." She'd find the sarcophagus to get her butt back to her *real* mother, and maybe that would lead her to her *real* father.

She held back a tear as a memory of her mother surfaced that felt more real than any of the memories she had of her fake mother and fake father. Fake, if S was truthful, but the feelings arising in Ali told her S was speaking the truth.

"Do you see this, Ali?" said Helen, holding up a black and white picture of Ali as a teenager standing next to a row of tall corn.

Ali was in a classroom, and university students were piling in. "Mom, I have to teach a class in a few minutes. Can you stay and talk after?"

Helen tapped the upper corner of the picture. "What's that light?" She pulled away, her lips scrunched up. "I mean, seriously. I notice that light every time I look at the picture. As you know, they never found your father, and you've been telling me about these strange Anunnaki that you've been translating from those tablets. Do you think they took him? Do you think that's where he went?"

Ali peered closer and furrowed her brow. The light Helen pointed to was a round orb that shone brightly. Ali didn't know what it was at the time and figured her mom was grasping at straws, trying to find reasons to keep her missing husband alive.

Ali knew what that orb was now.

It was a ship, one she had never seen before. From the air, it was clear it watched, perhaps scouting her father and her as well.

She shook her head, getting her mind straight. Memories were distracting, and she had a mission to get to Mount Gabriel. She couldn't let anything stand in her way.

She resumed her stroll down the corridor, sniffing the aromas that called to her from the cafeteria just around the corner.

She'd been searching for Daf, and thought maybe she'd been eating dinner.

She walked into the crowded cafeteria and looked around.

"Ali?" William waved his hand. "Over here."

He sat at a table, eating some type of mash.

Ali's stomach growled, and for some reason, her heart fluttered. The guy was handsome, but she had no time to flirt.

She took a step forward and hesitated, her heart skipping a beat. Daf scooted next to him, chomping, her arm a little too close to William's.

Daf set her hand on William's forearm playfully, and then acted like she didn't mean to and set it beside William's arm, still touching.

Ali frowned. *Nice touch, Daf. Guild dammit, I'm jealous?*

She almost laughed. Jealousy didn't normally run through her veins, but something about William and Daf sitting next to each other disturbed her.

She feigned a smile and walked toward William.

"There she is," said someone at a table she walked by, laughter coming from the area a moment later.

She stopped and turned. Hank's bloodshot eyes stared at her, his teeth dotted with specs of food.

"A seat, my love?" He patted an empty chair next to him at a table full of techs.

"I have other plans, Hank. We've already talked about this crap, haven't we?" She took a step away from the table, and a hand smacked her rump.

Ali spun to see a wide-eyed Hank and her fist coming down hard on his face, knocking him sideways.

His elbow hit his plate, shattering it across the floor, the noise echoing loudly throughout the cafeteria, and silencing the room.

She grabbed Hank by his greasy hair and slammed his face onto the tabletop. She held it there, then bent over and whispered into his ear, "This is your last warning, techie. You try this again, and I promise the results will be worse."

Continuing to hold his hair, she stood erect and glared at the other techs. "You like how Hank treats the ladies?" She pointed a finger at one of them. "If I ever, and I mean *ever*, see any of you treat a woman like he did, I'll give you the same experience I just gave him, got it?"

They nodded their heads in stunned silence.

She released her grip, and Hank lifted his bloody face. He wiped his nose, blood streaming from his nostrils and dripping off his chin. He rose, his legs wobbly, and waddled out of the cafeteria.

A pang of guilt hit her. Yeah, he deserved it by invading her space, but she'd punished him harshly, maybe too harshly. Hopefully, he was headed to medical, and while he was there, they could give him a new attitude, so she didn't have to go through this mess again.

A hand touched her back. She spun, her hands in fists, ready to strike anyone who dared confront her.

Crap.

She dropped her arms. It was Diana.

She grabbed Ali's wrists, squeezing tightly, her voice quiet and sharp. "What is going on here?"

Ali yanked her arms away and hurried toward the cafeteria doors. They whooshed open, and she exited, entering the corridor.

Diana charged after her. "You do not turn your back on a superior, especially when questioned."

Ali spun and planted her feet. "Superior?" She snorted. Talking to her mother, let alone a superior like this, would get anyone else a year in jail, but she didn't care. She'd had enough. "Superiors teach respect, which is something you haven't taught your techs."

"Do I have to ban you from the cafeteria, too?"

Ali took a charging step forward, her index finger pointing toward the ground. "'Too?' What do you mean by 'too?'"

Diana stood her ground, her voice monotone, her face stern. "You are forbidden to enter Tech Quarters."

"Why? What are you so scared of?"

"You know what you were doing." Diana tipped her head, her face flushing red. There was a glint in her eyes as if she knew what Ali was uncovering.

Diana didn't say anything about staying out of the docking bay where Wrench was working a mech with missile turrets and guns for arms.

Maybe she still didn't know about the mech, but Ali wasn't going to press her luck and accidentally clue her in.

Instead, Ali turned, heading toward her sleeping quarters. There, she could lock the door and shut Diana out.

"Stop," said Diana.

Ali continued forward.

"I have ordered you to stop, and you are required by Star Guild Law to do so."

Ali halted with a grunt. She twisted around, her heart burning. She walked slowly toward Diana, pointing a finger against her chest. "If you think you're going to use Star Guild law on me—"

Diana gently pushed Ali's finger down, her face softening. "Look, I'm on your side. If I wasn't, you'd have been thrown in the brig by now. I'm not trying to make you suffer like you think I am. You always seem to forget that—"

"You're on my side? I haven't seen you in I don't know how long and you're suddenly on my side? I know which side you picked."

Diana went rigid. "What do you mean by which *side* I picked? I disobeyed a direct order and risked my life to come down to Eos to save you."

Ali didn't care what order she disobeyed or if it was a direct order or not. "Tell me the truth, once and for all. Who is my *real* mother?"

Diana stood still like a stone warrior studying her opponent. She didn't flinch or budge as if what Ali said wasn't a surprise to her. Perhaps she'd somehow seen the conversation Ali had with S. "It's not what you think. *They* want me to ki—" She stopped.

Ali's face hardened, her heart sinking. "They want you to kill me?" She glanced around. "Is that what you were going to say?" She shook her head furiously. "No, skip that question. Let's get to the bones of the matter, *Diana.* Who are *they?*"

Diana straightened in her posture and lifted her chin. "You have to realize I'm trying my damndest to keep you alive, so you better shape up and obey."

Ali felt her pulse rising. "So, *they,* whoever *they* are, want me dead. Were you sent to kill me rather than save me?"

Ali's lips began quivering uncontrollably. It *was* true. Not only did *they* order Diana to kill her, but Diana also wasn't her mother. Diana had known it, and now Ali did too.

Diana looked away, then back at Ali. "I do care for you. That is why I am keeping you alive."

A tear trailed down Ali's cheek. "You never showed me an ounce of love." She thrust her fists by her side. "And you're not stopping me from lifting this shroud you assholes forced on me. I'm going to find the entire Guild'n truth."

Diana lowered her head, slowly shaking it. She touched the silver comm band on her shoulder. "Guards, please come to the corridor adjacent to the cafeteria. We have a situation."

Ali wiped a tear and let out an exhale. If she wanted to stay out of the brig, she needed to do what Diana asked. At least, she had to *act* subordinate. "Okay, okay. I'll stay in my room and find some other crap to do."

Diana cocked her head to the side. "I'll be watching you. Last warning." She walked past her, touching her comm band and calling off the guards.

Ali watched her disappear around the corner.

She eyed the ceiling and sniffed the nice cafeteria smells, her stomach growling, and knowing she'd have to skip dinner.

She walked toward her sleeping quarters so she could gather herself, wait a couple of hours, and then head to Mount Gabriel tonight.

44

KODA

Starbase Matrona

Koda leaned his back against a tree, his legs crossed.

He was just outside the infirmary and let his thoughts drift as he peeled an orange.

He was the Prime Overseer of Sphere Nine, the youngest Prime Overseer in the history of the starbase.

He didn't know if all the Spheres were rioting, on lockdown, or in pieces, and it scared him. He wanted the people safe and to understand the situation to be prepared for any possible future attacks. He needed to be on the holochannels to let the starbase know, step by step, and day by day, every update he could give them.

He glanced down at his hand. It was empty, but the handgrip from the gun he held a few days ago remained fresh in his palm.

Was it two days ago? Maybe just one?

He shook his head and rubbed his eyes. Everything else was becoming a blur, but he remembered he had held a gun.

At the time, he was ready to blast anyone trying to get into the hospital room he and Devon, plus the *Brigantia* and *Taranis* Guard were in.

To his luck, or perhaps to the enemy's luck, no one barged into the room, guns blazing.

"Can I sit next to you?"

Koda glanced upward to see Devon glaring down at him, his eyebrows high.

The kid looked as if the trauma from the last few days haunted him. He'd been through a lot, just as Koda had, and much of it together.

Koda patted the ground. "Sure. What's on your mind?"

Devon sat next to him. "How do you know something is on my mind?"

"It doesn't take a photon scientist to see it in your eyes, Devon."

Devon sighed. "Yeah, it's just…well, there's this woman I can't seem to find, and I need to know—"

Devon.

Koda lurched forward, accidentally slapping Devon's chest. A female voice rang through his mind, calling for Devon.

He shook his head, pressing on his ears with his hands. "Did you hear that?"

Devon scrunched his nose. "Hear what?"

"Nothing." The events in the past week must have set his mind on overdrive.

Koda patted Devon's knee. "How is your body holding up? The Suficell Pods are healing me up quickly."

Devon nodded. "Yeah. Me too." He looked down, drawing a smiley face with a rose next to it in the dirt.

"Whoa," said Koda. "Are you a Robert Rose fan?"

Robert Rose was the most decorated and anonymous artist on the starbase. No one knew who the artist really was, but the guy was brilliant. Some said Robert could foretell the future and painted the prophecies in his art, and Devon had just drawn the signature Robert signed on his art perfectly.

Devon nodded. "I like Robert a lot. But Robert is a pair of people, not just one. A man draws and paints, and the woman is the teller of truths."

Koda showed his palms. "Teller of truths?"

"You know, the prophecies."

"How would you know this? No one knows a thing about Robert, other than he's the greatest artist of our time."

Devon shrugged. "Anyway, about that woman. Is there a way to—"

Devon.

Koda pushed up to a standing position, his hands on his hips. "You can't tell me you didn't hear that?" He looked around the tree he'd been leaning against. No one was there, except a vast pond and more trees.

Koda threw his hands up. "Who said that?" He glanced at Devon, wondering if the guy was some type of ventriloquist.

Devon shrugged. "Said what?"

Koda glanced to his left and right. Several guardsmen stood at their posts. None were women.

"What are you hearing?" asked Devon.

"Your name." Koda tapped his head. "In my mind, and it sounds like it's coming from someone standing right next to me."

Devon pointed at his chest. "You hear my name?"

A man in *Brigantia* fatigues walked by, carrying a loaf of bread. Koda hailed to him. "Sir?"

The guard stopped. "Yes?"

"Did you hear someone call his name?" Koda gestured toward Devon.

"I don't know his name, sir."

Koda scratched his temple, then lowered his voice, making it strong like the guard's to gain rapport, a stupid politician trick. "It's Devon."

The man shook his head. "No. Sorry."

Koda swept the air with a wave of his hand. "Move along, soldier."

The guard gave him an odd look and went on his way.

Devon.

Koda jumped, spinning in a circle, looking for the source of the voice. Was this a practical joke the Guards were playing on him? "What?"

Devon stood and touched Koda's shoulder. "Maybe we should get you back in an infirmary room so you can rest for a bit?"

Devon.

The voice was louder.

Koda pulled the back of his hair. "What is it?"

The nearby guards turned, tilting their heads in inquiry. Koda waved them off. "At ease." They all gave him an odd look and faced back around, except for one.

Sergeant Manning.

Manning spoke into his shoulder band comm device and strolled over to Koda and Devon. "What seems to be the issue?"

Koda's hands began to shake. "Sorry, no issue."

Manning eyed Devon and then Koda, clearly not buying it. "Well, okay. If there isn't an issue, I do have a question for you two, if you have time?"

"Sure," Devon said.

Koda shot him a look, not wanting to deal with anything but the voice screaming in his head.

Manning crossed his arms. "The papers you had in your hand when we found you the other day? Why were they so important?"

Koda's eyebrows rose. "You don't know?"

Manning shook his head. "That's why I'm asking."

Koda grimaced, his head down, his finger jostling his ear.

"Seriously, are you okay?" asked Manning.

"Yeah, why?" Koda looked away. "I'm fine." He stood straight, remembering how tough he'd had to be in Star Guild Academy all those years ago to get respect.

"Sir," said Manning. "If you need to get rest, you can do so. We won't think less of you."

Koda exhaled loudly. "Yes, I'm fine. Totally fine. I couldn't be better. I was trained for this *stuff*, just like you."

Manning crossed his arms. "I see. You're a tough guy. I get it." He pointed at his fellow Guardsmen. "Is that why I saw you ordering my men around?" He winked, leaned closer to Koda, and whispered, "Right now, my friends over there think it's funny, but if you keep trying to boss them around like you've been doing these last couple of minutes, the comic relief isn't going to last much longer. Catch my drift?"

Koda's face softened. "Yeah, yeah."

Manning continued, "We all thought you two were tough guys when you did what you needed to do by leaping out of that building and making it to the forest alive. The two of you don't need to prove anything to us after pulling that stunt."

Devon nodded. "Thanks."

Koda nodded as well.

"Good. Now, about those papers?"

Koda motioned toward Devon. "He can tell you."

"Um...well...how do I say this..." Devon looked at the partially eaten orange in his hand as if it was going to somehow advise him. "Those papers are the reason we jumped out of the building. I had hacked into Prime Director Zim Noki's HDC through the holonet. I translated and transcribed what I thought was junk data going across the holowaves, and during the process, I found something called *The Kill-Off*. After I decoded the message, Savanna and I read—"

"Stop," interrupted Manning. "All I want to know is, what did it say?"

"That batrachotoxin would be released into our air and water supply within two weeks' time, but a message was sent out three days before we found it and it's been several days since, so, when counting..." he paused, counting on his fingers, "...we have seven days before they release batrachotoxin into the population."

"What is it?"

"A nasty toxin."

Manning jerked back. "You've got to be screwing with me."

"I wish," said Koda.

Manning ground the heel of his boot into the grassy moss. "Well, why not? I guess that'd be as good a way as any to kill us." He moved his hand to his holstered pistol, and then let his hand fall. "What I'd do to have Zim alone in a room."

Devon ran his hands through his hair and cleared his throat. "But we don't have an antidote. It's a deadly toxin, and I don't know where to start looking for a cure, or if one even exists."

"We won't die like this, you two. We'll survive. You both or someone else will find an antidote," said Manning.

Devon's shoulders slumped. "They've done this before, Manning."

"Poisoned us?"

"No." Devon shrugged. "Well, not that I know of, but according to the documents, this isn't the first time they've killed humans en masse."

"Like, in the past?" Manning shook his head. "I don't remember reading anything about that at the academy."

I have the antidote.

"You have what?" Koda stared at Manning intently, trying to determine how his voice could have changed from male to female.

Koda rubbed his temple hard. That voice couldn't have come from Manning.

Was he going insane?

Manning rested his hand on Koda's shoulder. "Are you okay?"

Koda shook his head, his face twisted in confusion. "I don't know. I'm hearing things."

Please escort me to Admiral Lutz, said the female voice.

"Where?" Koda looked around, trying to locate the source of the voice.

"What?" asked Manning and Devon at the same time.

Biosphere, Door One, and bring some Brigantia *Guards with you.*

"Dammit," yelled Koda, his face reddening. "I'm hearing a female voice in my head. She's telling me she has the antidote and wants me to—"

"Stop." Devon put his hand up. "Tell her to send an image to you."

Koda rubbed the back of his sweaty neck. "An image?"

Devon nodded frantically. "Yes, just do it. Close your eyes and ask for an image."

Maybe Devon knew a trick to stop this insanity. Koda closed his eyes and asked for an image. A rose popped in his head, one so bright he had to open his eyes.

"What did you see?" questioned Devon.

"I…uh…a rose?"

Wide-eyed, Devon almost tripped over his own feet, his face beaming with a smile. "I know who it is."

"Who?" Manning stood and grabbed Devon's shoulders. "Now, you're both freaking me out, man."

Devon frantically shook his head and pointed at his forehead. "No, you don't understand. Her voice is usually in my head when she's looking for me, but for some reason I'm blocked, maybe? She's getting through to me via Koda."

Koda narrowed his eyes. Now Devon had clearly joined him in the insane club. "What?"

"A woman I know can do things like that." He was obviously embarrassed. "What else did she say?"

Koda blinked several times, doing his best to remember. "She said biosphere door one, and she has the antidote."

Devon turned and rushed toward the biosphere forest, yelling over his shoulder. "We have to get to her. She will save us."

Manning and Koda gave each other a blank expression. Devon ran back in their direction, and grabbed Manning's arm, pulling him toward the biosphere forest and in the direction that led to door one.

Manning tapped his shoulder band. "*Brigantia* Guard Team Nine, I need you stat." He glared at Devon and pulled his hand free. "You better not be crazy, or my guys will hang me for this."

They rushed forward, and Koda hurried after them, wondering how a woman could possibly send her voice to his mind. "The attack, the toxin, and now this?"

He jumped over a fern and saw a group of *Brigantia* Guard, Team Nine, heading their way, and then veering off toward Manning.

45

EDEN

Orbiting Eos—Adarta Sector, Orion Spur

Eden stared through *Swift's* viewing screen in awe of the beautiful golden planet before her, its aura grabbing her and beckoning, seducing her to come and land on its ebb-filled surface.

She smiled and held in a tear. "I'm back," she whispered to herself. Though it wasn't Starbase Matrona, she considered Eos her second home.

She had left this planet, this sector, not in death, but by surviving miraculously, thanks to the Space Templars.

Her heart shifted and became heavy. She searched the vidscreen, eyeing the world before her and the space around Eos.

Death hovered everywhere.

Ships' armor floated in Eos' orbit, scorched from a quick burn, and then a quick freeze.

Broken cannon barrels dotted the area, lit up like small stars from the sun's shine as if the cosmos was showing Eden the failure of Star Guild to protect the sector.

A knot formed in her throat. She didn't know what else to do or how to react to the bleak emptiness in front of her.

A loud beep sounded on the bridge.

She flinched, then twisted around.

Skye stood on the landing, studying the vidscreen. His eyes moved to hers, somehow instantly calming her with his gentle gaze. "We have scavengers. I need you to change the view to the upper left quadrant and zoom in."

As you command, Swift replied.

A box materialized on the screen in the upper left quadrant and zoomed in.

A large ship, its wings extended like a bird with its tips pointed upward, hovered in the distance in front of them. It had an orange underbelly that protruded like a pregnant woman and a red, flat-top roof that extended a quarter of a starship's length.

The craft was long and thin.

It sucked up a chunk of floating metal into its belly, perhaps a piece from a destroyed Thunderbird.

A soft finger touched Eden's forearm. It was Nyx, her eyes sparkling, intensifying her stare. "They're hailing us." Nyx turned and gave a nod to a bluish-cat like humanoid, a Sirian, sitting at a station.

The big cat returned the nod, pressed a button, and glared at the screen. "The scavenger's captain is on the screen."

Eden gave the Sirian a double-take. He had spoken without moving his lips.

She blinked several times and then turned her attention to the screen. A human with narrow, steely blue eyes, a long face, and blonde hair stared back at her. He wore a silver robe with a tight-fitting collar accompanied with a round, white insignia with three blue dots on the front of the robe.

He held a scowl. "I…Y'taul an…do…du...here. Who mi...u be?" His lips didn't move in concordance with his speech, as if he had some type of language translator, one that didn't work very well.

He closed his eyes and bowed his head. Another man came into view. He had similar features and wore an identical robe. He whispered in Y'taul's ear, then walked away briskly as if he didn't want to be backhanded by the guy.

Y'taul opened his eyes and swayed side to side. "Your…ship not detected...by...radar. Invisible? What technology...this?" He scratched his chin. "Ship... new design. Where you dwell?"

Skye stepped forward. "We are from Aurora. We are the Space Templars, and if anything, this ship is not new. It is ancient, well beyond your years, and beyond mine."

Y'taul stepped back, his hand coming to his heart. He gave a long, low bow. He tapped his insignia. "The Space Templars are renowned. I am humbled by your presence. I now see you are speaking in the native human tongue. I've adjusted my translator accordingly."

He made a sweeping gesture with his arm. "I know all about the Space Templars. However, I'm baffled by your ship. It's not one I have seen before." He leaned toward the screen and raised a brow. "I can see that it can't take that much damage."

Skye bowed back. "Our ship's name is *Swift*, and I'd suggest you not underestimate her." He motioned to Eden and the crew. "Or me and my crew."

Y'taul scratched his chin a second time. "Interesting. Can we do a trade of some sort?" He clapped both hands together and brought them to his chest. "Perhaps we could trade mono-atomic gold for information about your ship, such as its stealth abilities and how it works?"

"That knowledge is beyond your understanding, Y'taul." Skye walked closer to the screen and stopped next to Eden. "You are in a dangerous sector. I wouldn't be here too long if I were you."

Y'taul innocently waved his arms in the air. "We collect junk, turn it into treasure, and trade. We're harmless."

"I understand," said Skye. "But I suggest you move on until we've deemed this area safe. This is a war zone."

Y'taul stiffened. "I know when I'm safe and when I'm not." He dipped his head. "Farewell."

His image blinked off the screen, switching to a view of Y'taul's ship.

A Thunderbird's broken hull was sucked into the scavenger. Apparently, another treasure for Y'taul.

Skye shook his head. "I've heard about Y'taul. I was told that he was difficult to deal with. The rumors are correct."

Eden shifted in her seat. "Who is Y'taul?" She wasn't getting a good feeling about the guy. She eyed Eos, itching to get planetside and save any survivors if there were any.

"He's a Plearian, but a scavenger of his race. The Plearians are quite advanced, evolved in thought and spirit, but what I've heard of Y'taul is that he's part of a vast scavenger network who aren't that advanced, except in technology. They spend their time collecting and becoming wealthy, their prime pursuit materialistic happiness, I suppose. I don't give them much attention, even though they deal in a lot of illegal activity."

"Illegal? There are space laws?"

Skye tilted his head at her like a teacher to a student who should know these things. "Yes, there are laws in the galaxy. A vast consortium of races came together long ago and agreed upon laws that limit Beings from doing this or that, such as murder, theft, hoarding resources…" he pointed at the debris in front of them, "…wars."

He paused in thought. "Also, there is a higher law governing all Beings. It's a law created by the Divine Spark, known as God, the Great Spirit, or All that Is. I could go on providing the names each culture has invented to describe the divine intelligence that created us all.

"Nonetheless, the laws governing all beings is Universal Law. This law connects us all, because what we think, say, and do has a corresponding effect on others and the entire universe. The Space Templars abide by those laws."

Eden pursed her lips. "Should I know these laws?"

"You know these universal laws. They are endowed in each of us by our Creator." He put his finger up as if he was going to give another long speech. "One such law, the law of non-interference—"

"Wait," interrupted Eden, giving Skye a blank look. "The law of non-interference? I'm glad of it, but you clearly interfered with our race by rescuing me and destroying those pyramid-ships."

Nyx rolled her eyes and sighed. "Your fleet admiral, Shae Lutz, sent out a distress beacon. You should know *that* better than us."

It was true, he did, but that still didn't answer her question. They interfered, regardless of who called upon them.

Eden relaxed. In truth, she didn't care. The Space Templars had saved many of her people.

"With every law, there is an exception," continued Skye. "This exception is if you ask for help, you will receive it. And so we assisted."

A loud beep reverberated across the bridge's walls.

"We detect a nuclear weapon on Y'taul's ship. I suggest crippling the ship and boarding her."

Eden turned. The voice came from a beige furred Sirian.

Skye moved quickly up the stairs, his brow wrinkled. "Hail Y'taul."

Y'taul appeared on the screen, his fist raised. "I will not stop scavenging."

Skye dipped his head. "Good on you, but that's not why we hailed you."

Y'taul calmed and smiled. "So, you have changed your mind. Send us your ship's schematics, and you can have five million units of mono-atomic—"

"That is not what we would like to exchange schematics for, Y'taul."

"Oh?" Y'taul put his hands together in prayer and touched the tips of his fingers to his chin. "Forgive me. Then, what would you like?"

"We will discuss our ship's technology once you hand over the nuclear weapon, a weapon that violates the Plearian Treaty and about fifty other laws." Skye folded his hands in front of him. "Does that sound reasonable to you?"

Y'taul stiffened. "We don't have a nuclear weapon on our ship. I'm sorry, but you're mistaken."

"*Swift's* sensors are never mistaken. Please hand over the nuclear weapon, or we will be forced to take it from you."

Y'taul glared at Skye, his lips straight. He turned and communicated with someone off-screen, then glanced back at Skye. He straightened his robe. "You have my permission to board and look for yourself. You can bring whatever sensors or devices you'd like." He massaged his chin. "But only you."

Skye let out a huff. "Understood. Prepare for boarding."

Eden glanced between Skye and Y'taul. She then eyed Eos, wishing it was Starbase Matrona, where her people were. But Eos' glow reached out and hugged her like a mother to a daughter, asking Eden to land on her, to search her terrain for Eden's people, for any potential survivors.

"I will see you soon," said Y'taul, blinking off the screen, his ship reappearing.

He's actually going to board?

Eden stood, her mind spinning, thinking of a hundred bad ideas about Skye boarding Y'taul's ship.

"You're going alone?" Eden would prefer he'd take a contingent of Sirian and human Marines if they had any.

He winked. "You don't think I can handle myself?"

"They seem hostile. Let me or someone else go with you."

He shook his head. "I'll be fine." He turned to exit the bridge.

Eden grabbed his arm. "I don't trust them."

Skye let out a chuckle. "Neither do I. I would appreciate your company, but you need to lead the bridge. I know I took over just now, but ultimately, *Swift* is your ship."

She quickly let go of his forearm and took a step back. "I don't entirely know what I'm doing on the bridge. I can watch and learn from you."

Hence, she thought, you should stay.

"I trust you." He turned and walked off the bridge, the door shutting behind him.

She backed up, wiping her hands together. *What do I do now?*

The bridge was quiet, and the crew stared at her, most likely wondering what her orders were going to be.

She sat down, her eyes on the screen. She leaned over, talking out of the side of her mouth. "Is he really boarding Y'taul's craft, or was he just bluffing?"

Nyx brought up a hologram of *Swift* from her chair's armrest. It spun slowly, and a golden dot blinked on the starboard side. "You see that? He's in *Swift's* launch bay." She lowered her eyes at Eden, her voice lowering as well, with an air of dismay. "He'll be flying an Aven to board Y'taul's ship."

Nyx either didn't like her, or she was impatient with Eden, not liking Eden's questions and novice approach as a captain on the bridge. "Skye doesn't bluff. He's activated his Aven now and will be heading Y'taul's way soon."

"Oh," said Eden, and rested her chin on her hand. "Bring up the scavenger ship."

Swift displayed the craft on the screen.

Eden leaned in and studied the ship. It floated in space, ignoring the debris field, waiting for Skye to dock.

It tilted and then reset itself, although slightly. Eden caught it. It did it again. And again.

It hadn't done that previously.

"Can *Swift* bring up thermal imaging infrared sensors?"

The vidscreen changed, and Y'taul's ship was a green mess of energy. Except for a rear, starboard booster highlighted in red, along with a bow thruster on the ship's port side.

The heat source, said Swift, is an activated booster on low burn and a port booster, keeping it in a stable floating pattern. If my sensors are correct, they are gearing up to fly as fast as possible, and soon.

Eden squeezed her eyes shut and pinched the bridge of her nose. "In other words, they're letting Skye board, and once he does, they'll take off."

Another booster, this one on the port side, went red along with the thruster near the front, starboard side.

Skye's ship came into view, an orb-shaped Aven, heading toward Y'taul's ship.

Nyx turned to a Sirian. "Get Skye on the comm."

Skye's face appeared on the screen. "Yes?"

Nyx stood. "Skye, they are planning on taking you hostage. Their engines are on, readying to take off the moment you board."

Skye huffed. "Of course, they would." He turned away, shaking his head. "I can't turn around. I don't know what they'll do with the nuclear device. I have to neutralize it."

Nyx went rigid, her hands curling in fists by her sides. "You're risking your life." She pointed at Eden. "That greenie is right. You need more of us to board with you."

"Wait," said Skye, studying his instrumentation and then his HDC screen. "I don't think they are waiting for me. In fact, I think they used me as a diversion."

Afterburn expelled from Y'taul's ship, and his craft blasted forward, a streak of light zipping by *Swift's* view screen, heading for Eos.

An alarm rang out on the bridge. Nyx sat hard, eyeing the viewscreen, her eyes on Eos. "We have incoming."

"Get Skye back on *Swift*," yelled Eden, her fingers squeezing the armrests. "And target those missiles."

A flash of light burst through the atmosphere, and then another, heading for *Swift.*

Swift adjusted its position quickly. Cursors surrounded the missiles and blinked when the missiles came in range.

"Fire," ordered Eden.

The craft vibrated as cannon fire littered space. An explosion went off, and then a second, and a third.

"Skye is on board," said a Sirian.

"Excellent," said Eden. "Let's—"

"*Swift*, evasive maneuvers," interrupted Nyx, her eyes narrow, focusing on the screen. "Now, find the scavenger ship."

On the screen now, said Swift.

"Pursue," ordered Nyx.

Swift blasted forward like a bat out of hell, speeding toward Y'taul's smaller ship, and was on its tail within seconds.

Eden's mouth widened. "Holy..."

This ship was fast. Almost too fast.

They soared through Eos' atmosphere, and *Swift* jerked to the side as streams of red tracer fire flew by, barely missing them.

Swift dodged again, avoiding a large cannon burst near them, the shots clearly coming from Eos' surface.

The vidscreen flashed red, and the bridge beeped as many sounds as it could.

Eden's eyes widened, and she pressed her back against the chair. "Oh, no."

Missiles, red tracer fire, and cannon slugs in the thousands were heading their way.

46

ZIM

Starbase Matrona

A rope secured loosely around Zim's neck held a burlap sack on his head. The burlap's coarse weave trapped the moisture from his breath, blinding him from everything but small rays of the hallway's light poking through the weave.

He was being led through the capitol building. Fury burned his veins, and his mind was dizzy with confusion. Days ago, he'd been in charge of Starbase Matrona, manipulating the people like puppets in a play, and now Sabra was in charge of him.

He didn't like Sabra.

He stopped. "Where are we going?"

A gun's muzzle pushed against his back. "Move."

The voice was gruff. Male.

He stepped forward and down the hall, wanting to kick his leg backward and hit the male where it counted.

He also didn't want a bullet in his back. He kept moving, and a hand gripped his elbow to steer him around a corner.

Zim knew the capitol building like the back of his hand, having been the Prime Director and practically living in it for over thirty years. He knew exactly where they were going, the parking garage. He didn't know the final destination, though, and he didn't like not knowing. It was like an ice pick jabbing at his insides.

Entering the parking garage, the sound of rumbling engines filled the air. "Why are we here?" He curled his fingers into a fist. "And where are we going?"

A door slid open in front, and a sharp shove to his back had him tumbling forward and landing on his side. He let out a grunt when he hit the ground.

Someone grasped his feet and shoved his feet and legs toward his body.

He was now in a fetal position.

"Dammit, what's going on?"

The door slid shut and clicked loudly. Locked.

Even though he knew the capitol building like the back of his hand, driving through the city was different. Chaotic, in fact.

After a while, Zim couldn't remember the many turns and lost his mental map.

The hovervan abruptly stopped, and the door slid open. "Out," said the same male voice that led him out of the capitol building.

Hands grabbed his arms and legs, pulling him out of the van and to his feet. They pushed him forward and up several steps into another building.

They halted, making Zim stay in one spot.

A bright light flashed on through the burlap sack. "Well, for galaxy's sakes, where am I?" He went to lift his hands, and they tugged against the cuffs.

A heavy hand landed on his shoulder and shoved him into a chair. They uncuffed him, and he brought his hands up to massage his wrists when they pulled his hands and arms down and strapped them to the chair.

He stiffened, flexing his muscles, and tried to pull away. He barely budged. "This is nuts. Let me go."

They loosened the rope around his neck and pulled the sack off his head. He squinted from the bright light. "Where the hell am I?"

"You're here to deliver a speech to the entire starbase."

He shifted his eyes to the shadow in front of him, waiting for his vision to adjust. "Sabra?"

She leaned forward. "Dim the light."

The lights dimmed. In front of him sat Sabra.

"I didn't agree to this."

Sabra smiled. "Just speak the truth. Tell the starbase exactly who you are, what you're here to do, and name your superior."

He shook his head. Screw her. "You're not getting your way on this." Enlil would torture him until Zim couldn't take it anymore, and then Enlil would wait a while, and torture him some more. "I'm not saying anything."

He gazed around the room. Leafy vines curled around the walls, and glow lights lined the edge of the ceilings. "I'm in Savanna Leven's meeting room, Sphere 6. Why am I here?"

Sabra's tone rose, and her voice was sharp. "Because Savanna and Koda were the only Overseers you couldn't buy. We're safe here, and more people in *this* Sphere despise you than fear you. Here, we'll be able to broadcast, and you can explain to Star Guild and the starbase why you had Savanna killed."

Zim held back his shock, but not his wicked smile. "So, she *is* dead."

"You didn't know?"

"I tried to kill her and her friend, but they went missing after the attempt. I'm glad to hear my efforts didn't fail after all."

Sabra crossed her legs. "You couldn't wait to kill her with the rest of the population when you released the toxin?"

Zim scanned the room, glad he could finally see everything. "I don't have free reign on who I can get rid of. It's your brother's call. Get a hold of him if you want to complain."

He continued to look around.

The men who had captured him by gunpoint in his office had their bandana's off. They were the same size as the men in his office, who were all smaller than him.

If they untied him, he'd rip them apart, and right now, that was all he wanted.

In the corner, Sabra sat on a couch, and several holocams hovered around him. He was going to be recorded if he wasn't already.

He stretched his neck to the side. A loud popping sound echoed in the room. "What the ebb are you doing, Sabra? You've broken more laws than I can count, and I can't wait until Enlil has you and your servants for lunch."

She narrowed her eyes. "Why did you kill Savanna?"

"You know what, Sabra? Just kill me. Get it over with because you're not going to get a damn bit of information from me."

Sabra gave a man in the corner of the room a nod. She turned her eyes toward Zim's. "But killing you would deny you a valuable soul lesson, hard-earned by your evil deeds. Perhaps it's time for you to examine your conscience just a bit?" She signaled to one of the men in the room. He walked over to a table against the back wall and picked up a gold helmet.

It was laced with clear quartz crystal and shimmered when it caught the light.

Zim furrowed his brow. "What is that?"

Sabra winked. "It is the Crown of Accountability. It was created eons ago to ensure those who wanted to rule would do so for the right reasons."

Zim pulled back, sucking in a big breath of air. "That's a myth." The Crown of Accountability, so the legend went, was a crown activated only by an anointed one, someone of the royal bloodline. When placed on a person's head, they could only speak the truth, no matter how harsh.

To Zim, the idea was absurd, but as he stared at the object that fit its description perfectly, he thought there might be something to the myth.

Sabra took the crown and slipped it onto Zim's head, covering his entire head and face, except his nose down to his chin.

A zap went through Zim's body, and he bolted up straight, his posture perfect. A tingling went down his spine and to his sacrum, and he instantly relaxed, though keeping his posture erect.

He let out an easy breath.

He felt good like he'd just taken a nice, long shower after a hard day on the job.

Sabra sat down on the couch. "Why did you kill Savanna Levens?"

Zim almost laughed. She wasn't going to get the answer, no matter how good this crown made him feel. "In truth, I don't know who killed her because it wasn't with my hands." Wait, why was he speaking? Why were these words coming out of his mouth? He tightened his body, and the crown sent another sensation down his spine. He relaxed again. "I was ordered to kill her because she broke into my HDC and decoded *The Kill-Off.*"

"What's The Kill-Off?"

She knew damn well all the information about The Kill-Off, but she was recording him to get this information out to the public.

He grunted and moved in his chair, doing his best to release himself from the restraints. Not having any luck, he pushed down his answer and fought every inch of the truth trying to spray out of his mouth.

A memory surfaced of a time he held a gun to a woman's head and told her to obey. If she didn't, not only would she die, but so would everyone she loved, even Fleet Admiral Shae Lutz.

He'd given her no choice, and in the interview with Lyle Gellers, she and Stan did all he asked, except when she didn't.

He punished her with a few blows to the stomach after the interview. He would have killed her had she not just been on the holochannels. The population would suspect something odd, and he couldn't afford any more riots.

A pain ran across his heart as he remembered, and the helplessness and anger she felt toward him stamped into his chest.

He leaned over as the agonizing sensation of her fear encompassed him.

What was this crown doing?

He shook the feeling off as another memory surfaced, one of Savanna Levens. She was running, her chest heaving in and out, knowing she didn't have much left in her. She was in an alleyway, and a man grabbed him...no...grabbed her.

He was in her body? He was experiencing what she had experienced? How?

A gun lifted to her head. It was dark out, but she could see the man's face. Zim reeled back. It was Payson? He hadn't ordered Payson to kill her. In fact, Payson was supposed to be underground, not released until he gave the order.

He never gave that order.

A blast went off, and every ounce of what Savanna tried to expose and tried to prevent from happening rushed through her, and then into Zim. He felt all of the sorrow that she failed.

She gasped for her breath, for her heart to keep fighting, to survive the bullet wound Payson had sent into her, and the same sensation ran up and down Zim.

He let out a scream, and perspiration now dotted every millimeter of his body. He couldn't take it anymore.

Another memory surfaced, and deep down, he knew these memories could go on forever.

He lurched back. "Okay, I'll talk."

"The Kill-Off, Zim." Sabra cupped her hands over her knee. "To help you out a little, I'll explain it. In five days' time, with a push of a button, you are going to send batrachotoxin across the entire starbase complex. What exactly is that?" She stood and waved a hand over the golden helmet.

Zim relaxed. Whatever Sabra had just done, felt good. "It's a toxin. Once the water and air systems are completely repaired, we're turning off the filtration system and releasing the batrachotoxin over the entire starbase. It kills quickly, and everyone who tastes it or inhales it will die. Any that somehow survive will be found and killed by gunshot."

Sabra again waved her hand over the crown.

He relaxed more.

"Who is your superior?"

He sat straighter. "The Monarch."

"What is the name of the Monarch, and where can he be found? Where is this Monarch's base of operations?"

Zim shook his head, grimacing. He wasn't going to give up Enlil. That would be suicide.

"Speak."

A sharp stabbing sensation, like a spear through his eye, penetrated his skull.

He screeched, his fists clenching as spittle shot from his mouth. His muscles spasmed, and he gritted his teeth.

The agony ceased just as quickly as it came, and he took a huge gulp of air.

"Tell me the truth," said Sabra.

Zim shook his head, and another wave of hell washed over him. He yelled, stuffing the truth as far as he could, and bit his lip.

Sweat dripped from his nose, over his lips and the floor. He began convulsing, his body shaking. "I…can't tell…you…or…I die."

A third wave hit him, and he screamed again as his eyes rolled to the back of his head. He no longer cared about luxuries and bonuses for successfully committing genocide on the humans. He cared about nothing but a quick, painless death to rid him of this torture.

He couldn't take it anymore.

Then it stopped.

Sabra nodded at a short man standing next to her. He grabbed a bucket from the floor and tossed the contents at Zim.

Ice water. It stung, and Zim tensed as the water slid down his face and his body, washing away the slobber drooling from his lips.

The holocams were recording him, and he no doubt looked like a fool, but the water eased his pain, and when Sabra waved her hand above his head again, he relaxed.

Silence filled the room.

Sabra broke it. "We've been recording you for the last two days. Everything. Every word you said against the human race, and every misdeed we caught, whether it be documents you signed in secret and rushed through the governance or your personal guard you lent to Captain Stan Jenkyns to kill Admiral Shae Lutz in the infirmary."

Zim jerked his head up and glared at Sabra. "I didn't send Payson and his team with Stan. I never did that. They aren't supposed to be let out from their lower levels in the starbase unless something terrible has happened, such as the toxin not being let out properly or it being stopped from releasing."

"So, they were ordered by someone else?"

Zim looked down. "No. Neither the Monarch nor I sent them an order." He wanted to cross his arms, but the restraints held them at bay. "Payson and his team have gone rogue."

"Then we'll pursue them and stop them," said Sabra. She motioned to another human standing near a door. "Get the Space Templars."

The man dipped his head and pressed on the control panel next to the door. The door opened, and he rushed down the hall.

Sabra ran her finger over her neck. "Turn the cameras off." She leaned forward. "Enki, the Space Templars and I have plans for you. If you cooperate."

"Doesn't seem like I have a choice." Since the crown prevented him from lying, he was stuck between a rock and a hard place. When, or if, Sabra planned to release this video to the public over the vid channels, if she hadn't already, he'd be done as a politician and most likely soon dead by Enlil's assassins.

Somehow, he had to get to Enlil and let him know what had happened, and that none of this was his plan or desire. Perhaps Enlil would know about the Crown of Accountability, and he'd just give him a slap on the wrist.

He rolled his eyes. It was Enlil. He'd strangle Zim to death. That's how the guy worked. He was dead one way or the other. His only chance was with Sabra, and how he loathed that option, but there was no other choice. "When do I go public?"

"Turn on the holodisplay."

A large man walked to an HDC against a wall and flipped a switch. The screen materialized, and on the screen was Zim talking with Sabra. They were in his office, and their conversation from the other day streamed across the screen.

Zim shifted in his seat. "Why am I seeing this?"

"This is the first phase, Zim. The second phase will be a public apology from you, in addition to other things. The third phase is, well, it's not here yet."

"What do you mean, 'the first phase?'"

"The first phase consists of our conversations mixed with some of your conversations we specifically selected and recorded, all telling the truth one way or another. Next—"

"What do you mean?"

A wicked smile formed on Sabra's face. "I mean to say everything you've said today, and since you've been with me, will be showing or is showing on the vid channels."

"Now? This minute?"

"Yes, as of fifteen minutes ago, we started streaming. Now, we're going to tell more truth." She steepled her fingers. "Get ready for the next question."

47

KODA

Starbase Matrona

Koda ran around a tree, his feet pounding against the forest floor, dirt pressing downward at every step.

Guards were behind him, keeping with him step by step. They were trusting Devon to find someone they didn't know, someone he didn't know, and someone who spoke to him in his mind.

Impossible.

Manning's rifle muzzle came into view, and Koda watched as Devon's eyes grew bigger.

Koda grew up an athlete and enjoyed the rush of a run, his adrenaline peeking.

Devon's breaths came heavy, obviously as far from an athlete as possible. "I feel her."

Manning kept his eyes forward. "What was that?"

"Nothing."

Koda heard him. He felt her? What did he mean by that? He jabbed Devon's arm with his elbow, getting his attention as they trekked quickly through the forest. "You feel her?"

Devon grimaced, not wanting to explain, but he did. "It's a strange feeling, man. I know it sounds strange, but I feel her...you know...a pulling." He paused and took several heavy breaths. "The only thing I can compare it to is a gravitational pull that slowly turns friction hot the closer I am to her." He shook his head. "Nah, I'm not describing it correctly."

Koda glanced over his shoulder at the *Brigantia* Guard close on their heels, following Devon. "Okay, I think I understand, but who is this woman?"

"Naveya."

"Who?"

"The other part of Robert Rose. Robert is the artist. Rose is the futurist, the prophet, the seer."

Koda blinked several times as he jumped over a shrub.

Devon took a quick left, sidestepping a downed branch. "This way."

Koda planted his foot and pushed off, shifting to the left and jumping over a rock and landing in a puddle of dirty water.

A beep sounded on Manning's wrist. "Devon, stop."

Devon skidded to a halt. He leaned over, breathing quickly, his face flush.

Koda halted next to him, his hand on Devon's back. "Breath slowly. Calm that body of yours."

Devon put his hand on his stomach. "It's coming from my solar plexus, my gut. I can feel her, we're getting closer. We need to keep going."

"No, we're staying here for a moment. Don't move." Manning glanced over his shoulder at a soldier. "Lance, you got a hit on that?"

Lance walked forward, staring at a rectangular device in his hand. A holovid projected a map of the biosphere a few millimeters from the device, and several red dots blinked wildly. "Someone tripped the wire we set in this vicinity." He shook his head, staring intently at the map. "I see a handful of signatures." He looked at Manning. "Are any of the *Brigantia* or *Taranis* Guard on patrol over there?"

"If there was, the tripwire's laser wouldn't be live," said Manning.

The little Koda knew about security systems and tripwires when something or someone interrupted a tripwire's laser beam, the beam stopped sending to the receiver for a mere second, changing the voltage output. A change would be sensed, and the system would bounce back a warning signal.

Apparently, several people had just tripped the wire.

Devon back peddled, his lips downturned. Koda could tell he didn't want to be involved in another firefight.

Manning held out a pistol, eyeing Devon, then Koda. He handed it to Koda. "Take it."

Koda grabbed it and held it by his side, his fingers curled around the handgrip.

Manning motioned for Lance and a few others to spread out to his left and motioned for several soldiers to his right. He slowed his pace and leaned up against a tree, his eyes narrowed, his rifle butted up against the crease between his chest and shoulder and aimed his weapon.

Koda crouched as his eyes searched the area, less for Naveya and more for the Matrona Guard if that was who tripped the wire.

Devon crouched next to him, his face pale.

Lance pointed toward a swath of trees. "They tripped the wire in that direction."

Manning nodded, and rushed toward another tree, getting low and hugging up against it. He tipped his head to the side a few times, and the rest of the soldiers rushed forward and hid behind cover.

"Devon, back up." Koda slowly moved back toward the infirmary, squeezing his fingers tightly around the gun's grip, Devon following him. He figured the last thing Manning and his troops wanted was for him and Devon to get in the way. Guild, that was the last thing Koda wanted, too.

One false move and a bullet lodged in his neck wouldn't be a good way to go.

It's best if we go back.

A low growl and Koda and Devon stopped. Koda turned and watched Manning advance forward with his men, slowly and cautiously.

Another low growl.

"I know that sound," Devon told Koda. "MiMi?" he whispered loudly, scanning the underbrush.

"Mimi?" asked Koda, his voice hushed.

A small, black and white dog stepped into view, pushing away a thick fern with its nose. It let out a soft whine.

"Is Naveya okay?" said Devon.

MiMi turned quickly, then twisted around to face Devon. She dashed off, then stopped and looked at him again.

Devon's eyebrows drew higher. "Naveya's not okay."

MiMi rushed forward, heading away from Devon.

Devon ran after her, jumping over a fern, and sidestepping a small tree, smacking the branches with his arm.

"What is he doing?" Koda huffed and ran after him, jumping over the fern and down a small decline.

MiMi jumped through more brush and moved right down a dirt path.

Devon followed, and Koda did as well, catching up to Devon as fast as his feet could take him.

A loud crack pierced the air. Gunfire. Then more cracking, and tracers zipped in front of them.

They both slid to a halt, Koda's feet flinging upward and into the air. He landed on his back, and the gun slipped out of his hand.

He picked up the gun and rolled off the path and into the thicket, pulling Devon to the ground. He lay partially on Devon's back to keep him down and covering his own ears from the loud gunfire.

He moved off Devon and crawled deeper into the brush, the soil clinging to his hands, chest, and knees. "Devon, come on."

A bullet whizzed by, scraping off a chunk of bark from a nearby tree.

He covered his head and dropped to the ground, his stomach churning. Devon hugged to the ground next to him.

"Naveya. She's so close."

Koda glanced at Devon and then crawled toward the path. He narrowed his eyes, surveying the area, then stopped. Something moved. A body? He leaned forward, squinting.

Was that a woman, lying against a downed tree?

Devon gasped. "It's her. She needs help. I have to go for it to get her out of the crossfire."

"Not yet. It's not safe. Let Manning deal with the immediate danger."

A handful of dirt exploded in front of Devon and splattered against his face.

He jerked back and wiped his face. He took a deep breath and bolted forward, his arms and legs pumping fast.

Koda reached for him. "No."

Devon jumped over a stump, brushing his hand along the grooved wood, and landed on his feet.

"You idiot." Koda pushed up and ran for him, doing his best to catch him and tackle him to the ground.

"Koda," Manning yelled.

Blood splattered against Koda's face, and his arms flailed outward. He tripped over his feet and landed on his side, tumbling, the gun somehow still in his hand.

He turned to see an open-eyed Matrona Guard staring at him, blood trickling out of the side of his head, lifeless. It was this soldier's blood across Koda's face.

Koda lay on the ground next to him, taking shallow breaths.

Nausea immediately took hold. He'd never seen someone die, at least not like this. Some guards died when he had jumped from Savanna's office, but he'd been in too much pain to notice.

This was a dead body, someone who was just alive a second ago and now wasn't. Yes, he'd been Star Guild academy-trained, but he'd never seen death close up, even during the attack.

Footsteps pounded toward him, getting louder by the moment.

He turned and crawled as fast as he could toward Naveya, swallowing vomit and doing his best to stay focused, to keep the image of a dead man, brains blown out, from his mind.

This woman was important to Devon, and they were almost to her. He craned his neck and saw Devon bear crawl past him.

Koda picked up his pace, then got to his feet as more fire echoed across the biosphere.

She was only a few meters in front of them, her eyes closed and her body curled into a ball. She wore rags, like a homeless person, though a hood covered her head.

She opened her eyes and thrust her hand toward Koda and Devon, her jaw clenched. Energy, similar to wind, swept around his feet and made them ten times as heavy.

He tripped and slid across the ground. "What the hell?" Devon fell as well.

Tracers flew a meter above them, sinking into a tree.

He went to move, but couldn't, as if a hundred pounds were sitting on each of his arms and legs.

Am I paralyzed? Was I hit?

He grunted. Why couldn't he get up?

A foot landed on him hard, and he let out a loud, "Oomph."

"Get off of him," shouted Naveya, the sounds of her steps rushing in his direction, branches snapping underneath her feet.

A thud and the foot lifted off of him, along with his paralysis, and he twisted on his stomach toward Naveya. Her hood was off. She was older than he expected, maybe middle-aged, or perhaps a little younger, her long strawberry blonde hair graying at the roots.

His mouth gaped when he realized what she was doing.

She had a Matrona Guardsmen in a chokehold. His face was reddening, and his hands squeezed her forearm, trying to get her arm off his neck.

His body went limp, and she let go. She got up and stood over him, her chest heaving. She wiped her lips and put her hand out toward more oncoming guards. "Stop."

It was Manning and his soldiers, their rifles aimed at Naveya.

Devon rushed forward and jumped in front of her, gun in hand. "This is Naveya, the woman we came to find."

Manning and the men quickly halted and relaxed, lowering their weapons. Manning saw the Matrona guard Naveya had choked, and raised his gun, inching forward.

Nevaya reached out and placed her hand on Manning's chest. "He's out cold, but alive. He's the last of the crew that came in." She frowned, shaking her head. "There'll be more bloodshed, but none right now. Take this one as a prisoner."

Manning motioned toward the downed guard. Lance and a few others lifted him and dragged him toward the infirmary. "How did they get in here?"

Nevaya put her hands together. "They were in here when I entered. I apologize. Even though I have skills, I couldn't take them all by myself. I needed your help."

Manning gave her a look as if what she said was as odd as a fish speaking to him. He shook his head and thumbed over his shoulder. "All right, sure. Now, let's get back."

Nevaya stepped forward. "I need to see Admiral Shae Lutz. It's urgent."

"Everything is urgent, lady. Get in line," said Manning. "He was just dealing with a group of..." Manning paused, looking as if thinking of the right word. "Super soldiers who broke into the infirmary, and—"

Naveya cut him off. "Super soldiers? Zim's personal guard? Was it a troop of guardsmen he or you had never seen before?"

Manning nodded. "Yes, ma'am."

She pressed her fists firmly against the sides of her head. "Oh, no. Don't tell me it's a group led by a guy named Payson."

Manning lowered his chin. "It is."

Koda slipped his finger through his gun's trigger guard. "I'm guessing that's not good."

Naveya shook her head slowly and glanced at the forest's canopy. "He's the last person we want here. He's a last resort, the finishing touch. He'll find any way to convince Shae that he, Payson, is on Shae's side. When he does, he'll strike when Shae's guard is down and then find a way to let out the toxin." She hurried toward the infirmary, Devon and Koda by her side. "Don't trust a thing he says, no matter what he says. He's a master at this, a master at ending a cycle when everything else has failed. It's a game to him." She went into a run. "Killing off humanity is ingrained in his DNA."

"Who are you?" asked Koda.

She turned and looked at Koda. "Thank you for being a clear channel." She shifted her green eyes to Devon and smiled. "I couldn't get through to this silly young man." She gently rapped her knuckles on top of his head. "We've talked about fear before and how it holds us back. It also drains us and leaves us closed inside. To remain open, focus on the positive, no matter how difficult life is." She glanced at Koda. "During the right moment, you were open, and thank the Space Templars, you received my thought packets."

Koda tilted his head. "Uh…no problem? And, again, who are you?"

Naveya placed her hands together at her heart and bowed. "I'm Naveya Lightwind, member of the Space Templars. I've been stationed on this starbase, masking as a homeless woman, observing your people, and reporting back to my Templar team." She grinned at Devon. "And in the process, I made a good friend." She spun around, hurrying toward the infirmary and patting the side of her leg. "MiMi, let's go."

A dog jumped out of the bushes, barking several times and ran by her side.

She patted her leg again. "Yo, Devon. You and your friend coming?"

Koda nodded. "We're on our way." She had a lot of questions to answer, like how the Guild did she have those strange powers? Or, had he imagined a wind coming from her, making his feet heavy and toppling him to the side just in time, so a bullet didn't stick into the side of his head?

He nodded, heading after her and answered his own question. "I'm imagining things."

48

SHAE

Starbase Matrona

"We need a way to stop the toxin." Shae massaged his neck, the raw skin nearly rubbed off a few days ago by Payson's attempt to kill him by strangulation.

If not for Louise and her quick action, she and the Guards would have come into a dead admiral on their watch, and he'd have no one to blame but himself.

He shouldn't have talked one on one with an advanced killer like Payson. Louise was letting him know about it now.

She stood in front of his desk in the infirmary, her hand in a fist, steadying her breath in order to keep herself calm. "Forgive me, Admiral. I'm a little confused about why you went against instinct and protocol and put yourself in such a dangerous situation." Her cheeks flushed red as her tone rose. "It was careless and put you and all of us in jeopardy. I can't—"

Shae raised his hand to halt her tirade. She was his best officer, but she wasn't an officer at the moment. She was a friend. A friend he needed, but a friend speaking to a superior officer a little *too* directly.

He tilted his head. "Be careful, Louise. I know I made a mistake. The good news, if we can call anything good news these days, is that

Payson and the rest of his crew are in the basement, heavily guarded and now double cuffed. Thanks to you."

Louise gently palmed her chest. "I'm your XO. I'm your second conscience, Shae, trained to be the eyes on the back of your head. Please use me more effectively and—"

A knock on the door cut her off.

Shae shifted his gaze and blinked at what he saw. "Koda? You're up and walking."

Koda looked from his uncle to Louise, a holopad in his hand, and took a limping step inside, his eyes full of excitement. "I hurt my ankle pretty bad, and I'm heading to the Suficell Pods, but on my way I saw...well..." he pointed a thumb over his shoulder, "...you have to see this. Both of you."

Shae stood. "What is it?" The last time someone told him he had to see something was when his daughter, young and vibrant with a twinkle in her eyes, wanted to show him how well she rode her bike.

It had been the first time she was able to do so without assistance.

Shae shook his head and cleared his throat.

Bike?

He didn't know what a bike was or why this mysterious daughter continued to infiltrate his thoughts. For the last time, he didn't have a daughter. Why wouldn't his mind accept that?

Koda backpedaled in a limp out the door. "Zim is on all of the holovid channels, confessing your innocence, and there's this woman named Naveya that—"

Shae's heart nearly stopped. "What? My innocence?" He stepped around the desk, ignoring his nephew's limp. "Show me." He walked out of the room, breezing past Louise and picking up speed with every step.

Louise followed him as he entered a large lobby where hundreds of soldiers were gathered in the halls or leaning on the railings on the landings above, staring at a holoscreen.

Shae gave a sideways glance at Louise. "Aren't all of these people supposed to be on duty?"

Louise gave a nod.

Shae dipped his head. "Round them up and—"

He paused when he saw Zim on the holodisplay. The guy wore a strange golden helmet inlaid with specks of sparkling clear rock.

"Yes, I will say it again," said Zim. "Enlil and I set up Fleet Admiral Shae Lutz. We wanted him to go down in flames, to be mistreated, and his credibility stained...destroyed. We were then going to kill him via a gas chamber. Captain Jenkyns was in on it as well. Now things are different, and I no longer want to end Admiral Shae Lutz's life. I've changed, I've 'seen the light' as they say, and in so doing, things will get better around here. I'm clearing Shae of all charges. He is innocent in all of this and should be championed a hero."

Shae gripped his nephew's forearm. Innocent in all of this? And who in the Guild is Enlil?

His face lifted into a smile. He couldn't help it. A weight he'd been carrying for some time lifted off his shoulders. But was it true or just another trick?

He asked Koda. "Did I hear that correctly?"

Koda patted his uncle on the shoulder. "Like I said, he announced your innocence."

Shae went to turn to shake Louise's hand and thanked her for putting up with him. He halted when her name came out of Zim's mouth.

"Executive Officer Louise Stripe?" Zim said, responding to a woman's question who was not on the screen.

Zim continued, "She was close to Captain Stan Jenkyns, but no, she wasn't part of the original plan." He cringed, as if in pain.

"Keep going, Zim," said the woman, offscreen. "This device will be more kind if you don't fight to tell the truth."

Zim let out a loud breath. Perspiration formed on his lips. "Fine. Okay, when we asked Louise if she'd cooperate by lying during an interview, she assured us she would."

He shook his head, his breathing noisy. "She, of course, did just the opposite. She started to say things we didn't want her to, so we stopped the cameras, and I forcefully stopped her."

"Forcefully?" asked the woman. "Did you kill her?"

Zim shook his head. "I didn't kill her, but I roughed her up a bit."

"What do you mean?"

Zim's face contorted, agony piercing his eyes. He moaned and leaned forward, gasping.

"You attempt to lie, the hurt will get worse, I assure you," said the woman. "Answer my question now. What do you mean by roughing her up, Prime Director?"

He glared at the interviewer, his chest heaving up and down. "I took her to another room. I threatened her with a gun. I slammed my fist into her stomach many times. She's a tough chick and took it like a warrior. I would have killed her had I not had an urgent summons from Enlil. I remember thinking it would be a bad idea to kill her as it could bring up suspicion. I had a few Guards watch her until I returned. When I did return, the guards were unconscious, and Louise was gone."

The vidscreen switched from Zim to an empty podium with the Starbase Matrona symbol painted on the wood stand.

Shae jerked back and turned to Louise. She gave him a nod, and he could see the pain in her eyes.

He gave her a reassuring smile as Zim's voice boomed through the holoscreen. Everyone quieted.

Shae turned.

Zim stood on the Matrona podium, the device no longer on his head. "We've been playing that vid on a loop for several hours now, and yes, that was me." His face was flush and exhausted.

He interlinked his fingers. "I'm ashamed of what I have done. I didn't recognize any of you as sentient Beings, but as a herd of animals to be used and slaughtered." He coughed into his hand and took a sip of water from a cup on a table beside him. "I've told you about the attack and about Enlil, who is my boss. He has orchestrated this scheme from the very beginning of your race's development on Eos and Starbase Matrona. I told you a few reasons as to why you mined ebb for us, and I spoke of Fleet Admiral Shae Lutz's innocence."

He pulled a handkerchief out of his pocket and dabbed at the perspiration on his cheeks. "When I was first introduced to the concept of revealing the truth, I mocked it. The idea was absurd. It would mean my death. Because of what I have done in the past and what I was planning to do in the future, in my heart…" He stared off-camera, as if not believing what he was about to say. "In my heart, I had already died. I had committed untold atrocities to countless people, and I didn't care."

He raised his fingers, mimicking quotes. "I was just doing my job."

He shifted on his feet. "The last task of that job was to kill you all by poisoning you through the air and waterway systems. That was to occur five days from today, which was the estimated time those systems would take to be repaired."

He looked deeply into the camera. "That has now been canceled. All of the toxin will be collected and jettisoned into deep space. From this moment forward—"

Someone shook Shae's shoulder. "We have a problem."

He wanted to raise his finger to shut the man up so he could hear the rest of Zim's speech, but a problem was a problem, not something an admiral could ignore.

He turned to see Manning, the guy's face stern and pissed. "Don't trust Payson, no matter what. A woman we've just found—"

A guard came up to Shae. "I'm sorry for the interruption, sir, but Payson and the prisoners are making a racket. They are demanding to see you. They say if they don't, they have ways to kill us all and that they can get out of their cells whenever they want."

Shae creased his brow. "All right. Gather some men, and I'll follow you."

Manning put his hand on Shae's chest, stopping him. "No, sir. We have information about Payson that you need to hear."

"Can it wait?"

Manning stepped back. "It can, but let me accompany you."

"You and your men are accompanying me whether you like it or not." He waved his arm. "Let's go."

Manning signaled several of his men. They exited the lobby and marched down a hallway, to stop in front of a large elevator. Manning pressed the elevator button and led them inside, motioning for Shae to enter first.

"Stay in the back, Admiral." Manning handed the admiral a rifle. "Just in case."

Shae inspected the weapon. It was black metallic and lightweight, yet it didn't feel metallic. "Who issued this to you?" It was a weapon he'd never seen before.

"It was Payson's and packs quite the punch. It's yours now."

The elevator dinged and opened to a dimly lit basement. It was large, about the size of the upper floors of the infirmary. Various doors lined the walls and signs with arrows pointed in several different directions, marking Surgery, Psych Ward, Medical Records, and more.

They headed to the psych ward.

Turning a corner at the end of the hallway, Shae heard a commotion up ahead, like a group of people kicking at their doors.

Manning whistled softly to two men standing near the psych ward entrance, their rifles pointed at the closed entrance door. They returned with a similar reply.

Manning nodded and motioned for Shae and his troops to follow.

"What's going on?" asked Shae, approaching the guards.

"Sir, they're getting out of control, slamming things and kicking the walls and doors. They want to speak with you."

Shae wasn't going to make the same mistake twice. "Are they on the other side of that door?"

The door had one window, but he couldn't see anyone except a room with ebb flooring, and a portion of another door beyond.

A guard shook his head. "No, Sir. They are locked up in several psych ward cells, but are kicking the ebb out of them right now."

Shae stepped forward. "Open the door."

A guard pressed his hand on a control panel. "Open."

The door opened, and Manning pushed Shae aside as he and his small team fanned out, their rifles extended, and fingers on the trigger.

Shae pointed his gun outward and walked in cautiously.

The ward was full of empty desks and seats, and lined by dozens of doors, all with single windows. The doors were thick and well built.

"Shae, there's something going on out there," said Payson, his voice echoing through the ward from behind his cell door. "We can feel it, Shae. It's excitement, but your people are cheering a fallacy."

Shae made his way toward Payson's cell. "A fallacy?"

"Yes," said Payson. "Whatever the excitement your people are experiencing above, they're excited over a lie."

49

KODA

Starbase Matrona

Koda groaned and hobbled to a Suficell Pod, one of many lining a pod room in the infirmary. The room was pale white with nothing more than pods hooked up to a large outlet system in the middle of the room. Tubes and wires for the outlet system traveled from the ceiling, down a pillar, ending and inserting into plugins.

He had screwed up his ankle during the skirmish out in the woods, and he needed to get away from that Naveya woman and stop thinking about the strange magic he saw her do, let alone her voice in his head.

He held a holopad in his hand, ready to access more documents Devon's software program had decoded, documents he hadn't looked over yet.

This way, he could think of something else.

He opened a pod door and ducked inside. Pain encircled his ankle, and he winced.

He shut the door and rubbed his foot. He set the holopad on the floor and sat next to it.

The other day, Koda had read about pad flight schedules and daily ebb quantity charts, data that meant absolute squat. It was mundane but important, yet he hadn't found the most important aspect.

He didn't know what that "important aspect" was, but he knew it was there. Something ate at him, and he knew a clue hidden from his people was somewhere in those documents.

Call it intuition. It *was* there.

He lay on his side on the floor, the pad's squishy gel releasing a lavender aroma.

He yawned and ran his fingers under sentences, this portion of the document proving more boring even more than the last.

It's here, he told himself.

He pulled his eyes away to look at an old elbow injury healed years before in one of these pods. He'd fractured it while participating in one of the annual Star Guild Academy Games when he was training to be a hotshot pilot.

Another hotshot had slammed him to the ground in a wrestling match, breaking his arm.

All the better. As a politician, if the governance still considered him one, and even if they didn't, he would dedicate his political career to freeing the public of the shitshow of the usual politicians; liars and thieves receiving constant bribes from special interest groups.

He glanced at a metallic box hanging from the center of the pod's ceiling. Dozens of wires originated from the box and encircled the pod, fastened to the walls, and went into the pad's base perimeter, which then sent healing energy frequencies and vibrations through the pad and to the patient.

The metallic box's digital display lit up, displaying three numbers, four-thirty-eight. It was the designated healing frequency for the wounds in his body, a frequency for tissue repair.

He scratched the back of his head and wondered if they could find a frequency to neutralize the toxin if it still by chance was released onto the population.

No one seemed familiar with that particular toxin, so there was nothing they could experiment with to formulate the frequency.

He went back to reading, pushing a swath of black hair out of his eyes.

He pursed his lips as he read something odd. *Eos Two? What the Guild is Eos Two?*

He continued reading and scrunched his brow. "All ebb is transferred to Eos Two before it's sent to Star Guild supply?"

He pushed up and sat on his knees, glaring down at the holopad. "Where the hell is Eos Two?"

Skimming down, his eyes widened. "Past the radiation zone?"

Nothing could survive, let alone exist, past the radiation zone. It was fatal if crossed into, even in a mech.

Heck, the stories he'd read in history books and what had been told in biology class about people crossing that zone were horrendous. When he was young, they showed him and his classmates images of mech pilots who had accidentally walked their mechs into the radiation zone.

The pilots were disgustingly disfigured and mutated and died a disgusting death.

According to the media, the history books, and the doctors who spoke at the schools and academies, stepping inside that zone created a nasty, grueling, disfiguring end to your life.

Unless those pictures were faked.

He didn't know what was real anymore.

"The purpose of Eos Two is threefold," he read out loud. "One, ebb is stripped of two minerals—crystal and gold. Two, the gold and crystals are transported off-planet. Three, Eos Two is the Monarch's home, the Prime Director's superior."

The Monarch?

A sound beeped in the Suficell Pod. Koda glanced up to see the pod's HDC blinking one minute.

How long had he been reading?

It didn't matter, he kept going.

"Mono-atomic gold," he read.

He rested his hand on the back of his neck. *What the heck was mono-atomic gold?*

Reading more, the process consisted of heating the gold to a super high temperature, turning the gold into ash, and subsequently creating a mono-atomic element called mono-atomic white gold powder.

Shortly after, the powder was sent to a classified destination.

Maybe Devon knows what that element is?

Another beep sounded, and the box sending the frequencies into the pod turned off.

He stood and stretched. His wound felt good.

He stepped out of the pod and swiped the hologram to the next page. He squinted at the title. ***MONARCH BLOODLINE IN HUMAN SUBJECTS. CONFIDENTIAL MATERIAL. ACCESS PASSWORD: NIHCTIS.***

He walked forward, heading toward the exit. "This is for Devon."

If anyone can access anything, it was that young man, especially if Savanna Levens used him as a tech advisor. *This* was the important piece of this document he was looking for.

Koda hurried into the infirmary's lobby with the holopad in his hand. Some of the guards were still watching the looped holovid of Zim confessing.

Koda wondered how many of the starbase population had seen the looped holovid, and how they were reacting. He thought he should get on the screen himself and calm down his Sphere Nine citizens.

Who was he kidding? This was better, Zim blowing holes in the illusion that had covered the entire population for who knows how long.

He walked to the nearest guard. "Have you seen Devon?"

The man, full of muscles and with a hard face, grimaced, keeping his eyes on the holoscreen. "Who?"

The guy was of no use. He moved on to a woman. "Have you seen a young, brown-skinned guy with black curly hair, and—'

She shook her head before he could finish his sentence, her eyes glued to the holodisplay.

"Koda?" said a voice behind him.

He turned and there in the infirmary's entryway was Devon, Naveya dressed in rags by his side. Her dog was at her feet, its tongue sticking out, panting.

He stepped forward, his hand out, and presented the holopad to Devon. "Devon, I need you right now." His eyes swept by Naveya, observing her calm demeanor, but not wanting to speak to her. She talked through his mind, and if that wasn't freaky enough, she'd used some type of strange physics that paralyzed him.

Space Templars ran through his mind. Stories had been told in fairy tales about the knighthood manipulating physics like she did, and she claimed to be of that band of light warriors, but regardless, it was all myth and folktales.

Devon huffed, his eyes drawn toward the floor. "Can you give me a minute?"

Koda crouched and reached his hand out to the dog, petting the scruff under its chin. This dog, for some reason, was enchanting. "Not really. I have something I think is important." He wiggled the holopad in his hand at Devon.

Naveya crouched as well, and stared eye to eye with Koda, somehow sending a feeling of peace through his body. "He's just seen something he doesn't want to ever see again, the death of those Matrona guards. He'd never seen killings up close and personal. It made it *real* for him."

Devon ran his hand through his hair and rested it on the back of his neck. "I don't want to relive it." He eyed the holopad in Koda's hand, zeroing in on the words on the hologram. "That says confidential material." He snatched it from Koda, his mouth gaping open. "It even gives a password?" He rushed toward the hallway.

Koda shot the woman a look, noticing a gun holstered at her hip. "Why do you have a gun?"

"I'm a Space Templar. Sometimes it's useful."

He shrugged her answer away. In times of battle, guns were always useful. He turned and followed Devon down the corridor, the dog close behind, wagging its tail. "I think Devon is about to do some magic with an HDC."

"I'm certain he will," said Naveya.

Rounding a corner and into an office, Koda nearly bumped into Devon at a desk.

Devon's fingers were working furiously on the holodisplay, moving icons, and accessing another HDC labeled Zim.

Program Decode displayed at the top of the holoscreen.

Koda felt a weight against his leg and glanced down. The dog was on its haunches, staring up at the screen as well.

Naveya crossed her hands in front of her. "What have you found, Devon?"

Devon put his finger up. "Just a second."

Koda slowly wiped his hands together, waiting, wanting to find out exactly what MONARCH BLOODLINE IN HUMAN SUBJECTS. CONFIDENTIAL MATERIAL meant.

Was it useful or something tossed out long ago, maybe an experiment that Zim and his superiors tried?

Devon moved Zim's HDC icon on the screen into the Project Decode icon. The screen brightened, and data from Zim's HDC blared in front of them.

"Pulling up the search bar." Devon tapped another icon and typed in **monarch bloodline in human subjects**. A password box appeared. Devon cracked his knuckles and stretched his neck left and right as if he was about to jump into a fight and teach some poor sucker a lesson.

He keyed **nihctis** into the password box.

ACCESS GRANTED blinked on the screen, and paragraphs of information fed down the holodisplay.

Koda clapped his hands together with a smile. Perhaps he found something that could help his people.

Naveya stepped back, her head nodding up and down. "They took more humans with the royal bloodline from another planet and sent them here." She pointed at the floor, indicating *here* as the starbase.

Koda read the information in front of him and stopped on his uncle's name. "Wait, what's it saying?"

Devon put his hand to his mouth. "It's saying that Admiral Shae Lutz was never born on this starbase. They've been monitoring him ever since they placed him here, experimenting with how an old war vet on another planet could lead Star Guild."

Koda's mouth gaped open. "What planet? What are you talking about?"

Devon shook his head. "I don't know what planet." He scrolled down and continued reading. He pointed at another line. "But here it says it's the planet of human origin." He turned in his chair, facing the woman. "Humans aren't from here?"

She pursed her lips. "I'm sorry, Devon. It's not for me to say. It's for you to uncover. All I can do is help in small ways."

Koda eyed the lady and then Devon, not knowing what she was getting at. "Hold on. So, if my uncle isn't from this starbase, does that mean he's not my uncle?"

Naveya dipped her head. "Not by blood, but blood doesn't matter in this context. He treats and loves you like an uncle to a nephew would."

Koda looked at the floor, his mind spinning. "Wouldn't my dad know? Why wouldn't he tell me?"

"Right here," said Devon, his eyes focused on more data plastered on the screen. "They paired him with your dad, making them brothers. Your dad is from the starbase, but Shae isn't. They look alike, though. How they pair them is by this process, apparently." Devon tapped on a highlighted word, **CONDITIONING**.

The screen changed, and more paragraphs appeared on the screen.

Koda read, and the more he read, the more his shoulders drooped forward. "They're mad. How many of us have they done this to?"

Naveya sighed. "A lot, but they only do it on a large scale at the beginning of each new cycle. Do you understand the cycles, Koda?"

Koda thumbed over his shoulder at the woman. "How does she know so much?"

"She's a Space Templar here to help us," said Devon.

"That simple, huh?" She knew more than she should, and yet she never let those on Matrona in on it? What kind of jerk would do such a thing? Right now, he didn't need to get into a question and answer session with Naveya, but he'd get to it later. He crossed his arms and leaned against the desk.

"What I've read after I decoded a bunch of junk data," said Devon, "is that they end a cycle and bring in a new batch of humans. They start this process after the previous batch begins to wake up to the fact we are a slave race, or they end the cycle when they feel the current batch has become too lazy or something."

"That's the gist," said Naveya.

"But, this royal line is new to me." Devon rubbed his eyes, yawning, clearly exhausted from all that had gone on for the last many days. "They've taken a few people from another planet that had some Anunnaki blood and placed them here? And not too long ago?" He glared at the holodisplay. "It says that your uncle arrived around twenty-two years ago."

Koda peered at the screen, reading. "By 'conditioning' they manipulated my dad and my uncle with drugs. They also restructured their DNA and implanted false memories into them?" Koda put his hands up. "That's insane. What about my dad's parents and my mom's parents? What about my other aunts and uncles? What about other people who knew my parents? They couldn't have *conditioned* all of them without them knowing it. I mean, what about my uncle's past memories on that other planet? Did they wipe those too?"

Naveya put her hands on Koda's shoulders. Her hands were warm, and strange energy came over him, relaxing him and calming his mind, slowing his heart rate down from the peak rate it had reached.

He let out an easy breath.

"Listen, Koda," said Naveya, "the answer to your questions is all a resounding yes. They *conditioned* all of them. It's a process, but the Anunnaki have done it for thousands upon thousands of years, and they have gone through almost a hundred of these cycles, their beginnings, and endings. It used to be gruesome. A lot of surgeries. A lot of mistakes. Now it's fast, and no surgery is required. A DNA manipulation can be done with simple lasers and specialized HDCs." She reached down and patted her dog's head. "To say the Anunnaki are masters at this conditioning process is an understatement."

"And my uncle's past memories?" He threw his hands out, his pulse rising again. "Wiped?"

"No, they can't ever wipe a memory. Memories are always latent in the mind and can resurface, which may be happening with Admiral Lutz."

"Whoa, guys, guys." Devon pushed out from the chair, his eyes like saucers. "What the Guild?" He pointed at the screen.

Koda moved forward to get a closer look at what Devon was freaking out about. There were more paragraphs with small, unreadable maps underneath.

Koda read quickly and stepped back, his eyes wide like Devon's. "What?"

Devon wiped his face with his hands, clearly in disbelief. "Shae had a daughter from the same planet he was from, and she was snatched as well, taken to the starbase four years ago. The daughter was planted with a well-to-do family like Shae, though a different family altogether."

Koda leaned in. "What family?"

Devon looked over his shoulder, eyeing Koda. "She was placed with Captain Diana Johnson. And we all know who Ali Johnson is."

Yes, Ali. The well-publicized daughter who went against her mother and decided to take on mech mining instead of following her parent's footsteps to join Star Guild military. "Where is my uncle. We have to tell him."

Devon tapped on the screen, and the maps enlarged, showing two maps, each with one blue blinking dot. He scrunched his brow. "Wait a minute. Is that?" He nodded. "It is."

One map was of the infirmary and the biosphere around it. The dot on that map was labeled **SHAE**. The other dot was on planet Eos and labeled **ALI**.

Naveya eyed Shae's map. "He's below us?"

Koda walked toward the doorway. "Yes, and I'm going to get him up here now. He's apparently having a visit with Payson."

Naveya stiffened, grabbing Koda's arm. "Payson is down there? Is he locked up?"

"I'm fairly sure he is," said Koda.

She unholstered her gun. "We need to hurry."

50

SHAE

Starbase Matrona

Shae walked slowly toward Payson's door. The guy leaned his face against the striated ebb window and watched Shae like a deranged lunatic.

Shae eyed Payson as he came closer and then looked past him at several other men sitting with their backs against the wall.

Payson's face lit up when he saw Shae's rifle. "You have her. You're keeping her safe and well cleaned, I assume?"

Shae disregarded Payson's comment. "You feel a fallacy? What do you mean?"

"Zim is executing a well-planned lie, and you and your people are falling for it." He turned, gesturing to his cellmates. "They feel it too. So do all of our friends in the adjacent cells." He cocked his head to the side.

"How do you know what Zim is saying?" asked Shae.

"Because I know the plan. I know the next steps to loosen your population, to get them to trust the Prime Director. By now, you realize this isn't the first time a genocide process has occurred on your starbase, correct?" He didn't wait for Shae's reply. "He's leading you all to your graves."

He could feel it? That didn't make any sense to Shae.

Shae glanced at Manning, who shrugged. "Right now, the only one I trust is my Guard and me."

Payson rolled his neck around, cracking several disks into place. "Zim will still unleash the toxin. We need to stop him. We need to kill him. We need to save our race." He gave a side glance to his friends, who nodded in agreement.

The admiral snapped his fingers. "You'd kill him just like that?"

Payson grunted. "Yes." Payson snapped his fingers, imitating Shae. "And he'd kill you and the human population just like that."

"We'll let this play out for a little longer. If in time, we need to eliminate Zim, we'll give him a public trial for his crimes."

"Let us out, Admiral. We'll make it simple for you. We'll take care of business the best way we know how. He'll be dead by morning."

Shae eyed Manning again, and Manning slowly shook his head as if telling Shae not to trust the man.

Shae brought his eyes back to Payson. He rested his hand on his neck, touching the raw, red skin. "This is what happened to me the last time I trusted you. I should trust you again? I don't think so."

Payson started to breathe heavily, pressing his hand against his head. "Listen. I know you're a good man, Admiral. I know you're on the starbase for a higher reason, but understand Zim is an evil that needs to be eliminated. We could have escaped long ago, but we wanted you to trust us. But now..." The weapon in Shae's hand wiggled. It flew out of his hands into a hover and turned to face Shae. "My gun is an extension of me. It holds my DNA. I can command it with the power of my mind."

Shae raised his hands as Manning inched his way toward Payson's cell, his weapon pointed at Payson. "Make that thing stop floating, Payson. Do it now, or you'll get a bullet in your head."

Payson's cell opened, creaking slowly as it slid into the ceiling.

More creaking sounds filled the ward, and a slow stream of elite soldiers with their arms held up walked out of the cells.

Shae quickly looked around. "Who opened the cells?" And how did they uncuff themselves?

"Don't worry about that," said Payson.

Shae glared into Payson's eyes. "Don't do this. If you attack, this will be a blood bath."

"I'm here to help you, Admiral, even if you don't want it." Payson nodded to his friends. "Take their weapons."

All of the Guards moved back and thrust their guns at Payson's oncoming men.

"Get back," shouted Manning.

Shae backed up near Manning, his hands up in fists.

A shot fired somewhere in the room.

Manning pressed his trigger several times.

A captive slid under the shots and swiped Manning's leg out from under him with a spinning low kick.

Manning flew into the air and landed on his back, still managing to hold his rifle. He got quickly to his feet, fire again, and still missed the attackers.

A foot came up and kicked his weapon into the air, to be caught a moment later by one of Payson's men. A knee slammed against his stomach, and he buckled over and fell to the floor. A foot came down on him, a gun now pressed against his forehead.

Shae eyed the attackers, waiting for one of them to come his way and do the same. He was old, but he could scuffle well.

"Look at your friends," said Payson, walking toward Shae with the rifle now in his hands. "You can't beat us. It's like a game where we see ten steps ahead."

Shae's Guards were sprawled out on the floor, their weapons seized and muzzles pointing at them. "Leave my men and take me."

"Maybe later, but right now, me and my team need to go."

Shae didn't move, staring stone-faced at Payson. Maybe if he could stall, he'd somehow convince this madman to stop his chaos. "Who are you?"

Payson scowled. "I'm human. I'm Payson. You know this."

"But where do you come from?"

"If you're asking if we're built by your enslavers, the answer is yes."

Shae dropped his arms by his side. "Do you work for Zim?"

"We did, but not anymore. We've woken up, and we can no longer allow any more human cycles."

"And so you're going to kill Zim, and then what? Take over the governance?"

"No more governance, Admiral. That ship has flown. I'm taking it under my wing to run a pure and ethical civilization." He pointed to his chest, holding his weapon with one hand. "I'm running it my way."

Shae stiffened. "I—"

"Enough." Payson sliced his arm through the air. "We're losing valuable time." He turned toward one of his men. "Royce, watch over them. The rest, follow me."

Payson and his men rushed out of the room and rounded the corner, out of view.

The room filled with silence except for a lone man pacing, his boots clacking at every step, his gun pointed at Shae.

Manning slowly sat up.

Royce shifted his gun toward Manning. "One false move, boy, and..." he pointed his empty hand at Manning while mimicking the act of shooting a gun.

Manning kept his eyes on Royce and spoke to Shae, "It was a mistake to bring you down here, sir. I should have known that." He slowly stood his hands up.

"Manning, sit down," ordered Shae. He gave Manning a slight head nod, telling him to do the opposite.

Manning would be a good distraction, and Shae could end this Royce guy quickly.

Manning curled his lips, most likely wanting to tear Royce apart, bone by bone. "I'm sorry, Admiral."

Shae slid his hand to his holster, feeling his gun against his fingers. "Don't do it, Manning." He gave a slight head nod again. *Don't do what I say, Manning.*

Manning slowly nodded back. "Shoot him now."

Shae pointed his gun, and Manning lunged toward Royce.

A shot rang out.

51

ALI

Planet Eos, Starship Sirona—Adarta System, Orion Spur

"I'm going to Mount Gabriel now," Ali said into the HDC, glancing over her shoulder.

She was in Tech Quarters, and a light was on in the corner of the room, where a tech was working. She knew it wasn't Sleuth, Diana's right-hand man. She had secretly watched him enter his sleeping quarters for the night before she made her way here.

Some of my race is still out there, replied S. **Please wait until I give you the ready. As I've said before, my brother likes to take his mech out for a ride every so often. If he decides to go on a mech stroll soon, I can no longer control his weapon and systems in his mech or his starfighter.**

"What does your brother look like?"

If you're asking if he's the redheaded, red-bearded man who has shown his face on your holodisplay, then you are correct. That is him.

Ali gritted her teeth. The red-headed giant was more than a nuisance to her. She wanted to erase that guy from her brain.

No, erase him from existence.

Ali, you must stay here until I tell you it's safe to go. It shouldn't be much longer.

Ali didn't know how long she could keep sneaking into Tech Quarters. The more often she did, the more she chanced her mother—no—Diana throwing her into the brig. And that would be that. She'd be stuck on *Sirona* until Guild knows when. With some strange weapon on its way, Ali had to get out of here and now.

Yes, it was a huge risk, and she was bargaining everything, her life included, on S' words, a stranger, but she had to go.

If S was telling the truth and there was a sarcophagus somewhere in the tunnels, how was she going to find it? And how was she going to find the people in the mountain that could help her and the people on *Sirona*?

It didn't matter.

"I'm sorry, but I must go."

My race may kill you, Ali.

"I know, but I have to go. I have to."

S didn't reply.

Ali cocked her head to the side, pursing her lips. She still had questions and wanted some answers.

"S?"

Yes.

"Deep down, I think I know a little about your race, but I don't know how. What's the name of your race?"

We are the Anunnaki from the planet Nibiru, a race vastly older than yours.

A zap hit her heart. The Anunnaki. That name rang familiar.

"I know that race."

You used to study them. Our blood runs through you, hence your interest in us.

"How does your race's blood run through me?"

You come from a long line of royal blood. My ancestors spliced Anunnaki genes in select humans eons ago. As those humans bred, more with that gene spread over a certain area of your planet. They are still very few, as throughout history, my race

kidnapped humans with royal blood to experiment on. This Anunnaki gene runs through you. You'd be considered a very distant cousin to me.

"Yes, the Anunnaki. I knew about them before I came here. I'm certain of it, but why do I feel this way?"

Before S answered, an image popped into Ali's mind. She sat at a desk as a professor at a college, the only female professor at the time.

She didn't know why she was the only female, but it didn't matter. She was transcribing a picture of a tablet, translating it into her own language—a tablet about the Anunnaki.

A rush of adrenaline hit her, and she lurched back in the chair with a quick breath.

"Why do I keep having these memories?"

What was your memory?

"I was a professor at a college. I was transcribing an ancient tablet."

Oh, yes. You were ahead of your time on your world, Ali. You were a professor, and as a female, that was nearly unheard of since the position was mostly granted to men. These memories are from that world. They are inside of you and will continue to open up and reveal more. The more that is revealed, the clearer you'll become in your mind and in your heart.

"What do you look like?" Her archaeology mind started to take over, and her curiosity for these Beings overrode her angst to leave Tech Quarters before her mom found her here.

Imagine the most beautiful women and men of your race. We're very similar to them and to you. Your race would consider our features very favorable to yours. None of us have flaws or asymmetrical features, nor do we age like your race. The biggest difference, however, is that we range from nine to twelve feet in height.

Ali nodded, hearing something in the corner of the room. She had been talking to S too long, and any minute now, Diana would probably walk into Tech Quarters and reprimand her.

But her busy mind wanted to know more. "What is your race's average life span?"

That's complicated, and you may not believe the answer I'm

about to give, but most races, including the Anunnaki, live thousands of years. We have technology to extend our lives.

"Like the Suficell Pods?"

Similar, but easier. A quick DNA manipulation of our genes enhances our longevity and erases any disease or illness. If we die, it's either by old age—again, thousands of years—or by war.

"Does your race war a lot?"

We used to war with ourselves until a king, an ancient relative of mine, united us. We then took to technology and explored the stars. There, we warred as well. We won many battles. Our scientists started manipulating other races, including yours. We've since stopped that practice and stopped many wars, but not all.

Ali shifted in her seat. "You sound like the bullies of the galaxy."

The bullies of the galaxy were the Reptilians, but we weren't that far behind them. Over the years, we calmed our desire to run the galaxy and enslave races. Only my older brother, Enlil, the redhead you have seen, continues to control slave populations. He does so to keep Nibiru, our people's home planet, from dying. Our atmosphere needs a continuous stream of mining products your people mine in order for us to stay alive. Our people long to use a different technology, though my father still holds on to my brother's means of keeping our planet alive. Most of my people are against my brother's ideas and consider it outdated. I, for one, am trying to stop him.

"Are there other ways to fix your atmosphere?"

The best way is with white powder gold, as it also extends our lives. Our race has found other places to live, and many have moved to those planets, but our home is our home, and many of my race intend to keep it that way regardless of the failing atmosphere. Since white powder gold does its job, my race is content and happy. We know of plenty more methods of extracting white powder gold by using robots and not a slave race, but my brother insists a slave race is the best way to mine. Most of my people are against his idea, almost all except the military brass and the head politicians.

"Why?"

The military uses your race to practice combat. The new recruits learn from battling humans. The politicians see your race as something to continue to experiment on, but as I said, most of my people are against this. Riots have ensued on Nibiru to stop the needless battles and experimentation.

A loud clank echoed in the room, knocking Ali back to her senses. No more chit-chat with S, no more questions. She had to get going.

"Look, I'm going to Mount Gabriel soon, but isn't there any way you can scramble their weapons if I encounter a mech or a starfighter?"

There was a pause from the other end of the screen as if S was considering her question.

I can attempt, though I'm certain the attempt will be for naught. Right now, I'm far from planet Eos, so there will be some interference and lag time. I'll do my best.

"Thank you. Where are you?"

I'm on a starship orbiting a green planet.

"Why are you so far away?"

To tell you now is a distraction from the task at hand. I need to focus on keeping you alive. After tonight, all Anunnaki patrols will cease for training purposes, giving you ample time to travel safely in the morning. But if you must make a trip tonight, then follow your intuition.

"I'm running out of time on this starship. My mother knows that I know more than I'm supposed to. I could be thrown in the brig at any time."

Then go.

END COMMUNICATION blinked on the screen, and Ali closed her eyes. *Am I really going to do this?* She leaned back in her chair and ran her hands through her red hair.

Her fingers trembled, and she looked at them. "Shit, I'm nervous." She put her hand on her heart. It was beating hard.

She ignored the pounding sensation and went with her gut. "I have to go."

She stood and moved quickly out of Tech Quarters and down a corridor toward one of the starship's launch bays.

The door opened, and Wrench sat on a stool, his head resting on a workbench, snoring softly.

"Wrench?"

He sniffed a snore and smacked his lips together, continuing to sleep.

She patted his back and wiggled his shoulder, jostling him. "Wrench."

Loudly, she whispered, "Wrench!"

Wrench jumped to his feet, his eyes half-open. "Yeah, boss? Get ya some brew?" He nodded and smiled, fixed his crotch, and sat down, laying his head back on the workbench.

"No, Wrench. It's me, Ali."

"Hmm?" He adjusted in his seat, smacking his lips again. "Ali?"

He yawned and lifted his head, gazing at her. He stood straight away. "Egad, woman. Ya so beau—" He caught himself and cleared his throat. "Aye, Chief Petty Officer Ali Johnson, Wrench at yo service." His wrinkled faced beamed like a light in the darkness, his gray brows nearly topping his bald head, his fingers at his forehead in salute.

Ali grinned back, though her heart told her to get on with it. "Are the mechs ready?"

"As ready as ever."

Ali crossed her arms and leaned on one leg. "Why are you standing at attention? You know I hate that crap."

He relaxed. "Forgot, ma'am." He smirked. "I hate that crap, too."

She rubbed her hands together. "I'm taking my mech out for a spin tonight."

His mouth formed a straight line. "Ya not serious?" He grabbed a tool hanging on the wall and let out a chuckle. He paused and eyed her for a moment. "Guild'n dammit on a heartstring, ya *are* serious." He shook his head, his lips downturned. "Please don't go out there by yo'self, Ali. Wait for your ma' to approve this so we can send starfighters out at the same time, ya know. I still have some fixin' to do, and it's not safe out there anyways."

"I know what I'm doing."

"So, ya know when luck arrives 'er leaves, do ya? Luck didn't always swing in yo favor, such as it was in yo favor when ya got here."

"It's not luck, Wrench. I'm very skilled in one of those and—" Ali pointed to a mech, her eyes going wide. "Are you kidding me?" She was so focused on Wrench, the mechs had slipped her sight when she walked in.

Wrench folded his arms across his chest, and leaned back, almost patting himself on the back. "No, I'm not kidd'n ya. Look at what I've got there, will ya?"

Two mechs had missile launchers taken from Thunderbirds installed on each shoulder, and one of each mech's arms had been converted into cannons. They stood against a bay wall, a few meters from a row of Thunderbird starfighters.

Wrench walked toward them, swinging the bulbous tool in his hand. "It took nearly the whole crew ta' assemble those. Puttin' in a weapons system was faster than I imagined."

He climbed up a couple of footholds on one of the mechs, opened a panel, and checked a hip gyro. "Ya know, ya and Daf are the luckiest people I know. Ya survived the impossible gettin' from yo warehouse to here." He pressed the tool against the gyro. The tool vibrated. "Well, we're lucky any of us on this starship is still alive."

Ali widened her stance. "Don't throw that *luck* crap at me, Wrench. I'm going out tonight."

Wrench glanced up at the missiles mounted on the mech's shoulder. "We haven't tested any of the weapons yet." He threw an arm out wide. "None."

"Then, I won't use them."

"That's another risk. What if ya encounter somethin' out there and ya need to shoot the Guild'n nuts out of that somethin'? Ya set your target, aim, fire, but nothin' happens, makin' ya an easy target?" He snatched a rag out of his back pocket and wiped his instrument, then examined something else in the mech's hip.

Ali ignored his statement. She'd be careful, and if S was able to help in some way by scrambling enemy systems, then all the better.

She had to get to Mount Gabriel, and for some reason, she had to get there tonight.

"How is Daf's mech?"

He dropped his head in defeat. "What do ya mean? Daf ain't jumpin' a mech outta this ship, either."

Ali bit her cheek. "How is her mech, Wrench?"

Wrench blew through his teeth. "Both mechs are ready."

Ali forced down a smile. "Good. I'm getting Daf, and we're moving out tonight."

She turned on her heels, wheeled out of the bay, and the door shut behind her. Entering a corridor, she headed toward Daf's sleeping quarters, convincing herself everything was going to be fine.

"Ali," yelled someone's voice, thick and angry.

Ali halted. "Son of a…"

Diana was in the corridor, resting her hand on her holstered pistol. Daf strolled up beside her.

52

ALI

Planet Eos, Starship Sirona—Adarta System, Orion Spur

Ali froze, not believing her eyes. "Daf, you're *in* on this?"

Daf stood an arm's length from Diana, leaning away from her, her eyes moving from Diana to Ali. She pushed out her bottom lip, clearly confused. "In on what?"

Diana glanced from Daf to Ali, her fingers curling around her gun's handgrip. "I got word you were in Tech Quarters again, Ali." She cocked her head to the side. "Why are you exiting the launch bay?"

Ali noticed Diana's fingers twitch around her weapon. "What are you going to do with that gun?"

"I can't keep letting you do this. You're going against my orders. You're becoming a problem, and you know me well enough by now I can't stand problems." She paused, her chin trembling and a tear welled in her eye. "And I'm supposed to—"

Ali pointed at Diana's pistol. "Daf, get the gun."

Diana lifted her weapon and aimed the pistol at Ali.

Daf lowered her shoulder and bull-rushed Diana, knocking her against the corridor wall.

Diana kicked Daf away.

Ali leaped, bringing a fist down on the gun and knocking it to the floor.

The weapon bounced and slid toward the opposite wall.

Diana threw an uppercut, and Ali swiped her arm down to block Diana's punch, then sent a hard elbow to Diana's temple.

Diana grunted from the hit but recovered quickly, positioning a leg behind Ali's foot and pushing as she connected both palms against Ali's chest.

Ali tripped, landing on her back, her head cracking against the floor.

Diana twisted around and dove for her weapon.

Ali pushed off the ground. "Get her."

Already in place, Daf sent a flying knee into the admiral's chin.

Diana went limp on the floor, her eyes shut, her breaths slow, and her fingers millimeters away from the gun.

She was out cold.

Daf gasped. "Oh, my Guild." She pulled her hair back. "I'm in deep shit. I'm going to be…" she shook her head, her voice rising, "…I don't know what they're going to do to me. This is probably on a holocam. Everything has been recorded. I guarantee it. What do I do?"

Ali hurried to the gun, then rushed to unstrap Diana's holster. She hastily put it around her waist and slipped the gun into the holster. "We have to go. Now."

Daf yanked Ali's arm. "No. I need to explain to the guards that I—"

Ali pulled Daf toward her, her nose close enough she could almost feel Daf's skin. "You stay, and you'll be locked up for a long, long ass time." She pointed an index finger at Diana. "Or that bitch kills you. If you come with me like you *wanted*, you have a chance to live."

Daf glanced at an unconscious Diana and then at Ali, bobbing her head up and down. "Okay, yeah. You're right."

"Let's get to the bay. We're heading for Mount Gabriel."

Wrench stood on the other side of the door into the launch bay, holding a long, metallic tool, ready to belt whoever walked through.

He relaxed when he saw Ali and Daf. "What the hell was all of that commotion out there?"

Ali hurried toward her mech. "Stay in here, Wrench. You don't want to be implicated in anything."

"Implicated in what?"

Ali stepped on her mech's foothold, eyeing Daf stepping up her mech as well. "The less you know, the better."

Wrench folded his arms and widened his stance. "Your ma' and ya ain't on the same page when it comes to these mechs, are ya?"

"She knows nothing about your and your crew's work on these mechs, Wrench." Ali stepped over the lip of the cockpit, one leg dangling inside. She touched the mech's arm cannon. "I'm sorry. I wasn't a hundred percent clear about who was ordering you to build these mechs. It wasn't Captain Diana Johnson. It was me."

Wrench glanced down, nodding. "I figured." He looked up, his face stern. "I guess that's why she was surprised when she saw my men building one of these."

"She saw this?"

"Yeah, she's the captain. I told her I was tinkerin', thinkin' she knew yo idea, but she must'a thought my crew and I were doin' this on our own accord to enhance our defenses."

Ali let out a breath of relief. Had Diana known the truth, shutting this experiment down would have been a pleasure.

Wrench glanced up at his modified mech creations. "Let me and my crew build more of these mechs. I mean, hell, all the mechs we need are at the warehouse no more than ten meters away from *Sirona.* We could have an army of these bad boys, and I'd feel safer with ya out there."

Safe? The only person who ever made her safe was her and herself only. She'd gone through this life by herself, making ends meet by her lonesome. It was hard enough to have Daf go with her. The last thing she wanted to be was a babysitter. "I don't think so, Wrench. We're getting off this starship, just Daf and me. Got it?"

Wrench huffed. "Fine." His voice lowered. "Be careful out there."

Ali gave him a thumbs up. "I plan on it."

Ali jumped into the cockpit and strapped in. She powered on the HDC, checking the auxiliary fuel pump, heat sinks, and water reserves.

All full.

She turned on the comm. "Daf, you all set?"

"All a go."

Ali turned on the HDC and saw Wrench through the cockpit window. He was hunched at his workbench, an HDC in front of him, and leaning into his comm mic.

"Both of ya, listen up," said Wrench. "I installed a weapon operating system. It's easy to find. It's labeled weapons on yo HDC's. Ali, you were a starfighter pilot, so use the targeting system and launching system the same way. Ya don't have much ammunition, so be wise if anything tries to bother you out there, and by all that's good, I hope nothing does."

Ali's heart raced. She wanted to get out of here before any guards came in to stop her from leaving. "How many missiles do we have?"

"Twelve in each rack, and ya have two racks. One on each shoulder."

"It's time for us to go," said Ali. "Are you ready, Daf?"

"Ready."

"Ali, no, wait. We need to go over—"

"No, Wrench. I'm sorry, but you have to open the launch bay door. We have to get out of here."

Wrench shook his head. "All right. Be lucky out there."

The launch bay doors opened.

Ali twisted her mech and walked it quickly across the ebb flooring and down the ramp leading outside, Daf on her tail, and both heading into the shadowy world outside.

It was past midnight, and the sun was on the horizon. The ramp sucked into *Sirona's* side, and Ali and Daf pushed forward, moving along the edge of the cliff face at the base of the plateau they had jumped from many days ago.

Ali walked around a boulder. “Be ready for anything, Daf. According to S, there are still some patrols out here, so keep a good eye on your radar.”

She didn’t mention that the red-haired giant in her dreams might be out on a mech stroll as well.

“I figured,” said Daf. “You watch out as well.”

“On it. Let’s keep walking to the mountain. Commlink me when you want. No comm restraints, all right?”

“Got it, Chief.”

They walked in silence for nearly a half an hour before they ascended a long incline in the side of the plateau that led to a high ridge.

They continued along an irregular edge, doing their best to conceal themselves within the shadows that were everywhere, from the tall spired ebb rock to the giant-sized rocks littering the ground.

Ali tapped her HDC, bringing up her map. She nodded to herself and drew her lips close to her mic. “Keep following the base of the ridge. It slopes down to Scythe Straights, then we’ll cut over to Gutter’s Pass.”

“Aye, Chief.”

Gutter's Pass was a large canyon with a wide overhang on one side that extended the entire length of the canyon. When it rained, water flooded over it like a clogged warehouse rain gutter, creating a wide waterfall.

Daf’s cockpit moved up and down, matching every footstep her mech made. “When we get to Scythe Straights, we'll move slowly from spire to spire.”

“Yep, got it.”

Ali gasped, and a chill ran up her spine. A thought hit her like lightning hitting a tree. “How did they always know where…” she cut herself off, shaking her head and pursing her lips.

It couldn’t be, but it was true.

No matter where she was, she was found. By her mother. Every time. In Tech Quarters, in the corridors, in the cafeteria. Everywhere.

The last time Diana confronted her, she again had found her and this time, in the corridor.

"Were you going to say something?" came Daf's voice over the comm.

Ali shivered. "The last several times I was attacked, they found me easily. When you dragged my damaged mech to mech bay, they found me. When we snuck over to Starship *Sirona,* they found us. When we made it to *Sirona,* my mother knew where I was at all times."

"What are you saying?"

Ali paused, all sensations draining to her feet. "Be aware of everything and watch your radar with all the senses you have."

"Ali, you're scaring me more than I already am. What's going on?"

"Daf, you may want to turn around. No matter where I am, they know. No matter where I go, they monitor me." She clenched her jaw and pushed her mech faster, a fury rising from her belly. "I'm being watched all day, every day. There is a tracking device in me. There has to be. "

53

EDEN

Planet Eos

An explosion jostled *Swift*, and Eden held onto her restraints, the ship now in a fast dive.

Eden stared at the vidscreen. *Swift* was so close, she could reach out and almost touch Y'taul's ship.

His ship moved just as fast as it dove toward Eos' surface, blue flames blasting out of its boosters and pushing it forward.

Swift shuddered again and spun out of the way of more cannon fire coming from Eos.

Eden gritted her teeth. How she'd love to skip this chase and head toward the mech warehouses to see if any of her race survived the onslaught and if so, pick them up and get them out of here.

Apparently, retrieving a nuclear weapon was more important.

Swift continued chasing Y'taul's ship, keeping snugly on its tail.

Y'taul's ship careened and plummeted into a clump of thick, white clouds.

Nyx thrust her fist toward the retreating craft. "After them, *Swift*."

It will be my pleasure.

A burst of white filled the screen, and the bridge shook from a nearby slug cracking open and splattering shrapnel in the sky.

The cloud whisked outward, twirling like smoke as *Swift* broke through.

The ground rose toward them, though many kilometers away, they were heading right for it. Cannons, large and bulky, sat positioned in rows between high spired buildings, tall landing pads, and large palace-like structures.

Eden's eyes widened. A small city? She'd never been shown or told of such a place on Eos.

She gasped and pushed her feet into the floor as if pressing on a brake. She wanted *Swift* to stop, to pause the scene, so she could examine the buildings.

Where were they? This couldn't be Eos, but it was. Structures, other than warehouses, water stations, and a few towers here and there hadn't been built on Eos, especially not a damn city.

"Y'taul's ship disappeared," said Nyx. "Where did they go?"

Eden gazed at the screen. The cannons continued to pound the sky from the ground, sending hot, red slugs *Swift* dodged, the shrapnel rarely making contact. "*Swift*, do a search."

Scanning, replied Swift. I don't see them anywhere. There isn't a signature anywhere on Eos or in the exosphere around the planet.

Swift pulled up and leveled out, pushing more power into her boosters, and heading away from the city.

Nyx slammed her hand on her armrest. "How did they disappear like that?" She turned. "And where is Skye? He should be in here by now."

Eden blinked several times, and her heart skipped a beat, thinking about the city below. A city below? There was an entire city. With that many structures, it had to have been built years ago, and right under Starbase Matrona and Star Guild's noses.

Or, maybe the city was there longer than she thought. Could it have been there for hundreds of years?

A massive explosion boomed through the cockpit, and the ship rocked back and forth, then dipped.

I've been hit. My engines are malfunctioning. I'll be offline in order to concentrate all energy and energy reserves on fixing this. Hold on, said Swift.

Nyx jostled in her seat. “Pull out of here, *Swift.*”

No response.

“You can fix yourself when we’re out of target range.”

The craft dipped again, the nose pointing toward the ground as the cannons and the city came closer.

“*Swift,*” screamed Nyx. “Fix…later.”

The ground was approaching at a whipping pace, the ship heading right for a skyscraper.

Eden closed her eyes. “Pull up, *Swift*. Pull up.”

The building continued to get bigger the closer they came.

Eden grimaced, her neck muscles tightening, and she pulled back on her armrests, trying to will *Swift* to veer right, or do anything other than slam nose-first into the skyscraper. “Pull up.”

Swift slowed, and barrel-rolled away from the building, then leveled out.

My apologies for the close call. I’m back online.

Eden wiped the perspiration off her brow and tried to slow her breathing.

Swift flew toward a mountain range, the range’s red and gold rock glistening in the sun’s light.

She flew over a large peak, and ducked behind it, hugging the mountain terrain as close as she could and moving quickly away from the city.

Alarms blared on the bridge. Enemy ships approaching fast. ETA, four seconds.

Another boom echoed throughout the bridge, and the ship rattled. *Swift* shifted course.

A quick, triangular craft flew by, the same type of craft Eden had seen fighting during the first attack.

Another craft came into view. *Swift’s* crosshairs highlighted the craft just as a missile launched from the enemy ship’s wing, and then a second missile.

Eden braced. She wasn’t used to having a self-controlled ship doing almost everything for her, or in this case, for the crew. “Twelve o’clock, *Swift.*”

I see it.

A quick cannon burst of purple bolts, and the missiles erupted into a fiery explosion. *Swift* moved her targets to the oncoming craft, now spitting red tracers *Swift's* way.

"What did you just shoot at the missiles, Swift?" asked Eden.

Plasma bolts. It's a new technology to you, but understand it's old technology to the Space Templars. Adjusting forward graviton shields, and sending a present to the enemy craft now.

Swift sent plasma bolts toward the oncoming ship.

A direct hit and the craft split into several pieces, its wings twirling in the air, and the cockpit turning it into a ball of fire.

We have incoming. Too close in range. Hold on.

A missile flew by, and *Swift* dodged cannon slugs, starboard side.

I'm going low, said *Swift,* hugging the mountain range and heading for the lowest peaks.

Nyx wrapped her fingers around her shoulder restraints. "*Swift*, I'm getting tired of this. Get us on the ground. At this rate, we'll be flying, dodging, and shooting down endless streams of ships all day. Plus, Y'taul's ship somehow blipped out of existence."

As you command. I'm going to straighten out for a smooth landing.

Eden glared at the vidscreen, watching the lower peaks of the mountain range getting nearer and nearer.

Underbelly thrusters are fully operational. I'll angle them in for a good landing.

Nyx gave a nod. "No problem. Thank you, *Swift*." She placed her palm to her chest and raised her chin as she looked at Eden. "Prepare for battle. They'll be upon us as soon as we land. After the battle, I imagine you want to find some of your friends?" She cracked her knuckles and rolled her neck. "Everyone, prepare for the ground game, our specialty. This ought to be fun."

"Should we just blast out of here and find Starbase Matrona?" asked Eden.

"Too easy," said Nyx. "Your heart sent us here. We'll figure out why soon enough."

54

ALI

Planet Eos, West of the Radiation Zone—Adarta System, Orion Spur

Ali stepped over a mound of ebb rock. "We have to hurry to Mount Gabriel before they show themselves."

She hoped she could get there before the Anunnaki or before that weird red-haired giant decided to track her, or whatever it was they did to always find her.

"Ali, I think you're overreacting. How could they possibly know where you are all the time?"

Ali butted her mech up against a red rock that jutted toward the sky. "I don't know. If I did, I'd rectify that issue and shove it up their asses."

"They'd have to place a beacon on you, somehow. When would they have done that? I don't see any flashing devices on your clothes, do you?"

Ali paused and tilted her head. Daf had a point. She touched the skin on her wrist and inhaled sharply. "Guild." She swallowed hard. "I'm telling you, it's probably in me."

"I doubt it."

Ali moved her mech toward the next spire, this one taller and twisting its way toward the heavens. "The beacon. Maybe they inserted it in my skin when they nabbed me from Earth. I don't know, but I know they track me. They have to. There isn't any other explanation for how they always know where I am."

"All right," said Daf, her voice soft. Ali could tell she didn't believe her. "If that were the case, they would have killed you by now."

"They tried. My mom, I mean Diana, must have wanted to keep me alive for some selfish reason, and then suddenly she wanted to kill me." Her chest burned, anger rising. "If that S character is telling the truth, she scrambled the enemy's operating systems and kept us alive."

Ali leaned forward, her mech mimicking her, and peaked around the rock.

They were in Scythe Straights, full of knife-like spires scattered throughout the bottom of a canyon, the rocks stabbing at the firmament. Each behemoth was twice as wide as a mech, and on average, two-hundred meters taller.

Ali narrowed her eyes as she surveyed the terrain. It was empty and lifeless, except for ebb rock and more ebb rock.

If Daf was right and Ali wasn't being monitored, this place would be a decent area to conceal themselves. And heck, moving between the great ebb jags might interfere with the Anunnaki's radar.

If they used radar.

Ali's comm crackled. "I'm getting a heat signature two kilometers west. Do you see that?"

Ali searched the holographic map on the holodisplay. The heat signature blinked, faded away, and then blinked again. Ali tapped her HDC. Was her computer fizzing out on her?

"Yeah, I see it. It just showed on my map now." She rubbed her brow, studying the signature.

"Daf, the signature is stationary. Let's keep an eye on it."

"Aye, Chief."

They walked from spire to spire, and Ali glanced from the terrain in front of her to her radar, back and forth, keeping tabs on the stagnated signal.

Reaching the edge of Scythe Straights, they entered an open field of ebb rock, Ali's mech's feet cracking chunks of ebb at another old mining spot.

Ali took a drink from her water tube. She swallowed, the cold calming her down. "We're getting closer to Gutter's Pass, and beyond the pass is a route to Mount Gabriel."

Once she arrived at the mountain and was in its tunnels, she'd search for the sarcophagus, and hopefully, find a group of people who could help her own people, and then everything would be shits and giggles from that point forward.

Happily ever after.

She rolled her eyes. Nothing in her life was ever close to happily ever after.

She thought of her mom, her real mom, Helen. She imagined her smile, her tears, and her long hug when she saw her again. She imagined years of memories flooding back when they reunited.

All she had to do was step inside the sarcophagus like that redheaded bastard did with Ali over his shoulder when he snagged her from Earth.

I'll see you soon, Mom.

She couldn't help but smile when her dad came to mind and how kind he felt in her memories. She couldn't wait to see him too, but deep down knew he wouldn't be as easy to locate as her mom.

She was determined to find him, though, and to hug him as long as he'd let her.

The mech lurched, and Ali put her foot forward, stopping her mech from falling face first.

"Pay attention, Chief. The ebb is uneven here."

"I can see that." Ali trekked onward and glanced up. The overhang above her was another sweet place to walk and hide since it cut off the view from satellites and ships if she didn't have a tiny beacon in her body. If she did, hiding wouldn't matter.

"I can't wait to see William's face when we see him again," said Daf.

Ali's stomach hardened. *William?* "Uh...why is that?" She pushed out a breath to kick out the jealousy overcoming her.

Right now, she should be scared shitless that an attack on her location could spring at any instant, and concentrating on walking, hiding, and on her destination, not worried over a stupid, handsome man Daf could easily woo over her.

Ali was beautiful, but Daf was a goddess, the type of woman who glowed when she walked into a room.

"He doesn't know we left, so he'll be looking all over for us. He'll do his cute little doctor thing, you know, being worried about our safety and well-being and all that."

Ali kept her mouth shut and paced her mech forward, though her heart ached.

It didn't matter. He was a distraction, and Ali didn't like distractions, especially not here. Not right now.

Daf continued, "Sitting on the couch next to him last night was bliss, holding hands." She hesitated. "And then we kissed."

Ali's breaths shallowed. "All right, enough of the love talk."

Daf laughed. "I'm just kidding. We didn't do anything. He's a great guy and breathtaking with the looks, those eyes and smile could melt stone, but it doesn't matter. If you weren't so off in your own little corner of the ship and so much inside of your head all the time, you'd see how he looks at you and blushes when he talks about you. He shines whenever you walk in a room."

Ali's mouth slackened, and she shook her head. *Concentrate.* "That's great. I hope he enjoys himself."

"He's a good man. If you could let him into your life a little more, you'd see that."

"Let's get off this topic."

"Sorry." Daf sighed. "I just wanted to get our minds off of our nerves. If you don't give him at least a few minutes of your time when we see him again, I'm going to kick your ass, okay?"

Ali cracked a smile. "All right."

The problem was Ali wouldn't be back. Daf would, and she could have William all she wanted. Ali was going to jump through that portal to back home where she belonged.

She couldn't wait to tell her mom her husband, Ali's dad, was still alive and they'd find him.

Where the hell could he be?

Three dots blinked on Ali's radar. Ali jerked back. "Shit. Three crafts approaching. Shut down your mech, Daf, now."

"I see them too. Shutting down." They weren't overheating, so their mech's heat would dissipate much faster. Ali didn't know if switching off the mech would do any good, but it had the last time they were somewhat hidden under the eve of a flat rock that sat on top of two vertical rocks, much like a giant ancient Irish dolmen back on Earth.

She paused.

An Irish dolmen? What the Guild was a dolmen?

A clear picture popped in her mind of two vertical megalithic limestone rocks supporting a large flat horizontal capstone, looking somewhat like a table with ancient bones buried inside.

She shook her head and squeezed her eyes shut, bringing herself back to the present. *Focus, Ali. Focus.*

She had a memory of her other life, the life she was about to return to: Earth, her mom, and eventually, her dad.

She swiped her finger across the holoscreen and flicked her finger on the engine's icon.

Her engines turned off, and the cockpit eased, ceasing its constant vibration. "Keep communication at a minimum right now and radar on and available."

She eyed the radar, which being on, may be detected as well. She huffed, but she needed to see the enemy like the enemy may be seeing her. She crossed her fingers. All she had was the hope S had scrambled the Anunnaki's sensors.

The three ships flew closer and moved fast. In a way, that was good. Maybe they were on a joy ride or flight practice, and they'd fly over them without notice.

They slowed, inching closer and closer on the radar screen.

Ali rubbed the sweat off of her palms and let out a jerky breath. *Come on. Keep going. Fly right by.*

They slowed more, and Ali leaned forward, craning her neck to try and peer at the ships. The rock gutter was in the way, cutting off any view of the sky.

The ships halted to hover directly above them.

She stood still, keeping her eyes on the radar.

Don't talk, Daf. Don't say anything.

In the back of her mind, she pleaded to S, hoping S had been monitoring the situation and scrambling the ships' tracking systems.

The rock wall and the ebb her mech stood upon began to shake.

Oh, no.

It meant the ships were lowering, perhaps landing or investigating the terrain more closely. The enemy had spotted something.

A wing came into view, the rest of the ship blocked by the gutter.

Ali hovered her finger over the engine icon, ready to activate her mech. "Daf, we have to run for it."

55

SHAE

Starbase Matrona

A shot echoed in the room, and Shae winced, lowering his weapon.

He wasn't the one who fired a shot.

Royce's head jerked away, and the guy went limp, tumbling to the floor as blood seeped from a wound in the side of his skull. His legs twitched, and his eyes fluttered.

Royce had died instantly and his body reacted, nerves shooting electric-like synapses throughout his lifeless muscles and tendons.

Shae's jaw dropped, and he held his breath, turning his attention toward the sound of the gunshot and aiming his weapon in that direction.

A woman stood just beyond the room's entryway in front of Koda and Devon, a dog by her side, held out a pistol, still pointing it at Royce.

She shifted her eyes to Shae. "Where is Payson?"

Shae's eyes widened. Who the heck was this woman, and how did she know Payson? He glanced at Koda, who gave him a head nod, telling Shae she could be trusted.

Shae nodded back and eyed the woman. "He left and went to kill Zim."

The woman tilted her head and lowered her gun. "You can't trust Payson no matter what he says. He's a cold-blooded killer. He's a sociopath, along with the rest of his team. To him, this is all a game, Admiral." She stepped into the room. "He could have killed you at any time, but I guess that wouldn't fulfill his plan or whatever he is doing to keep you alive."

She walked athletically toward Shae, revealing that she wasn't as homeless as she looked.

Shae holstered his gun. "How do you know Payson?"

She waved off his question. "No time for that. Right now, we need to know where he is." She bowed. "I'm going to have to find him and kill him. If I can't kill him, he'll release the toxin."

Shae took a step forward, glancing at Koda and then back at the woman. "Who the hell are you?"

She reached underneath her raggedy shirt's collar and pulled out a pendant. "I'm Naveya, and I'm here to help."

Shae stiffened. He touched his pendant behind his shirt, feeling the cold steel against his chest. She had the same pendant as he did.

She was a Space Templar.

Naveya walked toward him, extending her hand for a handshake.

Shae took her hand and shook it, then gasped. A zap went through him and rushed to his brain, tingling every brain cell he had.

A memory opened up of a young girl, Alison, a name he knew well as it was the name he and his wife, Helen, had named their only child.

His wife? Helen? He didn't have a wife.

But wait.

He did. He knew he did.

Alison had been his child, his daughter. He knew it but didn't know how.

Alison stood in a field under the blazing summer sun, the heat sweltering.

He was there, watching her, observing how she played and enjoying it. A sensation deep in his gut told him he always enjoyed it when she was around and loved it when she played.

Michigan came to mind. They were on a farm, his family's farm.

But where was Michigan? It wasn't on the starbase. He was on a farm, on a planet, with a real sun beaming light down on him, unlike the artificial sun in the biosphere.

Alison stood in a massive field and in the only dirt patch around. She held two dolls, not playing with them the right way, not the way a good girl should play.

He strolled over to her, squinting under the sun's rays. He touched her back and leaned down. "You're playing like a boy."

She wrapped her small fingers around a doll's arm and threw a punch at the other doll.

"No, no, no." Shae frowned, rubbing her back. "Girls play with tea. They don't box with dolls."

She looked up at him, her innocent eyes studying him. She was smart and an independent little one at that. "How come, Daddy?"

He shrugged. "It's just the way it is."

She looked back at her dolls and wiped the dirt off a doll's face. "It's fun, though."

"It's not for a girl."

She frowned. "But why, Daddy?"

He didn't know, other than societal reasons. He didn't have any qualms about it. It was just the way it was, and people would look at him differently if they saw her play fighting with dolls. They would judge him, and worse yet, they would judge her.

He had to protect her.

He reached down to take the dolls from her and scold her, but something within him told him it wasn't right. Looking into her eyes, he could tell it wasn't right from her perspective as well.

He let out a huff, going against every reason in his gut. If a girl wanted to box, a girl should box. And he'd teach her.

He grabbed a doll's arm with his finger and thumb and jabbed a punch at her other doll. "I got you." He winked.

Alison laughed, and leaned against his leg, her sweet touch bringing him a smile. They boxed with the dolls back and forth, laughing and making funny sounds.

From that day forward, Alison was going to be Alison, and it wouldn't be him or anyone else if he could help it, who was going to tell her what kind of girl she was supposed to be.

Naveya snapped her fingers next to his ear, and he came back to the present.

Then it hit him like a hovertrain barreling into an ebb wall.

He had a daughter, one that he had loved, one who meant the world to him. His recent memories and his recent thoughts weren't crazy. It wasn't because of stress. It wasn't because of the attack.

Alison was his daughter, and he missed her dearly.

In another life, in another time, he thought about her every day, watching her play in the field and on the hay bales. He would worry about her safety, like a good father to any child.

Then he disappeared from her life and that world like a flash in the night.

How did he disappear, and where did he disappear from? That memory hadn't surfaced. Was Alison alive today? If so, how the Guild could he find her?

His heart ached, and he yearned for her, to feel her lean against his leg again, to see her sweet, innocent eyes, and to read books to her before bedtime.

The way things used to be.

He dropped to his knees, and tears came to his eyes, his bottom lip quivering. He touched his chest. "Where is she?"

Koda hurried to him and crouched by his side. "What happened? Are you okay, Uncle?"

Nevaya nodded. "He's just had a clear memory of his daughter."

Shae wiped a tear and nodded. He looked around the room. He had just made a fool of himself, and the soldiers looked at him as though he'd become an alien. The woman just said he had a daughter, and they all knew here on Starbase Matrona, he didn't.

"I'm sorry." His voice cracked.

Manning touched his back. "Let's get you out of here."

He pulled Shae to a standing position and led him to the doorway where Devon stood.

"Thank you," said Shae. "All right, you all. Let's find Payson."

And I'll see if I can figure out how to find my daughter.

He stopped in front of Devon.

The young man half-smiled, wanting to look away but couldn't, his innocent eyes matching the memory of his daughter, Alison's innocent eyes.

"Admiral," said Devon, "we have some important information for you. We know exactly where your daughter is located."

56

ALI

<u>Planet Eos, West of the Radiation Zone—Adarta System, Orion Spur</u>

Ali's finger hovered above the engine icon, readying to activate her mech. The ground shook from the starfighters overhead, most likely about to investigate what was beneath the rock eve Daf and Ali were hiding under.

"On my count, Daf. We activate our mechs and run."

"Got it, Chief."

The canyon vibrated more intensely and then stilled.

Had the starfighters landed on the gutter rock above them?

Ali pulled her finger away from the icon and eyed the radar. The blue dots indicating the enemy above were flying away, heading north at a fast pace.

Ali let out a deep breath. "Oh, my Guild." She touched her chest. "Thank you, S."

It had to be S' intervention. She had to have screwed with the enemy's radar, glitching it.

That was a close call, and if they had been located, they were literally stuck between a rock and a hard place.

Maybe I should have taken Wrench's advice and waited until we could have an army of these weaponized mechs.

She cringed at the thought. If she waited, the secret weapon that S told them about would pulverize Starship *Sirona,* ending her and everyone on the ship.

She couldn't have that.

The commlink crackled. "What the Guild just happened? If they hovered, they'd obviously spotted something."

Ali let out a sigh of relief. Whoever or whatever it was that helped her, she wasn't going to question it. "Let's get moving."

"All right. Activating engines," said Daf.

"Activating engines," repeated Ali.

They walked through Gutter's Pass until they reached a smaller version of Scythe Straights, aptly named Little Scythe Straights.

She entered the valley with Daf on her tail. They butted up against the first knifed rock they saw. Ali glared at the radar. "All clear."

"Yes, all clear."

Ali pulled up the map on her holoscreen and swiped her finger across the distance and time icon. "Four kilometers and eleven minutes until we get to Mount Gabriel."

"Thank Guild."

They moved from spire to boulder and boulder to spire, taking it slow and easy.

Ali's radar beeped, and her heart skipped. She glanced at her radar, but nothing was there other than Daf's mech.

Shaking it off, she rounded a boulder, her mech jostling up and down from each. She picked up speed, heading toward another spire.

Her radar beeped again, and a blue dot pulsed near her location then faded away.

She paused, glancing through her cockpit window, surveying the landscape.

Nothing.

"Daf, did you see that?"

"See what?"

Ali continued to study the terrain. "Never mind. False alarm. I think I have a little bit of a radar malfunction, but keep your eyes on yours, okay?"

"They are practically glued to it."

"Good."

The blue dot blinked on her screen a third time, then disappeared.

She glanced out her cockpit window.

Just ebb rock and spires.

Nothing more.

She grunted. Her radar's wires must be crossed with all of its new enhancements.

Concentrate, Ali, she told herself.

Daf came over the comm. "Did I ever tell you about the time I cut all power to our mech warehouse?"

Ali leaned her mech's back against a spire. "That was you?"

The power going out only happened once on Ali's watch, and Ali had been a mech miner longer than Daf, so Daf was most likely talking about this *specific* time.

Daf giggled. "Yeah, I hated mining. I wanted to go back to the biosphere to be with the plants and animals, so I cut the power."

Ali grinned.

At the time, she had assumed someone was the culprit and not a power facility malfunction. "How badly did you cut it? It took them like a week to get it back online. As per a Chief's responsibilities, I had to train new employees at another warehouse while you all stayed on the starbase."

She hurried to another spire and hid against it.

"I cut the shit out of it. Literally. I chopped the cables with our mech's mining cutters and smashed the generator and the transformer. My reward was spending time in the biosphere swimming and canoeing."

Ali shook her head, remembering that day and that week. She'd worked like a dog while the rest of the crew vacationed. "I can't believe that was you. How'd you get past the holocams? They record everything at the plants, you know."

"Well, I had a friend help me. It was Savanna Levens' assistant,

Devon. He hacked into the system somehow and looped a vid stream or something. I don't know exactly what he did."

Ali moved cautiously to another boulder, Daf close behind. "He cost us a lot of money is what he did, and he could've been thrown in jail. How did you get him to do that?"

"You don't want to know."

Ali rolled her eyes. "You slept with him?"

"What? You think I slept with him?"

Ali eyed the radar. It was all clear, and she rumbled to another large rock. "Okay, you didn't sleep with him."

"Heck, no." She paused. "I let him paint me."

Ali's eyebrows rose. "Paint *on* you, or paint a picture *of* you?"

"Of me. Nude."

Ali smiled knowingly. Of course, a catch. "Okay, why?"

"He told me I was model material, and he needed, well, a model."

"You better hope my mother—" Ali caught herself. Diana wasn't her mother. "You better hope Diana doesn't have that painting of you hanging in her office."

She was half-joking, but Diana had paintings and sculptures all over her office, and she wouldn't be surprised if a gorgeous woman like Daf was in one of them.

"There's more. When Devon paints, he goes by the name of Robert Rose."

Ali raced to another spire, but couldn't help but make a face. "Yeah, and I'm Fleet Admiral Shae Lutz."

Robert Rose was the most famous painter on Starbase Matrona. Robert Rose never showed his face, so painters in the hundreds had said they were him over the years.

"I saw the painting. There's no doubt in my mind he's that Robert guy. I saw other paintings he did, too, but they weren't released to the public."

"Devon is not Robert Rose."

"How do you know? Why can't Devon have an alias?"

"Because he's not Robert Rose. You got duped Daf. I don't know what got you to take your clothes off, but—"

"It's art, Ali. Nudity is art if viewed from an artist's perspective. From what I saw of Devon, he has the eye and the skill for it."

Robert Rose had an uncanny way of predicting the future with his paintings, which was probably why the guy hid.

Why didn't he predict this fight, this war?

Maybe he did.

It didn't matter. Devon wasn't Robert Rose.

"Okay, you keep thinking that. He's simply a good artist that got *you* to take your clothes off. I've been—"

An explosion hit the ground, jostling Ali's mech. Rocks ricocheted off her window and against her mech's chest and legs, pounding against her like a hammer to metal.

"Take cover." Ali twisted her mech around, not knowing where the shots had come from and curled her mech behind a spire. Her eyes darted from her radar to the terrain in front of her.

There was nothing.

"Daf, you still with me?"

"Here, Chief. I can't locate the shot's point of origin."

"Ready weapons." Ali swiped across her weapon's icon and tapped on her arm cannon. Her holoscreen changed, adding a crosshair and the number of cannon shells in her mech's mag.

"Aye, Chief, but I still can't locate the enemy."

Another blast slammed into a boulder several meters away, sending chunks of rocks and dust flying through the air.

"Why don't we see them, Chief?"

"I don't know. Use your eyes and survey everything in front of you. Our HDC maps are being messed with. I'm going to peek around the rock."

Before she could, her holoscreen changed, and the man with the red-beard appeared. "Haraje." He grinned. "I'm not going to let you live, Alison Johnson. And you know what? My sister can't help you anymore."

Ali lurched back. She tightened her muscles, the veins in her neck bulging. "You piece of shit. You think—"

His image blinked off the screen.

“Screw you, asshole.” Ali peaked around the corner. “Are you kidding me?”

There he was and in a mech twice her size. He stood in the open, his mech’s cannons for arms and missile turrets on its shoulders, pointed directly at her.

It was *that* mech again, the exact same one that tried to kill her on her way to *Sirona*.

His cannons flashed, and she quickly ducked back around the boulder. A slug whizzed by, impacting a rock and cracking off a few pieces.

Ali leaned into her comm mic. “Daf, target the mech on the other side of my boulder. He’s facing me, not you. Once you let him have it, I’ll engage.”

“Okay, Chief.”

She flexed every muscle in her body. She couldn’t wait to end this creep.

“On my mark, take him down in three…two…one…”

57

EDEN

Planet Eos

Swift's thrusters kicked on, bringing the ship into a quick hover.

Eden relaxed her grip on her armrest and watched the vidscreen as *Swift* descended behind a large hill, surrounded by a red mountain range.

She squished her eyebrows together. They were in the radiation zone, and what should be a dead landscape on the flatland they were about to land upon teemed with small trees and lichen, some grass, and a river in the distance.

It wasn't a dead zone like the history books, and the governance swore by. No. In fact, the zone where humans were allowed to mine, had built their mining warehouses and had perspired like biosphere waterfalls in the stifling mechs while they worked tirelessly, was the real dead zone.

She'd been told another lie. Did these lies ever end?

How she'd love to take them, ball them up, and throw them at Zim and the rest of the governance.

Everything was quiet now. *Swift* wasn't being shot at with volleys of cannon fire and missiles. "Why aren't they firing at us?"

Nyx gave her a look that said Eden should already know the answers to these questions. "*Swift,* pull up rearview."

The vidscreen split, and behind them, dotting the mountains and several grassy hilltops, were burning flames that sent thick smoke twirling into the sky.

Swift touched down, and the bridge jostled for a moment. Eden unstrapped, and walked slowly toward the vidscreen. "Are those starfighters?"

"Anunnaki starfighters, to be exact," Nyx told her, walking beside her. "*Swift* can do a lot of damage in a battle. A lot more than most starships, especially with her laser and plasma weapons."

Lasers too? Skye hadn't schooled her on *Swift's* weaponry.

Nyx flared her nostrils and reached under her robe, pulling out a small and sharp silver sword from a sheath on one side of her hip, the metal gleaming with a blue sheen. With her other hand, she unholstered a pistol.

She smirked, the scar on her cheek raising when she did so. "You ready, Eden?"

Eden slowly shook her head, a ball forming in her stomach. "Not really." She was a good shot with a weapon, but other than that, she didn't know how to fight on the ground. "Can't we take *Swift* back into the air and out of here?"

Nyx gestured with a side dip of her head toward the bow of the bridge. "I don't have the patience to answer every question you have, child. Listen, you come with us and live, or you stay here and wait it out on *Swift.*"

Nyx walked toward the nose of the bridge, and the crew followed her, a dozen humans and Sirians. They held swords shining like Nyx's in one hand, and pistols in the other. Skye wasn't anywhere to be seen.

A tall blue furred Sirian tossed a pistol at Eden. "I'm Jantu. Stay behind me, and I'll keep you safe. What you now have in your hand is a plasma blaster. It'll do more damage than a gun housing bullets."

She caught it, taken aback when he talked without moving his lips.

"Stay behind you?" She looked around the bridge and noted the exit on the other side. "Shouldn't we go that way?"

The floor shuddered, and the bridge quickly descended like an elevator, moving quickly, and stopping when it touched the ground.

They were now on Eos soil.

The walls lowered to the ground, exposing them to the elements. A breeze ruffled her hair, and she took a deep breath, smelling the sweet, fresh oxygen.

Then she froze and covered her mouth.

She breathed on Eos. Impossible. Breathable air didn't exist on this planet.

Yet, it did.

She kicked at the floor, and let out a loud grunt. She wanted to yell to the hilltops and strangle the bastards, any bastard that told her people Eos was uninhabitable and deadly without an oxygen device of some sort.

Nyx holstered her pistol and put her hand on Eden's shoulder, her eyebrows furrowed. "We have to go. Enemy troops are on their way."

Eden took a deep breath, filling her lungs to capacity and let out a gush of air. She shook her head, her lips straight, her eyes practically shooting beams of fire. "I'm breathing. I shouldn't be able to breathe." She lowered her shoulders. "Why didn't Skye tell me?"

Nyx shrugged. "I don't know. And I don't care. Why he'd make you the captain of this ship is beyond me. You're not fit. But, right now, come with Jantu and me." Nyx looked at the rest of the crew. "Everyone, fan out in threes. Stay undercover and wait. They'll be on us soon."

I'm not fit?

She wanted to punch Nyx in the gut. Eden had experience, and while yes, she probably required more training to be a captain, she'd led squadrons against pirates and potentially saved Starbase Matrona and Star Guild from terrible destruction.

"Let's go, Eden." Nyx and Jantu hurried off, heading for the ship's stern.

Eden followed her. "Where's Skye?"

Nyx picked up her pace. "Knowing Skye, he probably took an Aven out for a ride and is having a great time while the rest of us are here under *Swift*." She eyed the landscape as she jogged toward a landing skid.

"When did he leave?" asked Eden.

Nyx rolled her eyes. "All right, Miss one-hundred questions. He left the starship when we landed. He'll hold off any oncoming craft, giving us more protection than we probably need."

"Where's everyone else?"

"Oh, my Shimmermist." Nyx stopped jogging and turned. "Are you going to shut that trap for just a second? Please?" Her shoulders heaved up and down.

"I ask questions because I need answers," said Eden. "Don't give me that shut your trap crap."

Jantu motioned toward the landing skid. "Show her kindness, Nyx."

Nyx sheathed her sword and lowered the pistol to her side. "What do you mean by 'where's everyone else?'"

"This ship holds thousands of people, so—"

Nyx held up her hand. "We're the only ones on the ship."

"What?" Eden wanted to pull out her hair. Why would they leave planet Aurora with this small of a crew? Now they were going to take on an army heading their way? They couldn't take on an entire army with just a dozen people. They had no chance of surviving.

Jantu laughed. "We weren't expecting a fight. We were going to take you on a joy ride to show you the ropes and get you used to *Swift*, but by the looks of things, your heart had a different idea."

My heart?

Before she could reply, Jantu turned and started off again, moving faster toward the tail of the ship.

"No more questions," said Nyx, twisting on her heels and following Jantu.

"All right," Eden said under her breath and jogged after the two.

Up ahead, Nyx and Jantu crouched next to the landing skid towering high above their heads. They eyed their surroundings.

Eden did the same, leaning her back against its metal.

"Here." Nyx threw her gun at Eden, who gracefully caught it with her free hand. "Can you handle two plasma blasters at the same time?"

Eden puffed out her lower lip, looking at the gun she'd caught. "I don't know."

"Then holster one, and use the other."

Eden didn't have a holster.

Nyx, staring straight ahead, pointed. "Here they come."

In the distance, two mechs walked down a hill and toward their position.

The mechs were the same as the mining mechs Eden had seen on many occasions, though twice as wide and tall, and their arms were cannons and had missile turrets attached on top of their shoulders.

They weren't at all like her people's mining mechs.

Accompanying them were dozens of giants suited in gray and green uniforms with masks covering their faces. They each carried a spear that glowed red at the tip.

And they were coming fast.

58

ALI

Planet Eos, West of the Radiation Zone—Adarta System, Orion Spur

"Go," yelled Ali.

The mech on the other side of the rock, the one driven by S' brother, stood still, not moving.

He obviously didn't know about Wrench's lethal upgrades to Ali's and Daf's mech.

Daf pushed forward, rounding the other side of the rock, and moving out of Ali's view.

"Missile's launched," said Daf. "Direct hit. Go, Ali, go."

Ali curled around the boulder, aiming her cannon at the Anunnaki mech.

The enemy had turned, twisting its torso to face Daf as chunks of armor slipped off its back, some melting and dripping to the ebb ground, and sending black smoke swirling into the air.

Daf's shots were as good as they could have been and had done a lot of damage, more than Ali expected.

She swiped her finger over the trigger button, and her cockpit hummed, jostling back and forth. Cannon slugs shot one after the other, followed by a flash of fire exiting the muzzle, rocketing yet another forearm sized bullet the Anunnaki's way.

The slugs slammed, one by one, into the enemy mech. Sparks flew at the mech's hips, and more armor flung and plummeted to the ground.

The Anunnaki stepped to the right, keeping upright. He thrust out both arms, pointing one at Daf and the other at Ali, ready to send hot hell their way.

"Head to cover," yelled Ali.

Ali twirled her mech to the side and dashed toward the rock she had just come from.

A ping, loud and eerie, reverberated off Ali's cockpit walls, and her mech shuddered. It tipped to the side from the blasts, and Ali widened her stance, the mech copying her, and staying on its feet.

She reached her mech's arm forward, grasping the rock and pulling the mech closer to the boulder. She held her other arm out, sending more slugs at the Anunnaki, most likely missing, but hopefully messing with the guy's aim.

She slipped behind the boulder and rested her mech's back against the rock. She breathed heavily, sweat now dripping from the tip of her nose to her chest.

"Daf, you with me?"

"Here, Chief. Right next to you."

Ali turned her head. Beyond the cockpit window, not more than five meters away, stood Daf. A small fire raged on her mech's shoulder, and wires stuck out of its missile turret, half of it blown to nothing.

"Don't worry, Daf. I think we have the upper hand. My guess is he didn't know we had weapons."

"Or he would have brought more of his friends."

Ali gave a thumbs up. "Exactly."

The rock jerked forward, pushing against Ali and vibrating her cockpit like pepper in a shaker.

Rocks tumbled down the boulder, clanking off of the cockpit's dome.

He had fired at the rock, trying to blast it and dwindle it down to expose Ali and Daf.

The cockpit beeped, and a dot blinked on the radar. Ali bit her lower lip, nearly biting through it. "Crap, we have another enemy mech coming. Perhaps he realizes we're a bit more than he can handle."

"What do we do, Chief?"

"We go for it."

"Go for where?"

"Mount Gabriel." She paused, wondering if she was thinking straight. "We make a mad dash, and send as many slugs and missiles at him as we can."

She could see Daf shaking her head, not liking the idea. "All right, it's better than nothing, I guess."

"Rush to the rock across from you, and send some cannon shots his way. It doesn't matter if you hit him or—"

The giant popped on Ali's holoscreen, his lips curled in a frown. "I have spoken with Zim. Your entire starbase, including the Star Guild Starfleet you so love, is gone." He leaned in, his eyes the only part of his face filling the screen. "Vaporized."

Ali punched through the hologram, her fist merging with the light colors between the giant's eyes. "You lie."

He raised his brows. "Do I?"

He blinked off the screen.

"Who was that, Ali? I heard him. I saw him."

"It doesn't matter." Heat rose from her belly, matching the stifling temperature in the cockpit. She lowered her head like a bull. "He messes with my friends, he messes with the worst part of me."

She pushed forward, headed around the rock she hid behind. "Go, Daf. Pound the shit out of him," Ali screamed and raced forward, targeting her missiles, the crosshair positioned firmly around the Anunnaki mech in front of her.

Cannons from Daf's mech smacked the Anunnaki's side, and missiles hit square on its chest.

The Anunnaki mech took a step back, sparks spraying from a busted compartment in its torso.

The mech backpedaled and aimed its cannons. Fire erupted out of the muzzles, and shells littered the ground as slugs blasted outward, heading for both Ali and Daf.

Ali twisted her mech's torso, and the shots soared past her except a few clanks against her mech's shoulder and arm. Several hit the side of the cockpit dome, ringing the cockpit like a bell.

Ali sidestepped, keeping upright and ran to a nearby spire.

A violent bang sounded in her cockpit, and a loud boom from several missiles connecting to her mech's back rocketed her into the spire.

The cockpit rattled, and her HDC blinked off, as nearly all systems went offline.

Her mech went limp and slid against the rock, cracking and crunching pieces of spire until she hit the ground, sprawled out like a dead soldier.

Everything shuddered and then went still.

Ali glared at the blue sky, her restraints keeping her from falling into the back wall.

"Guild dammit," she cursed. "Daf, are you near me?"

"Yes, and I'm hitting him with everything I got. He's slowing down." A pause. "No, wait. He's turning around and facing me."

"Get out of there, Daf." Ali reached toward the HDC to turn the mech back online.

"I'm ducking around a boulder. He's out of view now. Where are you?" Daf's breaths came heavy.

"Hold on." Ali pressed an emergency override button, which should act like a shock wave to the mech's system.

Nothing happened.

"Shit." She flexed her muscles and made a fist. She punched at the air, her nostrils flaring. "Daf, get out of here and get to the mountain. I can hold him off."

She knew she couldn't. She'd be a pile of dust here soon, but at least it would give Daf time to find those people inside the tunnels in Mount Gabriel. S made it clear they could help the people on Starship *Sirona*.

"What are you talking about? Let's go together. We might be able to outrun him."

An explosion of rock tumbled from the spire and covered Ali's cockpit window, dimming the light from outside.

"Go, Daf. Now."

"No. Where are you? I don't see you on the radar. All I see are the incoming mechs and this prick out here."

"How close are the other mechs?" asked Ali.

"Not far."

"Then go Daf. Get out of here."

"That's a negative, Chief. I'm not leaving you."

Ali grimaced. She had to get Daf out of here. She dragged her into this mess, and the last thing she wanted was her dying like Hendricks had in front of her.

She wouldn't be able to see her mother again, or her father, but that paled in comparison to saving thousands of lives on *Sirona*.

"I will catch up to you."

Daf sighed. "All right, but hurry. I'll get a head start, but I expect you to be no more than five minutes behind. Got it?"

Ali swallowed the sorrow trying to move up her throat. "Got it."

"I'll see you soon, Chief."

"See you soon." Ali blinked away her lie. For a few minutes, everything went quiet. No Daf. No concussion blasts. Just her and her downed mech.

She lifted her hands in front of her face then dropped them to her side. "Well, I almost got to reunite with mom and dad."

Ali's mech lifted in a diagonal position, the mech's heels the only thing touching the ground.

"Here we go." Ali's lips downturned, and she whispered to herself, "Save all those on *Sirona*, Daf. It's all in your hands now."

The rocks and dirt rolled off of her cockpit window, and the light peered in. She squeezed her eyes shut. She knew what was coming. A storm of point-blank cannon fire.

She'd be dead in a minute, maybe two.

59

ALI

Planet Eos, West of the Radiation Zone—Adarta System, Orion Spur

Her mech moved backward, its feet dragging across the ground.

Why hadn't the red-headed giant killed her yet?

She opened her eyes, seeing the Anunnaki mech slowly moving toward her, sparks flying off it, and its armor hanging like ripped clothes.

She was pulled around the spire, and the enemy mech disappeared out of view.

Wait, how did I see the enemy mech when it's pulling me?

Her eyes widened. "Daf?"

"I got you."

Daf leaned her up against the spire, pressing her mech's arm against Ali's chest, keeping her mech in a standing position.

"I turned on my rear cams and saw you weren't holding him off at all," said Daf. "From this point forward, don't lie to me, Ali. This isn't just you against the world. This is us against the world. We work as a team, do you understand? Not until you're dead do I move on. Got it, Chief?"

Ali nodded. "I was trying to save you and—"

"Don't give me that bullshit, Chief."

"All right, I got it."

"Good."

This was the second time Daf had saved her butt.

"Ali, unstrap your restraints and override the system."

Ali shook her head. "I tried."

"Hurry, Ali. He's coming closer."

"I'll try and get Wrench on the line."

"Fine. I'll hold this bastard off." Daf let go of Ali's mech, and the mech toppled to the ground to land on its side. Ali jostled left and right in her restraints, and hung toward the side wall.

More explosions, but she had to ignore them and get Wrench on the line.

She tapped on her comm line, bringing up several numbers. She patched in Wrench's number to his workbench comm, crossing her fingers.

"Wrench here." His voice was higher than normal, more spirited. But why?

"Wrench, I don't have time—"

"Sleuth, how ya doing, man? I've got yo specs ready for HDC transfer. What else ya need?"

Ali creased her brows. What was Wrench talking about? She wasn't Sleuth.

"No, Wrench. It's me, Ali. I'm in a major pickle, how do I—"

More explosions rocked the area.

"Oh, ya, Sleuth. An emergency? Ya, the captain is right here next to me. I'll send her yo way."

Ali kept her mouth shut. Her crap for brains, fake mother, was in the launch bay. No wonder he was odd on the comm.

"Okay, this is Wrench. The coast is clear. Yo mother wouldn't leave my side, interrogatin' me about—"

"Wrench, listen up," interrupted Ali. "I don't have time. My mech is out of commission, and I need to override the system right now."

For a moment, silence filled the comm. The silence felt louder than the cracks and booms echoing outside.

"Wrench?"

"I was thinkin', but I got it. Okay, unstrap and get yo'self to the HDC console."

Ali unstrapped, her feet landing on the side of the cockpit. She took a few steps to the console. "I'm here."

"Good, now punch off the compartment underneath the console. Got it?"

"Punch it?"

"Ya don't have the right tools. So, kick it, punch it. Do what ya gotta' do to get 'er off."

Ali nodded. She pounded the console with her hand, seeing screws were keeping it in place. She wanted to kick it, but it was too high, so she continued to pound it with the side of her fist.

The console began cracking where the screws met. One more hit and the console went flying, ricocheting off the cockpit window and to the floor.

"It's off."

"Do you see the lever?"

In front of her were wires upon wires, holocomp chips, and plugs. In the middle was one lever, small, but a lever nonetheless.

She touched it. "Yes."

"Flick it off. This shuts down all safety controls that keep yo mech in the off position when yo mech's computers show it to be in engine danger. It's a safeguard. When ya turn that safeguard off, it'll keep yo mech activated even if ya mech overheats, and even if ya mech's engine is about to seize up or explode."

"Got it." She flicked the lever. The HDC turned on, and the engines revved, humming beautifully. "It's on."

"I hit him hard," said Daf.

"What was that? Are ya in physical danger?" asked Wrench.

"No time to talk. Sorry Wrench." Ali turned off his comm channel and strapped in. She swiped across the holoscreen, activating her mech's gyros and joint functions.

"Where did you hit him?" asked Ali, pushing her mech into a

standing position. She swiped across the weapon's icon, readying her arsenal.

"I hit him with a few missiles in the middle of the chest, and he's moving even slower now."

Ali walked her mech to the other side of the spire and peaked around it. The Anunnaki was maneuvering behind a rock as well, most likely waiting for his reinforcements.

The reinforcements.

She pulled up the radar and saw they were still a ways off, but a ways off didn't mean much. Maybe ten to fifteen minutes until those jerks were here.

The enemy mech then dashed behind a spire. It rounded their position, probably trying to cut them off from to the mountain. "Did you see that, Daf? He is flanking our position."

"I saw him."

Ali brought up her cannons. "Blast him when he goes for a run again."

The guy rushed his mech toward another rock. Ali let off several cannon rounds but didn't know if she hit him or not. "I thought you said you slowed him down?"

"Apparently, I was wrong," said Daf.

"He's trying to block our escape to the mountain."

Ali studied the area, seeing rocks everywhere, all big enough to hide behind. "We have to close in on him and engage. I'll move forward, but in a short arc to his left. You do the same but on his right. One of us will get him on his rear, hopefully. Use as many boulders for cover as possible."

"All right."

Ali moved toward the giant's location, spotting a rock for cover. She dashed toward it, and then behind it, watching her radar. "He's not moving."

Maybe his mech was out of commission.

Ali moved to another rock, then halted quickly, splintering a small clump of rocks and sending rocks like shrapnel in the air.

She faced the redhead's mech. Its cockpit window was cracked open, and the occupant, the piece of ebb who'd haunted her dreams for years, was either unconscious or dead, hanging out of the window, his arms dangling.

He had to be lifeless. If not now, he would be in a minute or so, since there wasn't breathable oxygen on this planet.

Ali walked her mech toward the guy. "I think he's dead. I'm going in for a closer look."

"On better thought, let's get to the mountain. We have inbound mechs, the heading is twelve degrees west, and still on their way. They'll be here in ten minutes, maybe sooner, maybe later. I don't know."

Ali tapped her head, trying to get her mind to work correctly, and the mech mimicked her, jerking her back on contact. She hated it when she did that. "You're right, let's get going and fast."

They moved their mechs through Little Scythe Straights, exiting the straights and trekking up a barren hill.

Ali pulled up rear view cams and gasped. The man who she thought was dead, who had been hanging out of his cockpit no more than a few minutes ago, was running after them, a glowing red-tipped spear-like weapon in his hand.

"Holy Guild. He's on his way, and he's fast."

"Who?" said Daf.

"Look in your rear cam."

"What the ebb'n hell? How is he breathing? How did he live?"

Ali took her eyes off of the holoscreen and saw Mount Gabriel in front of her, so close she could almost touch it. "We're minutes away from the mountain, maybe closer. Let's pick up our pace."

"You don't have to tell me twice."

Ali's mech shuddered as an explosion beneath her rocked her upward, jolting her head backward and then violently forward.

For a brief second, she eyed her radar. Another mech had sprung out of nowhere.

A second blast and all systems went down, and static blared over her commlink and throughout her cockpit.

Instinctively, she knew even the override lever wouldn't do anything now.

Black smoke rose in front of her window, and clanks and grinding sounds filled the cockpit.

Her mech tipped backward, and she grabbed onto her restraints, her head and neck whiplashing a second time when the mech slammed into the earth, sending a dust cloud into the air.

She unstrapped and rushed to the window, trying to get a clear view of Daf and how many mechs were out there.

She pressed her cheek against the window, trying to gain a better angle. When she couldn't get a good look, she moved from the window and fussed with the comm, trying to fix it.

A loud clank sounded against her mech, something bumping up against it and hard. Her heart pounded, and she shifted her eyes back to the window. She touched Diana's gun, holstered at her hip.

Her mouth dropped open. A giant mech's foot was coming down, ready to smash her inside her cockpit.

She took in a deep breath and pressed the hatch button, opening the dome at the apex of her mech's head.

Heat rushed in, stirring gently across her skin, and she scrambled out of her mech onto the hard, rocky Eos surface. The mountain loomed over her.

So did an enemy mech.

The mech's foot came down on her mech's cockpit and smashed it like a pancake. Fire and sparks flew outward.

The concussion blast threw her off of her feet and somersaulted her in the air. She landed on her back, then tumbled head over heels, sliding across the ebb surface.

She dug her feet in the ground to stop herself and looked up. She had to get to Daf to survive, but where was she?

The Anunnaki mech twisted around, bolting after another mech—Daf's.

Daf's mech hurried toward the mountain, walking backward, her cannons pointed directly at the oncoming mech.

"Daf," screamed Ali. She breathed hard and heavy as Daf, and the

Anunnaki mech began shooting, the sounds twice as loud outside and the explosions twice as bright.

Daf was outmatched, not by weapon power alone, but by the other mech's size.

Daf ducked away from a barrage of missiles by millimeters if that. She continued to trek backward, and fired a volley of missiles of her own, hitting the enemy squarely in the chest.

It stopped and swayed, teetering to the side, then managed to straighten itself as cannon fire littered its hips and legs.

Ali swung her hands out wide. "Go, Daf, go. Get out of here."

Daf shot another round of cannons and another at the stationary mech. She hurried forward, blasting the mech in front of her.

Armor scraped off the Anunnaki, plummeting to the ground and sending small poofs of dust into the air.

Ali reached her hands out. "Turn around, Daf." She raised her hands in the air, jumping up and down, doing her best to will Daf away from the mech and get her toward the mountain.

She had to save *Sirona.*

Daf bull charged, firing one cannon after another, then sent a missile the enemy's way.

More armor flew, and smoke streamed from the Anunnaki mech, but Ali knew that Daf's full-on charge wouldn't work against the much larger opponent.

The opponent waited, taking the brunt of her rage, and when Daf closed in, the enemy raised its cannon arms and slammed them against her.

Daf's cockpit window burst open, sending shards of striated ebb glass through the air, and littering the ground. Her mech tilted and toppled hard on its back.

Ali ran for Daf, then stopped dead in her tracks when the Anunnaki lifted its mech's foot and brought it down on Daf's cockpit, the sound of metal against metal soaring to her ears.

She dropped to her knees, her hands in fists. "No. Daf, no."

She had just brought Daf to her death. If Ali had listened to Wrench and waited for him to make an army of mech soldiers, they would have had a chance to survive this mess and overrun the mechs they had just faced.

She'd been selfish and stupid.

She pounded the ground, then reeled back. "How am I breathing out here?"

She gazed around, her eyes wide, her breaths coming easy and quick. The air was fresh.

"I can breathe. What the Guild?"

Footsteps pounded behind her.

She turned to see the red-haired asshole cresting a small hill.

Ali jumped to her feet and slid to an indentation in the ground, surrounded by a clump of ebb rock.

She eyed the man scanning the area, no doubt looking for Ali and Daf.

When he noticed the two downed mechs, he walked down the hill. His laughter carried across the valley. He lifted his spear in the air. "Haraje."

Ali shifted her gaze to the enemy mech. It peered down at Daf's mech, then turned and walked in the opposite direction, obviously not seeing the Anunnaki giant walking with the spear.

The giant picked up his pace, running after the Anunnaki mech. "Stop, you imbecile. I'm Enlil, your damn Monarch." He halted as the mech disappeared behind a hill. "You better not let me find out who you are, or I'll slit your throat, along with every one of your family members." He shook his head. "You blind rookie."

Ali lowered her position to her stomach and eyed the ground for a moment. There was too much going on. She needed to calm down and gather her bearings.

"What the heck?" She touched the rock. The land all around wasn't how she had seen it when she was in her mech.

But how?

Yes, there was the plain red, gray, and black in the ebb rock and in the landscape, but now it shimmered with gold and clear rock.

She peeked above her hiding spot. Enlil was walking away from her. At his feet, the ground was packed with the gold and clear rock, sparkling as far as the eye could see.

"What is this?" Why didn't this gold and clear, glittering rock show up in all the walls, ships, and mechs built from ebb?

Where did those parts of the rock disappear to? Did they simply meld into the finished product, disappearing after the rock was melted and formed into whatever was needed?

That really wasn't the question. Why couldn't they see it when looking through a mech's cockpit, or in a ship, or peering through a warehouse window?

She paused, glaring at Enlil's back. He strutted toward Daf's mech.

Sparks and smoke rose from Daf's cockpit, and she thought she saw movement. If Daf had somehow survived, Ali had to save her.

She aimed her gun, pointing it at Enlil's back, and pulled the trigger.

Her gun recoiled, and a bang echoed, making it twice as loud as it should have been.

Enlil yelped and lifted his leg and twisted around. Blood splattered, and he fell to the ground, grasping his hamstring.

He lifted his spear and shot wildly.

Ali ducked, keeping her head out of the open.

The shots ceased, and she peeked over the lip of her hiding spot.

Enlil dragged himself up a small incline and moved behind a pile of unused mined ebb.

Ali took another aim and pulled the trigger. It went wide just as Enlil concealed himself behind the rocks.

Ali ducked back down, and silence filled the valley.

She couldn't help but think, as impossible as it sounded, that Daf lived and probably needed help.

First, she had to get rid of this Enlil guy.

She huffed. It was the last thing she wanted to do, but survival was survival. "Guild, here I go."

She crept out of the indentation and hurried toward the small incline topped with the unused mined ebb, where Enlil hid.

She held out her gun and making sure she wasn't in Enlil's sight, went as quietly as possible.

At the base of the incline sat a mound. She leaned against it and peered around.

Enlil hadn't shown himself and hadn't poked his spear out.

She eyed the ground. Blood trailed behind the mined ebb.

She had hit him well. Hopefully, he bled out.

She bolted out from behind the mound and up the incline, resting her back against the mined ebb, which was nothing more than a pile of large slabs thrown on top of each other.

She was now on one side of it, and Enlil on the other.

Silence pierced the air.

No movement.

The guy had to be dead or dying, but she had to make sure.

She took a step on the ebb, and proceeded to climb, moving quietly, cautiously. Reaching the last portion of ebb, she aimed the tip of her weapon over the edge.

Again, nothing. No return gunfire, no shift or movement.

She took a quick glance.

He wasn't there.

She looked around the area, surveying it.

A streak of blood showed his path around another pile of ebb in the distance. He was retreating.

So be it.

Ali turned and rushed toward Daf's downed mech.

The smoke had grown thinner. Good. She ran faster and jumped back as a small internal explosion lifted the cockpit's HDC column into the air, flipping it to the ground.

If Daf lived through the mech crunching her cockpit with its foot, there surely wasn't any way Daf had lived through the internal explosion.

She ran to the cockpit and grabbed a handhold, pulling herself up and onto the window frame. She looked down.

A spark from a broken wire fizzed brightly, highlighting Daf. She was unstrapped, her eyes closed, and laying against the back corner of the cockpit, a portion the enemy mech didn't trample and compress fully to the ground.

Luck had been on Daf's side.

Ali jumped into the cockpit and crouched. Daf's chest moved up and down, breathing, bringing a smile to Ali's face.

A clank from outside reverberated in the cockpit, and Ali glanced up, gasping.

Enlil pointed his spear at her head, his lips also forming a smile. "Hello, Alison."

60

ALI

Planet Eos, West of the Radiation Zone—Adarta System, Orion Spur

Ali lurched out of the way as a shot rang out from Enlil's spear, pinging loudly into the back of the cockpit and singeing the ebb wall.

As Ali moved, she raised her gun, pointing her weapon at Enlil. She pulled the trigger several times as Enlil leaped back to safety, but not before a bullet caught his spear, splitting it in half.

The spear fell to the floor, broken.

Ali moved away from Daf, catching a glimpse of Enlil's shoulder as he hurried around the window frame toward the top of the cockpit's dome.

She pressed the trigger twice, sending one bullet and missing. The second trigger pull only clicked, and her gut wrenched.

The gun's magazine was empty, and she didn't have any spare bullets on hand.

Enlil hopped into the cockpit, his body twice her height and width, his eyes menacing. He took a step forward with a limp and grimaced.

"You hurt me, little girl."

Ali held her gun out. "Don't take another step."

He limped onward, regardless. "I know you're out of ammo."

Ali took a step back. "Why do you want to kill me so badly? Why have you been watching my every move?"

He rubbed his hands together. "I'm a scientist, above all else. Let's just call you, and your father, an experiment."

Ali took another step back. "My father? You *know* my father?"

He shook his head, his eyebrows rising. "It doesn't matter who I know. What matters is that I can't have you here anymore. You were my pet project, and kind of my baby. I watched, monitored you, gave you the best circumstances possible when I brought you here." He reached down to the back of his leg and brought his fingers up in front of him, blood dripping. "I detected a part of me in you. I wanted to see how well you did in this world. I didn't like what I saw."

She took another step back, bumping into the wall. Her hand came down against her holster.

She almost flinched. Did she just touch a magazine? She adjusted her fingers, slowly swiping up, keeping her facial features calm.

She momentarily paused between a breath.

She *had* swiped against a magazine in the holster. This could be the first time she'd ever wanted to thank Diana for anything.

She put her gun above her head. "I surrender." She pressed the magazine release, and it dropped from the gun to bounce against the floor. She lowered it, pointing away from him, and cleared the gun by pulling the slide back. "It's empty."

He took another step in her direction, cocking his head to the side, eyeing the magazine on the floor. His eyebrows furrowed. "What are you doing?"

"I'm surrendering."

"That doesn't change anything." He brought his eyes up to hers. "You have my race's blood in you, and I've been finding that the few on the starbase and in Star Guild with my blood are less controllable. I can't have you spread my race's seed in the human race if you know what I mean."

She lowered her hand to her belt and pulled the magazine out of its pouch. She thrust it into the magazine well, and slammed her palm into it, simultaneously pressing on the slide lock, automatically closing the slide and loading a round.

Enlil lunged for her gun, and Ali pulled the trigger, expelling a hot bullet his way. He twirled around, blood splattering from his arm.

Ali pulled the trigger again, slamming a bullet in his rear. He yelled in pain and pulled himself up and over the cockpit.

Ali let off another round, hitting him in the back before he jumped to the ground.

She holstered her gun and pulled herself over the lip of the cockpit. He was hobbling away, heading for the incline he'd hid behind earlier.

A trail of blood lined the ground, and he held onto his leg and back. There was no way he'd survive. He'd bleed out in no time.

She dropped back down, her hands and arms shaking, adrenaline mixed with fear coursing through her body. She wanted to throw up but held it down. She had to get Daf out of here before anymore Anunnaki showed up.

She shook Daf. "Wake up."

No response.

She pulled Daf closer to her and tapped her forehead. "Daf, it's me. Ali. You're safe and alive."

Nothing.

Ali let out a low growl. This was the last thing she needed, especially right now, in the middle of a fresh battle zone.

She couldn't pick Daf up and throw her over the lip of the cockpit without a step ladder, so she pressed the hatch button. The dome unlocked with a hiss and opened.

Ali backed up and lifted Daf's limp arms by the wrists and pulled her out of the mech.

She glanced behind her at Mount Gabriel. It was right there. "Here we go."

She lifted Daf and leaned her against her shoulder, then brought her forearm between her legs and lifted her body onto her shoulders.

She hurried toward the mountain, Daf's body pushing down on her like a ton of bricks.

Ali went into a slow, unsteady jog. "I thought you'd be lighter."

She kept her eyes on the mountain, getting closer with every step, her breaths fast and heavy.

She had to get to the tunnel, and she knew exactly where it was.

Heading up an incline, her legs gave way, and she dropped to a knee and tipped to the side. Daf fell on the ground with a thump.

Ali lay on her back, resting, the mountain's shadow keeping her cool.

She rubbed her face. "Oh my Guild, Daf. Wake up." She wiped the spit from her mouth. A loud sonic boom echoed in the distance.

Starfighters.

They were getting louder, heading her way.

"Guild dammit." She grabbed Daf by the arms and pulled her up the slight incline toward the tunnel, her mind spinning on overdrive, and her heart nearly beating out of her chest.

The starfighter's engines rumbled louder, and she looked up in the sky. They were dots now and a ways away, but that wouldn't last long.

Daf's hands slipped from her grip, and Ali dropped to her rear. She bent over, her head between her legs and her hands on her knees, moaning.

She had to keep going. She couldn't stop here.

She slipped her arms under Daf's armpits and pulled her some more, watching the girl's shoes scraping across the ebb ground and listening to oncoming fighters coming to kill them.

Her legs burned, and her head pounded. She glanced at the sky. Starfighters, and coming in fast. She had a minute, maybe less to find cover before they strafed her position.

She looked over her shoulder, recognizing a boulder in front of the tunnel entrance. "Ten more meters."

The starfighters grew nearer, and the ground began to shake.

She hurried behind the boulder as the crafts thundered overhead. She held her breath, waiting for them to turn around, to search for her and Daf, or to land near the downed mechs.

They did none of that and continued to soar onward.

"Thank you, S." Maybe it was S that scrambled their heads up display or not, but she had to thank someone. No way could she have lived through this on her own, even with Daf's help.

She slid to the ground, crossed her legs, and let her head fall into her hands.

She let out a cry, then more, letting the deep bellows of sadness and fear escape from her belly.

It was short-lived.

The starfighters' engines growled loudly again, and she gaped her mouth open. They had swung around and were coming in for another pass.

61

EDEN

Planet Eos

Jantu and Nyx walked out from under *Swift* and into the open, watching the coming mechs and troops. There were a lot of them, more than Eden thought the small group of humans and Sirians could take on, but that wasn't the top of her worry list.

She had to find someone, anyone on this planet who might have survived the onslaught. They were probably in the warehouses, and Eden and her new crew needed to head there if they survived.

She shifted her focus to the enemy grunts walking on land that sparkled like glitter. Skye was right. Ebb was full of crystals and gold, not just the red, black, and gray she'd seen her entire life.

Eden walked on the hard ground and stopped next to Nyx.

Nyx stood straight and tall, turning her back to Eden. She extended her arms behind her back. "Help me with my robe."

"Huh?" Eden blinked a couple of times. "Why?"

"It gets in the way."

Eden eyed the oncoming small army. They were getting closer. This wasn't a time for a wardrobe change.

"Hurry it up, Eden," blurted Nyx.

Eden reached forward and pulled off Nyx's robe, expecting a half-naked woman. Thankfully, Nyx was fully clothed, wearing a silvery armor-like cloth.

A small, metallic bow, thin and flexible and arrows were secured to her back by a silver cord strung around her torso and waist.

The arrows were tipped with red, round heads.

As quick as a flash, Nyx grabbed the bow with one hand, pulled an arrow with the other, and brought them in front of her.

She aimed and shot.

Ali followed the arrow. It headed straight for a mech, moving at speeds that rivaled a bullet.

A loud concussion and fire blasted outward at a mech's shoulder. It rocked back, an arm falling to the ground in a heap of metal. A mounted missile turret followed, breaking into pieces and exploding when it hit the ground.

Another arrow was fired by Nyx, and a fiery mess erupted from the mech's other arm, where it and the other missile turrets broke and fell.

The mech stopped, now weaponless.

Eden eyed Jantu, the blue-furred Sirian. He towered over her and gave her a side grin, then nodded toward Nyx.

Eden turned to see Nyx launch a third arrow and shatter another mech's cockpit window, followed by a larger ball of fire bursting out of the cockpit.

The mech fell back, landing hard and smashing rock.

Nyx grabbed another arrow and notched it against her bow. "I only have four arrows left." She closed her eyes, whispering something inaudible. She opened them, an evil grin growing on her lips. "Skye is on his way."

Did they even need him? She looked around, noticing a few humans with their own bows and arrows, readying to send them like a hellstorm upon the approaching troops and mechs.

"The enemy is in firing range," said Jantu, calm and patient, as if in the middle of a meditation.

Eden twisted around. The giant troops ran toward them faster, their spears raised.

Blasts exited the spears' tips.

Nyx pulled Eden closer to Jantu. "Shields."

Jantu crouched and held his forearm outward, touching a brass-colored band on his wrist. A blue bubble of some type expanded around them, and Nyx drew Eden closer, nearly hugging her.

Sparks riddled the bubble, blocking any and all bullets from penetrating.

Nyx crouched as well and aimed an arrow at a mech. "Eden, have your guns ready. As soon as there's a lull, we'll return fire. Got it?"

Eden nodded, her stomach twisting and turning. Would there ever be a lull?

Nyx closed one eye, targeting an enemy. "Now."

The bubble disappeared, and Nyx laid into the oncoming mech, sending arrow after arrow to topple the beast over.

"Fire, Eden. Fire."

The giant grunts rushed onward, yelling, and firing. Rocks burst in front of them, throwing some of them into the air, their arms flailing until they smashed onto the ground.

Eden targeted a giant that ran through a dust cloud and pulled the trigger.

She missed but looked at her gun in surprise. It didn't recoil, and instead of a bullet, it expelled an indigo bolt of some sort. Was that plasma?

She raised the blaster again, aiming at the soldier she had just missed.

Nyx's arm came across Eden's chest. "Stop. Jantu's out there."

Jantu hurried toward the oncoming men, sword in hand, the blueish blade shimmering against the sun's rays.

His robe blew in the breeze like a cape, whipping behind him. The soldiers fired at him, and he blocked each shot with his shield.

He jumped and somersaulted in the air, landing a couple of meters from a giant.

The enemy slashed its spear, and Jantu swung his sword, cutting the spear in half.

The giant reared his broken spear above his head and came down, swiping fast and hard at Jantu.

The grunt was too slow.

Jantu ducked and sideswiped the giant's legs with a low kick, sending him on his back.

The Sirian pulled out a small, round device with a pointy stem from under his robe. He slammed it into the ground, turned and fled, bullets whizzing by him.

He dove onto the ground, activating his shield again.

Nyx turned her back to Jantu. "Close your eyes."

Eden dove to the ground and closed her eyes.

A bright light flashed all around, and everything went silent.

Nyx stood from her crouch. "All is well, now, Eden. Get up."

Eden turned, staring at the open field in front of her. Jantu walked slowly toward them with long, athletic strides as if today had been nothing more than a walk in the park.

Behind him were enemy soldiers lying motionless on the ground.

"What did you do?" Eden studied the downed troops, straining to see any movement.

Nyx punched Jantu in the arm. "He showed off in front of you, *that's* what he did."

Jantu rubbed his arm, looking at his feet. "I tend to get carried away at times."

"Carried away?" Nyx shook her head. "That's an understatement."

Eden motioned toward the soldiers. "Are they dead?"

Nyx crossed her arms and sucked in a deep breath, her chest out, obviously proud at what she was going to say. "It's a stun light. We usually save that for the last arrow."

She pulled a small, wooden item shaped like a pencil from a pouch on her thigh and waved it in front of Eden.

Eden flinched when the item quadrupled in size, forming a long shaft.

Nyx reached behind her back, grabbing a bulbous, round silver ball from her belt and twisted it onto the shaft. "You screw one of these bad boys on here and shoot it high into the air. Drop it right in the middle of any crowd. The light shines, and everyone within a thousand-meter radius that sees the light at its full glory falls down in a state of paralysis or sleeps. They won't be able to move for a day."

Eden put her hands on her hips. "Wouldn't it have been easier if we had just done this right away?"

"The mechs aren't affected by it. The drivers are seated behind tinted cockpit windows. Most of the troops behind the mechs could have been shielded, as well." She tapped Eden's elbow, then walked toward the middle of the ship. "We only have a few stun lights, so we use them at opportune moments." She grinned. "Let's go. Skye is here."

She surveyed the rest of her crew now waiting in a circle just below the belly of the ship, some squatting, others leaning on a bent knee, some breathing heavy, some calm. Most importantly, they were alive without a scratch or a ruffle on any of them.

Strolling up to the group, Nyx placed her hand on Skye's back and gave him a nod. "And, where were you during all of this?"

He folded his hands in front of him, looking at Nyx, then Eden. He dipped his head. "I think I know why Eden's heart steered us to Eos. I came upon a starship sitting at the base of a ridge. It had *Sirona* written on it—"

Eden's mouth opened, but no sound came out. The news struck her like a hard punch. She pictured a crashed starship, its hull busted open and people lying on the ground, dead and burned. She didn't want to ask, but she had to. "Are they okay?"

"They don't look like they've taken critical damage, but as I flew further, I saw a massive war machine with an equally massive cannon mounted on it. It was approaching *Sirona*, moving slowly across the plateau. If it maintains that pace, *Sirona* has a day, maybe two tops before it gets there."

Eden threw her hands to her face and rubbed her eyes. "We have to stop it."

"That's what we intend to do." He rubbed the back of his neck. "It's our job to protect and assist. After all, we are the Space Templars."

62

SHAE

Starbase Matrona

Shae stood in an infirmary room with HDC's lining the walls. He pointed at a blue dot on the holoscreen in front of him. The dot was on planet Eos and at the base of a mountain. "That's her? That's my daughter?" He shot Devon a look. "If so, why is she at the base of a mountain?"

Devon shrugged. "I don't know, Admiral. But she's moving, which means she's alive."

If he could see her on the screen and he could see himself on the screen beside it, then whoever inserted a device in him, perhaps a small nano-chip, and in his daughter, had been monitoring both of them as well.

He didn't like that feeling. In fact, he wanted to scratch through his skin to find the tracking device and stomp it into the ground.

On his way to this room, he had Koda contact Louise, and asked for her presence. She was on her way.

Shae raised his voice. "If my daughter is alive on Eos, she'd have to be in a ship or a mech."

Naveya and Koda stood in the room as well, and Naveya put her finger up. "There is ample oxygen on Eos, enough for you and me, and everyone else to breathe."

Shae almost laughed. How little this woman knew. Did she figure Shae was an idiot? "Naveya is your name, right?" He waited for her nod, then continued, "I'm sorry, but Eos hasn't had oxygen for as long as humans can remember."

Koda shifted on his feet and let out a little chuckle. "My uncle is right, ma'am. If there was oxygen on that planet, we'd be living on it."

Naveya jabbed a tongue against her cheek, clearly in disbelief at their response. "I see. And, how about those Space Templars? Your governance was pretty open about them too? And, extraterrestrials and other *Beings* out in the cosmos? Those who attacked you were simply a figment of your imagination?"

She crossed her arms. "How about those Suficell Pods? Do you really think after five anti-aging sessions with a pod, extending your life by nearly a hundred and forty years, you really can't use them for anti-aging anymore? No. You can use them limitlessly." She huffed. "Do you want me to keep going?" She dipped her head toward the holoscreen. "You can either trust me, and trust your memories of your daughter, Admiral, or you can stay here and always wonder."

As much as Shae wanted to fly his butt to Eos and meet his daughter, and get her back here in one piece, and as much as he wanted to believe that Naveya was telling the truth about Eos, he couldn't leave.

He had a starbase to save. With Payson on the loose, and if Naveya was also telling the truth about Payson wanting to unleash the toxin, he had to stay here and stop the psycho from killing everyone.

Devon tapped the screen, his fingers going through the hologram. "She's moving again."

Naveya leaned forward, resting her hand on a table next to the HDC screen. "Admiral, I think it would be wise for you to be with your daughter as soon as possible. Your reunion will spark more memories in you and her. Together, both of you would be a force to reckon with. You both have royal blood in you that will help with your rebellion. It will enhance your abilities more so upon meeting your daughter."

Shae cocked his head to the side. "A rebellion? Blood? Enhanced abilities?" He wanted to roll his eyes but refrained. "Look, we're not starting a rebellion. We're simply trying to survive the attack and the resulting aftershocks." He didn't even want to comment on the royal blood and enhanced abilities.

Nevaya cleared her throat. "You are starting a rebellion, Admiral. You're fighting back and figuring out a truth that has eluded you for centuries, that you're a slave race. You have masters, even if you can't see them. You mined ebb for them, for reasons you're also uncovering."

She continued, "As a slave race, you are breaking your shackles and are in the process of fighting for your freedom. Even if you don't want to admit it, you're the leader of this rebellion. As the leader, you need to do everything in your power to overcome the evil that has kept you enslaved for a thousand years. That is why you have to see your daughter. It's not a wish, and it's not a pie in the sky hope. It's a must."

Shae rubbed his face. He was already overstressed, constantly weighing his decisions and options during this war and wondering how many of the choices he made had killed innocent lives.

Louise walked through the door and stopped abruptly when she saw Naveya. "You? I saw you helping Manning on the vids." She gave her a double-take, then walked to Shae. "Are you okay?"

Shae nodded and looked her up and down, remembering what Zim had said about her, and done to her. She was a hero to Shae, someone who tried to spill the truth over the live news channels and almost died for it.

He jabbed a thumb over his shoulder, motioning toward the holo-screen. "I'm being tracked. No matter where I am, the assholes know."

Louse backed away. "Are you sure?"

"Positive."

She eyed the monitor more closely. "That's you, the blue dot?" She gestured toward the screen with the map of Eos. "Because whoever is tracking you is doing a shitty job. You're not on Eos, Admiral."

"That's my daughter."

Louise's mouth dropped open. "Excuse me?"

"I have a daughter, Louise." Shae forced down a smile.

Louise glanced around the room. They nodded back to her, confirming Shae spoke the truth.

Louise put her hands out. "Since when?"

"It's complicated," Shae said.

"Obviously." She massaged her temple. "Do—" she huffed, not able to find the right words, or perhaps unable to unscramble the thoughts screaming through her mind.

Naveya clicked her fingernails against the table. "He has to see her as soon as possible. It's for the good of your people."

"And who is this individual? I watched her on a vid doing things to the Matrona Guard during a gunfight. What she did was uncanny. She was fast, and—"

Shae ran his fingers through his black hair. "Again, it's complicated. Her name is Naveya, and she's with us."

Louise's mouth formed an 'o'. "Are you thinking of going?"

Shae shook his head. "If what Naveya states is true, then I must go. It will benefit us all, somehow."

Koda raised his hand, as if still in the academy. He dropped his arm just as quickly. "You have to stay, Uncle. We need you. People take orders from you, and believe in you." He cleared his throat. "More importantly, we have to stop the toxin."

"That's right, the toxin." Naveya tapped her fingers against the desk. "I can't stay here any longer, Admiral. I have to find Payson and stop him. I implore you to please, for the sake of humanity, find your daughter and reunite with her. It will change everything. Trust me. What seems insurmountable with this war now will not be so difficult once you two see one another. There was a time, and in a different land and on a different world, where you were sought after to lead an army because you could think faster and react faster than most. You were always successful. Here, on Starbase Matrona, you were purposely altered and slowed. Meeting your daughter will quicken your thinking and your reaction time." She slapped her hands together and hurried toward the doorway. "Do this for your people." She stepped out of the room and rushed down the hallway, yelling over her shoulder. "Devon, soon, I'll send you the antidote to the toxin just in case. Be open and ready."

"Will do," Devon yelled back.

Shae didn't move his eyes from Louise, a strange sensation pulsing through him, telling him Nevaya was right. It pricked at his heart and went up and down his spine.

He'd had those *knowings* before, but they were always brief. This one lingered. "What does Executive Officer Louise Stripe think?"

She wiped her hands together, thinking. "What do I think?" She motioned toward the doorway. "Who the hell was that woman is what I'm thinking."

Devon chimed in. "I know Nevaya, and she's never wrong. She says strange things, but the years she's helped me, and I've helped her, she just *knows*. I don't know how to explain it or how she does it, but she has this ability to—"

Louise swiped her hand in front of Devon, cutting him off. "Who the hell is she?"

Shae pulled his pendant from underneath his collar. "She has one of these. She's a Space Templar."

Louise physically gulped. She hurried to the doorway and peeked into the hall. "She's gone." She walked back into the room, sighing, as if not wanting to say what she was about to say. "With what I saw on the vid recording, she must be a Space Templar." She paused. "Which means, I'd say do what she says."

Koda shook his head wildly. "No. Uncle, you have to stay here."

Shae leaned back in thought. "Thank you, Louise. I value your opinion above most, and I agree."

Koda stepped forward, a vein bulging from his forehead. "Do not leave your people."

Louise held her chin high. "They're not *his* people. They're *our* people." She stepped forward to stand eye to eye with Koda. "Trust me. I'm an executive officer with a lot of experience. We can find Payson, we can find Zim, and we can defeat this threat. We can. If she's truly a Space Templar, and I feel odd for saying this, but I think she is, then we do what she says."

"And I go see my daughter." Shae let out a long breath. "You all heard what Naveya said. I can help us more by reuniting with her. I'll be back soon, and apparently, more quick-minded than before."

Koda nodded.

Louise jabbed her index finger at Koda. "Get a transport ready with NMJ drive capabilities. There should be a few of those in Sphere One in the launch bay."

Koda dipped his head. "Yes, ma'am." He raced out of the room.

Shae glanced at Devon. "Get me on the comm line to the hoverstation. I'm getting a private hovertrain to Sphere One." He motioned toward a silver band on his shoulder. "Contact me on my commlink and let me know what ship Koda has prepared for me. Also, upload the holomap on the ship's holopad so I can successfully track and find my daughter." He walked over to Louise and put his hands on her shoulders, squeezing gently. "Thank you, Louise. I'll see you when I get back."

He walked out of the room and around the corner. "Both of you. Tell no one where I'm going. No one."

He marched down the hallway, a smile forming on his face and a pins and needles sensation in his hands and feet.

He was going to see his daughter, and if memory served him right, she was one of the biggest loves in his life. After many years, a love he'd finally see again.

63

ALI

Mount Gabriel, Eos

Ali gripped Daf's wrists and pulled her past the boulder. She stumbled backward into the mouth of the tunnel.

The starfighters zoomed overhead, flying by and circling around again.

She pulled Daf further into the dim tunnel, and the further she pulled, the darker it became.

She laid Daf on the ground and leaned against a wall glaring at the entrance, looking for any signs of movement.

Daf moved and poked her head up, glancing around. "Why is it so dark?"

"Shh," whispered Ali. "Keep your voice down."

"Where am I?"

Ali leaned over and stroked Daf's hair. "Keep your voice down. We're in the tunnel."

"I can barely see anything." Daf blinked several times. She went to get up, but dropped back down, grabbing her leg. "Holy Guild, my leg."

Ali gently touched Daf's thigh. "This one?"

"Yes, just below the knee. It's on fire."

Ali moved her hand over her knee, feeling the heat. It was inflamed. "Can you move it?"

Daf cringed. "Yes, but it hurts. Where's your flashlight?"

"In the mech."

"You don't have it clipped to your buckle?"

"No. You have yours?"

Daf felt her buckle, then nodded. "Here."

Ali unclipped it, turned it on, and pointed it at her knee.

"Am I okay?"

"Yeah, you'll live. No blood." Ali went to help her up.

Daf yelped and flinched. "Damn, there *is* something wrong with it."

Great.

Ali swept the light down the tunnel to see where it turned. She stood and walked a few steps.

"Wait," called out Daf. "I'm breathing. I'm outside, right?"

"Yes, for some reason, we can breathe on Eos."

"You're kidding me."

Ali shook her head. "Are you breathing? Then no, I'm not kidding."

Daf pressed her palm against her head. "Another day, another lie exposed. Oh, my Guild."

Ali held up her hand. "Shh." She bent and examined the ground, then lifted the light to look down the tunnel further. "Footprints."

"Footprints?" Daf touched her lower leg, wincing.

Ali tilted her head, studying the tracks. "Dozens of them heading that way." She pointed her flashlight down the tunnel. "They look like children's feet, but wider."

"That rules out the Anunnaki."

Ali nodded and moved over to Daf. "I'm helping you up, and we're following these to wherever they go, even if I have to carry you on my back."

"You had enough rest yet?" Ali beamed the flashlight down the tunnel, studying the trail in the dirt.

It had been ten minutes of walking, and if Ali remembered correctly, she was heading for the glowing door she'd seen during one of her treks many moons ago.

Daf gave Ali a haughty look, sitting on her rear and leaning against a tunnel wall. "You hop on one leg for this long and then tell me how you feel, okay?"

It was pitch black, other than where Ali pointed the light.

That was good. Thank Guild the Anunnaki hadn't followed her.

She helped Daf to her feet, placing Daf's arm around her shoulders. Daf hopped, moving onward.

"We're heading for a door?"

Ali shrugged. "Yes, and I think this is the way." She pointed the flashlight at the dirt. "They tread lightly."

Daf frowned. "What?"

Ali halted and examined another footprint. "It means they walk softly, even carefully. Whoever these footprints belong to, they must be short and stocky, because their soles are wide and the toes are thick." She paused, examining them more. "They also walk toe to heel, instead of the other way around."

"And that tells you they walk softly?"

"More like they're careful about where and how they walk."

"Obviously, not careful enough to cover their tracks."

"Yeah, I'm puzzled by that, too." Ali patted Daf's hand resting on her shoulder.

A hollow sound echoed to the side of them. Ali aimed the light in the sound's direction.

Daf went rigid, her arms tightening around Ali's shoulders. "What is it?"

She pointed her flashlight at the sound, and the beam landed against a large, silver door, the one that had pulsated blue, and shown her where she had come from, displaying images of her home planet, or so she had thought many weeks ago.

Ali walked forward cautiously, Daf hopping by her side.

Ali touched the door, and a soft light shimmered from it. The door was cold and glassy to the touch, sending a shiver down Ali's back. The hairs on her arms raised.

A moment later, the door changed colors: gold, then purple, electric blue, and then green.

Daf blinked several times. "That's beautiful."

The door faded to black, and Ali held her breath, a tingling sensation building in her gut.

Something was about to happen.

A galaxy appeared. Stars and gases of different colors formed in a spiral, spinning.

Ali didn't flinch. "This is what I was telling you about."

A star system zoomed in as an asteroid zipped by a green planet, a planet with a vertical ring surrounding it, then the scene zoomed by more planets, all different colors and sizes.

The scene slowed, moving beyond a red and tan planet, and halted at a predominately blue world.

Every muscle and bone in Ali's body seemed to vibrate, and goosebumps stood on end all over her skin. "My home."

The door shuddered, and the scene blinked away, changing back to a metallic silver door.

Daf fumbled, and took a step back on her bad leg, and yelped. She fell down, holding her shin. "What was that?"

Ali reached forward, touching the door, her mother and father coming to mind. "It's my family." She turned. "My mom and dad are there on that blue planet you saw."

The door made a clanging noise at it unlocked. It shook, and clanked again, then creaked loudly as it began to open.

64

EDEN

Eos

An Aven, an egg-shaped Space Templar starfighter, flew overhead, its hum barely audible, Skye its pilot.

The starfighter was invisible, able to camouflage itself, matching the sky above or the ground below. Eden imagined if she were looking down at it from a starship, she wouldn't see an Aven. She'd see the ground beneath it, the top of the Aven duplicating the terrain below.

Eden glanced forward, eyeing the many cat-like Sirians in front of her, all with belts, holsters, and plasma blasters. They were tall, athletic, and beautiful.

The human Space Templars were just as gorgeous. A handful was in front of her, bow and arrows strapped to their backs, also carrying belts around their waists with guns holstered at each hip.

Eden walked along Eos' ebb landscape. Even after nearly half a day of walking, she was still having an issue with the oxygen.

Not that it was hard to breathe, because it wasn't. In fact, it was easy, but it was eating at her mind.

Her entire life, she'd been told that Eos wasn't habitable, except to the few sporadic trees or plants, and to the carbon dioxide breathing drudges, which were creatures similar to biosphere squirrels, though the size of a large dog.

They ran around once in a while and were harmless.

It didn't matter, because right now, she realized it had been her entire life she'd been lied to, about everything.

She kicked a rock on the ground, watching it tumble forward and bounce against a pile of mined ebb that hadn't been carted off the planet yet.

Nyx was by her side, a warrior with sparkling skin and a glow that made her mesmerizing to look at.

Jantu marched next to her as well. He held himself strong, and every step he took was just as silent as Nyx's.

The guy had blue fur, yellow cat-eyes, and towered over them both. He was calm, cordial, and now that Eden had seen him in action, taking out enemy grunts easily, he was someone she felt completely safe around.

Jantu's whiskers twitched, and he gazed up at the Aven. His lips didn't move, though Eden could still hear him speak. "It must be nice to sit and fly above us. You wouldn't want to get your feet dirty, eh?" He winked at Eden and pointed to the Aven flying overhead, poking fun at Skye.

Nyx huffed. "He's keeping us safe, Jantu. Any craft that comes by to send some cannon fire our way, they'll have to deal with Skye first."

Jantu chuckled. "They'd be balls of flames before they'd even get a peek at us."

They continued to walk toward *Sirona*. It wasn't Eden's starship, but she couldn't wait to see some of her Star Guild Military members.

She eyed the humans and Sirians in front of her, thinking maybe they could fix whatever was wrong with *Sirona* and get them back into the air. More importantly, the crew on *Sirona* could tell her where Starbase Matrona had gone, along with the rest of Star Guild military.

She couldn't wait to see Fleet Admiral Shae Lutz again. He was the father she never had.

She took in a deep breath, filling her lungs with fresh air. "I'm breathing on Planet Eos. Holy Guild." She glanced up at Jantu.

He smiled back at her, giving her a decisive nod. His long strides were slow, his muscles flexing through his fur-covered legs.

Eden shook her head and snorted. "And I'm talking to a tall, blue cat."

"I'm a Sirian, Eden."

She patted his arm, grinning. "Yes, that too, and a damn great one at that."

He dipped his head, slowly closing his eyes, sending out a soft purr. "Thank you."

Nyx walked forward at a quicker pace, flicking a look over her shoulder at Eden. "Charming the big tyke, I see? He doesn't need charming, you know. He's a big boy."

Eden ignored her, continuing to walk, the sun beaming hot rays on them. A soft breeze whisked her hair back and died down a moment later.

A breeze never occurred in the starbase's biosphere.

Oh, the biosphere.

Her nostrils flared, and she curled her fingers in a fist, wishing she could be with her people on Matrona, and could go back in time to warn them about the Anunnaki piece of ebbs before the attack happened.

Nyx halted and faced Eden. "I sense more anger in you than usual." She put her hand out, placing it on Eden's heart, more annoyed than anything else. She closed her eyes. "Calm, Eden. Please calm down."

Nyx's palm was soft and warm, and strange energy came from it.

Eden relaxed, letting out a soft breath.

Then a rage overtook her as Zim's face jumped into Eden's mind.

Nyx opened her eyes. "Don't fight it."

Eden shook her head. She wanted to kick the Prime Director's butt from here to the moons and back. All of the Prime Directors, in fact. They lied to her people. For centuries, and probably longer.

Then they tried to kill her damn race.

She growled, and let out a ferocious yell, her body tightening and her face reddening.

All the humans and Sirians stopped, and the Aven slowed to a hover above them.

Eden dropped to her knees, and Nyx went to her knees as well, keeping her palm placed firmly on Eden's chest.

Eden thrashed, and punched, connecting with Nyx's outstretched arm. She wrapped her fingers around Nyx's forearm and attempted to pull it away.

It didn't budge.

Eden grasped Nyx's shoulders, squeezing. "Get. Your. Hand. Off. Of. Me."

Nyx closed her eyes and exhaled. "Don't fight it."

Zim entered her mind again. She watched him on a holovid while in class at Star Guild Academy, which felt like eons ago.

Zim held up a picture of Eos. There, in the picture, was a mech mining ebb. "Be grateful our mechs are well built and able to sustain little to no damage from the dense gravity on Eos. If you took a step outside your mech, you'd crumble to the ground, feeling a force like a ton of ebb pushing down on you. You'd be dead in less than two minutes if the lack of oxygen didn't kill you first."

A deceitful pile of ebb-shit lie.

Lie. Lie. Lie.

That's all the Prime Directors did.

Gravity probably didn't even work that way, and hell, she was on Eos now without a mech, and other than the threat of being attacked by Zim's Anunnaki race, she was doing fine and dandy without a mech.

She dropped her hands by her side, a rush of relief washing through her, the anger exiting her heavy heart.

She dropped her head in her hands and sobbed.

Nyx rubbed Eden's heart. "Now, do you feel better?" She wiggled her hand in the air and wiped it with her other hand as if dusting off Eden's residual anger from her own.

A lightness overtook Eden like a million kilograms of ebb lifting off her shoulders. She stood, nodding. "I feel much better."

Nyx jabbed a thumb over her shoulder. "Now that I've helped you, hopefully, you'll be less of a pain and maybe more fit to be a captain." She rolled her eyes at the thought. "Let's keep going. You've held everyone up."

They walked onward for hours, and Eden took in the newness around her.

She gazed at the falling sun and knew soon the sun would dip even lower on the horizon, only stopping to show a sliver of itself until it rose again in the morning.

It was becoming as dark as Eos was going to get, and the shadows on the ground from the mountain peaks, and the larger boulders were growing longer.

It wasn't as cold as the climatologists on Starbase Matrona had always claimed it would be at this time of evening. Perhaps this was an anomaly, but she supposed it was just another false claim, something the weathermen and women were told to say, also believing in the lie.

They headed toward the edge of a cliff, and several Sirians slowed and crouched at the edge of the drop-off.

They pointed, spotting something. They then dropped flat on their bellies.

Eden's eyebrows came forward, and she hurried to the edge and crouched next to them. She went to her stomach and inched her way to the drop-off, pining to see what the Sirians, and now the humans, were observing.

A blast of wind came from behind her, sending small rocks down the canyon wall.

The wind didn't blow like this on Eos, and she glanced over her shoulder to figure out where the strong breeze had originated.

She nodded when the Aven's camouflage dematerialized, and the craft changed to a soft silver metallic color, its landing sleds touching the ground behind her.

The wind ceased as the thrusters deactivated. A hiss and the ramp descended, clanking against the ground.

Skye walked down the ramp wearing a purple robe, his hood off, and chestnut brown hair bouncing with each step, his hands tucked into his sleeves at the waist.

He went on his stomach next to her and reached into his robe, pulling out a pair of glasses. He placed them over his eyes and peered down the steep cliff. "The starship is down below." He took off his glasses, giving them to Eden. "Put these on and follow my fingers. *Sirona* is a little beat up, but still intact."

She placed the glasses over her eyes and flinched. The glasses lightened the shadows around her, changing everything from evening to day in a snap.

Below Starship *Sirona* sat, dented, and scorched. The good news, however, was Skye had been correct.

It was intact.

She took the glasses off, holding them in her hand. "What do we do now?"

"We wait. My Aven's radar picked up a craft headed in *Sirona's* direction. It was small, so it shouldn't pose a threat to the starship, or to us."

The ground began to vibrate when he finished his sentence, and as if on cue, a small transport ship lifted above the cliffs. It was quiet, though not as quiet at the Aven.

The ship didn't have lights, and it looked like a flying shadow.

It slowed in speed when it reached *Sirona*.

Eden put the glasses back on to see it in better light. Skye's fingers touched the top of the rims, and the lenses magnified the scene in front of her.

It was now as if she was standing next to *Sirona*.

The small ship hovered above *Sirona*, and near a hatch on the roof. A platform descended from the transport ship, carrying a tall, wide man. It stopped and landed next to the hatch.

The hatch opened, and out came a woman.

"How do I zoom in?" asked Eden.

"Like this." Skye's fingers adjusted the top of the rims, and the view became sharper and magnified even more.

Eden gasped. "What the…"

She eyed the woman exiting *Sirona* and watched her walk onto the platform and bow to the large man. He dipped his head in response, and the platform raised, swallowing the two individuals into the ship.

Eden backed away from the edge and moved the glasses away from her eyes. "That's a human, but who is that?"

Whoever it was, they held themselves like royalty. Even though she could only see a silhouette of the individual, even close up, she could tell that it was a woman.

A twinge of shock ran through her as the name "Captain Diana Johnson" rang through her mind.

The small ship turned one-hundred and eighty degrees and sped up, shooting toward the sky and disappearing beyond a mountain range.

Skye cocked his head to the side. "Did you get a good look at the person?"

"We have to warn *Sirona's* crew."

"Yes, that was an Anunnaki ship, Eden, but we can't give away our position. Right now, we rest and wait until the morning. We'll park the Aven near a boulder where it will mesh, camouflaging itself.."

Eden shook her head. "No, we let them know now. We let them know someone on the starship, someone high up, is not on their side. There is a traitor in their midst, and if my eyes weren't deceiving me, that traitor is Captain Diana Johnson."

65

KODA

Starbase Matrona

Koda watched as his uncle marched down the hallway and out of the lobby, heading for his daughter.

He stood staring through the large pane window, his eyes on Shae disappearing in the thick biosphere forest. He sat on a chair and leaned back, reflecting on what had just happened.

His uncle had a child but from another world? He shook his head. Everything that had gone on in the past several weeks was insanity, and it wasn't over. Now some lady named Naveya was going after Payson. Again, insanity.

Koda yawned and closed his eyes. He had to do his job as a politician and help his people, and to him, finding the truth and letting his citizens know was the best way to do so.

More importantly, he couldn't find the truth if Payson remained alive and stopped his efforts. If Naveya spoke the truth, Payson would attempt to finish humans off with the toxin.

The more Koda dug, the more truth revealed itself. Payson had to be eliminated somehow or another.

Devon came to mind, and he opened his eyes. He needed his

hacker friend. He looked around, wondering why Devon hadn't followed him.

Getting up, he made his way down the hall, checking several rooms until he saw Devon standing in front of an HDC, decoding more junk data.

A holoscreen was on in the corner of the room, a few *Brigantia* and *Taranis* Guards watching the news. Zim was on the monitor, speaking about humans being a slave race, created to serve the Anunnaki. "No longer will you serve this purpose," Zim's voice boomed over the holochannel.

Koda scratched the back of his head, turning toward Devon. "What are you doing?"

Devon's eyes went wide, and his face went slack as he stared at the HDC screen in front of him. "Holy hell."

"What is it?" asked Koda.

Devon lurched away as if Koda had frightened him. He gave Koda a double-take, then blinked several times. "I'm piecing several things together." He eyed the corner of the room where Zim was on the screen, continuing to speak. "Hey, can we turn that off? I need to concentrate." He glared back at his HDC screen.

The guards either didn't hear the young man or ignored him.

Koda stepped toward them. "Sirs, I'm Prime Overseer Koda Lutz, and I need you to leave this room and watch the news elsewhere. We have important political business to attend to and need quiet."

After a few grunts, they moved out of the room, several craning their heads toward the screen to get as much information as possible. Koda closed the door.

"Thank you," said Devon. "I may need your help with this."

"You need my help? You can use your brain magic on this stuff better than I can." Devon was a genius hacker, and Koda just liked politics and helping the common human.

"Maybe."

Koda tugged at his lower lip, eyeing the screen in front of him. He leaned in. A holographic document labeled *Ebb Quarries* was in front of him. He read the first couple of paragraphs. "It explains how to mine ebb. So?"

Devon nodded. "Yeah, I know. But after reading all of that boring trash, you finally arrive at *this* page." Devon swiped across the screen, pulling up another page. "Eos Two."

Koda had read about Eos Two before, but only skimmed over it. It was a place the Monarch, who Zim called Enlil, lived and ran his slave operations from. He had no idea where Eos Two was. "What about Eos Two?"

Devon tapped on the holographic page. It zoomed in on a paragraph. "Starhawk Transports group four, which includes Starhawk Transport V76, V77, V78, V79, V80, V81, and V82, reports on day five of each week, at zero-seven-hundred hours, to Ebb Quarry warehouse Nine, located on Eos One."

He pointed at another line on the page. "Here they are to load three-point-eight tons to four-point-three tons of ebb. Then all Starhawks must leave Ebb Quarry warehouse Nine and head to Outpost Settlement Eighteen at twenty-one hundred hours on Eos Two and unload ebb tonnage."

Devon continued, "The following day at zero-seven hundred hours, Starhawk Transports must deliver new material to target Destination N. Starhawk Transport group five, which includes Starhawk Transport V83, V84, V85, V86, V87, V88, V89, and V90, reports to Outpost Settlement eighteen at zero-eight hundred hours to extract unwanted ebb remnants. Then they transport to Starbase Matrona's Sphere One at eleven-hundred hours."

Koda narrowed his eyes, thinking, what were unwanted ebb remnants? Is that code for something?

Devon cleared his throat and took his eyes from the screen. "Starhawk Transports take off from an Eos Two facility with these unwanted ebb remnants, but where do they go from there?"

Devon shuffled through several documents on the holomonitor. "I can't find any explanation of where it is actually delivering the mined goods. All we see is Destination N, but not where that is or why they are going there."

Koda shook his head. "What are these ebb remnants?"

"Yep." Devon pulled up another holographic page and pointed. "Read."

It was titled *Crystals and White Powder Gold*. Koda scanned four paragraphs and then froze. "What the…"

Devon nodded. "Yes. They separate the gold and crystals from the ebb, then load crystal on Starhawk Transports and gold on the other Starhawk Transports."

Koda crossed his arms. "But they say that they turn the gold into powder?"

"Have you ever seen gold or crystals on Matrona or on Eos?"

Koda frowned. "Never."

"Exactly."

Koda let out a slow breath, eyeing one of the paragraphs. "What's Destination N?"

"That's what I want to find out, and more." Devon put his fingers over his lips, thinking. "The only way we can do this is if we go to the source. My software program works well, but it's limited, not able to access everything."

"And the source is Zim's office." Koda dipped his head. "Great, now, lead the way."

"Right this second?" Devon bit his lip. "Can we sleep on it instead?"

Devon looked just as tired as Koda felt.

"Listen, Devon." Koda's lips downturned. "If I can stay up, you can too. We have more uncovering to do, and in the name of serving humanity, it's our job."

"Why the hurry? Everything is getting better by the moment."

Koda stood taller, his chest out. "Look, I'm a politician, but I'm not like the rest. We're supposed to serve the public the best we can, and the best way I can right now is to understand this information so I can give it straight to the people. They have a right to know everything."

Devon tapped his lips with his finger. "But why the hurry?"

"Because what if Zim's HDC gets corrupted or the junk data stops or is deleted? We don't have all the information yet. And we need that information." He paused. "Can it be deleted?

Devon yawned. “I’m tired.”

Nerves tingled in the pit of Koda’s stomach. He didn’t know much about HDC’s or how they worked, but he knew a lot about politics, and a politician who didn’t want something seen could easily have that something deleted.

If by chance Zim or one of his higher-ups wanted to cover their tracks, they could turn off the junk data stream any minute.

Why this junk data was still running, Koda didn’t know. What it did tell him was perhaps the Monarch, Enlil, who really ran things, didn’t know Zim’s HDC had been hacked.

“You didn’t answer my question. Can it be deleted?” asked Koda.

“In a sense, yes, but data is never completely gone. It would be hell trying to find it if they turned the stream off, though.”

Koda grabbed Devon's forearm, pulling him out of the room and into the hallway. “Let’s go.”

Devon almost tripped, trampling down the hall and knocking Koda’s arm off of his. “Where are we going?”

“We’re going to the source.”

“The source?”

Koda quickened his pace, heading for the infirmary’s lobby. “Zim’s office.”

Devon yawned again and rubbed his eyes. “Okay, but if I fall asleep, you’re carrying me there.”

Koda nodded, pursing his lips. “I’ll do whatever it takes. We have to figure this shit out.” He tugged on Devon’s forearm. “Now, let’s go.”

Koda pushed open the lobby doors, and they exited the building.

Koda went into a run as ideas of Zim’s HDC being turned off or destroyed entered his mind.

He raced across the biosphere grass, heading for a biosphere forest, Devon running just as fast behind him.

Devon picked up speed, now running beside Koda, and jumping over a downed branch once entering the forest. “It’s not about you trying to impress the people to become the next Prime Director, is it? If so, then we can easily take a nap and get to this after we wake up.”

Koda rolled his eyes. “It’s about helping humanity.” There was some truth to Devon's words, but not entirely. If Koda could dig up something so important, so incredible from Zim's office, Koda would be lauded as a hero, as one of the best politicians ever to grace Starbase Matrona.

He knew that at Zim's office, he'd find more treasures, more than the people would ever need. He just had to avoid Payson, but with Naveya on Payson's butt, the guy probably didn't have much longer to live.

A crack pierced the forest, and Koda stopped in the shadows of several trees. He threw his arm out, halting Devon as well.

His eyes went wide when he saw him, and he gulped hard. *You have to be kidding me.*

There in the distance crouched Payson and a few of his men, perhaps scheming over their next move. Payson turned and focused on Koda's position.

66

EDEN

Eos

Eden woke with a start. It was dusk, and she had been resting her back against the Aven's landing gear, her butt on the ebb ground.

Yawning, she rubbed her eyes and glanced around at her companions.

The humans, Sirians, and even Skye were fast asleep, laying on the ground, their breathing slow and easy.

Good idea.

Exhausted, she closed her eyes to get some more shut-eye.

Something nearby rustled, and Eden froze, her eyes opening wide. It couldn't have been the wind that made that sound.

She heard it again. This time it was more clear, boots sliding on the ebb surface.

Maybe some of the humans or Sirians were up and walking around, scouting the area to make sure they were safe?

She slowly turned her head. Skye opened one eye, bringing his finger to his lips.

She saw a boot out of the corner of her eye, just beyond the nose of the Aven starfighter.

Even though the starfighter was camouflaged, hidden in a hologram beaming a boulder all around them, someone or something could bump into it and figure it wasn't the shape the Aven projected.

A second boot came into view, both gray. A third and fourth, slid across the ground, stopping next to the other boots, dust swirling around them.

A creepy sensation prickled her spine, and she looked back at Skye; he was on his back, feigning sleep.

She fought the urge to warn everyone, doing as Skye asked, and remaining quiet.

Looking around the landing sleds, she saw several more boots appear.

A hand covered her mouth, and her eyes about popped out of her head.

She tried to move, but someone had pinned her body against the sled. Twisting her head, she saw Nyx's face.

Behind Nyx were a handful of men and women, each with a bow on their backs and arrow between their teeth, crawling silently on the ground toward the boots.

Nyx dropped her hand from Eden's mouth, then whispered into her ear. "We're silencing the perimeter."

Eden nodded. All who were on the move were on all fours, crawling, even Skye.

Jantu moved into a crouch, waving her to come his way.

Eden slid past Nyx, moving quietly in Jantu's direction. Jantu closed his eyes, pointing at his eyelids. "Close your eyes," he said, his mouth not moving, though his voice boomed in her head.

A loud thud sounded and a shriek. A bright light flashed, and there were several thumps that sounded like bodies hitting the ground.

"We could have done without the loud scream," said Nyx.

Eden opened her eyes.

A man, who had just been outside of the hologram, ducked his head back in. "I'm sorry, Nyx. I scared the water right out of that one."

He pointed to a giant on the ground, wearing a green and gray tight spandex-like outfit. He had peed himself.

The Templars dragged eight large bodies under the Aven.

All of the sleeping giants wore tight green and gray suits with masks that had black, buggy eyes.

They looked human in every way, except for the masks. Eden walked toward one of them, curious to see if they had human faces or if they *were* bug-like.

Maybe these soldiers were crossbreeds of some sort.

"If you want to take a look under their masks, just look in the mirror. They look like you, just twice your size." A yellow-furred, female Sirian stood over an unconscious Anunnaki, eyeing Eden. "Ugly buggers, if you ask me." She winked.

"Get your gear on, my friends," said Skye. "We're going to Starship *Sirona*."

Everyone grabbed their packs and weapons, following Skye through the hologram and onto the wide plateau.

Jantu put his hand on Eden's shoulder. "Are you coming?"

She nodded. "Yeah."

Nyx tugged on Eden's arm. "Then let's go. You're holding us up." She walked through the hologram.

Eden hurried through the hologram, eyeing the troops walking behind Skye.

She surveyed the land before her, taking steps forward, following the group.

The terrain was dotted with heavy boulders and ebb rock heaps, unused mining ore. Small trees grew about sporadically, and red ridges and mountain ranges lined the backdrop.

Steam lifted from the ground as the sun rose above the horizon to the east.

It was morning, and the temperature was warm and nearly perfect.

A good day for a stroll, thought Eden, wishing she could have built a house down here and enjoyed the luxury of a fresh environment.

Skye picked up the pace and started jogging.

"Here we go," said Nyx, a few meters in front of her. "Start running, Eden. We'll get there sooner if we run. It doesn't take a galactic-net hacker to understand that."

"It doesn't take a galactic-net hacker to see you're an asshole," Eden said under her breath.

Jantu pointed forward. "To Starship *Sirona*." He slowed, and faced Eden, jogging backward. "If you need me to carry you on my back, I can."

Eden glanced at Jantu's shoulders, seeing how muscular they were. For a moment, she considered it.

He thumbed over his shoulder. "Can you keep their pace?"

Eden's lips curled downward. "Probably not." She started to jog anyway.

Eden jogged, her shoulder nearly hugging a rock wall that went up hundreds of meters, if not more. Sweat dripped from her face and perspiration wetted her back like she'd taken a shower with her clothes on.

Her breaths came quickly, and her heart nearly beat out of her chest, but Guild, she felt incredible.

It had been nearly an hour, and *Sirona* was in view, its vast body like a small bug in the canyon it was nestled in. She couldn't wait to get to her.

Eden stumbled her last steps to Starship *Sirona* and plopped on her rear, her head between her knees.

She spat and wished she had a bag of water she could gulp down.

She squinted against the sun gleaming off *Sirona's* dented and bruised exterior.

She shook her head at the Space Templar. Were they perfect Beings or something? They looked unaffected by the run, and from what she could see, barely broke a sweat.

A loud hissing sound erupted next to her, and she flinched, relaxing an instant later when one of *Sirona's* launch bay doors opened, and a ramp extended, crunching against the ground.

A man, old and weary, wearing an oxygen mask, stood at the opening, and a woman, tall and healthy, stood next to him, wearing an oxygen mask as well.

Several *Sirona* Guards were behind them in masks and helmets, pointing their rifles.

Eden stood, moving toward *Sirona*, her hands in the air. "Don't shoot. We're here to help." A wave of happy nerves ran through her veins, and her body nearly exploded with excitement.

Here she was, standing in front of her people again. She couldn't help but smile.

The guards slowly moved their weapons in her direction and took a step forward. The woman standing at the top of the ramp had her hand on her holstered sidearm, and the old man watched Eden curiously.

Eden halted. "My name is Major Eden Gains, pilot and officer from Starship *Brigantia*."

The woman lifted her hand up and lowered her arm. The guards lowered their weapons.

The old man rushed down the ramp, his long and thin gray hair edging his bald head bobbing against his shoulders. He headed for Eden.

Reaching her, he wrapped his arms around her.

Eden jerked back, then calmed. "Wrench?"

Wrench was an old friend and someone she'd known since her beginning days at Star Guild Academy nearly fifteen years ago.

He cleared his throat, and she could see a stream of tears through the glass plate on his oxygen mask. "The one and only."

Eden touched his mask. "You can take this off."

He touched her face and then her lips. "I thought I was just imaginin' things. It *is* ya. And by golly, ya don't have a breathin' apparatus on."

Eden smiled wide. "That I don't." She took a deep sniff. "You can breathe on Eos, Wrench. You can actually breathe."

Wrench shook his head. "Are ya sure this isn't no dream?" He pinched himself. "What the Guild'n motha' lichen is going on?" He slowly took off his mask and took a quick breath. He wiped his tears with his sleeve and took another breath, this one deeper.

He paused, his brows drawn forward. His lips slowly upturned. He spun around, waving at the woman and the *Sirona* Guard, laughing like a kid with a nasty cough, but laughing nonetheless. "Take those off. I can breathe. I can really breathe."

He faced Eden, his lips turning into an 'o'. He backed up, seeing something or someone above and behind Eden. "What'n the Guild 'er that?"

Eden turned, patting Jantu's wrist. "He's my friend. His name is Jantu."

Wrench took a step forward and gave Eden another bear hug, then stepped back, looking her up and down. He patted her shoulders, standing proudly. "How the Guild are ya alive? We got information ya'd disintegrated. I even watched it on the HDC, and boy, did I cry!" His face contorted for a moment, and he bit his cheek, taking in another breath. "And since when does Eos have oxygen?"

"Always," said Skye, walking toward Wrench. "Even before Star Guild and Starbase Matrona were ever a thought in anyone's mind."

Wrench gave Skye a double-take, almost as if he'd just seen an angel. He shook his head.

"Inside, everyone. Being outside probably ain't the safest place to be." Wrench gestured for them to follow him up the ramp. "We need to get y'all out of sight."

Up the ramp and into the bay, Eden, Skye, and Nyx, along with the rest of their crew, stood next to each other. The *Sirona* guard eyed them, as if unsure what to do, or not sure if Eden and her friends would jump them any minute.

The ramp sucked in, and the bay door closed.

Nyx let out a snort, eyeing a guard. "Ooh, you're all so menacing." Her tone was filled with sarcasm.

A woman walked toward Eden and took off her mask. Eden held in a gasp at the traitor, her happiness dimming a few notches. It was Captain Diana Johnson. The captain's lips were flat, and she had dark circles under her eyes as if she hadn't slept in days or weeks.

Eden immediately stood at attention, not because she wanted to, but she had to. She'd rather spit at the traitor's feet.

"Relax, Eden," said Diana. "Who are these..." She paused, obviously at a loss as what to call the furry Beings. "Who are your friends?"

Eden shifted on her feet. "They are Sirians and humans. They are the Space Templars." She leaned in and spoke in a warning tone, "You don't want to mess with a Space Templar. I've seen them in action."

Diana took half a step back after Eden said "Space Templars." Her upper lip twitched, and her eyes widened for a moment. She cocked her head to the side. "Space Templars?"

Eden bobbed her head up and down, wanting to out Diana more than anything. Here she was, finally with her people, and she had to stare at this creep. "Yes. I didn't believe they existed either, but here they are, existing."

Skye walked forward, his hand outstretched.

Diana took his hand and shook it.

He wrapped his other hand on top of hers. "The light in me bows to the light in you." He dipped his head. "That is what we say where I come from. I respect your inner light, and I hope you respect mine."

"Okay." Diana let go of Skye's grip. "That's wonderful." Her voice was flat. "Wrench, get these people and..." she hesitated, her attention landing on a Sirian, "and *them*, some food and drink."

"I'll get the cooks right on it, Captain." He gave Eden one long stare like she was a long lost granddaughter and walked out of the launch bay.

The door shut behind him.

"Is there a place we could speak, Captain?" asked Skye, his voice serious, his tone a bit troubled. "We witnessed something last night I'd like to go over with you."

Eden stiffened. What happened to keeping quiet about what we saw last night?

Diana puffed out her lower lip. "Uh, sure." She gave a sideways tip of her head to her *Sirona* Guard, perhaps telling them to stay sharp and to be ready for anything. "Just you and me, Skye?"

"I'd like Eden and Nyx with me if that is all right."

"I'll have a couple with me, as well." She turned on her heels and headed to her quarters. "Follow me, gentlemen...and ladies."

They walked through the launch bay and down several corridors. Eden passed the cafeteria, smelling the wonderful food cooking.

Several Star Guild men and women strolled by and gave her nods. She bit her lip, doing her best not to look like a fool and smile at everything and everyone.

She wanted to yell and throw her hands in the air. Though this wasn't Starbase Matrona or Starship *Brigantia,* she'd made it back to her people, and most of them looked healthy and safe.

She rubbed her hands together and gave Skye a sideways glance, her eyebrows high. He gave her a nod back as if saying congratulations for finding it back to her comrades.

She mouthed, "Thank you."

He put his hands together at his chest and dipped his head, mouthing back, "It wasn't me who got us here. It was you." He grinned.

She was here, back with her friends, and soon, they'd get this big heap off the ground and to the stars, destination: Starbase Matrona.

Diana looked over her shoulder as she continued to walk down the long corridor lined with doors. "If you don't mind me asking, what do you want to talk to me about?"

Skye walked close behind her. "A few things. My Aven's sensors detected this ship as operational and ready to go. If there is anything preventing you from leaving, I'd like to assist and get your starship into space right away. Two, you have a traitor amongst you. I'd like to out that traitor immediately. It will hasten my first objective to get these people off this planet and back home."

67

ALI

Eos

Ali jumped back. "Daf, get up."

"I'm trying."

"Are you seeing what I'm seeing?"

Daf nodded her head, her chin nearly hitting her chest. "Umm…I, uh…"

In front of them was a stone path lit by bluish-white lights that hung like torches on the rock walls lining the stones.

Ali stood motionless, her eyes darting left and right, and her legs were bent in a defensive stance, her hands in fists by her face.

Something pulled her like a moth to a flame, and she wasn't turning around no matter what. No, she was going to march forward and head for her destiny, whatever destiny it was.

Ali took a giant step toward the opening. "I'm going in."

"No, Ali. What are you doing?"

Ali ignored her and continued on, taking her first step onto a square stone, and then another. She glanced over her shoulder. Daf hopped behind her, using the wall as a crutch, and biting her bottom lip in obvious pain.

Ali stopped and looked forward, her eyes locked on the view in front of her, a long, wide tunnel that curled after twenty or so meters.

Daf draped her arm around Ali's shoulders and leaned into her. "Fine, take me with you."

Daf didn't have much choice. Even if Ali wanted to turn around, something she couldn't explain had grabbed hold of her.

Ali advanced down the path, her strides matching Daf's hopping.

Ali put her hand up and halted. "Do you hear that?"

Daf shook her head. "Hear what?"

"Shh."

There it was, a faint pounding sound of metal slamming against rock in the distance.

Daf nodded. "I hear it."

"Come on." Ali walked, staring at the walls. She'd been in tunnels like this before in Peru and Scotland, both areas thought to be carved out by Dwarves long ago.

She quickly inhaled. What were Peru and Scotland, and what were Dwarves?

She released her breath. It didn't matter. It must have been something she studied on the other world, on Earth, when she lived there.

Ali slid her fingers on the walls. "These walls were made, not formed, and whoever made these were experts. But it wasn't with laser technology or machines. It was with pick-axes. You can tell by the grooves in the rock."

She stopped and inspected what looked like a door in the wall, small and wide.

She continued.

Daf remained quiet, looking all around, her eyes wide, ready for an attack, or something or someone that might jump out of nowhere and surprise them.

Rock against rock reverberated off the walls. "Vothuten."

Ali glanced left and right, but no one was there.

Breathing came from behind her and pierced the tunnel. Ali's spine tingled. She slowly raised both hands.

"Re."

Ali slowly turned with her hands still raised. She looked down and shuffled back a step at what she saw.

A short man, stocky with a thick beard and a heavy brow. He stood next to what Ali had suspected was a door, and by the new opening in the side of the tunnel wall, she had been right.

The man's head came to about the top of her waist, and one hand was on his hip, the other holding a pickaxe over his shoulder.

He held a scowl.

He shoved his pickax in front of Ali's face. She flinched and put her fists up, bringing her back leg more behind her, ready to kick the little man if she needed to.

"Ka," he grunted.

Ali tilted her head. What was he trying to say?

She glanced at Daf, who was wincing in pain and doing her best to keep herself upright and protecting herself at the same time by holding her bad knee up and leaning against the rocky wall.

He shoved his tool closer. "Ka."

Ali unclenched her fists and raised her arms again, nodding. "Okay."

A grunt behind her reverberated against the walls.

"Guild," whispered Ali. "There's more of them."

She cautiously turned and froze.

Standing before them were a handful of little, wide men. All with thick beards and mustaches, their eyebrows curled upward and meeting with their long, unkempt hair. Like the dwarf behind them, they had dark green outfits that looked like thick, heavy dresses that stopped just above their ankles. Tools were attached to belts that rounded their bellies.

Their bare feet were caked with dirt.

A few held thick swords and a couple held axes, while one cradled a pickaxe in his arms.

The blunt end of a pickaxe poked Ali in the back and pushed her forward. "*Uhnegrin pra thergetyr barhutol.*"

Daf hopped in Ali's direction. "What the Guild is he saying?"

"I don't know, but I think he wants us to follow his friends."

Ali nodded at the men standing in front of her. Their faces were solemn, their brows furrowed and practically frozen in place.

Ali took another step forward, Daf hopping next to her.

"Veryrant." A man with blond hair, the only blond in the bunch, raised his hand, palm out. *"Veryrant."*

Ali stopped.

"Ka," grumbled the man behind them, nudging Ali again. She walked forward.

"Veryrant." The blond lifted his hand, palm outward, his voice louder.

Ali folded her arms. She had about enough of this. "Can I help you?"

The man behind her shoved her hard, his strength twice the power she expected. She tripped and fell to the stone path.

"Hey," shouted Daf. The little man swiped her standing leg out from under her. She landed on the ground next to Ali, a pickaxe pressed against her neck.

"Daf, don't move."

A loud clang echoed, and the pickaxe pressed to Daf's neck went flying out of the man's hand to clatter across the stone flooring.

"Veryrant," said the blond male, this time calm and commanding, his posture strong and his chest outward. His arm was extended, and the pickaxe in his hand was missing.

Ali followed to where his arm pointed. He had thrown his pickaxe at the other man's, hitting with pinpoint accuracy and knocking it away from Daf's neck, not harming a hair on Daf's head.

Small, but strong fingers pressed into Ali's arm, gently lifting her to a standing position.

They then helped Daf, lifting her to her good leg.

The blond pointed to his chest. "Thun." He walked over to the man who swiped Daf's leg and slapped a hand across the guy's chest. "Harak."

Ali dusted herself off, glaring at Harak. "Tell Harak he's a jerk." She touched her chest. "Ali." She pressed on Daf's shoulder. "Daf."

Thun grunted and dipped his head, his lips flat. He eyed Harak.

Harak lowered his head and walked to the pickaxe on the ground and picked it up.

Thun took a small hammer from his belt and threw it at Harak. Another loud clang and Harak's pickaxe jumped out of his hands, and slid across the stone path, bouncing off a rock wall.

Harak held up a fist, grunting.

Ali put her hands on her hips. "He's got some good aim there, Daf. Lucky for you, or your head might have a dent in it."

Daf touched her temple and rubbed it, obviously not liking the thought.

"Welcome." An abnormally tall man in a brown robe with reddish hair and blue eyes appeared from around the corner. He bowed, his hands pressed together at his chest.

He was an Anunnaki. Ali raised her fists.

He smiled. "I mean you no harm. I'm Chan-Ru, counselor to the throne of Niburu. You may call me Chan."

Ali tilted her head and lowered her arms. "What's happening right now? Did S send you to help us?"

Chan cocked his head to the side, pushing his lower lip out. "Who's S?"

Crap.

"She sent us here. She told us we could get help for our people." She jabbed a thumb over her shoulder. "There is a ship in the distance at the base of a plateau with thousands of people on board."

Chan tilted his head more. "I don't know it."

Ali sighed. "We need help. The Anunnaki are coming with some type of secret weapon to kill everyone on that ship."

Chan nodded his head. "Yes, my people, the Anunnaki. They like to kill, experiment, and play games with your people. Let's see if we can get you help."

He turned.

"Where are we and who are…" Daf waved her arm around the assembly of little men, "…these guys?"

"Daf…" the last thing Ali wanted was a conversation. They didn't need talk, they needed help.

Chan nodded his head. "You're close to Dirn Garum, which I'm learning has quite the history. Its other name is quite simple, the City in the Mountain." He touched his chin. "I'm new here, too, but not as newly arrived as you. I came to this planet with some companions not too long ago, and they were killed. I escaped and found this tunnel."

Chan pointed at Harak and Thun. "As you can tell, those two don't see things eye to eye. They are brothers, sons of King Gilrak." He grinned. "Keeping these names straight is certainly a challenge. The others have names too. We have—"

Ali threw her hand in the air, cutting Chan off. "I'm sorry, but we don't have time. We need to hurry."

Chan dipped his head several times in quick succession. "Yes, yes. You're right. Follow me."

Daf put her arm around Ali's shoulder, and Ali helped her hobble around a turn in the tunnel, the small men behind them laughing and grumbling about something Ali couldn't understand.

Ali's heart lurched forward, almost as if grabbed, and something similar to a pulse shot from her heart.

She let out a loud breath and almost lost her balance, taking Daf with her. Daf held her steady with her one good leg.

Ali's eyes blurred, and she shook her head. "What was that?"

Chan halted and walked toward Ali. "Are you okay?" He rubbed her back. "We have to keep moving. I know my race, and they can be callous, especially the one named Enlil. I have no doubts what you say is true, and if we want to stop that weapon, then as you said, we need to hurry. I will help you convince Gilrak to assist you and your people."

The sensation in Ali's heart ceased, and her eyes cleared up. She nodded. "Thank you."

Another pull snagged her heart like a hook to a fish. She let out another loud breath. "Dammit." She just wanted to get help, not experience a heart attack.

"Ali, what's wrong?" Daf's face contorted in worry.

"I don't know."

They walked past an opening in the side of the tunnel, and Ali stiffened, her eyes widening. She reached out, her hands shaking.

The opening was tall and wide, and inside granite walls made up the room.

Her heart lightened, and her body strengthened. She shook Daf off of her, focused on what was sitting in the middle of the room.

A sarcophagus.

Daf leaned against the wall. "Ali, what are you doing? We have to hurry."

Ali ignored her and bent next to the sarcophagus, touching the lid. It bore the same hieroglyphs she touched in her dream. No, in her memory.

Was this the sarcophagus she came to this world through?

Laughter erupted behind her and in the tunnel as the little men approached, then silence.

Thun rushed into the room, his hands up. "*Veryrant, veryrant.*"

Ali traced the hieroglyphs with her finger, and Thun pulled her away.

Chan stepped between Thun and Ali, separating them. "Let her be."

Ali raced back to the sarcophagus, and followed a line in its side, her finger touching a keyhole.

She eyed Chan. "Where is the key?"

"Ali," said Daf. "We have to get going."

Ali shook her head. "I need the key." She was here, in the room that would take her back to her mother. Helen would give her love, and she'd be as happy to give it back, the way it used to be, the way it was supposed to be between a parent and child.

And her father. She'd find him, and they'd reunite.

This wasn't her world. Not Eos. Not this tunnel. Not Star Guild or Starbase Matrona. None of them were her responsibility and never were.

She could go home. She could be happy again.

But where was the key?

She stood and searched around the room.

Chan stepped in front of the exit into the tunnel, blocking Thun from leaving the room. "Thun, give her the key." He pointed his index finger at Thun's belt.

Thun patted his belt and shook his head.

Ali eyed Thun's belt and spotted the key hanging from it, attached by a thick string. His back was to her, and she quietly walked toward him.

Chan crossed his arms at his chest. "Thun, please."

Ali snagged the key and ripped it off the string. She rushed to the sarcophagus, and the key flung from her hands and slipped inside the keyhole.

Thun grunted loudly and ran toward her.

The sarcophagus' lid rose, and a bright light flashed. Thun skidded to a halt.

The lid moved to the side and dropped to the floor, a thud echoing in the room. The light brightened from inside the sarcophagus, shooting colors everywhere.

Ali stepped forward, her eyes on the prize, the portal that would take her to her family, her real family.

She was going home, and she couldn't wait a moment longer.

68

KODA

Starbase Matrona

Koda stopped in the trees' shadows, Devon by his side. They stood still, eyeing a killer.

Payson.

A hand came up and covered his mouth, pulling him down and against something soft, another body.

Devon had been pulled to his butt as well, a hand around his mouth.

"Shh," said a female voice. "The last thing you want is to grab their attention."

The hand released Koda, and he turned.

"Naveya?"

She nodded, her voice in a hush, MiMi by her side. "The one and only." She pointed to Payson and his men. Though they were far off in the distance, huddled in a clearing, Koda wouldn't be surprised if Payson had bionic hearing as well.

"You almost walked into a death trap. They would have killed you two quickly," Naveya said.

"What are you doing?" asked Devon.

"Waiting for the right moment. I kill Payson, the rest of the team crumbles. I kill a team member, the pack continues as if nothing happened. It's just how Payson and his guys work." She tapped her gun holstered to her hip. "I want to do this quickly and easily."

Payson stood, looking around as if he heard something, and the rest of the men went quiet.

"Stay low," whispered Naveya.

Payson stepped through the long blades of grass and over a fern in Koda's direction. He slid out a long knife as he walked cautiously forward, a gun in his other hand.

Two of his men followed.

Naveya pulled out her gun and aimed. "One shot between his eyes."

Naveya pulled the trigger, and the gun recoiled just as one of Payson's men pushed Payson out of the way, taking the bullet in his shoulder.

"That didn't go well," Naveya huffed. She stood. "You two and MiMi, get behind the trees."

Koda and Devon rushed around the trees and crouched low, her dog by their side. Koda inspected the area. Payson and two of his men were now in a defensive formation, rushing from tree to tree, taking cover, then advancing.

Where had Naveya disappeared to?

"I don't see her." Devon's voice shook.

Payson and his men crept closer. Koda fumbled for a gun and quickly realized he didn't have one. He made a fist, grimacing.

"I think we need to back up and run out of here," said Devon.

Koda dipped his head. "I think you're right."

Devon went to pick up the dog.

"Shoot them," yelled Payson.

Gunshots went off, and Koda and Devon ducked to the ground, the tree in front of them shedding splinters from several well-placed bullets.

Koda looked up, preparing for the worst. Behind the trees and in the shadows stood Payson and two of his men, their guns extended, searching.

Payson spotted Koda and pointed his weapon.

There was a rustling in the trees, and Payson looked up, his gun following.

Naveya jumped from the trees, landing on top of Payson, and throwing him to the ground.

His two men quickly aimed their weapons at Naveya, and she threw her hands out, fingers splayed. The men were lifted off the ground and landed on their backs, their gun's flinging out of their hands.

Koda's eyes widened. There it was again. Naveya somehow manipulating physics and tossing those stooges around like dolls.

Naveya leaned her knee against Payson's chest, her gun at his head. She somehow got his gun as well and tossed it over her shoulder. The knife he had wielded was half-buried in the ground, next to his leg.

How she'd done that, and so quickly, Koda didn't know. She was a Space Templar, and according to the old stories, they were more advanced than any warrior in the galaxy.

Now he saw why.

A gun cracked in the distance, and Naveya rolled back, the bullet whizzing by her and connecting to a tree, splitting off a chunk of bark.

Payson rushed away from her, moving fast. Naveya leaned against the tree and pulled the trigger several times. The two other men who accompanied Payson jumped in the way just in time, blood splattering outward.

They lay on the ground, dead, and Naveya pushed to her feet, shooting several more bullets at a dodging Payson.

She missed.

Payson and the rest of his men rushed onward, disappearing down a hill and out of view.

Naveya palmed her forehead. "Now, I made a mess, didn't I?"

Devon walked forward, his hands shaking. "I thought you did good."

Naveya nodded, MiMi licking her dangling fingers. "You two, continue that way." She pointed in the opposite direction Payson had gone. "I have to follow those bastards. This time, they'll be ready, so I have some planning to do before I attempt another assassination."

She cringed, shaking her head. "How did I miss? How did I screw that up?" She stood tall. "It won't happen again. I have to get to him before that XO of yours takes her Marines and hunts for him. I don't want any more of your people dying." She bounded off, MiMi in tow, headed in Payson's direction. She looked over her shoulder. "Stay away from Payson, all right? And don't pick up that gun. Live by the gun, die by the gun."

Koda had been thinking of retrieving it, having seen where she threw Payson's weapon. He bit his lower lip, not wanting to obey, but again, she was a Space Templar, she probably knew a hell of a lot more than he did.

Naveya disappeared down the hill, but Koda couldn't shake the feeling this wouldn't be the last time they saw Payson.

He took a long, deep breath, wagging his head back and forth. "You don't see that every day." He turned to head in the opposite direction of Naveya. "All right, back to our regular programming."

He blinked several times, trying to get the image of blood flying everywhere out of his head.

That fight had come out of nowhere, and he shook his head, still not believing a middle-aged woman could take on Payson and his men like that.

He pushed the thought away as they walked through the forest and into a clearing until they faced a biosphere wall, a wall that went on for kilometers around the internal starbase.

It went from ground to ceiling and blocked any view of the cities on the other side. Windows lined the inner wall where the rich lived, or big businesses had their offices. Some political types had offices in the wall, including Savanna Levens.

In front of them stood the door that led to Sphere Six, and just above it was a broken window, its glass shards splattered over the biosphere grass below.

Koda stood next to Devon, rubbing his knee, and remembering the pain from the landing after jumping through that exact busted window.

"Where next, Koda?"

"Through the door right there." They'd head to Zim's office in Sphere Eight where they could hack the data stream and figure out where Destination N was located, and gather more information they could spread across the channel streams to the masses.

He'd have to look through the Prime Director's files, scour infovid backlogs and basically tear Zim's office apart.

It wasn't going to be fun or pretty, but it'd give him more pieces to a puzzle.

"We should have walked more westerly. We need Sphere Eight, not Six."

Koda gave a slight head shake. "It'd be another day's walk. We hop onto a Sphere Six hovertrain, we get to Sphere Eight in forty minutes."

"That's if hovertrains are functioning."

"Let's hope."

Devon rubbed his pant leg. "Let's hope there aren't any rogue Matrona Guard out there too. You know, guards who haven't gotten the info that Zim cleared your uncle of all charges."

Koda massaged the back of his neck, a smile creeping on his lips. Shae was innocent, and Zim had finally let the starbase and all of Star Guild know.

But like Devon mentioned, what if some of the Matrona Guard hadn't gotten the news? What if, beyond the doors to any and all Spheres, there were guards ready to blow holes in them?

He eyed Sphere Six's access door. It was a sphere loyal to Savanna Levens, wherever she might be. Hopefully, she was alive. Sphere Six, he'd heard, hadn't participated in the short civil war between the Matrona Guard and the *Brigantia* and *Taranis* Guard.

In fact, Sphere Six's legion of Matrona Guards stood down, their sergeants and sergeant majors not trusting Zim's lies about Fleet Admiral Shae Lutz.

They were probably ordered to stand down by Savanna herself.

Koda walked toward Sphere Six's door. He took out his ID card and mentally crossed his fingers. "If this still works, I'll kiss you. If it doesn't, we're getting in through that window somehow." He pointed to the window he and Devon had jumped.

Devon shook his head. "I'll pass on the kiss."

Koda shrugged, swiping the card on a console next to the door. "I agree with you on the kiss." A beep sounded, and the door slid open. He let out a sharp breath. "We're in." He gave Devon a wink, sweeping his arm through the doorway. "Shall we?"

They hadn't been outside of the biosphere in a week. He let out a groan, seeing a world of ebb streets, buildings, and sidewalks.

The biosphere was beautiful. The world outside was ugly.

Koda stepped through, taking his first steps on the street, and headed for a sidewalk.

The city was quiet, and it was late, so people were probably sleeping, or tossing and turning from all the information coming over the holochannels from Prime Director Zim Noki.

"What time is it?" asked Koda.

Devon glanced around, staring at the red and gray ebb buildings. "Maybe midnight or a bit later?" He stopped in stride. "Are we that off with our time?"

"Maybe."

"Shall we act normally?"

"You? Normal? Impossible." Koda winked. "The hovertrain station is this way. Come on."

He hurried down the sidewalk, ready to get as much information as he could, to be the politician his Sphere had elected and a damn good one.

He knew deep down in his heart he was the champion of the people, and he was happy to fulfill his destiny.

69

SHAE

New Starbase Matrona Sector Territory

Shae sat in the cockpit, eyeing the view screen in the small four-seat jumper craft.

He ran his finger up the screen, splitting it into two halves. "Rear cam, left screen."

Starbase Matrona came into view, shrinking the further he flew.

He sighed. "I'll see you again shortly, beautiful."

He switched off rear cam and glared at a full screen of stars and distant planets in front of him as he thought of his daughter.

He smiled at the potential of seeing her, then straightened his lips. Even though happiness swelled in him, he pushed it away. A major threat to the starbase and his people still loomed, one that needed to be dealt with, and now.

He had confidence in his officers and Marines. They'd get the job done.

They had to.

He pushed the throttle forward, initiating thrusters to take him faster.

He tapped on the flight console and brought up NMJ drives, and locked in the location. "Here goes nothing."

He activated the drives, readying the ship for a fast hop into another sector, his old stomping grounds, his old home.

The jump sequence initiated, and everything moved slower for a moment, then the cockpit stretched in front of him, moving outward and expanding.

A loud pop sounded and then silence as the vidscreen lit up in white streaking stars that zoomed by, becoming lines, bright and thick.

Static filled Shae's ears. There was another pop, and everything was right again—the flight console, the viewscreen, the entire ship.

He let out a quick breath at the planet before him, planet Eos, it's golden aura like a wide halo, welcoming the admiral back.

"Nice to see you, old friend."

He brought the ship into a forty-five-degree angle, setting the craft for stable planet entry. He brought up the map Devon had installed on his craft, sent from the holocomps in the infirmary to this small ship.

A map of Eos came to view, and his daughter, Alison, came on the screen in the shape of a blue dot. He furrowed his brow. She was now deep inside the mountain. Finding her may not be easy.

The ship shuddered when it hit the Eos atmosphere. In minutes, he'd be flying into potentially dangerous territory. Being in a small ship, though weaponless, had its benefits; the enemy might not be able to track him easily if they were around.

Ten minutes later, gliding in, he pulled back on the throttle at the behemoth mountain below, Mount Gabriel. He glimpsed the map, seeing the blue dot on one side of the mountain and navigated his way to the southeast base of Gabriel.

He pitched the craft back and slowed for a landing, then hovered the ship, his mouth turning into a frown as the skids extended, and the craft touched down.

It wasn't the skids extending or the landing causing his unease.

Smoke fluttered off of two objects toward the sky. He'd been paying so much attention to the map and mountain, he hadn't seen downed mining mechs in the ebb field nearby, blown to shreds.

He swallowed hard, thanking his lucky stars no enemy had come around, at least not yet, because whoever met the enemy in those mechs hadn't fared well.

He unstrapped and walked to the back of the ship, grabbing an EMU, Eos Mobility Unit, made for dense gravity and pulled it over his jumpsuit, strapping on specially made EOS boots, and snapped them onto his lower pants, sealing them.

He took the helmet off the rack and shoved it over his head, sealing the helmet to his suit as well.

With a hiss, fresh oxygen filled his helmet, clearing up the fogging visor.

He hurried to the flight console and pulled off an attached holopad, transferring the map on it, which displayed his daughter's location and route of entry she took to get inside the mountain.

He grabbed a rifle and shouldered it, then slapped the button near the door panel. "Open."

The door flipped upward, like a wing on a bird about to fly, and he hopped onto the thin Eos dust covering the ebb terrain.

He rushed toward the mountain base with the rifle strapped to his shoulder and the holopad in hand, trekking in the direction his daughter had gone.

The ground rumbled, and the sky roared. A rush of adrenaline took over as several starfighters zoomed overhead, seeming to come out of nowhere.

He thanked his lucky stars they hadn't spotted him.

He jumped up a small rock base and ascended, viewing parted sand in a long line that led to the opening in the mountain. He paused, halting for a moment, and studying the track.

Had someone been dragged into the mountain? Had it been his daughter?

He'd have to hurry.

He ran to the opening, and turned his helmet light on, lighting up the darkness.

He took a step inside and stopped again. He saw boot tracks, but something else quite odd. "Bare feet?"

Small, wide feet, with small wide toe tracks, led down the tunnel, and boot tracks looking more fresh followed the bare feet.

Three boots instead of four?

He moved down the tunnel and nodded to himself. "Someone is injured." It was clear from the tracks someone was helping another, perhaps someone had broken a foot or leg, and those people had been in the destroyed mechs outside.

He quickened his pace, shining his light on the ground, moving his eyes from the holopad to the trail in front of him.

He was getting closer.

He slowed as a thought struck him. What if she didn't remember him? What if she saw him as a stranger? Did she have memories like him?

She had been so young when he'd been taken and sent to Starbase Matrona, the kidnapping he still didn't have a memory of, and she probably wouldn't either. If it took twenty years after Shae had been stolen for him to remember his daughter, surely it would take her just as long, and she hadn't been kidnapped from her home planet that long ago.

He curled his fist and shook his head, grunting loudly. "It doesn't matter."

He rounded a long, winding corner and came to an abrupt halt, gasping loudly.

On the side of the tunnel stood a long, wide door. He paused, watching it glow and change colors, as it seemed to bulge in and out.

He took a step forward and put his hand on it, then stepped back when a click echoed across the tunnel and the door vibrated open, creaking loudly.

He looked at the holopad and studied the map, the blue dot still in one place. A line passing through the doorway indicated she passed through and wasn't far from him.

His stomach churned, butterflies seeming to want to break out of him and flutter down the path in front of him.

He took a step forward and then another, moving cautiously, keeping his eye on the path and the wall.

He stopped and inched backward. He heard voices up ahead, some loud, some low and dull.

He placed the holopad under his armpit, squeezing tightly and unstrapped the rifle from his shoulder, pointing it forward.

He walked slowly, taking deliberate steps.

The voices rang louder.

He curled around a long, wide turn in the tunnel and froze, his rifle pointed at the back of several small men, one large and tall, and a woman clearly favoring one leg and leaning against the wall.

He tilted his head. She wore a mech miner jumper, but what was most peculiar was she didn't wear a helmet.

Yet she breathed.

He jerked back, remembering what Naveya said about Eos. It had breathable oxygen. He had forgotten and hadn't needed this suit at all.

"Ali," the woman yelled, lifting a hand and waving.

He lowered his weapon and took a few more steps to look into the room where lights were shooting from some type of ancient, open rock casket.

Standing next to it was an older version of Alison. Her red hair, which if memory served him right, always baffled him. If he recalled, her mom had blonde hair, and his was nearly black.

They shrugged it off, figuring it had to be a genetic thing since a few people in his family were redheads.

He walked closer and reached out, his shaky hand wanting to touch her, to bring her in for a hug like he used to do when she was little.

He gasped again, a low bellow blurting out of his mouth as he reached toward his daughter. "Alison, no. Don't do it."

70

ALI

Mount Gabriel, Eos

Ali loomed over the sarcophagus and peered into the portal. Rainbow colors swirled from the middle until it cleared, showing her a view of the room she had stood in before coming to this world—the tomb in Southern Iraq.

The ruins of Madkhal.

One step inside, and she'd be in Southern Iraq, back on Earth, where she could find her way to Michigan and her mother.

My mom.

She touched the sarcophagus, and the view changed to her mother, Helen.

Helen sat in her living room, on the magenta couch they had since Ali had been a child. She held onto Ali's college graduation picture, looking at it with love.

Sunlight streamed through the window, highlighting Helen's face. She had a tear rolling down her cheek. "I miss you, dear. So, so much."

Ali reached out. "Mom." She wiped a tear from her own face and set one foot on the thick, wide edge of the sarcophagus and then the other foot. "I'm coming."

The scene switched to the tomb at Madkhal, where Ali was

headed. She wished she could transport to her mom's living room in the blink of an eye, but of course, her mom didn't have a sarcophagus.

She shook her head. Why was she thinking silly thoughts at a time like this?

Just jump through, Ali, she told herself.

She dangled her foot over the edge.

"Ali," yelled Daf.

Ali flicked a look over her shoulder. Daf stood there, waving a goodbye, her lips straight. She could tell she was holding back tears of her own.

But why? She was Chief Petty Officer Alison Johnson. No one liked her. She was boring, a piss-ant, and most of all, a nobody.

Yet, there Daf was, and from what Ali could tell, she'd miss Ali.

Strangely, Ali would miss Daf too.

Chan stood next to Daf, his hands folded into his long, thick sleeves. He dipped his head as if saying that whatever her decision was, it would be okay.

The small men fidgeted with their tools, and Harak cleaned his teeth with a long, silver dagger. The only one who paid attention was Thun, who watched wild-eyed at the spectacle in front of him.

Ali waved to Daf. "Goodbye."

Maybe she'd be back someday, to check on everyone, to see if Star Guild and Starbase Matrona survived the Anunnaki. Or if they didn't.

She gulped hard. What if her friends and crew didn't survive the Anunnaki? What if they succumbed to slavery again, or worse, were completely annihilated?

She couldn't have that.

Hell no.

She looked down into the sarcophagus, seeing the Madkhal tomb, inviting her to step through the portal and arrive in Iraq, back home where she belonged.

She thought of her mother again, and the scene switched back to her. Helen now leaned her back against the couch and stared out of the window.

Ali needed to jump. She had to, in order to save her sanity, save her mom and find her dad.

Her mother was safe, but her people on Starship *Sirona* weren't.

She made a fist and grunted loudly. *Dammit.*

She had to stay. She had to see this through this and help. "I love you, mom. I love you so much."

She went to take a step off the ledge and set her feet onto the floor. She wasn't leaving Eos, or Star Guild, or the people she'd come to know so well.

"I'll see you soon, mom. I promise." She blew her a kiss. "When I come back, we'll find dad together."

Her foot touched the floor while the other was still planted firmly on the sarcophagus edge when a simple thought pulled at her.

She lurched forward and threw her hands on the sarcophagus to keep herself from falling into it. "Show me my father."

Clouds formed, white and puffy, and the scene burst through the clouds and moved quickly toward a topographical view of Mount Gabriel, moving closer and closer.

The view changed and zipped through the tunnel system inside the mountain, stopping at the back of a man in an EMU suit and a lowered rifle, helmet on, staring at Ali, Daf, the little men, and Chan.

She squinted and cocked her head to the side. That scene was happening now.

She pushed away from the sarcophagus and pulled her gun out of her holster, pointing it at a man wearing the same suit she'd just witnessed in the sarcophagus. "Don't move."

Chan and the little men turned, and Daf stood frozen, the closest to the man.

He slowly crouched and set his rifle on the ground. He kicked the rifle toward Ali, to show her he didn't mean harm.

Several foreign words came out of Harak's mouth, and he stepped forward, his weapon raised high. The man in the suit stepped back, his arms still high, and Thun jabbed an elbow into Harak's chest, grunting several words.

Harak stood down and huffed.

Ali stood still. "Who are you?"

The man lifted his hands toward his helmet and unsealed it from his suit. A hiss and he pulled off the helmet, his eyes glued to Ali, his lips straight.

Ali dropped her weapon, her mouth open. "Admiral Shae Lutz?"

She'd never met the guy or spoken a word with him, even over the comm lines, not that she had the credentials or position to do so.

He took a step forward, his chin trembling. "Is your name Alison?"

Ali nodded. "Alison Johnson." She stood straighter. "Are you and the rest of Star Guild here to help Starship *Sirona*?" If so, this would be easier than she thought.

His eyebrows raised. "Starship *Sirona*?" He then lowered his chin, as if remembering. "Oh, yes. Good, they are alive."

Ali furrowed her brow. "You're not here for them?"

He shook his head. "I'm here for you."

She touched her chest. "Me?"

He looked away as if not wanting to answer. He took another step forward and cleared his throat. "I'm not from this world, and neither are you."

Ali blinked several times, trying to comprehend what he just said. Were they both from Earth? If so, wonderful, but Ali wasn't going back until she helped save *Sirona*. "I'm from Earth, but I'm not going back yet." She turned, giving the sarcophagus a glance and then turned back. "Are you leaving for Earth?"

He halted, shaking his head. "You need to listen to me, Ali, and I know this is going to sound absurd, but please believe me."

The small men shifted on their feet, a few grunting loudly. They looked bored, and Chan put his hand out, shaking it back and forth, telling them to calm down.

"Okay, I'm listening." What would the fleet admiral of Star Guild have to say to her that was so important he needed to come in person? She froze. "Wait, how did you find me?"

"You and I are both tracked. We have something similar to a homing beacon implanted in us. A few people in tech found the signal, and long story short, I followed the signal to find you."

Ali touched her gut, feeling a sensation hit her in the stomach. She had been right. *They* were tracking her.

Shae continued, "For a while now, I've had these memories." He paused, gathering his thoughts. "I had a farm in a place called Michigan. I had a daughter. She was young, vibrant, and had red hair. She had a mom, and her name..."

Ali put her hand up. "Is this a joke?"

"Ali, listen." He looked deeply into Ali's eyes. "I was taken from you and your mother. I don't know when or exactly how, but I was in the military. I was an admiral in that military, as well. And, if you have any memories of that place, our home, then please try to remember me." He took a step forward, moving closer. "Do you remember anything of what I'm referring to?" He eyed the sarcophagus. "You mentioned Earth, so you have memories, I assume."

Ali rubbed her temple and looked at the dirt covering the rock floor. Was he trying to tell her that he, the fleet admiral of Star Guild, Shae Lutz of all people, was her father?

"Do you remember any of this, Ali?"

Ali looked up. "Some. Are you my..."

Shae nodded, now only a few steps from her, a tear welling in his eye. "I'm your dad. I used to teach you how to punch with your dolls. I taught you how to throw rocks and skip them in rivers, I—"

A rush of memories flooded her mind, and she fell to her knees, Shae moving to his with her.

She flashed to her dad showing her how to ride a horse for the first time, the many hugs he gave her, playing with her dolls with him, driving a tractor with her by his side, and the memories went through her like a slideshow, all attached with emotions, ups and downs, good and bad.

The images stopped, and she found herself looking into Shae's eyes, feeling the same love, the same touch she felt back then. "Dad?"

Shae nodded. "I can't believe it either, but yes, you're my daughter." A tear streamed down his cheek as his hand came to her shoulder. "I've only remembered you for a short while, but know that I loved you so, so much. You were my everything. I love you just as strongly today. It's what brought me here."

Ali stood and helped him stand as well. She wiped her tears and let out a laugh pulling her dad into a hug.

He wrapped his arms around her tightly, and she rested her forehead against his shoulder, crying.

She gently pulled away and sniffed. "Mom misses us."

"I would think so." He let out a little laugh. "We'll see her again."

She wiped her eyes with her forearm. "What now?"

Shae grabbed her hands. "We win this war, and then head back home. Deal?"

Ali lifted her lips into a smile. "Deal."

EPILOGUE

Ali helped Daf down the spiraling path, the air around them getting colder. It took a little convincing to get her father on board with following her to some unknown city in the mountain, but eventually, he did.

"Where are we going again?" asked Daf.

Chan, continuing to walk, glanced over his shoulder at the small men who spoke to each other in a low hush, their eyes darting from Shae to each other and then back.

"The city inside the mountain. It's called Dirn Garum," said Chan.

Ali eyed Shae, who walked behind her, the suit now off. "Are you confused as to how we're breathing on this planet?"

He gave a sideways grin. "It's a long story, but no, I'm not."

Ali nodded. "It's nice to see you."

His grin grew. "You have no idea how good I feel. For the first time in my life, I feel whole. I feel put together. Strangely enough, I can think more clearly."

She took in a deep breath, realizing she had the same sensations. Before, life had missing parts. Today, those parts had come together like a puzzle, and here she was, reunited with her father, a father she hadn't seen since he left on some mission to a place called Haiti when she was twelve-years-old.

"They can still track us."

Chan chimed in, "The Bawn people can trace the chips' locations, and deactivate them in your bodies. I wouldn't worry."

Ali frowned. "The Bawn people?"

Chan threw a thumb over his shoulder as he continued to lead the way. "Yes, the small people with us. They are called the Bawn."

"They have the technology to deactivate a chip?" asked Ali.

"They are more advanced than you'd think."

Interesting, thought Ali. An advanced civilization had been living in a mountain underneath her nose the entire time she'd been mining on Eos.

As if life hadn't already thrown her a million curveballs.

Curveballs?

She figured it was a term she used on Earth.

"So, we help *Sirona* and get back to the starbase," said Shae, following closely behind.

"Yes, and apparently, these Bawn people can help us." So said S, and S had been right more times than not.

It all seemed surreal.

She felt she had to help these people, but once everything became right again, if it ever had been, she and her father would leave this hell-hole of a sector where slavery reigned and truth suffered, and head home.

Life would be peachy, and she'd live happily ever after.

She rolled her eyes at the thought, Daf hopping next to her. Nothing was ever peachy, but maybe for the first time in her life, something would be easy.

She almost laughed. Easy didn't exist for her.

She shook her head as they continued to walk, the tunnel spiraling and descending at a slow grade.

A pain grabbed Ali's stomach. She stopped and bent forward, grimacing. Her dad came to her side, rubbing her back.

"What's wrong, Ali?"

Daf held on to her. “Is it your stomach?”

Ali bobbed her head up and down, another pain like a knife digging into her belly. “What the Guild?”

She straightened and let out a breath.

The pain subsided just as quickly as it had arrived. Ali rubbed her stomach. “I don’t know where that came from.”

Chan and the Bawns stared at her. Neither concern nor care was written on any of the Bawns’ faces.

Chan, on the other hand, stepped in her direction. “If you need help, you and Daf can lean on me.”

“Ali can lean on me, too,” said Shae.

Ali shook her head. “I’m fine. Carry on.”

Chan turned and walked, the rest following him. He gestured at the tunnel’s walls. “We're almost to the great cavern. I think you'll be amazed.”

A queasiness overtook Ali, and she slowed, swallowing vomit that was trying to force its way up.

Daf hopped onward, her arm clutching Ali’s shoulder. “Ali, you look pale.”

Ali shot her a look. “I’m a redhead. I always look pale.”

“True, but more pale than normal.”

Ali glanced down, moving her head back and forth and kept her legs pushing forward. “I don’t feel good.”

“Here it is.” Chan halted, his arms reaching upward.

In front of Ali stood the mouth of a gigantic cavern. Gypsum hung like chandeliers off the cave’s ceiling, white and glistening, branching twenty or so meters above, looking like thick, leafless branches covered in snow and ice.

A spectacle she’d seen before, but not on this planet or on the starbase.

“This is—” Ali doubled over, clutching her abdomen. She went to one knee, taking Daf down with her.

Daf leaned against the rock wall. “I think she needs help.” Daf’s voice was high.

Shae came to her side, but again, the agony quickly subsided.

Ali slowly stood, wanting to roll her eyes again. "Now what?"

She had dealt with almost being killed several times. She had dealt with her mother Diana not really being her mother. To top it off, her entire existence on this world had been a lie, plus she'd been kidnapped and taken to a slave race.

What else could go wrong?

Her stomach ached again, and she held down another bout of throw up. "Is the cavern affecting me somehow?"

Shae rubbed his stomach. "Something is starting to bother me as well."

Chan looked around. He paused, his finger up, and his eyebrows twitching. "Hold on." He shuffled into the cavern and touched a large, perfectly rectangular shaped rock in the wall.

Harak jumped, violently shaking his head as if he didn't want Chan to touch the rectangular rock. He spoke loudly in a language Ali didn't understand, grunting and spitting on the ground.

Chan raised his hand, palm out, a calmness to his voice, "Perhaps they are the Ones." He motioned for Ali and Shae to walk in his direction. "Come, come."

Ali glanced at Daf and then her dad.

Shae gave her a nod, telling her to proceed, his face gnarled in pain.

"All right." Holding her stomach, she moved past the Bawns and into the cavern. She stopped and gazed at the path's edge farthest from the stone wall.

She backed away.

Beyond the edge was a black, dark abyss, lining its perimeter was a spiraling path with bluish-white torch-like lamps lighting the way. It went on and on, disappearing into the bowels of the mountain.

Ali hunched over, feeling dizzy, and more nauseous. She blinked several times, trying to get the sensation to wane.

Chan stepped forward, placing his arm around her shoulders. She leaned against him for support.

Chan dipped his head toward the trail's edge. "The path is formed in a Fibonacci spiral." He turned and guided her to the wall.

"A what?"

"It's an obsolete term in your language describing the spiral of life. All of creation begins with it."

Ali's stomach tightened, and she winced just as a grinding sound pierced the air. She glanced up and jerked back, eyeing the source of the sound. "Whoa."

The rectangle had opened up like a French door, one side to the left, and the other to the right.

Inside the rectangle was a statue of a man the same size as Ali. He wore a helmet, one she recognized from the Space Templar fairytales she'd read a few years back.

Shae hurried toward the statue. "A Space Templar."

Chan dipped his head. "Correct, Sir."

A garbed, rock robe flowed from the statue's torso to his knees, exposing his calves and bare feet. The statue was polished as if it had recently been made or very well-kept throughout the years.

Chan touched the statue. "This is Gordwyn, Keeper of the Mountain, Guardian of All Beings of Light. The lore is that he was once a real Space Templar before turning himself into stone to wait."

"Wait?"

"Yes, to wait for the One."

Ali zeroed in on a sword sheathed in the statue's stone belt. A real sword, not one etched from stone. It gleamed from the lamps set against the wall.

Ali's stomach eased, and she took a deep breath as she stepped forward, drawn more to the sword than to the statue.

Her mouth gaped when the sword seemed to light up from inside the closer she got, sparkling and glistening. She reached for it, not wanting anything more than to touch it.

"Don't. I hear it can be dangerous to touch if you're not of the bloodline."

Ali turned, facing Chan. "The bloodline?" S told her about royal blood, but not the bloodline. Maybe it was one and the same.

The sword called to her, almost singing, and she twisted back around, her fingers getting closer to the metallic blade.

"Be careful," warned Chan.

She attempted to pull back, but her body wouldn't let her. "I can't control myself."

"What the hell is happening?" Shae walked forward, as if unable to control himself as well.

"Surrender, you two," said Chan. "Your bodies know."

She touched the sword, her father resting his hand on it a moment later.

A green light flashed, almost blinding her.

She closed her eyes and backed away, shielding her face with her forearm to block the light.

A beautiful hum that reminded her of the songs from the Earth monks in Tibet rang in her ears.

The light dimmed, and she dropped her arm.

Chan was gone, along with Daf and the Bawns, but her father stood next to her.

Her heart skipped a beat, and her eyes darted left and right, until she saw him—the Space Templar.

The statue wasn't stone anymore.

"Young warrior priestess and warrior priest," said the Templar, standing where the statue had been. He had human flesh, and his robe's material was now similar to brown wool.

She squinted, wrinkling her nose in confusion.

"Come closer," said the man, a smile on his face, his brown eyes beaming with compassion. "Both of you."

Shae and Ali took a hypnotic step forward.

He unsheathed the sword and lifted it in the air. "To one knee, please. You're both being initiated."

She went to a knee, Shae following suit.

She wanted to talk, to ask what was going on, but her mouth and tongue wouldn't cooperate.

She felt the sword rest gently against her shoulder. "I've been the guardian of this sword for centuries. Its name is Sol, the Sword of Light. Your destiny, both of you, from this day forward, is to protect the weak, to walk the path of light, to heal your sorrows and physical ills, and to help others in the same regard. If you accept your destiny, it begins this moment. Your bloodline, that from which I came, carries this legacy. I've beckoned to our bloodline for centuries, and finally, you, my young blood, have answered."

She blinked, and her knees went weak as she gasped for breath and fumbled to the ground. A loud clang sounded next to her, and she pushed herself up in a hurry, a sword now lying next to her.

She glanced up at the man. He was a statue again, or maybe he had always been a statue. She didn't know.

Had she blacked out?

She faced her dad, and from the look in his eyes, they both had the same experience.

Shae massaged his temples. "What was that?"

Chan pointed to the sword. "It's for one of you. It will remain with the one who picks it up."

Shae crossed his arms. "I have plenty of weapons at my disposal. I don't need another."

The sword tugged at Ali as if a string was attached from it to her. She leaned down and picked it up, surprised it wasn't heavy. She turned and lifted her gaze.

The Bawns were quiet, staring at her intently. Chan inched behind them, perhaps to give them a better look at her.

Thun went to his knees, placing his head against the stone path. "Sumyana."

Another Bawn did the same, until they all did, except Harak.

"Sumyana," they called. "Sumyana."

Ali curled her fingers around the handle, squeezing the hilt. Electric plasma-like energy crackled around the blade, blazing purple, and lighting the area around her.

Somehow she knew if she focused and pointed the sword, it would shoot a plasma bolt in that direction.

She lightened her grip, the plasma energy dissipating. She waved the sword from side to side. It felt right, almost like it was an extension of herself.

Daf leaned her shoulder against the wall. "What's happening?"

"I'd like to know, as well," said Shae.

Chan put his palms together in front of him. "The Bawns are saying Sumyana, which means 'Enlightened One' if I'm hearing it correctly. Well, Sumyana could also mean 'flying creature' in their language, but I don't think that's the case here. From what I can determine, you both are the heroes they've been waiting for, their fabled protectors."

Ali held the sword by her side and walked to the group, her body feeling better, her mind somehow more at peace. "Did you see what I saw?"

Daf pushed out her bottom lip and shook her head. "What do you mean?"

Ali gestured at the statue. "He didn't turn human and speak?"

Daf shook her head. "No."

Chan bowed. "You saw what you were meant to see, Ali. Leave it at that."

"I saw it as well," said Shae. "You're not crazy."

Harak crossed his arms, still holding his pickaxe. "I guess it's time." He spat on the ground. "They are sun lovers of all things. How could we be so cursed?"

Ali stood taller. "What did you call us?"

"You are all sun lovers." He spat a second time.

Chan giggled. "Daf is a sun lover, your dad's a sun lover, I'm a sun lover, and you're a sun lover. We don't dwell in the mountains is what he's saying, and he doesn't trust those who come from the *outside*."

Ali gave Harak a double-take. "Wait, you speak my language?"

"No. You now speak mine." Harak dropped his arms and patted his chest hard.

Ali touched her own chest. "I do?"

"I understand them too, Ali." Shae placed his hands on his hips.

Thun stood. "A curse, brother? They are a gift, and a gift shouldn't be judged by appearances. She holds the sword, Sol, which means she bears the blood. Her father also bears the blood and has a heart of gold for allowing her to have the sword. I hope you didn't forget the words etched in our stones. They are our guardians now. It won't be our father any longer."

Ali shuffled back. "What?" The last thing she was going to be was a guardian for these Bawn people. According to S, these people were supposed to help her, not the other way around.

"What are you saying, Ali?" Daf hobbled to her. "How did you learn their language?"

Ali shrugged. "I have no idea. I'm speaking in my language, not theirs."

"The Guild you are." Daf grabbed onto her arm. "You're speaking in a different language."

Thun took Ali by the hand. "Follow us. You, your father, and my father have a lot to discuss."

"Discuss what?" asked Ali.

"Ali, what are you saying?" Daf turned to Chan. "How is she speaking their language?"

Chan grinned. "There is much more to the Universe than meets the eye."

Daf shook her head, her hands flopping by her sides while hopping on one leg. "Okay, I give up."

Thun let go of Ali's hand and guided them down the trail. "Our race is similar to yours. We come from Earth as well, and someday, we wish to return to our homeland." He slammed his ax on the ground, his voice rising. "You and your father are the ones to lead us, Ali. You are the ones to defend our kingdom and to guide us by the light of your sword, Sol. But, first..." he turned and walked backward, his elbows wide and his chest thrust out. "When we are ready, we will turn those who stole us to this planet into ash."

Ali followed him down the spiraling path. "Turn *who* into ash?"

"The Anunnaki."

Ali bit her cheek. This wasn't the plan. All she wanted to do was save her friends on Starship *Sirona* and meet up with Starbase Matrona, not create another war and continue this tireless fight, and pound the bad guys into the ground. "They're too many, and we don't have the firepower."

Thun quickly nodded toward her sword. "We have more firepower than you can imagine. You have Sol."

She looked at Sol. "It's just a sword."

Thun grumbled and stomped his foot, continuing to walk backward. "It's not *just* a sword. No matter how many have tried, Bawn or other, it wouldn't allow us, them, or anybody to pry it out of the statue's sheath. But, you have it now, which means you've been chosen, along with your father. You're the Ones."

Thun bowed and twisted around, picking up his pace. "Sol's entire lineage is etched in stone. We will etch your name into the stone next." He brought his eyes to the sword. "Sol is wielded by the one destined to defeat our oppressors, as is also etched in our stones. You are of the bloodline that will correct the grievous injustice perpetrated on our two peoples. You and your father. You both are intermixed with the blood of the Anunnaki and the blood of the human race."

"All I can do is find a way off this planet. That I can do with my dad by my side."

Shae looked ready to go anywhere with his daughter.

How was she going to convince these Bawn to help Starship *Sirona*? They wanted to fight, to make mincemeat out of the Anunnaki. The last thing they wanted to do was help.

Thun's brows drew together and he frowned. "If a race is unjust, it's not only right for that race to be stopped, we are obligated to be the ones who stop them." He halted and wrapped his fingers around her wrist. "Come."

Ali stiffened. *What did I just get myself into?* They wanted all-out war.

They walked down the spiraling path, toward the city. If she could get the Bawn to somehow help her, then great. If not, she'd find her way back out of here and to *Sirona*.

She also needed food and water, and more importantly, rest and to catch up with her father.

She glared at the sword in her hand and lifted her gaze. She couldn't believe she'd survived and her dad walked by her side.

To the Bawn, she and her father were the Ones, whatever that meant, but being chosen ones didn't matter. Being whole did. With her father with her, she felt more complete than ever, as if a giant weight had lifted off her shoulders.

Shae wrapped his arm around her, bringing her in close as they continued down the trail. "This is the best day of my life."

She smiled and swallowed a cry. "This is the best day of my life too, Dad." She leaned her head against his shoulder. "Thank you for coming. We'll get back home together." She looked into her father's eyes. "I can't wait to see my mom's reaction when she sees us."

They continued walking, Ali leaning against her father, and Shae holding her tight, to Dirn Garum, the city inside the mountain.

The End

Enjoyed Veil Rising? If so, then turn the page to find your way to *Backlash Rising*: Star Guild Saga Book 2.

AUTHOR NOTES - BRANDON ELLIS

MARCH 12, 2020

I want to thank you from the bottom of my heart for taking the time to read book one, Veil Rising.

And, boy, do I have an interesting story to share about this book, but before I get to that, right now I'm living in Bali and want to share something else with you. It'll be quick.

As I type this, I'm in Bali and while I'm here, I'm recording my experience for authors around the world on my YouTube channel, "Bailing to Bali."

The link is further below.

My family and I decided to sell almost everything we owned, including one of our cars, all of our furniture, and what we couldn't sell, we put in storage.

We left our house of three years, a 2500 square foot beauty with four bedrooms, a huge garage, tall ceilings, and two creeks in our back yard along with a forest directly to the right of our house. To say it was hard to leave was an understatement, but we had a pull to Bali that we couldn't ignore any further.

And now Bali is where I'm writing my books while I adventure this incredible, unique island.

The YouTube channel is further down where you can watch short videos (four to ten minutes long, some a bit longer) of us preparing for the move, during our move, the flight, the triple whammy sickness I had the moment I arrived in Bali (thank God that's over), and see how much weight I lost. Wow!

You'll see incredible beaches, forests full of monkeys, the places we're staying, the happy people, and everything else we've discovered and continue to discover in Bali.

If you're interested in watching my Bali experience, here is the YouTube channel:

https://www.youtube.com/channel/UCJUzm6Su32UyaZO0a9sdlQw

And back to this book.

It was a journey, let me tell you. But it started out a little strange.

At my old house in Portland, Oregon, I laid down for a good night's sleep after a long day of work (I was a Sports Therapist before I became a full-time writer). I remember the year, 2013, and of all things, I remember the month—July.

So there I was, laying down in bed, and closing my eyes when BOOM!, an entire story…no…an entire series opened up before me.

Characters, ships, a starbase, aliens galore. I'd never written a Sci-Fi (turns out that's now my writing genre), but I had to get everything down on paper as soon as I could.

I scrambled out of bed, found my journal, and wrote, and wrote, and wrote. The next day I began my Sci-Fi writing life.

By 2014, I had written three books in the series, and nobody read them.

Why?

They were terribly written. I didn't know how to write Sci-Fi, I didn't understand the tropes, and most of all, I actually didn't understand how to write a book, let alone what good editing meant.

I learned quickly that friends, even though they tell you they are the best editors in the world, really aren't, unless they are a professional, which mine weren't.

I eventually took the series offline and out of the bookstores as I had it in mind that I'd rewrite the series.

And so, in the summer of 2019, I started book 1's rewrite, Veil Rising. About ten months later, thinking it'd only take me a month, I finally finished.

It took a lot of hard work, patience, and love. A lot of love from my family, from my author community, and from my fans cheering me on.

And it's fans, like you, that keep me going, along with keeping many of us authors going in the Indie publishing world. We couldn't do this without you, so we thank you, and like I said above, from the bottom of our hearts.

We deeply, deeply appreciate you.

With much Love and until next time, enjoy your reading, enjoy the next book in the series, and always and in all ways, love each other.

Brandon Ellis

www.brandonelliswrites.com

CONNECT WITH BRANDON

Enjoy the book? Then take a gander at Brandon's Facebook Group where you can help him and the rest of his rag-tag team of readers decide on pertinent information in the next books in this series or any other series he's writing... https://www.facebook.com/groups/EllisIsland/

His Facebook crew are fun, engaged readers, and can think of an alien race name for his books in a minute flat. There, you can read early chapter drafts for books Brandon is working on, join his ARC Team and read finished books before they are released, and much more. Again, here is the link: https://www.facebook.com/groups/EllisIsland/

And, join Brandon's Sci-Fi rebellion as well by subscribing to his newsletter. Brandon's a sucker for ancient alien information (is it real, or fake?), writing about ancient archeological sites that will blow your mind, and mixing in SciFi as well in just about every email he sends to you. Grab his free bestselling book, Starfighter: Freedom Star Book 1 (https://dl.bookfunnel.com/utmbp42qyd), to hop on his list. He doesn't spam, so sit back and enjoy the entertaining ride.

BOOKS BY BRANDON ELLIS

You can find a complete list of Brandon's books on his website here:

https://brandonelliswrites.com/books/
Or at Amazon here:

https://www.amazon.com/kindle-dbs/entity/author/B00BLVIYNW

OTHER LMBPN PUBLISHING BOOKS

To be notified of new releases and special promotions from LMBPN publishing, please join our email list:

http://lmbpn.com/email/

For a complete list of books published by LMBPN please visit the following pages:

https://lmbpn.com/books-by-lmbpn-publishing/

All LMBPN Audiobooks are Available at Audible.com and iTunes. For a complete list of audiobooks visit:

www.lmbpn.com/audible

CPSIA information can be obtained
at www.ICGtesting.com
Printed in the USA
LVHW041518030820
662267LV00005B/988

9 781642 028041